Oswald Joseph Reichel

The elements of canon law

Oswald Joseph Reichel

The elements of canon law

ISBN/EAN: 9783741175619

Manufactured in Europe, USA, Canada, Australia, Japa

Cover: Foto ©Andreas Hilbeck / pixelio.de

Manufactured and distributed by brebook publishing software
(www.brebook.com)

Oswald Joseph Reichel

The elements of canon law

THE ELEMENTS OF CANON LAW.

THE

ELEMENTS

OF

CANON LAW.

BY

OSWALD J. REICHEL, B.C.L., M.A.,

Sometime Vice-Principal of Cuddesden College, Oxford.

LONDON :

THOMAS BAKER, SOHO SQUARE.

1889.

ERRATUM.— Page 134, paragraph 1, line 5, for *invalid* read *valid*.

PREFACE.

WE all do err at times, and by God's grace may be raised up again and restored to newness of life. Yet is the Body of Christ Holy, and the aim of all its institutions is that its members may be sanctified through the truth.

Thus even that machinery, which at first sight seems to have least to do with personal holiness, is found to be really most designed to promote that holiness. For as it is ever difficult in this world to fathom the heart and to guage the moral guilt of sin in each particular case, so to do this generally (so far as that is possible) from a public or Church point of view is the hardest task of all. And this is the business of Canon Law, which not only seeks to regulate the organisation and the several duties of office within the Church, but also aims at controlling the administration thereof by distinguishing what is due to the individual and what is due to the Body as a whole. For as " we being many members are one Body and everyone members one of another," so " if one member suffer, all the members suffer together," and if one member

wilfully indulge. in sin the type of holiness is lowered
for all.

Moreover, sin is sometimes the outcome of general
weakness in face of strong temptation, and requires the
kindly help of others to be successfully overcome; whilst
in other cases sin is wilful, and to tolerate it is to do
harm to all the rest. Canon Law, which is the code of
rules elaborated by the collective wisdom of the past under
the guidance of the Holy Ghost, endeavours to show
within the range of cases which come under its cognisance, how truth may be elicited from the observed facts,
and how justice may be combined with mercy, so that
what is right and equal may be done between each individual member and the whole Body of the Church.

TABLE OF CONTENTS.

———◆———

A

THE ELEMENTS OF CANON LAW.

CHAPTER I.

THE RELATION OF CANON LAW TO OTHER BRANCHES OF LAW.

ALL laws are either of God's making or of man's making ([1]). Hence Law may be exhaustively divided into two kinds: (1) Divine Law; and (2) Human Law ([2]).

1. Divine Law is God's Law, whether as Creator or as

([1]) The following Schedule will illustrate this chapter:—

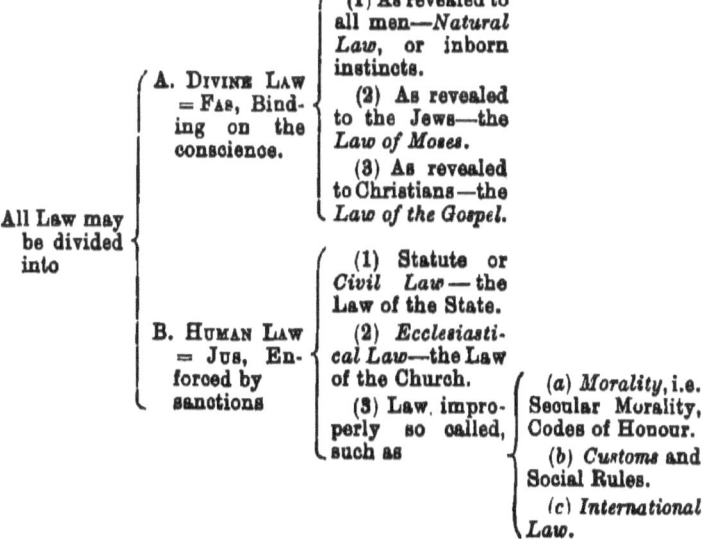

([2]) Gratian I. Dist. i. c. 1.

B

Moral Governour of the world.   In the one case it is termed Natural Law, in the other, Moral Law.

Natural Law (¹) is what God the Creator has implanted in us by nature, such as the instinct of self-preservation, of self-defence, of propagation, and the like—in short, all those natural instincts common to all men which spring from their physical condition.

Divine Moral Law is what God has revealed of His will touching human conduct either in Old Testament times or in the Gospels (²).

2. Human Law is Law of man's making.   When written it is more properly called Law, and when unwritten is called Custom.   Human Law is applied to two different sides of life : (1) the State, and (2) the Church.   In the former case it is called Civil or Statute or Common Law ; in the latter, Ecclesiastical Law.

Civil Law (³) is the Law of a Civil Community or Body Politic (⁴).   According to modern ideas it should aim at securing the well-being of the greatest number in and

(¹) Isidorus, c. 4. ap. Gratian I. Dist. i. c. 7 : Jus naturale est commune omnium nationum, eo quod ubique instinctu naturæ non constitutione aliqua habetur, ut viri et feminæ conjunctio, liberorum successio et educatio, communis omnium possessio et omnium una libertas.   Augustinus ap. Gratian I. Dist. viii. c. 1 : Jure divino omnia sunt communia omnibus : jure vero constitutionis hoc meum, illud alterius est.

(²) Joannes Chrysostomus mentions many things allowed in the Old Testament which are forbidden by the Gospel.   See Gratian Caus. xxiii. Qu. viii. c. 14.

(³) Isidorus, c. 5, ap. Gratian I. Dist. i. c. 8 : Jus civile, quod quisque populus vel quæque civitas sibi proprium divina humanaque causa constituit.

(⁴) It ought not, says Augustine, ap. Gratian I. Dist. ix. c. 1, to run counter to natural law.

through the State. Ecclesiastical (¹) Law is the Law of a Spiritual Society, the Body of Christ. Its aim is to promote the advancement in holiness of all the members of that Body with a view to their final salvation in the world to come.

3. Canon Law is of a composite kind, and consists partly of Divine and partly of Human Law. It includes :—

(1) What God has revealed of His will touching human conduct in the Holy Scriptures (²) ; i.e. the Divine Moral Law, and

(2) The Laws which the governours of the Spiritual Society, the Church, have from time to time laid down (³), viz., the Canons of Councils and the approved Customs of the Church.

(¹) Jus Ecclesiasticum is a term of wider extension than Jus Canonicum. See Von Schulte, *Geschichte der Quellen des Canonischen Rechts*, c. 30.

(²) See Gratian I. Dist. ix.

(³) Which have less weight than Holy Scripture, according to Augustine, ap. Gratian I. Dist. ix. c. 10.

CHAPTER II.

DIVISION OF THE SUBJECT.

1. THE subject-matter of Canon Law naturally falls into the following three divisions : (1) the first dealing with Canons generally and Canon Law ; (2) the second dealing with the general Government of the Church and Jurisdiction ; (3) the third treating of certain Essentials for the Church's holiness and maintenance upon earth ; to which may be added (4) a fourth, treating of certain extensions of Church organisation in mediæval and modern times.

2. In dealing with Canons generally and Canon Law, (1) first the meaning of the term, the source and authority of Canons have to be ascertained ; and then (2) the various steps to be traced, by means of which a species of Canonical Jurisprudence has grown up in the Church on the basis of isolated Canons.

3. In treating of the General Government of the Church, it will be necessary to consider, (1) the nature of Jurisdiction ; (2) the Officers through whom Jurisdiction is administered, viz., the Ecclesiastical Hierarchy ; (3) the Unit of Jurisdiction—the Diocese.

4. The Essentials necessary for the Church's holiness and maintenance upon earth fall under the three classes of Graces, Gifts, and Censures, and suggest as separate heads for treatment : (1) The Sacraments and all other means

of Grace ; (2) Spiritual Gifts, whether of Orders or
Matrimony ; (3) Ecclesiastical Censures, both private and
public.

5. The extension of Church Organisation in Mediæval
and Modern Times has principally affected three things :
(1) the Diocesan System, by creating Sub-units of Jurisdiction within the diocese ; (2) the System of Public
Worship, by substituting Public Worship for the Eucharist ;
and (3) the Administration of Discipline.

PART I.

OF CANONS AND CANON LAW.

BEFORE treating of Canon Law as a branch of Jurisprudence, it is well to consider the materials out of which it is constructed. Hence a twofold division of the subject suggests itself; the first treating of Canons generally, the meaning of the term, their sources and their authority; the second treating of Canon Law as a scientific whole.

DIVISION I.

OF CANONS GENERALLY—THEIR MEANING, SOURCES, AND AUTHORITY.

CHAPTER III.

OF CANONS GENERALLY.

1. THE term Canon, from the Greek word κανών, a carpenter's rule (¹) is ordinarily used to express a rule of conduct sanctioned by the Church at large, whether by

(¹)· See Schulte, *Geschichte der Quellen des Canonischen Rechts*, Vol. I., p. 29.

enactment or by custom (¹). The Church of Christ being a corporate unity—the Body of Christ consisting of many members (²), Canons of the Church is the name applied to the disciplinary rules regulating the outward conduct of those members whilst upon earth (³).

2. In the New Testament a rule of doctrine or article of faith is also called a Canon (⁴), and in this sense the term is used by the Tridentine Council, and in more recent times by the Council of the Vatican. It may therefore be employed indiscriminately to express a rule of faith equally with a rule of life.

3. Used in the latter, which is the more ordinary, sense, it may be defined as a disciplinary rule regulating the position and conduct of members, and the outward arrangements of the Church upon earth. Such rules when made by proper authority are styled Canons, and the whole of them Canon Law by analogy to their civil counterparts (⁵)

(¹) Gratian I. Dist. iii. writes : Ecclesiastica constitutio *canonis* nomine censetur. As to customs, Hieronymus ad Lucinium, Epist. xxviii., ap. Gratian I. Dist. xii. c. 3 and 4, writes : traditiones ecclesiasticas . . . ita observandas ut a majoribus traditæ sunt. Justinian Institutes Lib. i. tit. 2; *Ibid.* c. 6; Diuturni mores consensu utentium approbati, legem imitantur. *Ibid.* c. 8; Gregorius universis episcopis Numidiæ.

(²) Rom. xii. 5: οὕτως οἱ πολλοὶ ἓν σῶμά ἐσμεν ἐν Χριστῷ, ὁ δὲ καθεῖς ἀλλήλων μέλη· 1 Tim. iii. 15 ; ἥτις ἐστὶν ἐκκλησία θεοῦ ζῶντος.

(³) The definition given by the Roman Canonist Caisson in his Manuale (Pictavii, 1880), Vol. I., p. 3, is, Leges a quocumque potestatem legislativam possidente in bonum fidelium firmatæ.

(⁴) Thus Philip iii. 16 ; πλὴν εἰς ὃ ἐφθάσαμεν, τῷ αὐτῷ στοιχεῖν κανόνι·, and in Gal. vi. 16 ; καὶ ὅσοι τῷ κανόνι τούτῳ στοιχήσουσι, where Canon appears used to express the creed or rule of faith.

(⁵) See Austin's Jurisprudence as to the accurate and inaccurate use of the term Law.

which bear the name of Civil Law, or in England Common
and Statute Law.   But whereas Civil Law consists of the
rules which govern the conduct of individuals in their
relations to the Civil Community—the State, Canon Law
consists of those which are binding on the several members
of the Ecclesiastical Community—the Church.

CHAPTER IV.

THE CHURCH.

1. THE Church (¹) is a divinely instituted, voluntary Society of persons gathered out of the world (²) and placed in the way of salvation (³) by being admitted within its fold. It not only is called, but *is* the Body of Christ in such wise that all the persons composing it are branches in a Vine of which Christ is the stock (⁴) and members of a Body of which Christ is the Head (⁵).

2. The objects for which this Society has been called into existence are : (1) that its members may by means of Christ's holiness be themselves made holy (⁶) whilst upon

(¹) See *Lehrbuch des Kirchenrechtes aller Christlicher Confessionen.* Von Ferdinand Walter, Bonn 1871.

(²) Rom. viii. 28 ; οἱ κατὰ πρόθεσιν κλητοί· Rom. i. 6, 7 ; 1 Cor. i. 2, 24. Κλητοί are the summoned ones, collectively called ἡ ἐκκλησία, or the formally summoned assembly, including both those who obey the call and those who are disobedient.

(³). Termed σώζεσθαι, Eph. ii. 5 ; χάριτί ἐστε σεσωσμένοι, Luke xiii. 23 ; εἰ ὀλίγοι οἱ σωζόμενοι, Acts ii. 47 ; προσετίθει τοὺς σωζομένους . . . τῇ ἐκκλησίᾳ·

(⁴) John xv. 5 ; ἐγώ εἰμι ἡ ἄμπελος, ὑμεῖς τὰ κλήματα.

(⁵) Eph. i. 22 ; καὶ αὐτὸν ἔδωκε κεφαλὴν ὑπὲρ πάντα τῇ ἐκκλησίᾳ. Eph. iv. 15 ; Ὅς ἐστιν ἡ κεφαλή, ὁ Χριστός, ἐξ οὗ πᾶν τὸ σῶμα συναρμολογούμενον, κ. τ. λ. Col. i. 18 ; καὶ αὐτός ἐστιν ἡ κεφαλὴ τοῦ σώματος, τῆς ἐκκλησίας·

(⁶) Thus Rom. i. 7 ; 1 Cor. i. 2 ; Κλητοὶ ἅγιοι, called to be holy, and 2 Tim. i. 9 ; κλῆσις ἁγία· Also 1 Cor. vi. 1, 2 ; ἐκκλησίαι τῶν ἁγίων, and Eph. ii. 19 ; συμπολῖται τῶν ἁγίων, 2 Thess. i. 10 ; ὅταν ἔλθῃ ἐνδοξασθῆναι ἐν τοῖς ἁγίοις αὐτοῦ·

earth, and so fitted for final salvation hereafter, and (2)
that by incorporating others into the same Society they may
maintain its continuity to the end of time (¹), so that all
mankind may be partakers of a similar benefit. Its note is
therefore holiness.

3. The Church is moreover an outward and visible
Society (²), having an historical existence in time (³),
having Christ for its Founder from Whom it traces unbroken
descent, and being One and the Same throughout all ages.
Although it were possible to imagine a corporate society
founded by Christ, keeping up a continuous existence without apostolic intervention ; yet, as a matter of fact and
history, the Society founded by Christ was established

(¹) Matt. xxviii. 20; ἐγὼ μεθ' ὑμῶν εἰμι πάσας τὰς ἡμέρας ἕως τῆς
συντελείας τοῦ αἰῶνος· Matt. xvi. 18; ἐπὶ ταύτῃ τῇ πέτρᾳ οἰκοδομήσω μου
τὴν ἐκκλησίαν, καὶ πύλαι ᾅδου οὐ κατισχύσουσιν αὐτῆς·

(²) The term ἐκκλησία, a duly summoned meeting, could hardly be
applied to an invisible society, neither could the command to hear the
Church (Matt. xviii. 17). The various expressions in the New Testament—Acts v. 11, Great fear came upon all the Church ; viii. 1, A great
persecution against the Church; xi. 26, Assembling themselves with the
Church; xiv. 23, Ordaining elders in every Church ; xviii. 22, Saluting
the Church ; 1 Cor. xiv. 4, Edifying the Church—all imply a visible
society, and not merely an indeterminate body of men thinking
alike.

(³) The whole question as to the possibility of the existence of Canon
Law as a distinct branch of Law turns upon the view taken of the nature
of the Church. For if the Church be not a visible society, but only
what philosophers would call a subjective association, or the sum total
of those who think alike on certain religious matters, (who can, therefore,
never be known in this world), there can be no such thing as Canon
Law, and what is so called is only a subordinate branch of Civil Law,
and derives all its force from the civil authority. The same result
follows if the Church be considered as necessarily conterminous with the
nation, after the analogy of the Jewish nation of old. For a long time
it appears that one or other of these views largely prevailed in England.
Hence, in a great measure, the neglect of Canon Law.

through the agency and intervention of the Apostles (¹). Hence, no other but the society so founded and continuously maintained to this day constitutes the Church of Christ. And this Society is called the One, Holy, Catholic and Apostolic Church.

(¹) Matt. xxviii. 19: πορευθέντες οὖν μαθητεύσατε πάντα τὰ ἔθνη, βαπτίζοντες αὐτοὺς . . . διδάσκοντες αὐτοὺς κ. τ. λ. (Mark xvi. 15, Luke xxiv. 47.)

CHAPTER V.

THE CONSTITUTION OF THE CHURCH.

THE Society so founded derives from Christ Himself its Constitution (¹). This it cannot alter without being faithless to its trust or apostate; nor can any portion of the Church alter it without cutting itself off from the rest. According to that Constitution it is One, Holy, Catholic, and Apostolic.

1. The Church is *One*, seeing that there is " One Lord, One faith, One baptism" (²), and that Christ prayed that His disciples all might be One (³). Hence expressions like the Eastern Church, the Western Church, the Church of Jerusalem, or Antioch, are inaccurate and misleading so far as they seem to imply a plurality of Churches. For no such plurality can exist, the Body of Christ being One (⁴), of which they all are parts. Those who cause rents or divisions (⁵) in the Unity of that Body are called *Schis-*

(¹) The divine framework of the Church, established by the Church's Founder,—its Constitution, must be distinguished from its disciplinary laws, albeit the latter are given by divine guidance. The former is immutable; the latter may be changed by the same authority that made them.

(²) Eph. iv. 5 : εἷς κύριος, μία πίστις, ἐν βάπτισμα·

(³) John xvii. 21 : Ἵνα πάντες ἓν ὦσι· καθὼς σὺ, πάτερ, ἐν ἐμοὶ, κἀγὼ ἐν σοὶ, ἵνα καὶ αὐτοὶ ἐν ἡμῖν ἓν ὦσιν·

(⁴) See authorities, ap. Gratian Caus. xxiv. Qu. i. o. 18-34.

(⁵) 1 Cor. i. 10 : μὴ ᾖ ἐν ὑμῖν σχίσματα· 1 Cor. xii. 25 ; ἵνα μὴ ᾖ σχίσμα ἐν τῷ σώματι, ἀλλὰ τὸ αὐτὸ ὑπὲρ ἀλλήλων μεριμνῶσι τὰ μέλη·

matics. To establish and uphold this corporate Unity, Christ Himself ordained the Sacraments (¹).

2. The Church is *Holy*, because it is the Body of Christ. The holiness of the Head (²) sanctifies the members (³), and their sanctification is the object of its existence upon earth (⁴).

3. The Church is *Catholic*, which means (1) that it embraces men of all nations, herein differing from the older society of the Jewish covenant which was limited to one nation only, that of the Jews (⁵) ; and (2) that it consists of the main body of the Christian society, steadfastly cleaving to the Apostles' doctrine and fellowship (⁶), in contradistinction to the factions (⁷) which elect to strike out new lines of

(¹) Augustine, Tractat. xiii. ad c. 3 Ioannis ap. Gratian Caus. i. Qu. i. c. 56.

(²) Mark i. 24 ; Luke iv. 34 ; John vi. 69 ; ὁ ἅγιος τοῦ θεοῦ· Conf. Acts. iii. 14 ; iv. 27 and 30. John x. 36 ; ὃν ὁ πατὴρ ἡγίασεν· 1 Pet. i. 15 and 16 ; κατὰ τὸν καλέσαντα ὑμᾶς ἅγιον, καὶ αὐτοὶ ἅγιοι ἐν πάσῃ ἀναστροφῇ γενήθητε, διότι γέγραπται ὅτι ἅγιοι γένεσθε, ὅτι ἐγὼ ἅγιος· 1 Cor. iii. 17 ; ὁ γὰρ ναὸς τοῦ θεοῦ ἅγιός ἐστιν, οἵτινές ἐστε ὑμεῖς·

(³) Heb. x. 10: ἐν ᾧ θελήματι ἡγιασμένοι ἐσμὲν 1 Cor. i. 2 : ἡγιασμένοις ἐν Χριστῷ Ἰησοῦ· Jude. i. ; τοῖς ἐν θεῷ πατρὶ ἡγιασμένοις καὶ Ἰησοῦ Χριστῷ τετηρημένοις κλητοῖς·

(⁴) John xvii. 19 : καὶ ὑπὲρ αὐτῶν ἐγὼ ἁγιάζω ἐμαυτὸν, ἵνα καὶ αὐτοὶ ὦσιν ἡγιασμένοι ἐν ἀληθείᾳ·

(⁵) See the argument in the Epistle to the Romans, showing that the old Covenant was confined to Abraham and his seed, whereas the new Covenant is for all (iii. 22) ; εἰς πάντας καὶ ἐπὶ πάντας τοὺς πιστεύοντας· οὐ γάρ ἐστι διαστολή· (v. 18) ; εἰς πάντας ἀνθρώπους εἰς δικαίωσιν ζωῆς· The word Catholic does not, however, appear in the New Testament.

(⁶) Acts ii. 42 ; ἦσαν δὲ προσκαρτεροῦντες τῇ διδαχῇ τῶν ἀποστόλων καὶ τῇ κοινωνίᾳ καὶ τῇ κλάσει τοῦ ἄρτου καὶ ταῖς προσευχαῖς·

(⁷) Such as existed in the Corinthian Church, one calling himself of Paul, another of Apollos, a third of Cephas, 1 Cor. i. 12. These factions are referred to as heresies in 1 Cor. xi. 19 ; δεῖ γὰρ καὶ αἱρέσεις ἐν ὑμῖν ὑπάρχειν· See Peter ii. 1 ; ἐν ὑμῖν ἔσονται ψευδοδιδάσκαλοι, οἵτινες παρεισάξουσιν αἱρέσεις ἀπωλείας.

teaching for themselves, and are hence called *Heretics* (¹).
Catholic doctrine is the name applied to what in the New
Testament is called the Faith (ἡ πίστις) (²), and is that
which hath been ever and everywhere taught in the
Church (³), which is set forth more explicitly in the Creeds,
and which has been defined more closely from time to time
as heresies required it (⁴).

4. The Church is *Apostolic*. For it was by its divine
Founder committed to the care and guidance of the
Apostles (⁵). Through them it has received its form of

(¹) Titus iii. 10 ; Αἱρετικὸν ἄνθρωπον μετὰ μίαν καὶ δευτέραν νουθεσίαν
παραιτοῦ. See Hieronymus in Aggæum c. 2, in Amos c. 5. Concil. Laodicense Can. 32 ; Concil. Martini Can. 70 ; Leo Epist. xlviii. c. 2, and
lxxiii. Cyprianus contra Hæreticos. Gregorii iii. Lib. Dist. c. 80.
Innocentii Epist. lviii c. 8 : all ap. Gratian, Caus. i. Qu. i. c. 60, 61,
66, 67, 68, 69, 70, 72, 73, also Caus. xxiv. Qu. iii. c. 27 to 88. A list of
heretics is given by Gratian in Caus. xxiv. Qu. iii. c. 89.

(²) Acts iii. 16 ; ἡ πίστις ἡ διὰ Ἰησοῦ Χριστοῦ· Acts. xiv. 22 ; ἐμμένειν
τῇ πίστει, xvi. 5 ; ἐστερεοῦντο τῇ πίστει Rom. iv. 19, 20 ; 1 Cor. xvi.
13 ; στήκετε ἐν τῇ πίστει· Rom. xi. 20 ; 2 Cor. i. 24, xiii. 5 : εἶναι ἐν
τῇ πίστει· 2 Tim. iv. 7 ; τηρεῖν τὴν πίστιν· Col. ii. 7 : βεβαιοῦσθαι ἐν τῇ
πίστει· 1 Tim. iv. 1 : ἀποστήσονταί τινες τῆς πίστεως· Jude 3 : ἐπαγωνί
ζεσθαι τῇ ἅπαξ παραδοθείσῃ τοῖς ἁγίοις πίστει·

(³) Vincentius Lerinensis Augustin. ap. Gratian Dist. ix. c. 8.

(⁴) On the difference between Heresy and Schism, see Gratian,
Caus. xxiv. Qu. iii. c. 26.

(⁵) The charge given by Christ to his Apostles, Matt. xxviii. 19, was :
᾽Ἐδόθη μοι πᾶσα ἐξουσία ἐν οὐρανῷ καὶ ἐπὶ γῆς· πορευθέντες οὖν
μαθητεύσατε πάντα τὰ ἔθνη, βαπτίζοντες αὐτοὺς. . . . διδάσκοντες
αὐτοὺς . . . These words imply (1) that the plenitude of power
resides in Christ ; (2) that in the exercise of that power, the charge
was given to the Apostles (*a*) of gathering a Church together out of the
world by the rite of baptism, and (*b*) of teaching the members of that
Church to observe Christ's commands. That charge still rests with the
successors of the Apostles, *i.e.* the Collective Episcopate for ἰδοὺ ἐγὼ μεθ᾽
ὑμῶν εἰμι πάσας τὰς ἡμέρας ἕως τῆς συντελείας τοῦ αἰῶνος· Hieronymus
ad Titum, i. c. 9, ap. Gratian I. Dist. xcv. c. 5. See Chap. xxix.

government, which they who decline are called *Sectarians*.
It is seen in the New Testament that the Church was
administered by the Apostles themselves through priests
(called elders or bishops) and deacons (¹), and that over
these others, such as Timothy, were appointed (²) as over-
lookers, or bishops in the modern sense.

Thus Corporate Unity, and Holiness, Catholic Doctrine,
and Apostolic Order are the true notes of Christ's Church
upon earth.

(¹) The term πρεσβύτεροι, elders, is used to designate the προεστῶτες
(1 Tim. v. 17) who were appointed (καθιστάναι, Tit. i. 5), or chosen
(χειροτονεῖν, Acts xiv. 23), from Church to Church (κατ' ἐκκλησίαν, Acts.
xiv. 23) ; and from city to city (κατὰ πόλιν, Tit. i. 5). In the first notice
we have of them (Acts xi. 30) they appear as discharging functions similar
to those for which the deacons (Acts vi.) were appointed. On leaving
Miletus S. Paul entrusted to them their work (Acts xx. 17), the nature
of which may be gathered from Acts xx. 28 seq.; 1 Tim. v. 17.; James v.
14; 1 Pet. v. 1; and they are indiscriminately called there πρεσβύτεροι
and ἐπίσκοποι In Phil. i. 1, the ἐπίσκοποι are mentioned side by side
with the διάκονοι, showing that they are the same who elsewhere are
called πρεσβύτεροι So also in 1 Tim. iii. 2, compared with v. 8 ; and
Tit. i. 7, compared with v. 5 ; Clem. Rom. i. Ep. ad Cor. 42, writes :
κατὰ χώρας οὖν καὶ πόλεις οἱ ἀπόστολοι κηρύσσοντες καθίστανον τὰς
ἀπαρχὰς αὐτῶν ... εἰς ἐπισκόπους καὶ διακόνους τῶν μελλόντων πιστεύειν·

(²) See 1 Tim. iii. 15 ; ἵνα εἰδῇς πῶς δεῖ ἐν οἴκῳ θεοῦ ἀναστρέφεσθαι·
Tit. i. 5 ; Τούτου χάριν κατέλιπόν σε ἐν Κρήτῃ, ἵνα τὰ λείποντα ἐπιδιορθώσῃ
καὶ καταστήσῃς κατὰ πόλιν πρεσβυτέρους, ὡς ἐγώ σοι διεταξάμην·

CHAPTER VI.

THE CHURCH'S POWER OF MAKING CANONS.

1. THE Church has as well the ordinary right inherent in every Society, as also a special divine right of making rules and regulations (¹) for its own government. This right, however, exists, and may only be exercised subject to certain limitations (²).

The Church may not order anything contrary to its divine constitution or the divine laws established by Christ. Were it so to do, it would forfeit its character as the Church of Christ and become apostate, a fate from which Christ has promised it shall be preserved. But it has full power to change from time to time its disciplinary rules, not excepting such as were established by the Apostles themselves. For it is the function of the Church to educate its members in the way of eternal life, and of the best means thereto it is the judge.

2. To be of force, all rules and regulations must be made by the proper legislative authority within the Church (³) ;

(¹) Gratian I. Dist. iv. c. 1. Factæ sunt autem leges ut earum metu humana coerceatur audacia. Dist. xv. c. 1.

(²) Gratian I. Dist. iv. c. 2. Erit autem lex honesta, justa, possibilis, secundum naturam secundum patriae consuetudinem, loco temporique conveniens, necessaria, utilis manifesta quoque ne aliquid per obscuritatem in captionem contineat.

(³) John x. 1: ὁ μὴ εἰσερχόμενος διὰ τῆς θύρας εἰς τὴν αὐλὴν τῶν προβάτων, ἀλλὰ ἀναβαίνων ἀλλαχόθεν, ἐκεῖνος κλέπτης ἐστὶ καὶ λῃστής. See Gratian I. Dist. x. c. 5.

or else have by long custom and acquiescence obtained the force of such rules (¹).

Such rules must not be capricious, but must have for their end the furtherance of the object for which the Church has been placed upon earth, viz., the salvation of mankind by means of Christ's holiness (²).

8. The power that can make can also unmake. The Church has, therefore, the power of abrogating generally or of relaxing in particular instances (³) all rules of its own making. Such particular relaxations are called dispensations, but no dispensations can alter the divine constitution of the Church, nor the divinely-given laws by which it is governed (⁴).

(¹) Gratian I. Dist. xl. c. 5 and 7. Dist. xii. c. 3 to 9.

(²) The old definition quoted by Caisson in his Mnnuale, vol I. p. 146 : Potestatem jurisdictionis ecclesiasticæ esse potestatem regendi et gubernandi subditos in ordine ad vitam æternam. Gratian, Dist. x. c. 4 : Constitutiones contra . . . bonos mores nullius sunt momenti.

(³) Authorities ap. Gratian, Caus. i. Qu. vii. c. 11 to 15, and 23.

(⁴) Gratian I. Dist. xiii. and Dist. xiv. c. 2.

CHAPTER VII.

THE SANCTION ATTACHING TO CANONS.

ALL rules being admittedly inoperative unless there be some sanction attaching thereto, there must needs be some sanction attaching to the Church's rules. This sanction is of two kinds; (1) the inward sanction of Conscience, (2) the outward sanction of Spiritual Censure.

1. As to the first :—The pursuit of holiness (which is the end of the Church's existence upon earth) being to the individual a matter of conscience, no one can be conscious to himself of sincerely pursuing this end who wilfully neglects the means which the collective wisdom of the Church has prescribed for that purpose ([1]). Hence a duly published Canon is said to be binding on the conscience.

2. Spiritual Censure is brought into exercise ([2]) by means of ecclesiastical jurisdiction, when offence or scandal arises in the Church, and may be either in the form of penance, or in the form of excommunication.

([1]) See the language used by S. Gregory of the 4 General Councils in Gratian I. Dist. xv., *c.* 2. Sicut sancti evangelii quatuor libros, sic quatuor concilia suscipere et venerari me fateor . . . . Cunctas vero quas præfata veneranda concilia personas respuunt, respuo ; quas venerantur, amplector ; quia dum universali sunt consensu constituta, se et non illa destruit, quisquis præsumit aut solvere quos religant, aut ligare quos solvunt.

([2]) See Augustin. de verbis Dom. Serm. xi., ap. Gratian Caus. i. Qu. i. c. 61.

Penance, or partial exclusion from the Christian Society, is said to be exercised for the soul's health, when the aim of the Church is to reform an offender.

When Excommunication or total exclusion is applied, the aim is to remove from the rest a source of contamination to the Church's purity.

3. In the Middle Ages the Church also obtained Civil or Secular sanction for its Canons and administration ([1]), out of which grew (1) the establishment of National Churches, (2) Concordats, (3) the Confusion of Church and State.

When the members of the Church living within the limits of particular localities or nations formed themselves into groups apart from other branches of the Church, such groups were called National Churches.

Concordats is the name applied to agreements entered into between National Governments and branches of the Church locally situate within the territory of those Governments, whereby such National Churches surrendered in a great measure their freedom of administration in return for secular advantages being assured to them ([2]).

The confusion and intermixture of Church and State, which followed in consequence, was such that to some the invisible Church appeared merged in the world ([3]) and to

([1]) This happened as early as the 4th century, and was the rule throughout the Middle Ages.

([2]) See Part iv.

([3]) In the time of Gregory VII., Innocent III. and Boneface VIII., the Pope and the Emperor, were spoken of as the Sun and Moon of one World-Empire. See Roichel's *See of Rome* pp. 282 seq. Labbé xii. p. 476 and Decret. Greg. IX. Lib. i. Tit. xxxiii. c. 6.

have lost the note of holiness. Hence a reaction set in, one of the results of which was a falling back on unity of sentiment in place of unity of communion, and the setting up of an invisible Church of persons thinking alike in place of the corporate society actually founded by Christ.

CHAPTER VIII.

THE making of rules and regulations can only be exercised
in the Church by the Legislative power to which it belongs
of right, and they to whom it belongs of right are those to
whom it has been entrusted by Christ, *i.e.* the Apostles,
and those commissioned by them. At the Council of
Jerusalem "it seemed good to the Apostles and Elders
together with the whole Church " ([1]) to make the decrees,
whence it appears that the Clergy generally and the Laity
have a certain share in the making of Canons as well
as the Bishops of the Church.

1. The share of the Clergy generally and the Laity in the
making of Canons does not go beyond assenting to them
([2]) and such assent is necessary before Canons can be considered in force. At different times this assent may and
has been expressed in different ways. Usually it is not
more than receiving them submissively when made known,
as becomes sons in the faith, and is given at the time of the
Publication of a Canon. Hence the importance of Publication in Canon Law.

2. The initiative in ecclesiastical legislation, however,

([1]) Acts. xv. 22; ἔδοξε τοῖς ἀποστόλοις καὶ τοῖς πρεσβυτέροις σὺν ὅλῃ
τῇ ἐκκλησίᾳ·

([2]) Gratian I. Dist. lxii. c. 2.

rests with the Bishops as inheritors of the Apostle's commission; for Christ's commission (S. Matt. xxviii. 19, 20) was specially given to them, and they were chosen from among the other disciples (S. Mark iii. 18) to be Shepherds to feed the flock (Heb. v. 2).

3. It rests, moreover, not with the Bishops individually, but with the collective Episcopate ([1]); for Christ's commission was given to the Apostles, not individually, but as a body (S. Matt. xxviii. 19, 20; and xviii. 18).

In so far as the Pope was at any time the representative or proctor of the collective Episcopate, he may be considered to have rightly exercised the initiative in ecclesiastical Legislation. Hence the authority claimed for certain Decretals and Constitutions ([2]).

4. In an Ecumenical or General Council of the Bishops of the whole Church the voice of the collective Episcopate properly speaks. The decrees or canons of such a Council, therefore, when assented to by the Clergy and Laity are of full obligation for all Christian people ([3]).

A derivative Legislative power rests with the Bishops assembled in Provincial or National Council, such councils being deemed to represent the collective Episcopate, so far as the making of rules or Canons is concerned for the special

---

([1]) Hence the great importance attaching to gatherings of the Episcopate which were ordered to be held twice a year. See Leo I.'s letters in Gratian I. Dist. xviii. c. 2; and the various authorities there quoted, for compelling the attendance of bishops at these synods, and the consent of comprovincials necessary. Gratian I. Dist. lxv.

([2]) Gratian I. Dist. xix. and xx. Caus. xxv. Qu. i. c. 6-9.

([3]) Bishops were required to communicate to their Churches the decisions of General Councils. Gratian I. Dist. xviii. c. 17. Gelasius ap. Gratian, Caus. xxv. Qu. i. c. 1.

needs of the Provinces or Nations which they represent. Rules made by a Provincial Council are of force therefore in the district for which they were made. Elsewhere they carry weight by analogy only, as being utterances of the Episcopate, and believed to represent the Collective Episcopate until such time as it shall have expressed itself otherwise.

Rules made by a single Bishop are not Canons. Though made in a diocesan Synod, they are no more than Statutes of the diocese, and have force only within the area of the individual Bishop's jurisdiction, and in it on those only who are the subjects of that jurisdiction ([1]).

([1]) Gratian I. Dist. xviii; Episcoporum igitur concilia sunt invalida ad definiendum et constituendum, non autom ad corrigendum.

CHAPTER IX.

ECCLESIASTICAL JURISDICTION—THE DIOCESAN EPISCOPATE.

As it belongs to the Bishops collectively to initiate legislation for the Church, so the care of enforcing the observance of Canons when made rests with the Bishops individually within the districts or dioceses severally entrusted to their charge. This delegation of local administration is called Jurisdiction.

1. All jurisdiction is, therefore, derivative and not inherent, *i.e.*, it is derived from the Church as a whole, and is granted by the Collective Episcopate to Individual Bishops in the exercise of its care for the whole Church (¹). By virtue of his consecration every Bishop becomes a member of the Collective Episcopate, a joint-partaker and fellow-sharer in one undivided office, viz., the oversight of

(¹) Gratian I. Dist. lxi. c., 11. Dist. lxii, c. 1.; Dist. lxiii, c. 35.; Dist. lxiv., c. 4. Hence there may be Bishops who have no local jurisdictions, and there may be episcopal jurisdiction exercised by those not of the Episcopal Order. An instance of the former appear to have been the χωρεπίσκοποι or village-bishops, referred to in Canon VIII. of the Nicene Council, and Canon II. of the Council of Chalcedon ap. Gratian lxviii. c. 4. See also Canon x. of the Council of Antioch : Ii qui sunt in vicis vel pagis, qui dicuntur Chorepiscopi, etiamsi Episcopi ordinationem manuumve impositionem acceperunt, visum est ut suum modum sciant et sibi subjectas Ecclesias administrent nec presbyterum nec diaconum ordinare audeant absque Urbis episcopo, cui subjectus ipse et regio. An instance of the latter is the exercise of episcopal functions by a Chapter through a Vicar during the vacancy of a see. Chorepiscopi might be consecrated by one bishop. Gratian I. Dist. lxvii. 1.

the whole Church (¹). The division of this office for administrative purposes and the entrusting of the exclusive oversight
of the Church in any particular district to a single head is a
matter of ecclesiastical order (²).

Such a distribution of one undivided office had obtained
previously to the Council of Nicæa, and was expressly
approved by that Council (³) ; and such division has obtained
ever since. Nevertheless, the jurisdiction of individual
Bishops is always subject to revision by their fellow-bishops
in case of need.

2. The supervision and revision by the Coepiscopate is
exercised both by the necessity of their concurring in the
appointment of a new Bishop, and also by the power of
appeal, which is never dormant (⁴); in the first instance from
a single Bishop to his fellow-bishops next adjacent through
the Metropolitan ; in the next place from the Bishops next
adjacent to those of a wider circle through the Primate or
the Patriarch ; and ultimately to the collective Episcopate in
General Council assembled. Thus no Bishop stands alone,
although exercising direct jurisdiction over his own diocese ;

(¹) Cyprian ap. Gratian, Caus. vii. Qu. i. c. 6. Caisson Manuale I.
p. 171.

(²) Cyprian Epis. 55, ad. Corn. Pap. ap. Gratian I. Dist. lxv. and
lxvi. and lxxxi. Singulis Pastoribus portio gregis adscripta est, quam
regat unusquisque atque gubernet. See also Augustin. Epist. ad. Euse-
bium 84, and Canon ii. of 1 Council of Constantinople ; κατὰ τοὺς
κανόνας, τὸν μὲν ᾽Αλεξανδρείας ἐπίσκοπον τὰ ἐν Αἰγύπτῳ μόνον οἰκονομεῖν·
τοὺς δὲ τῆς ἀνατολῆς ἐπισκόπους τὴν ἀνατολὴν μόνην διοικεῖν· . . . καὶ τοὺς
τῆς ᾽Ασιανῆς διοικήσεως ἐπισκόπους τὰ κατὰ τὴν ᾽Ασιανὴν μόνον οἰκονομεῖν·
κ. τ. λ.

(³) Concil. Nicæn. Can. 4 and 6, ap. Gratian I. Dist. lxv. c. 6.

(⁴) Gratian I. Dist. lxv. c. 1. Concil. Nicæan. Canon vi. Gratian
I. Dist. lxiv. c. 5 and 6., also lxv. c. 4, 8 and 9.

but in every case other Bishops are associated with him, exercising, when required, a joint Episcopal control (¹) that so the rule of the collective Episcopate may be everywhere felt, and that no portion of the Church may suffer through the delegation of jurisdiction to individuals.

3. A local district entrusted to the charge of a single Bishop is called a diocese. When several dioceses are combined, the whole is called a Province, and the presiding Bishop a Metropolitan (²). When several Provinces within the limits of one nation are united, the whole is called a National Church, and the presiding Bishop a Primate. And when a larger group of Provinces are brought together under the presidency of one, the whole is called a Patriarchate, and the presiding Archbishop a Patriarch (³). These divisions and the graduated Hierarchy of Jurisdiction which they imply are purely matters of Church Order, and may at any time be altered as circumstances require. Thus five Patriarchates only were known to the Council of Constantinople ; to wit, Rome, Constantinople, Alexandria, Antioch, and Jerusalem. In later times other centres were added. In the mapping out of local jurisdictions the early Church usually followed the civil arrangements of the Empire. It, therefore, committed to a single Bishop a town (⁴) together with the adjacent villages, to a Metropolitan a more important city together

---

(¹) Gratian I. Dist. lxvi. c. 1. ; lxxx. c. 6 ; xcii. c. 8. ; I. Dist. xc. c. 11.

(²) Concil. Chalcedon. Can. 12, A.D. 451.

(³) Gratian I. Dist. xcix.

(⁴) Christianity appears to have been originally planted in the mother cities *metropoles*, whence it slowly spread to the *pagi*, or villages, the latter continuing heathen, and hence called *pagani* long after it was

with the presidency of the adjoining Bishops, to a Patriarch or Primate (¹) a Capital City together with the place of honour among the Metropolitans. And amongst Patriarchs stood pre-eminent the Bishop of the Capital City Rome (²), Patriarch of Italy and the West, and successor of S. Peter.

universal in the cities. It is highly probable that the nomenclature of the Church was taken from that of the synagogue as Owen, *Canon Law* p. 29, suggests.

(¹) Gratian I. Dist. xcix. c. and ci.

(²) Gratian I. Dist. lxxix. and xcix. c. 4., and xcvii.

CHAPTER X.

AUTHORITATIVE SOURCES OF CANONS.

ECCLESIASTICAL laws being only valid, when they are authorised by Legislative authority in the Church, it is well to inquire how this authorisation may be given. This may be done in one of two ways, (1) either directly and by enactment, in which case they may be said to be regularly made, or (2) indirectly and by sufferance, in which case they may be called irregular. To the former class belong (1) Canons of Councils, and (2) certain Papal Decrees and Constitutions; to the latter, (1) Local Customs, and (2) Rules of Law.

1. Canons of Councils, are either Canons of General or Canons of Provincial Councils. Canons of General Councils are of all the most authoritative. In them the Collective Episcopate legislates for the whole Church, and they therefore are of obligation for all Christians.

Of lesser authority are the Canons of Provincial Councils, or assemblies of Bishops of one or more Provinces. Within the Province or Provinces of the Bishops composing them, they are of obligation when published. Outside these Provinces they have no force necessarily, save as indicating the mind of the Episcopate, so far as the matters to which they apply have been brought under its notice. Under similar circumstances, and in default of other Canons, they may be applied elsewhere, and thus they may in time acquire elsewhere the force of accepted customs.

2. Not less authority was allowed in the Middle Ages to the decisions of the Roman Bishops ([1]), on the ground that they were not only the rulings of a great Metropolitan, but also of the Patriarch of the Western Church, to whom belonged a further undefined precedence as successor of S. Peter. These decisions are of two kinds, (1) Sentences or Decrees, and (2) Constitutions.

Sentences are the rulings mostly of the earlier Bishops of Rome, before the institution ([2]) of the College of Cardinals ([3]). They are called *Decrees* when they are decisions of a general character, made proprio motu, whether before a Congregation of Cardinals or not ; *Decretals* when they are sentences on particular cases given by request or after consultation with others; *Rescripts* when they are written replies to inquiries on doubtful points ([4]).

Constitutions are the Conciliar utterances of the Pope and Cardinals in Council assembled. According to the degree of formality with which they are issued, they are called either *Bulls*, when issued by the Chancellor of the Roman Church and sealed with a leaden seal, *Briefs* when less formally written and impressed with the seal of the

([1]) Gratian I. Dist. xix.

([2]) Caisson Manuale, vol. I. p. 32.

([3]) The College of Cardinals was instituted by Nicolas II. A.D. 1059. See the Decretum in Labbé xii. 50 quoted in Reichel's *See of Rome*, p. 192, note.

([4]) In case of Rescripts being at variance, see Decret. Gregory IX. Lib. i. Tit. iii.

Fisherman (¹), or *Encyclicals* when addressed as circular letters to the Bishops and Clergy.

Papal Decrees which have been accepted and acted upon, must be allowed to have at least the force of Customs, and Papal Constitutions to have not less authority than the Canons of Provincial councils ; and during the long time from the breaking up of the Roman Empire until the dawn of the Reformation, when the Popes were the *de facto* representatives and spokesmen of the whole Episcopal Body, they may justly claim a much higher degree of authority.

(¹)   Caisson Manuale, vol. I. p. 33.

CHAPTER XI.

BESIDES Canons made by regular authority there are other rules derived from subsidiary sources, having in themselves no direct authority in the Christian Church, but having by sufferance and long acquiescence acquired a kind of indirect authority, so that they are of the nature of Canons, and in practice are not distinguishable therefrom. They are of two kinds ; (1) Customs, (2) Rules of Interpretation.

1. Customs or Customary rules (¹) are such observances as have grown up and been generally acted on and received without any known initial authorisation. They are allowed either to serve as an authoritative commentary on Canons properly so-called, by way of extension or interpretation ; or, in certain cases, they may even act as general dispensations, when they run counter to them.

Customs are said to be Extensions of Canons when they go beyond them, and have been used in cases to which no

---

(¹) The following conditions of a valid custom are laid down by Caisson Manuale, p. 59; (1) They must have taken root in the community, or (2) at least the major part thereof; (3) they must be well-known; (4) have been publicly acted on; (5) freely; and (6) without interruption. There are many cases in which no prescription by custom is allowed. See Decret. Greg. IX. Lib. i. Tit. iv.

Canons apply, but to which they apply by analogy following in the same lines.

They are Interpretations of Canons when they agree with them, and therefore only explain them so far as they are doubtful or obscure.

They act as general Dispensations when they are opposed to Canons. Before being allowed to have this effect they must, however, be shown (1) to be reasonable, which means useful to the people without giving license to sin, and (2) to have sufficient Prescription (¹).

In allowing an indirect authority to Customs the Church appears to have kept in view the great aim of all its legislation, which is the advancement of holiness in the world ; considering it wiser to acquiesce in Customs shown to contribute to holiness rather than to insist on uniform rules which might locally fail of promoting it (²).

2. Where Customs do not interpret existing Canons, there Rules of Interpretation may be applied. These, as being the work of Judges and Lawyers, have likewise no direct authority, but only such indirect authority as arises from being generally received and acted upon.

Rules of Interpretation are manifold. Eleven are cited

(¹) A prescription of at least ten years is required when they are extensions of law ; and certainly a prescription of forty years is enough when they are against law. See Gratian, Caus. xvi. Qu. iv. In some cases a prescription of thirty years suffices as when one Church prescribes against another. See Gratian, Caus. xvi. Qu. i.i. Decret. Greg. IX. Lib. ii. Tit. xxvi.

(²) A custom may be determined (1) by a distinct Canon to that effect, or (2) by the growth of a contrary Custom. See Caisson Manuale, p. 68,

authoritatively in the Decretals of Gregory IX. (^{1}) and eighty-eight in the Sext of Boniface VIII. Very frequent appeal is made to the following four :

(1) The mind rather than the bare words of the Legislative authorities ought to be followed.

(2) The aim and object of the Canon is to be considered.

(3) In cases of doubt as to the meaning, words are to be taken in their usual and natural sense.

(4) A restricted meaning is to be given to Canons creating disabilities, and an extended meaning to Canons conferring privileges. Thus the Canon enacting that a layman striking a Clerk shall be excommunicated, being a Canon creating a disability for laymen, is construed strictly to mean striking only, to the exclusion of threats or violence ; but the same, being a Canon conferring privileges on the Clergy, is extended to all of the Clergy, including novices of a religious Order.

Canons spurious in their origin may in time come to be accepted as authoritative, as being Customs expressing the

---

(^{1}) The rules of Gregory IX. are the following :—Decret. Greg. IX. Lib. v. Tit. xli.

1. Omnis res, per quascumque causas nascitur per easuem uissoivicur.
2. Dubia in meliorem partem interpretari debent.
3. Propter scandalum vitandum veritas non est omittenda.
4. Propter necessitatem, illicitum efficitur licitum.
5. Illicite factum, obligationem non inducit.
6. Tormenta, indiciis non præcedentibus, inferenda non sunt.
7. Sacrilegus est offendens rem vel personam ecclesiasticam.
8. Qui facit aliter quam debet, facere non dicitur.
9. Committens unum peccatum, reus est omnium, quoad vitam æternam.
10. Ignorantia non excusat Praelatum in peccatis subditorum.
11. Pro spiritualibus homagium non præstatur.

As to the meaning of words, see Decret. Greg. IX. Lib. v. Tit. xl.

D

mind of the Legislative authority, and as such acquiesced in by that body and the Church generally. For it is immaterial what may be the source from whence the stream issues, so that the water of the stream be pure, and that all things be ordered for promoting holiness.

DIVISION II.

OF CANON LAW AS A WHOLE.

CHAPTER XII.

THE CANON LAW OF THE CHURCH A STREAM.

WITH progress of time there is also progress in ecclesiastical legislation. New laws are being continually wanted to meet fresh needs, and new customs are ever growing up.

1. The progress of legislation within the Church has in a great measure followed the accidents of the Church's surroundings in the world. It has, therefore, shown two rival tendencies and been in two opposite directions, one towards separation, the other towards centralisation. On the one hand, the more independent of one another and national localities become, the more do the ecclesiastical rules framed for the special needs of those localities become divergent and provincial. On the other hand, the more the several branches of the Church are brought into connection with one another, the greater is the tendency towards uniformity of rule.

2. On the breaking up of the Roman Empire, a great isolation ensued between districts which had formerly been under the same government. Out of this isolation grew up the varieties of the nationalities included in the Western Patriarchate. Differences of race, and custom, and climate

D 2

gave rise to special ecclesiastical laws. Ecumenical Councils for the time being fell into abeyance, and there was a large growth of distinctly Provincial Canons.

3. Unity, however, being a note of the Church, there arose with the re-establishment of intercourse between the different branches of it a desire to assimilate differences in a general uniformity of rule to which all might be subject. Out of this desire came the pursuit of Canon Law as a science. And thus Canon Law may be defined to be the amalgamation of all the Canons at any time in force in the Church, in so far as this has been done by competent authority.

4. Canon Law may therefore be compared to a stream continually increasing in volume and gathering into itself tributaries in its onward course, and also from time to time dividing and flowing in several parallel streamlets. The history of Canon Law shows it under both these aspects. It involves, therefore : (1) the collection of materials, and (2) the assimilation of the materials when collected.

On the one hand Canon Law is a gathering up from various sources in chronological order of the Canons in force in various parts of the Church. Such were the Collections and the Summaries or Abridgements of Collections made in different parts of the Western Church up to the 11th century.

On the other hand Canon Law is a fusing of materials into one, and a reducing them to order and system—in short, a Codification of all the Canons in force, or, in the words of Gratian, a *Concordantia discordantium Canonum.*

CHAPTER XIII.

APART from and in addition to the Collection known as the Apostolic Canons, accepted by the Western Church as to 50, and as to 84 by the Eastern Church (the ecclesiastical law of which it represents in the third century), the stream of Canon Law flowing in the Western Church had, up to the time of Codification, received the following tributaries : (1) The Code of the African Church; (2) The Collections of Dionysius ; (3) The Spanish Collections; (4) The so-called False Decretals; and (5) Sundry Minor Collections. A few words as to each of these.

1. The Code of the African Church consisted of the Nicene Canons, supplemented by those of native Councils. It was published by Fulgentius Ferrandus ([1]) in A.D. 547, under the name of *Breviatio Canonum* ([2]), and contained African decisions up to A.D. 427. Subsequently Cresconius,

---

([1]) Fulgentius Ferrandus was the friend and pupil of Fulgentius of Ruspe, and went with him to exile in Sardinia. On his return to Carthage he became a Deacon, A.D. 523, and died A.D. 551. See Schulte's *Geschichte der Quellen*, p. 44.

([2]) The Breviatio Canonum contained 232 Canons of the Councils of Ancyra, Laodicea, Nicæa, Antioch, Gangra, Sardica. It is published in Migne's *Patrolog*, 1848, vol. lxvii. p. 949.

an African Bishop, issued a fresh treatise (¹), about A.D. 690, called *Concordia Canonum*, representing the law of the African Church.

2. About A.D. 510 a Collection (²) was made by Dionysius Exiguus (³), a Scythian monk, living at Rome, based on the Code of the African Church, and including, (1) 50 Apostolic Canons ; (2) the Canons of the four General Councils, viz. those of Nicæa, A.D. 325, Constantinople, A.D. 381, Ephesus, A.D. 431, and Chalcedon, A.D. 451 ; (3) 138 African Canons and the Canons of Sardica ; and (4) Papal Decretals from Pope Siricius, A.D. 386, to Pope Anastasius II. A.D. 496. As revised and enlarged, and presented to the Emperor Charles by Pope Hadrian I. in A.D. 774, this Collection is known as the Adriano-Dionysian Codex (⁴), and represents the law of the Roman Church at the time.

3. Of the Spanish Collections (⁵), the first contained the Canons of Nicæa, and those of Ancyra of Neocæsarea and Gangra only (⁶). A subsequent edition, towards the end of the fifth century, contained also those of Antioch,

(¹) Bibl. Jur. Can. I. App. of. 33. See Schulte, p. 44.

(²) This collection was made at the request of Stephen, Bishop of Salone.

(³) Dionysius first published the Canons of Sardica, and by some authorities is stated to have composed them. He also first introduced the Cyclus Paschalis, in which the birth of Christ is taken as the starting point of chronology. He died about 550 A.D.

(⁴) Published in Bibliotheca Jur. Can. I. 101, and Migne's *Patrolog. Lat.* 1848, vol. lxvii. See Schulte's *Geschichte der Quellen*, I. p. 41.

(⁵) See Schulte, *Geschichte der Quellen*, p. 41.

(⁶) Its date is uncertain. The translation of the Nicene Canons was known in Gaul in 489 (Concil. Regense, Can. 3), and that of the Ancyran Canons was quoted in 517 A.D. (Concil. Epaonens).

Constantinople, and Chalcedon ([1]). A new Collection appeared in the seventh century, containing not only Canons of Greek, African, Spanish, and French Councils, but also Papal Decretals from Pope Damasus to Gregory I. It bore the name of Isidore, of Seville ([2]), who, however, does not appear to have been in any way connected with it. It represents the law of the Spanish Church.

4. All that was contained in the Spanish Collection, wrongly called after Isidore, and in addition the Canons of several other Councils, were included in a Collection ([3]) which appeared at Mainz about 843 A.D., with a preface at its head by one Isidorus Mercator, called by some Peccator, on the strength of which it was attributed to Isidore of Seville. This Collection is best known for containing the Decretals of the Popes from Sylvester to Gregory II. (died A.D. 731), among which are included 35 that are spurious, and 59 spurious letters of Popes from Clement to Melchiades. In consequence of these spurious additions it usually goes by the name of the False Decretals, or the Pseudo-Isidorian Collection ([4]).

([1]) Published from an Oxford MS. under the title of "Codex Ecclesiæ Romanæ." (Ed. Paschas Quesnell in Opp. Leonis, par. 1675, Tom. II.)

([2]) Isidorus Hispaliensis (of Seville), born at Carthagena about 560 A.D., a friend of Gregory the Great, presided over the Councils of Seville, 619, and Toledo, 633, died at Seville 4th April, 686, one of the most able, learned, and energetic bishops of the Middle Ages.

([3]) See Reichel's *See of Rome*, p. 89, seq.—"No doubt appears to have been felt as to their genuineness before the time of Nicholas of Cusa. The Magdeburg Centuriators thoroughly exposed the spurious additions."

([4]) More than 50 MSS. of this Collection are extant. The Codex Vaticanus, No. 630, of the 12th century, observes the following order:— After the Preface comes a letter of Aurelius to Damasus, and the answer

The object aimed at in this Collection appears to have been to put an end to the confusion and servitude of the Church and the uncertainty of the law, by introducing a uniform code of ecclesiastical discipline, clothed with the prestige of antiquity, and to protect local Bishops from the encroachments of the civil power by substituting for the jurisdiction of Metropolitans who were under that power the jurisdiction of the Roman Bishops who were independent of it ([1]). The articles, therefore, which tell in favour of the Roman Supremacy are not so much usurpations of the Popes as spontaneous acts of submission on the part of the Cisalpine Church, and derive authority, notwithstanding the fiction as to their origin, from having been generally accepted and acquiesced in. This Collection represents the received Canon Law of the Cisalpine Church.

5. Among minor Collections which were subsequently made, perhaps the best known are (1) the *Canonum Collectio*, in 381 titles, which was drawn up France at the end of the eighth century; (2) the *Collectio Ancheriana*, made in the ninth century; (3) the *Penitentialis* of Bishop Halitgar, of Cambray, dating from about 925 A.D.; and (4) the *Collectio Anselmo dedicata*, made between 883 and 897 A.D., and of Italian origin.

of the letter (both spurious); then the Ordo de Celebrando Concilio, borrowed from the 4th Council of Toledo; a list of Councils, and a spurious correspondence between Damasus and Jerome. There are two editions of the False Decretals, one in the Collection of Councils, by Merlin (Tom. I. Paris, 1523), the other in Migne's *Patrolog. Lat.* Tom. cxxx. See Schulte's *Geschichte der Quellen*, I. p. 43.

([1]) That is the view of Möhler, Walter, and Hefele.

CHAPTER XIV.

CODIFICATION OF CANONS.

By Codification we understand not so much a mere collection of Canons arranged in chronological order, as a grouping of them under heads according to their subjects, so that the law on any subject can be ascertained at a glance. Codification was not a work completed at once, but one which advanced by successive stages, (1) through the collections called Capitularies and Penitentials, (2) to fuller collections adopting more or less of methodical arrangement, (3) until Gratian's systematic method was reached.

1. Capitularies was a name commonly given to short summaries of law, whether of Canon Law which the Bishops reduced into articles for the benefit of their Clergy, or of Civil Law which the temporal lords drew up for the rule of the Laity. These, when ratified or confirmed by the sovereign, became laws of the realm.

Capitularies was also a name given to selections from the canons made without such sanction by individual Bishops for the regulation of their dioceses. In this sense capitularies had neither the force of statute law, nor any ecclesiastical validity outside the particular diocese for which they were framed.

Penitentials were instructions issued by Bishops to their clergy, giving lists of canonical offences, and the penances

to be imposed for the several violations of them. Among
such collections known in England are ([1]) : (1) that of
Gildas, drawn up about 570, A.D.; (2) that of Archbishop
Theodore, between 668 and 690, A.D.; (3) that of Beda, about
733, A.D.; (4) that of Egbert, between 766 and 791.

2. More definite progress towards Codification was made
in the tenth and eleventh centuries by works ([2]) such
as:—(1) The two books of Regino, abbot of Prüm,
compiled about 906, A.D., entitled *De causis Synodalibus
et disciplina ecclesiæ.* (2) The Code of Canons in force
in the Frankish Church drawn up by Burchard ([3]), Bishop
of Worms, between 1012 and 1023, A.D., and called *Liber
decretorum collectarium,* in twenty books. (3) The
Decretum and *Panormia* of Bishop Ivo of Chartres (died
A.D. 1117) ([4]) containing the Canon Law of the French
Church at that period. The Decretum which is in seven-
teen books is a collection of materials out of which the
Panormia is contructed, itself consisting of eight books.
(4) The collection made by Anselm of Lucca (died 1036,
A.D.) in thirteen books ; also the *Collectio duodecim partium*
(after 1023) and two collections of Cardinal Deusdedit,
each in four books (1086-87) for which the archives of the
Lateran were employed.

3. A Code of Canons available for the whole Western

([1]) These are printed in Haddan and Stubb's *Councils and Ecclesiastical Documents,* that of Gildas Vol. I., p. 113, that of Theodore Vol.
III., p. 173, and that of Beda Vol. III., p. 326, that of Egbert Vol. III.
p. 418.

([2]) These are given in Migne's *Patrolog. Latin.* Vol. clxi.

([3]) See Schulte's *Geschichte der Quellen,* I. p. 41.

([4]) See Schulte, p. 41.

Church being still a desideratum, and the need more pressingly felt owing to the revived enthusiasm for the study of Civil Law, Gratian, a monk of Bologna, produced about 1144 A.D. a work entitled *Concordantia discordantium Canonum*, better known in after times as the *Decretum Gratiani*. In this work old and new Canons are brought together, their discrepancies are pointed out, and their reconciliation is attempted. The Decretum was a great stride towards a science of Canon Law, and constitutes the first part of the *Corpus juris Canonici*.

CHAPTER XV.

THE CORPUS JURIS CANONICI.

1. *Corpus Juris Canonici,* or Code of Canon Law ([1]), is a name applied to the compilation begun by the monk Gratian in the middle of the twelfth century, and continued during the next two centuries by others, approved by successive Popes, and generally received as authoritative throughout the Western Church until the period of the Reformation.

2. The *Corpus Juris Canonici* consists of four chief, and of two subsidiary parts, the same degree of authority not being universally accorded to the latter as to the former.

The four chief parts usually accepted as Canon Law, are the following :—

    (1) The Decretum of Gratian.

    (2) The Decretals of Pope Gregory IX.

    (3) The Sext of Boniface VIII.

    (4) The Clementines of Clement V.

The two subsidiary parts, the authority of which is not so generally admitted, are called *Extravagantes,* and consist of—

    (1) The *Extravagantes* of Pope John XXII.

    (2) The *Extravagantes Communes.*

---

[1] The best modern Edition of the *Corpus Juris Canonici* is that published at Leipsic in 1839, by Bœhmer and Richter.

3. The principal Mediæval Canonists who have written treatises on the *Corpus Juris Canonici,* are—

(1) William *Durandus,* Bishop of Mende, called Speculator from the title of his book Speculum Juris. He died in 1287.

(2) Francis *Zabarella,* Cardinal Archbishop of Florence and often called the Cardinal of Florence. He died in 1417.

(3) Nicolas Tudeschi commonly called *Panormitan,* because he was Archbishop of Palermo, sometimes Lucerna Juris because of his learning. He died 1445.

(4) The Jesuit, John Cardinal *Turrecremata,* who died 1468.

4. In modern times perhaps the best known names of those who have dealt with the same subject, are—

(1) *Petrus de Marca,* Archbishop of Paris, who died A.D. 1662, the author of a Treatise, De Concordia Sacerdotii et Imperii.

(2) Louis *Thomassin,* of the French Oratory, who wrote L'Ancienne et Nouvelle Discipline de l'Eglise, and died A.D. 1695.

(3) Anaclet *Reiffenstuel,* who died 1720.

(4) Zeger Bernard *Van Espen,* who became a Jansenist, and was concerned in setting up the schismatical church at Utrecht, and died 1728.

CHAPTER XVI.

THE DECRETUM GRATIANI.

1. THE *Decretum Gratiani* constitutes the first part of the Corpus Juris Canonici. It was the work of an Italian Benedictine Monk, sometime the inmate of the Monastery of Classe near Ravenna, and subsequently of S. Felix at Bologna, where he compiled this work about 1144 A. D. ([1]). He is said to have afterwards become Bishop of Chiusi ([2]).

Making special use of the compilations of Burchard of Worms and Anselm of Lucca, Gratian aimed at grouping the existing Canons systematically according to subjects, making short comments on them, and reconciling them when opposed to one another. He himself called the work *Concordantia discordantium Canonum.* Pope Alexander called it *Decreta;* subsequent writers and Popes *Decretum,* which is the name it now generally bears.

2. The Decretum consists of three parts, called in Gratian's time respectively *De Ministeriis, De Negotiis, De Sacramentis.* They were afterwards called, and are now usually known as, *Distinctiones, Causæ,* and *De Consecratione.*

The first part was subdivided by Paucapalca, Gratian's

([1]) Between 1139 and 1151. See Schulte, p. 48. It was probably written between 1139 and 1142, and was known in Rome in 1144.

([2]) See Schulte's *Geschichte der Quellen,* I. p. 46.

pupil, into 101 Distinctiones. Of these the first 20 treat of the subject of law generally, of the various kinds of law, and of ecclesiastical law and custom in particular, and were often called the *Tractatus Decretalium;* the remaining 81 contain the rules regulating the appointment, ordination, qualifications, and duties of the clergy, and were called the *Tractatus Ordinandorum* (³).

The second part consists of 36 *Causæ* or *Cases,* each of which suggests a number of questions (*Quæstiones*), the answers to which are given from Canons of Councils or Decretals. This part illustrates the practical application of the law, and is the distinguishing feature of the book. Some of the cases bear special names. Thus the first is often quoted as *Causa Simoniacorum,* the twenty-seventh as *Causa Conjugii.* The thirty-third contains the long *Tractatus de Pœnitentia,* itself divided into questions, and the third question subdivided into eleven Distinctiones.

The third part treats of the Sacraments of the Church and their due administration. It was subdivided by Paucapalea (⁴) into five Distinctiones, each of them comprising a number of chapters.

3. The Decretum of Gratian soon superseded all other collections, and not without reason; for in it Gratian shows himself the real founder of Canon Law as a science. It passed through many editions, none of them being very critical, and all of them made without any attempt at

----

(³) See Schulte's *Geschichte der Quellen,* vol. I. p. 50.

(⁴) Paucapalea and other of Gratian's pupils added other Canons, taken from the Collections of Burchard, Ivo, and Anselm. These additions were not considered of force in the Schools.

verifying or correcting the quotations from older authorities. Anxious to have a more accurate edition, Pius IV. ·instituted for that purpose the *Correctores Romani*, who executed the task assigned to them by publishing a revised text in 1582, which has served as the basis of all subsequent editions.

CHAPTER XVII.

THE DECRETALS OF GREGORY IX.

1. AFTER the publication of Gratian's Decretum, Papal Decretals on points of discipline became so numerous that it soon ceased to be complete and new collections became necessary. Several such were made, the best known being the following:—

    (1) That of Bernardus, who died A.D. 1213 as Bishop of Pavia, called the *Breviarium Extravagantium.* It obtained the name of *Extravagantes,* because the Decretals subsequent to Gratian's collection were called *Tituli extra decretum vagantes.* The new material was grouped under five heads, treating respectively of jurisdiction, civil procedure, clerical offices and duties, marriage, and crimes; and this being the first collection of extravagantes was called *Volumen primum* or *Compilatio Prima.*

    (2) A fresh compilation was made by Petrus Collivicinus by order of Innocent III. containing his Decretals from 1198 to 1210 A.D. It was approved by the Canonists of Bologna, and is known as the *Compilatio Tertia.*

    (3) The *Compilatio Secunda* consists of the Decretals of the Popes from Alexander III. (A.D. 1181) to Celestin III. (A.D. 1198.) It was at first edited

by Gilbert and Alan, two Englishmen, but their edition was not received at Bologna until it had been revised by Johannes Gallensis.

(4) After the fourth Lateran Council (A.D. 1215) the *Compilatio Quarta* was made, containing the Decretals from 1210 to 1215, A. D. (¹)

2. In 1230 A.D. Gregory IX. directed his Chaplain, Raymond of Pennaforte (²), to make a new collection of Decretals arranged systematically. The result was the *Decretalium Gregorii IX. compilatio*, which in 1234 A.D. was submitted to the University of Bologna and by it approved. The Bull *Volentes igitur* which accompanied it directed that it should supersede the older compilations.

Gregory's Decretals are in five books. The first treats of the authority of Canons, the election, translation, and resignation of Bishops, of the Archdeacon's office and of delegated judicial offices, spiritual judges, proctors and arbitrators. The second of civil procedure, tribunals, witnesses, presumptions, prescriptions, and appeals. The third of clerical duties, of prebends, institution, chapters, parishes, tithes and vows, monks, patronage, and celebration of sacraments. The fourth of espousals and marriage. The fifth of criminal procedure, accusations, inquisitions, simony, heretics, homicide, excommunication, sentences, and rules of law.

(¹) These four compilations are given by Labbé, *Antiquæ Collectiones Decretalium,* Paris 1609-21.

(²) He was the third General Master of the Dominican Order. He is stated to have once crossed from Majorca to Barcelona in 6 hours, using his Friar's cloak as a boat. He died in 1275, being nearly 100 years old.

CHAPTER XVIII.

AFTER the supersession of the earlier collections by the Decretals of Gregory IX. in 1234, A. D. appendices and supplements were again added, first by Innocent IV. in 1245 A.D., and subsequently by Alexander IV., Urban IV., Clement IV. and Gregory X.

1. In 1298 A.D. a new collection was published by Boniface VIII. including all the post-Gregorian Decretals. It was called *Liber Sextus* or the Sext, because it was a complement to the five books of Gregory IX. It travels over the same ground with those five books, and is itself subdivided into five books to correspond with them.

2. After the publication of the Liber Sextus, a series of Decretals was issued by Boniface VIII. (among them being the celebrated Bull *Unam sanctam* directed against Philip of France, in 1302 A.D.) and by his successor Benedict XI. These are not included in the Sext They were united and published with comments by Cardinal Johannes Monachus, under the style of *Constitutiones Extravagantes Libri Sexti* and are found among the *Extravagantes Communes* in the *Corpus Juris Canonici*.

CHAPTER XIX.

THE CLEMENTINES.

In 1813 A.D., Pope Clement V., published a *Liber Septimus*, including the Constitutions of the General Synod of Vienne A.D. 1311, and his own Decretals. This book he submitted to the University of Orleans, then suspended its circulation and commenced a new one. The new collection was completed by his successor, John XXII., and sent to the Universities of Paris and Bologna. Accepted by them, it was received as authoritative in the Church, and is known by the name *Constitutiones Clementinæ*, or the Clementines.

Like the Sext, the Liber Septimus, or the Clementines is divided into five books, which correspond in subject-matter with the five books of the Gregorian collection.

CHAPTER XX.

THE EXTRAVAGANTES.

THE subsequent additions to Canon Law, commonly called *Extravagantes* rest on a somewhat different footing from the previous ones. Since the time of Pope John XXII. the papal power was not sufficient to secure for their decisions the force of statute law, neither can they have been said since then to have been universally received in the Western Patriarchate. In the absence of such reception, whatever may be their authority within the metropolitan jurisdiction of Rome, it is doubtful whether they can be considered as canonically binding elsewhere, albeit peculiar respect may be due to them, as being the utterances of the first Bishop of Christendom.

The Extravagantes are usually divided into two parts; (1) the *Extravagantes Johannis P.* xxii., containing twenty Decretals of that Pope under fourteen titles, and (2) the *Extravagantes Communes* embracing seventy-four Decretals of Popes from Urban IV. (A.D. 1261 to 1264) to Sixtus IV. (A.D. 1471 to 1484).

A subsequent effort was made by Gregory XIII. (A.D. 1572 to 1585) to codify later Decretals, which was brought to a successful issue by Clement VIII. in 1598 A.D. It contained the dogmatic decisions of the Councils of Florence and Trent, but it was soon withdrawn.

CHAPTER XXI.

AUTHORITY OF THE CORPUS JURIS CANONICI.

THE authority of the *Corpus Juris Canonici* (¹) may be considered under two aspects : (1) Legal or Civil ; (2) Ecclesiastical.

1. Legal or Civil authority can only be said to belong to Canons and Canon Law in so far as it is expressly given by the Law or the Custom of the Realm. Where it is so given, Canons are invested with a civil sanction either directly or indirectly.

2. Ecclesiastical authority belongs to Canons and Canon Law in all cases where they have been properly made, duly published, and continue to be enforced by local ecclesiastical authority, so that they cannot be taken to have fallen into disuse, or to have been superseded.

(¹) The best Editions of the Corpus Juris Canonici, are those of Lancelottus, published at Cologne, 1783, 2 Vols. 4to, and of Boehmer and Richter, published at Leipsic, 1839, 2 Vols. 4to.

CHAPTER XXII.

LEGAL OR CIVIL AUTHORITY OF CANON LAW.

1. No Canon Laws as such possess legal or civil authority. When legal authority is given to them Canon Laws become laws of the realm and can be enforced by state authority. This is advantageous in that it helps to enforce the discipline of the Church (¹), but disadvantageous in that it brings the Church's discipline under the control of the State (²).

Canon Laws may be enforced by the State in two ways, either directly or indirectly; directly by action before its own tribunal like other laws of the realm, indirectly by attaching civil penalties to the sentences of ecclesiastical tribunals. The latter is the more usual method (³).

2. The sanction whereby the State enforces Canons is generally by imposing certain temporal disabilities or by depriving of certain temporal advantages and civil rights those who violate them. These penalties it has

---

(¹) See Augustinus ap. Gratian I. Dist. x. c. 7.

(²) Concil. Carthagin V., Can. 9, A.D. 401, and many other authorities quoted by Gratian, Caus. xxiii. Quest. iii. c. 10, permit the Church to appeal to the civil power to protect its rights. Augustinus ap. Gratian, Caus. xxiii. Quest. iv. c. 41, and Quest. v. c. 4. See also Gratian, Caus. xxiii. Quest. v. c. 18-24, 32-35. 39, 40, 43-45.

(³) In ancient times the Clergy were not allowed to appear before a secular court without the Bishop's leave. See the authorities ap. Gratian, Caus. xv. Quest. 1., and particularly Concil. Agathense, Can. 32, A.D. 506, Ibid. c. 17. The aid of the civil power was invoked to enforce ecclesiastical censures, by Concil. Carthag. iii., Can. 38, A.D. 397, and by Gregory. See Gratian, Caus. xi. Quest. 1. c. 19 and 20.

carried so far as to include forfeiture of life and civil protection. So long as the Church possessed few or no temporal advantages, such penalties would hardly have touched its members, nor was legal authority wanted for its Canons, even if that could have been obtained. It was otherwise when the Church acquired extensive temporal advantages, such as the possession of property and the immunities of the Clergy. It then became of importance that the Church's rules should carry legal authority, or they would not have affected its temporalities. Hence the possession of temporalities has to a great extent brought the Church under the control of the supreme governing power in the State, and this must be the case as long as the Church possesses any worldly estate.

CHAPTER XXIII.

THE *Corpus Juris Canonici* when completed formed the prescribed standard of Ecclesiastical Law for the Church in the Western Patriarchate, and as such it was accepted by the Church.

1. By the Civil power it was not so received, except with certain restrictions and modifications varying from time to time and from place to place, and it was only invested with legal authority subject to these modifications.

These modifications were sometimes styled Concordats when they were put in force by special agreement with the Pope. More often they were called Liberties, when they upheld the cause of Nationalism in a local Church against foreign influences.

2. Such modifications existed in Germany, in France, in other European States, and in England ; and in each case the *Corpus Juris Canonici* had legal force only subject to these Concordats or Liberties.

In Germany the form they assumed varied from time to time. Thus :—

(1) In A.D. 1122 the struggle respecting Investitures was terminated by a Concordat concluded at Worms between Pope Calixtus II. and the Emperor Henry V.

(2) Three hundred years later, in A.D. 1418, a Concordat was concluded at Constance between Pope Martin V. and the Heads of the German nation.

(3) Again in A.D. 1447 and 1448, two Concordats were concluded called the Concordats of the German nation, the one by Pope Eugenius IV. ratified by Nicolas V. conceding the German demands and called the Frankfort Concordat or Concordat of Princes ; the other concluded by the Papal Legate with the Emperor Frederic III. and known as the Concordat of Aschaffenburg or Vienna.

In France it was held that the Decretals in the *Corpus Juris Canonici* were not of the same authority as the text, but only served as a written explanation of the law, and that no Canon Laws were of force which were contrary to the usages and Liberties of the Gallican Church. Under cover of this form of expression, French Courts refused to give coercive effect to Canons of the Church whenever they ran counter to French interests, customs, or wishes. Nevertheless :

(1) A Concordat was concluded at Constance in A.D. 1418 between Pope Martin V. and the representatives of the French nation, which received the royal assent in 1424.

(2) But in A.D. 1438, the King having by the Pragmatic Sanction of Bourges adopted the reformatory decrees of the Council of Basle as the law of the land, the Pope refused to acknowledge the law.

(3) On the other hand Pope Leo X. concluded a

Concordat with Francis I. in A.D. 1516, which was protested against both by the French Parliament and the University of Paris.

Among Concordats concluded with other States may be mentioned:

(1) That concluded with Savoy, in 1451 A.D.

(2) That concluded between Pope Innocent VIII. and King John II. of Portugal in 1486, which did not however, receive the approval of the Cortes.

(3) That concluded by Pope Adrian II. in 1523 A.D., with the King of Spain.

CHAPTER XXIV.

LEGAL AUTHORITY OF THE CANON LAW IN ENGLAND.

As in other countries, so in England the Canon Law was received as legally binding with limitations varying from time to time (¹).

1. Up to the early part of the 14th century it was acknowledged, at least theoretically, as binding, even in cases where the power of the stronger toned down its distasteful provisions : for :—

(1)   England was a part of the Western Patriarchate, and owed its Christianity to the Roman Church, ever since Augustine's mission in A.D. 596 (²) ;

(¹) In *Martin* v. *Mackonochie* 2 L. R., Adm. and Eccl., p. 116, the Dean of Arches observed : The peculiar character of the English people and the English Church is also strongly shown in their determination not to admit the general body of the Canon Law into these realms, but only such portions of it as were consistent with the constitution, the common law, and the peculiar usages of the Anglican Church. Neverthe-less, in 1848, in *Burder* v. *Mavor* 6. N. and C. 1, the perpetual curacy of Forest Hill was declared vacant by Mr. Mavor's acceptance of another benefice by the authority of the twenty-ninth Canon of the fourth Lateran Council, A.D. 1215.

(²) The various documents proving the early existence of Christianity in Britain, are collected by Haddan and Stubbs in *Councils and Ecclesiastical Documents*, Vol. I. The attendance of three British Bishops at the Council of Arles in A.D. 314 shows that at that early date the British Church was not independent of the Continental Church nor pretended to be of the Pope, since the Acts of that Council were submitted to the Pope for his approval. The inroads of the Saxons, however, in A.D. 449 drove the Britons, whether heathen or Christian, to the Western parts of the island, leaving the Southern and Eastern parts in undisputed

and the mission of Birinus, in 632 A.D. ; nay more, the reigning Norman dynasty had acquired its throne with the Pope's sanction (¹).

(2)   In acknowledgment of this debt King John had, A.D. 1213, surrendered his Kingdom to the Pope, to be held by him of the King in fee, subject to an annual payment of 1000 marks (²).

(3)   More than any other country, England had suffered from the abuses resulting from the practise of dilatory appeals to Rome. This gave rise to the rebellion against the Roman Curia, beginning with the Statutes of Provisors (³) and the Wycliffite (⁴) movement, and culminating in the Reformation.

2.   The *Corpus Juris Canonici* was however supplemented

possession of the heathen invaders. Augustine on his arrival in Kent in 596, and Birinus on coming to Mercia and Wessex in 632, found nothing but heathens to deal with ; and the overtures of the former to the Christians surviving in Wales were far from successful. Whatever claim may therefore be advanced by the Welsh, the Cornish, and the Strathclyde Churches to derive their Christianity from an earlier source, it is clear that Saxon England owes its first knowledge of Christianity to the missions of Augustine and Birinus. See Pearson's *Early and Middle Ages of England*, Chap. v. ; Reichel's *See of Rome in the Middle Ages*, Chap. ii. ; Owen's *Institutes of Canon Law*, Chap. xvii.

(¹) Alexander II. sent a consecrated banner to Duke William before he attempted the conquest of England. See Lingard's *History of England*, Vol. 1, Chap. vi., p. 186.

(²) See Rymer I., iii. 115 ; Lingard's *History of England*, Vol. II., Chap. v. p. 165 ; Reichel's *See of Rome*, p. 251.

(³) Passed in 1350 and 1353. See the Statutes quoted in Reichel's *See of Rome*, p. 632, and in Phillimore's *Ecclesiastical Law*, p. 1434, who quotes 27 Ed. III. St. 1. c. 1.

(⁴) See Reichel's *See of Rome*, p. 588, for one view of Wycliffe.

in England by two special tributary sources: (1) by Legatine Constitutions and (2) by Canons Provincial.

Legatine Constitutions were (1) those of Otho, the legate of Pope Gregory IX., made about A.D. 1237, and (2) those of Othobon, legate of Clement IV., made about 1268 A.D. in Henry III.'s reign. These Constitutions were annotated by John of Athon or Acton, Chancellor of Lincoln in the time of Edward I.

Canons Provincial were the decrees of Provincial Synods, held in the Province of Canterbury, under the 14 Archbishops, beginning with Stephen Langton, A.D. 1207, in Henry III.'s reign, ending with Henry Chichele, A.D. 1414, in Henry V.'s reign. These Canons were collected and arranged with extreme care by William Lyndwood, Archbishop Chichele's Chancellor, afterwards Bishop of St. David's, and were published about 1420 A.D. ([1]), and in 1462 A.D. they were accepted by the Province of York as authoritative for that Province also.

3. The Canon Law thus accepted in England has been from time to time curtailed by the action of the Civil power.

(1) By the Statute of Provisors ([2]) passed in 1350, which enacted, that the election to dignities should be free that patrons should enjoy their rights, and that, in case of the Pope's transgressing the Statute, the king should have the right of presentation.

(2) By the Statute 16, Rich. II., c. 5 ; commonly

([1]) Lyndwood's *Provinciale* was republished in 1664, with a selection of his notes, and the complete work in 1679.

([2]) See note 3 on page 61.

known as the Statute of Præmunire, which forbad the introduction of any Bull or Instrument from the Roman Court touching the King, his crown, and his realm, under pain of loss of the King's protection and forfeiture of lands and chattels.

(3) And again in 1418, by the Concordat concluded at Constance, between Pope Martin V. and the representatives of the English nation, which in several important matters restricted the power of the Pope.

(4) The most important restrictions were, however, made in the time of Henry VIII. and by many Statutes since then, so that the legal authority of the Canon Law is now confined within the narrowest limits.

CHAPTER XXV.

AUTHORITY OF CANON LAW IN ENGLAND AS AFFECTED BY
THE ACTS OF SUBMISSION AND SUPREMACY.

1. UNDER pressure from Henry VIII. and fearing the
penalties of a Præmunire, the Bishops and Clergy in Convocation assembled made submission to the King on the 11th
February, 1532, acknowledging the King instead of the
Pope as Supreme Head over the Church of England, so
far as the law of Christ would allow (¹). This submission
was made into law by the *Act of Supremacy*, 26 Henry VIII.
c. 1, passed in 1534, in which the limitation-clause was
dishonestly suppressed, and was still more trenchantly enforced by the Act 26 Henry VIII. c. 13, which made
it high treason to deprive the King of the dignity, title, or
name of his royal estates.

2. By a Form of Submission made 15th May, 1532, the
clergy promised *in verbo sacerdotii* never in future to enact,
put in use, promulge, or execute any new canons or constitutions, provincial or synodal, unless a license from the crown
had been first given to assemble their Convocation and
to make, promulge and execute such constitutions and
ordinances as should be made in the same (²). This Form

(¹) The qualification Quantum per Christi leges licet is said to be
due to Cardinal Fisher. See Dixon's *Hist. Ch. Eng.* Vol. I, p. 63.

(²) "We the Clergy do offer and promise *in verbo sacerdotii* here
unto your Highness, submitting ourselves most humbly to the same,

was embodied in the Act 25 Henry VIII. c. 19, commonly known as the *Act of Submission,* and passed at the end of the year 1533 (¹).

3. It was further enacted by the same statute, that a review should be had of the Canon Law; and till such review should be made, all canons, institutions, ordinances, and synodals provincial, being then already made and not repugnant to the law of the land and the king's prerogative, should still be used and executed. A *Reformatio legum ecclesiasticarum* was actually executed by a commission appointed by Edward VI. in 1551, but this review never having received any confirmation from higher authority, the legal position of the Canon Law in England would at present seem to be this (²) :—

(1) No ecclesiastical laws have legal authority which

that we will never from henceforth enact, put in ure, promulge, or execute any new canons or constitutions provincial, or any new ordinances provincial or synodal, in our Convocation or synod in time coming [which Convocation is always, hath been, and must be assembled only by your high commandment or writ], unless your Royal Highness by your Royal Assent shall license us to assemble our Convocation and to make, promulge, and execute such constitutions and ordinances as shall be made in the same, and thereto give your Royal Assent and authority."

(¹) After quoted this form the Statute runs as follows :—
Be it therefore now enacted, by authority of this present Parliament, according to the said submission and petition of the said clergy, that they, nor any of them, from henceforth, shall presume to attempt, allege, claim, or put in ure any constitutions or ordinances, provincial or synodal, or any other canons, nor shall enact, promulge, or execute any such canons, constitutions, or ordinances provincial by whatsoever name or names they may be called in their Convocations in time coming.

(²) The principal English writers on Church Law contented themselves with treating the subject from a legal, rather than a canonical point of view. Such are the writers of the following important and valuable works : (1) Godolphin's *Repertorium Juris, or Abridgement of the Ecclesiastical*

F

run counter to the law of this land or the royal prerogative, or have been superseded by Statute Law.

(2) The royal License is statutably necessary for "attempting, alleging, claiming, or putting in ure," as also for "enacting, promulging, or executing" any Canons whatsoever; but subject to this proviso, all canons, constitutions, ordinances and synodals provincial anterior to the statute 25 Henry VIII. c. 19, have legal authority, except such as have been subsequently superseded by Statute Law.

(3) No new canons have any legal authority, unless made after the Royal License has been first had and obtained.

Laws, 1687; (2) Bishop Gibson's *Codex Juris Ecclesiae Anglicanæ* (1713); (3) Ayliffe's *Parergon Juris Canonici* (1726 and 1734). (4) Oughton's *Ordo Judiciorum*, (London 1728). In modern times Sir R. Phillimore's *Treatise on Ecclesiastical Law*, besides many legal hand-books, by Cripps, Dale, Stephens, Hodgson, Blunt, and others. Robert Owen's *Institutes of Canon Law*, 1884, proceeds, however, on strictly canonical lines.

CHAPTER XXVI.

OF greater importance is the ecclesiastical and spiritual authority attaching to Canon Law. The ecclesiastical authority of Canons is twofold.

1. Such as embody a divine law are absolutely binding (') for all time and all men, whether they agree or not with statute law. They are unchangeable and cannot be dispensed with.

2. Such as establish rules of human devising for the disciplinary government of the Church upon earth stand on a different footing. They are binding whilst in force (²); if made by the whole Church on the whole Church (³); if made by a local branch on that local branch; but not till they have been published by due authority; and they may be changed (⁴).

3. In both cases the obligation is as well in *foro ecclesiastico*, or the Outer Tribunal (⁵) as in *foro conscientiæ*, or

(¹) Augustin. ap. Gratian I. Dist. xi. c. 9, and Dist. xv.

(²) See Leo Epist. li. ap. Gratian, Caus. xxv. Qu. i. c. 3 and 16 Hilarius in Synodo Romana Can. i. *Ibid.* c. 4.; Gregorius Lib. ii. Epist. 7. *Ibid.* c. 13, and Decret. Greg. IX. Lib. i. Tit. ii.

(³) Gelasius ap. Gratian, Caus. xxv. Qu. i. c. 1.

(⁴) Gratian I. Dist. xiv. c. 2.

(⁵) Concil. Chalcedon. Can. i.; τοὺς παρὰ τῶν ἁγίων πατέρων καθ' ἑκάστην σύνοδον ἄχρι τοῦ νῦν ἐκτεθέντας κανόνας κρατεῖν ἐδικαιώσαμεν·

F 2

the Inner Tribunal, but with this difference, that divine laws are always binding both in the Outer and Inner Tribunal without publication, whereas disciplinary laws although binding in the Outer Tribunal are not binding on the Inner Tribunal until by publication they have been brought under the notice of the individual.

4. Disciplinary laws duly made in the Church and having reference to matters rightfully of spiritual cognisance have ecclesiastical authority, although no civil sanction may attach to them, nay even although statute law should be repugnant to them ([1]).

([1])   Decret. Greg. IX. Lib. i. Tit. ii. c. 7 and 10.

CHAPTER XXVII.

CANON LAW AS A WHOLE.

1. So far as Canon Law does not directly express *divine* law, but establishes disciplinary rules for the government of the Church upon earth, it is not at all times one and the same, neither is it in all places one and the same.

2. Moreover, neither the *Corpus Juris Canonici* received by the Western Church, nor any subsequent collection, is so much a general code covering every case and decisive for all time, as a Collection of decisions which have been given from time to time as *need has arisen*. Canon Law is therefore the Case Law of the Church, *i.e.* a collection of judgments given by the Episcopate for the time being in the exercise of its power of determining what is most conducive to holiness, each judgment forming a precedent not lightly or without good reason to be departed from. Yet like all case law each decision stands on the merits of the authority from which it emanates.

3. There may also be included in the received collection of cases decisions which subsequent criticism has shown not to belong to those whose names they bear ; likewise decisions which contradict one another. For all that the mind and intention of the Church is to be found in its Canon Law. Where that mind varies, so have the circumstances and needs of the Church under which it was

expressed varied, so that the same divine guidance which at one time and in one nation has seen fit to prescribe one rule, has at another time and in another nation prescribed another rule as most conducive to holiness.

4. So long as the Church is in the world it will ever be so. Nevertheless as tribes give place to nations, and nations are brought more into contact with each other, and become more assimilated to one another in temporal matters, so do local and national differences in the Church tend to disappear. And when Catholicism which is perfect has come, then that which is partial and national shall be done away.

PART II.

CHAPTER XXVIII.

OF CHURCH AUTHORITY.

1. The Church being a divinely instituted Society has from its Founder, Christ, (1) a divinely-appointed Constitution by virtue of which it is One, Holy, Catholic, and Apostolic; and (2) a divinely given law including both natural law, and also the revealed moral law.

Besides these it has also certain rules and enactments of its own appointment. These go to make up what is known as Canon Law. They deal (1) with the general Government of the Church, and (2) with certain Essentials for its maintenance upon earth.

2. The Church's aim being ever to promote the salvation of mankind, and the holiness necessary thereto among its members, the first business of its positive rules is to prescribe the order which from time to time is found to be most conducive thereto. This involves determining principally three points :—

(1) The Nature of Jurisdiction.

(2) The Officers of Jurisdiction—the Hierarchy.

(8) The Unit of Jurisdiction—the Diocese.

3. The Church has further to legislate as to the administration of certain things essential to its existence upon earth. Hence its rules deal secondly with :—

(1) Sacramental Graces.

(2) The Spiritual Gifts of Orders and Matrimony.

(8) The Exercise of Discipline or Censures.

DIVISION I.

CHAPTER XXIX.

THE APOSTLES AND THE EPISCOPATE.

1. The Head of the Church, Jesus Christ, gave His commission to His Apostles in the following terms : " All power is given unto Me in Heaven, and in earth. Go ye, therefore, and teach all nations, baptizing them in the name of the Father, and of the Son, and of the Holy Ghost, teaching them to observe all things whatsoever I have commanded you : and lo, I am with you always, even unto the end of the world ([1])."

These words imply :—

    (1)   That the plenitude of power resided in Christ.

    (2)   That in the exercise of that power the charge was given to the Apostles (*a*) of gathering together a Church out of the world by administering the rite of baptism, and (*b*) of teaching the members of that Church to observe Christ's commands.

([1]) Matt. xxviii. 19.

(3)　That that charge still rests in the Church with those to whom it has been entrusted by the Apostles, and will so rest until the end of the world.

2. As Christ entrusted the charge of His Church to the Apostles as a College or Body and not to them individually, so the Apostles committed the same charge to the whole Body of the Bishops, and not to them severally. The whole Church, therefore, and each part of the Church is under the charge of the Collective Episcopate throughout the world (²).

3. Those only are deemed Bishops of the Church and members of the Co-episcopate, on whom the plenitude (³) of the priesthood has been specially conferred (⁴) after the Apostles' order (⁵).

(²)　See Concil. Nicæn. Can. 5.

(³)　See Caisson Manuale Juris Canonici § 855.

(⁴)　Not therefore the πρεσβύτεροι who in Acts xv. are called ἐπίσκοποι before ecclesiastical terminology had been accurately defined, nor the χωρεπίσκοποι of Nicene times who appear to have been identical with them.

(⁵)　And this statement is equally true whether the plenitude of the priesthood is a distinct Order, or whether it is only a gift of jurisdiction·

CHAPTER XXX.

· THE charge given by Christ to His Apostles was at once a conferring of Orders and a giving of Jurisdiction. The setting them apart as a special class of men to baptize and to teach, and the bestowal of a special gift for that purpose, was a giving of Orders. The sending them into all nations was a conferring of Jurisdiction over the whole world.

1. Between Orders and Jurisdiction there is this difference, that Orders are spiritual gifts bestowed on classes of men solemnly set apart to perform certain functions in the Church, whereas Jurisdiction is the reception of authority by individuals for exercising those functions. Orders may exist where there is no Jurisdiction for exercising them, as in the case of a Bishop who has resigned his see. And Jurisdiction may be held by one who has not yet received the Order to exercise it, as in the case of a Bishop elect and confirmed but not consecrated.

2. The spiritual gift conferred in Orders is given once and for all; and once given, it cannot be taken away although the exercise of it may be forbidden. But the authority to exercise it may be given or taken away, or superseded (as it is on appeal), or renounced (as by resig-

nation), or changed (as by translation), by the power from which it is derived ([1]).

3. From the earliest time the exercise of all spiritual functions has been limited in divers ways in the Church by those having jurisdiction, so that even Bishops, who as members of the Co-episcopate are charged with the care of the whole Church, are as individuals restricted in the exercise of that care. This restriction includes :

(1) A limitation within local districts, which are called Dioceses.

(2) A limitation of power within the Diocese, imposed both by the necessity of consulting the Chapter in ordinary cases, and the Metropolitan in extraordinary ones.

(3) A limitation in respect of persons, some persons and corporations within the Diocese being exempted from episcopal jurisdiction.

4. As to the relation of Jurisdiction to. Orders, three principal views are held by those who accept Orders as of divine appointment :

(1) The view that all jurisdiction necessary for the exercise of Orders comes from the temporal Prince. This view is called Erastianism. It

([1]) The difference between Orders and Jurisdiction is usually made clearer by remembering that Order is (1) a Spiritual gift imparted at Ordination ; (2) equal in all of like Order ; (3) perpetually inherent in those to whom it has been given ; and (4) incapable of delegation ; whereas Jurisdiction is (1) not necessarily conferred by Ordination ; (2) very unequal amongst those of like Order; (3) is not perpetual, and can be curtailed in various ways ; and (4) can properly be delegated. See Caisson § 256.

See Hieronymus, ap. Gratian, Caus. ii. Qu. vii. c. 85. Ambrosius, *Ibid.* c. 37.

makes of the Church a religious department of the state ([1]).

(2) The view that all jurisdiction comes exclusively from the Pope, to whom it has been committed by Christ. This is called Ultramontanism. It reduces all Bishops to the position of mere Curates and agents of the Pope, and makes of him a spiritual autocrat.

(3) The view that all jurisdiction was committed by Christ to the Apostles as a College and to their successsors, the collective Episcopal Body, from which it is derived to individuals through officers of its appointment. This is Catholicism, and considers all Bishops joint-Assessors with the Pope as their President in the one government of the Church.

([1]) See the anthorities showing the limits within which the civil power may meddle with the affairs of the Church in Gratian I. Dist. xcvi.

CHAPTER XXXI.

VARIETIES OF JURISDICTION.

1. JURISDICTION may be defined as the possession of authority to exercise spiritual functions for the good of the Church. All such authority comes from the Collective Episcopate as inheritors of Christ's commission to His Apostles. Its object is so to rule men in this life, that they may obtain life everlasting.

Jurisdiction extends to various classes of subjects, and includes :—

(1) The right to make laws for the Church. This belongs to the Collective Episcopate in Council assembled.

(2) The right to teach. This is specially the duty of the Diocesan Bishop and his deputies within his Diocese.

(3) The right to administer the sacraments, which is committed to the Bishops in common with all of the Priesthood.

(4) The right of spiritual censure, which is exercised under the Bishop by the spiritual Officer appointed for that purpose.

2. Jurisdiction may be exercised in several different ways, and according to the way in which it is exercised, it bears several different names. Thus it may be exercised :

(1) Either *publicly* or *privately*; publicly as when a sentence of excommunication is pronounced, privately as when a penance is imposed on a penitent.

(2) Either *informally* or *formally*, more usually called *voluntarily* or *contentiously*.

(3) Either by a *Principal* of ordinary Church appointment, hence called an Ordinary, or by a *Deputy*.

(4) Either *directly* or *intermediately*.

3. Where Jurisdiction is exercised *publicly*, as in the outward enforcement of discipline in the visible Church, it is termed Jurisdiction of the *Outer Tribunal*. Where it is exercised *privately* and in secret, and is binding only on the conscience it is called Jurisdiction of the *Inner Tribunal*.

4. Where jurisdiction is exercised formally with the observance of judicial forms, it is called *Contentious* or *Judicial* jurisdiction. Where it is exercised *informally* at the sole *will* of the superior and without judicial forms it is called *Voluntary* or *Extrajudicial* jurisdiction (¹). Such Voluntary jurisdiction is exercised at ordination, in collating to a benefice, in granting or withdrawing a license to preach. And there is this distinction between Voluntary and Contentious Jurisdiction, that Voluntary Jurisdiction may be exercised by a superior anywhere, whereas Contentious Jurisdiction can only be exercised within the territorial limits of the superior's jurisdiction.

5. When a well-ascertained and definite authority is attached by the Church to the holding of a public office, such

---

(¹) See Phillimore's *Ecclesiastical Law*, p. 1210.

authority is called *Ordinary* Jurisdiction (¹) or the Jurisdiction of one who ordinarily acts as a Principal. Such is that of a Bishop in his own Diocese, of a Metropolitan among his Comprovincials. When authority is delegated to a deputy (²) and is held by him subject to restrictions, it is called *Delegated* Jurisdiction, or the Jurisdiction of a deputy, and it is held subject to whatever restrictions the Principal may have imposed (³).

There are three points in which Ordinary and Delegated Jurisdictions differ :

(1) A Principal or Ordinary may delegate his jurisdiction, but a deputy may not.

(2) An Ordinary's office continues after the death of the granter, whilst the deputy's absolutely ceases ; for an Ordinary or Principal is a functionary of the Church, whilst the deputy is the delegate of an individual.

(3) A delegate for a single case ceases to have jurisdiction when that case has been settled.

There are nevertheless certain Ordinary Jurisdictions which cease with the granter's death. Such is the jurisdiction of a Vicar-General and Official of the Bishop (⁴) the reason being that these Officers are considered identical

----

(¹) On Ordinary Jurisdiction, see Decret. Greg. IX. Lib. i. Tit. xxxi.

(²) On Delegated Jurisdiction, see Decret. Greg. IX. Lib. i, Tit. xxix.

(³) See Phillimore's *Ecclesiastical Law* , p. 1211. Ayliffe's *Parergon*, 161, 163. In case one deputy is superseded by another, see Decret. Greg. IX. Lib. i. Tit. iii. c. 24.

(⁴) Where these two offices are combined in one and the same person, he is called a Chancellor. Ayliffe's *Parergon*, 163. Phillimore's *Ecclesiastical Law*, p. 1211.

with the Bishop and to make up but one person with him. So long therefore as these Officers hold office, their jurisdiction is an ordinary one and as such capable of being delegated. But inasmuch as they are Officers of the Bishop and not of the Church, and can be superseded by him at will, their office depends on the Bishop's will and terminates with his life. When however these appointments are confirmed by the Chapter, they become Church appointments, and as such are ordinary jurisdictions tenable for life (¹).

6. When authority is exercised *directly* and without a go-between, as by a Bishop over an individual in his own Diocese, or by a Metropolitan over his Suffragan, it is called Direct or Immediate. But the jurisdiction which is exercised through an intermediacy, as that of a Metropolitan over an individual in the Diocese of a Suffragan, is called *Indirect* or *Mediate.*

(¹) See Phillimore's *Ecclesiastical Law*, p. 1197 and 1207, and below Chapters xlv. and xlvi.

CHAPTER XXXII.

ACQUISITION OF JURISDICTION.—TITLES.

1. BEFORE anyone can be allowed to exercise Jurisdiction in the Church he must first have acquired what is called a *Title* thereto. Should, however, Jurisdiction have been exercised by one having no real title, the defect may in some cases be subsequently supplied by the Church. In order that this may be possible, it is necessary :—

    (1)   That the defect in title be one which is capable of being subsequently set right.

    (2)   That it is also one where there is a colourable claim of title.

    (3)   And that the colourable claim has been commonly admitted.

2. A title to Ordinary Jurisdiction is obtained by being advanced to some office to which it usually attaches, and possession of office is obtained by formal admission granted to a fit person, duly appointed, in the proper manner. A title to exercise Delegated Jurisdiction is conferred by the simple act of appointment by anyone having Ordinary Jurisdiction.

The establishment of public offices in the Church to which ordinary jurisdiction is attached is a matter of ecclesiastical order and of arrangements made by the Collective Episcopate. Without its active and passive concurrence no such new office can therefore be established, nor an old one abrogated. Hence it must concur in founding a new see or in dividing an old one.

3. Before anyone can be admitted to an office conferring jurisdiction it must be established to the satisfaction of the superior ([1]) :—

(1) That the appointment has been *actually* made by the person *entitled* to make it, whether by election or postulation as in the case of a see, or by collation or presentation as in the case of a benefice.

(2) That it has been *duly* made; an election, for instance, must have been free and regular, a presentation or collation without simony or corrupt motive.

(3) That the person appointed is a *fit person*, fitness having reference to both mind and body, age and morals ; without fitness the appointment is canonically a nullity.

4. These conditions being complied with, actual possession of the office is given by Canonical Institution or Mission, which may be defined as the formal assignment to a particular person of a particular office by one having jurisdiction for that purpose.

When Ordinary Jurisdiction has once been rightfully

([1]) Thus in England before a Bishop is confirmed by the Archbishop these points have to be established in his Court, or in the court of his Vicar for this purpose, commonly called his Vicar-General. The Vicar-General, as the Archbishop's deputy in spirituals, usually acts for him, and confirms the election. See Phillimore's *Ecclesiastical Law* p. 47.

acquired, it resides in its possessor until it be lost either by resignation, translation, or deprivation, or in certain contingencies *ipso facto*, or by death.

No holder of any office to which Jurisdiction is attached is permitted to overstep the limits of his authority (').

(') Decret. Greg. IX. Lib. v. Tit. xxxi. and xxxiii.

DIVISION II.

OFFICERS OF JURISDICTION—THE HIERARCHY.

CHAPTER XXXIII.

THE EXERCISE OF JURISDICTION BY EPISCOPAL
INTERMEDIARIES.

1. As the Collective Episcopate has received from Christ
the care and charge of the whole Church, it alone can be
said to have Universal jurisdiction ; and its jurisdiction can
only be exercised in a general Council. From the earliest
times, therefore, the ordinary administration of the Church
has been exercised by individual Bishops, assisted by advising
Clergy, to whom has been assigned a limited jurisdiction
within certain territorial boundaries. Jurisdictions thus
limited locally are called Dioceses, and those exercising
rule over them, Diocesan Bishops and Chapters.

2. In respect of jurisdiction a Diocesan Bishop is called
a Prelate or Superior ('), because he has been singled out
to exercise ordinary rule over others. In the place where
he exercises that rule he is called the Ordinary.

For the maintenance of the unity of the faith certain

(') See Decret. Greg. IX. Lib. i. Tit. xxxiii. de Majoritate et
Obedientia.

Diocesan Bishops have been charged with a supervision of their brethren as intermediaries between them and the Collective Episcopate (¹). Such intermediaries are termed Higher Prelates, and they exercise ordinary jurisdiction over others of the same order.

For the better government of Dioceses, the Church has also sanctioned a subdivision of the Bishop's jurisdiction by the creation of officers exercising it in part or in whole, but not of the episcopal Order. Such officers are called Lesser Prelates.

3. The whole body of these Higher Prelates, Diocesan Prelates, and Lesser Prelates constitute together what is called the Hierarchy, which is, therefore, the sum total of all officers exercising ordinary jurisdiction in the Church arranged one under the other in graduated ranks (²). At the head of the Hierarchy stands the Collective Episcopate, from which all jurisdiction flows. The lowest rank in the Episcopal Hierarchy is that held by a Diocesan Bishop, who has no other jurisdiction save that over one Diocese. Between the Collective and the Diocesan Episcopate come the several grades of Patriarchs, Primates, and Metropolitans, each of them exercising a jurisdiction of oversight over the group of Bishops severally belonging to his Patriarchate, or Nation, or Province, and each subordinate one to the other.

4. No member of the Hierarchy possesses any absolute jurisdiction over those whose superior he is; but the whole body under him have a joint jurisdiction with him.

(¹) Isidorus ap. Gratian I. Dist. xxi. c. 1.   Nicholas, *Ibid.* c. 6.

(²) Leo Epist. lxxxii. A.D. 446, ap. Gratian, Caus. ii. Qu. vi. c. 14.

He is their president, and, therefore, the acts run in his name. Nevertheless, his associated bishops give their votes and suffrages jointly with him, and their votes count equally with his. They are therefore called his suffragans (¹).

(¹) See Decret. Greg. IX. Lib. v. Tit. xxxi. and xxxiii. on Excesses of Jurisdiction. In the Province of Canterbury the Bishop of London is Dean; Winchester, Chancellor; Lincoln, Vice-Chancellor; Salisbury, Precentor; Worcester, Chaplain; and Rochester, Crossbearer.

CHAPTER XXXIV.

THE GREAT PATRIARCHS.

1. THE highest place in the Episcopal Hierarchy is occupied by the Great Patriarchs. Of these there were originally three, those of Rome, Alexandria, and Antioch ([1]). Subsequently two more were added by the Council of Constantinople, those of Constantinople ([2]) and Jerusalem ([3]).

2. The relation of the great Patriarchs to those under them was not everywhere the same, neither did they all stand co-ordinately as equals on the same footing, or even bear the same title. The bishops of Rome and Alexandria were properly called Popes, he of Antioch Patriarch, those of Constantinople and Jerusalem Archbishops ([4]).

3. Among the original three the Pope of Rome ever held a higher position than the others, and the Pope of Alexandria had ampler powers than the Patriarch of Antioch. The prerogatives of the latter were shared by certain Eastern

---

([1]) Gratian I. Dist. xxii., c. 1.

([2]) Gratian I. Dist, xxii., c. 3 and 6.

([3]) In viii. Synodo habita sub Hadriano II. Can. 21 ap. Gratian I. Dist. xxii. c. 7.

([4]) See Owen's *Institutes of Canon Law*, p. 30.

Metropolitans.   The Council of Constantinople (¹) assigned
to the bishop of Constantinople a rank next after that of the
bishop of Rome on the ground that his city was a new
Rome.

(¹) Can. 3 : τὸν μέν τοι Κωνσταντινουπόλεως ἐπίσκοπον ἔχειν τὰ
πρεσβεῖα τῆς τιμῆς μετὰ τὸν τῆς Ῥώμης ἐπίσκοπον, διὰ τὸ εἶναι αὐτὴν νέαν
Ῥώμην.

CHAPTER XXXV.

THE POPE.

THE greatest Patriarch of all is the Pope, who is also Primate of the whole Episcopal Order. This position he derives from two sources : (1) from the Lord's command ([1]), (2) from Canons of Councils.

1. As Christ's commission, which is called the power of the keys, was given to all the Apostles in the words : " Receive ye the Holy Ghost. Whosoever sins ye remit, they are remitted to them," and was confirmed to them by the sending of the Holy Ghost on the day of Pentecost, so it was thrice solemnly given to S. Peter ([2]), as their chief and leader, and is now in the possession of the whole Episcopal Body, of which the Pope is the head or president.

In the earliest times the Council of Arles A.D. 314, at which three British Bishops are believed to have been present, is found submitting its decrees for the Pope's approval. The Nicene Council A.D 325 recognises the Roman Bishop's authority over the Bishops of Italy, as a precedent to be followed elsewhere. That of Sardica bestows the right of entertaining certain appeals on the Roman

---

([1]) Gelasius ap. Gratian I. Dist. xxi. c. 3.
([2]) Augustinus ap. Gratian, Caus. xxiv. Qu. i. c. 6.

Pontiff—a right recognised by the Emperor Gratian in 378 A.D. and admitted by the Greeks.

2. The Pope is, therefore, not only the Bishop of Rome, Metropolitan over the six adjoining Saffragans and Patriarch of the suburbicarian provinces, which in time included the whole of the West (¹), but he is also the Primate of the Collective Episcopate throughout the world, in relation to which he is admitted to hold a superior pre-eminence (²). The extent of the privileges attaching to this Primacy and Pre-eminence have been matter of much dispute. It seems that they have varied at different times in the Church's history. They, however, distinctly include (1) a primacy of honour, and (2) a primacy of jurisdiction (³).

3. The Pope has undoubtedly the primacy of honour, and, therefore, should rightfully act as the President and spokes-man of the whole Episcopate in Council assembled (⁴).

4. He has also the primacy of jurisdiction (⁵), so that with him, as superior Metropolitan of the Church, it rests to preside over the court of final appeal over all Bishops (⁶).

(¹) Anacletus and Zacharias, A.D. 743, require all Bishops, qui ordina-tionibus apostolicis subjacent, to visit Rome once a year. Gratian I. Dist. xciii. c. 4.

(²) Iren. Contra Haer. iii., c. 3 : Ad hanc enim ecclesiam propter potiorem principalitatem necesse est omnem convenire ecclesiam.

(³) Authorities ap. Gratian Caus. ix. Qu. iii c. 10-21.

(⁴) Labbé Tom. II. fol. 1287. Tom iv. p. 838.

(⁵) Gregorius Lib. v. Epist. 26 ap. Gratian I. Dist. xciii. c. 2. Cyprianus, *Ibid.* c. 3 ; Qui cathedram Petri, super quam fundata est ecclesia, deserit in ecclesia se esse non confidat. This was at one time shown by conferring the pallium. See on this point the authorities in Gratian I. Dist. c.

(⁶) In matters of faith, the Church of Rome anciently claimed to be the bulwark against heresy. See authorities ap. Gratian, Caus. xxiv. Qu. i. c. 10-17.

As such president, his *ex officio* utterances may be called
infallible in the same sense that the sentences of the
highest civil tribunals are infallible, because upon earth
there is no higher court by which they can be reviewed on
appeal.

The election of the Pope, which was originally made by
the Clergy and People of Rome, and subsequently was made
subject to the approval of the Holy Roman Emperor ([1]), is
now made by the College of Cardinals ([2]).

([1]) See on this point the authorities in Gratian I. Dist. lxiii. c.
21, 22, 28, 28, 30, 31, 32, 33 : and the views disapproving of imperial interference, Gratian I. Dist. xcvii.

([2]) Rules for the election of a Pope of Nicolaus II. A.D. 1059, of
Stephen III. A.D. 769, of Boniface and others in Gratian I. Dist. lxxix.

CHAPTER XXXVI.

THE ROMAN CURIA.

To assist the Pope in so vast a charge the Curia Romana or Roman Court has been associated with him. It consists of three bodies :—

(1) The College of Cardinals.

(2) The Congregations of Cardinals.

(3) The Roman Tribunals.

2. The Cardinals are at least nominally the chief clergy of the city and province of Rome. Of these there are seventy according to the Constitution of Sixtus V. viz. six Cardinal bishops, fifty Cardinal priests, and fourteen Cardinal deacons. Their meetings for business purposes are called Consistories. The most important of their functions is the election of a Pope ([1]).

3. Congregations are Committees of Cardinals appointed for various purposes, the principal ones being :—

(1) The Congregation of the Consistory, which arranges the business to be transacted in Consistories.

(2) The Congregation of the Inquisition or Holy Office, which is charged with the trial of heresy.

([1]) Decretum Nicolai de electione summi Pontifices, ap. Gratian I. Dist. xxiii. c. 1.

(3)   The Congregation of the Index, which examines books suspected of heresy and condemns them.

(4)   The Congregation of the Council of Trent charged with the execution of the decrees of that Council.

(5)   The Congregation of Bishops and Regulars which determines disputes between these bodies.

(6)   The Congregation of Rites which besides determining the ritual appoints festivals and investigates claims to canonization.

(7)   The Congregation of Indulgences and Immunities, which inquires into matters of jurisdiction.

(8)   The Congregation for the Propagation of the Faith.

All these are considered to make one person with the Pope, so that there is no appeal from their decisions to him.

4. It is otherwise with Roman Tribunals, as certain Institutions are called, which carry through ecclesiastical business of a contentious or non-contentious character, and exercise an Ordinary Jurisdiction.   Such are :—

(1)   The Chancery which keeps a record of all that is done in Consistory touching the making provision for vacant sees.

(2)   The Datary which records all that is not done in Consistory.

(3)   The Penitentiary which takes cognisance of all cases touching the sacrament of Penance.

(4)   The Rota which judges all cases concerning benefices.

5. The Pope is also assisted by other ministers not of the Curia, such being :—

(1) Legates (') who are delegates sent to princes with full powers for certain purposes.

(2) Nuncios, who are accredited delegates with limited powers.

(3) Apostolic Commissaries, who are dispatched to judge on any business.

(4) Vicars-Apostolic sent to preside over the Church in places where no diocesan hierarchy exists, and are usually Bishops.

(5) Apostolic-Prefects who are priests sent to assist Bishops in colonies.

(') See Decret. Greg. IX. Lib. I. Tit. xxx.

CHAPTER XXXVII.

LESSER PATRIARCHS OR GREATER PRELATES.

1. AMONG lesser Patriarchs subordinate to the five great Patriarchates there existed several in former days. Others still exist now.

In the Western Church were those of Aquileia and Grado or Venice, to which Milan and Ravenna occupied at one time a position hardly inferior. In later times a similar rank was accorded to the Primates of Lisbon, of the Indies, of Pisa, Bourges, and Canterbury.

In the Eastern Church the chief Metropolitans of the sees corresponding with the capitals of civil government were at one time called Patriarchs. Subsequently these were styled Protothrones. Such were Caesarea in Cappadocia, Heraclea in Thrace, Thessalonica, and Corinth.

The Archbishops of Bulgaria, Cyprus, and Iberia ([1]) were independent of Patriarchal control, and were, therefore, themselves quasi-Patriarchs.

2. Below the Patriarchs stand the Primates, or superior Metropolitans of National Churches ; under the Primates, the ordinary Metropolitans of a Province ; and under these the Diocesan Bishops, in this relation called Suffragans

---

([1]) The Bishops of Cyprus obtained from the General Council of Ephesus (A.D. 431) the confirmation of their independence of the See of Antioch, the Council being at that moment in conflict with John of Antioch. See Routh's *Opuscula* on 8th Canon of Ephesus.

because they give their voices in Synod with their Metropolitan, and when not present themselves in and through
him (¹).

3. The chief duty of a Patriarch is to see that the Canons
of General Councils are observed, and to hear appeals from
Metropolitans where the custom prevails. The tendency,
however, has been to curtail intermediate jurisdictions, and
to carry appeals direct to the Pope (²). Foreign jurisdiction
is, however, disallowed (³).

(¹) See the authorities from Pseudo-Isidore on this point, ap. Gratian I.
Dist. xcix.

.(²) This Nicolaus did, soundly, rating Hincmar of Rheims. See
Gratian Caus. ii. Qu. vi. c. 13, and Caus. iii. Qu. vi. c. 10; Pseudo-
Isidore, ap. Gratian Caus. iii. Qu. vi. c. 5, 7, 9; Leo, Epist. lxxxii ;
Ibid. c. 8. It was one of the principal results of the False Decretals.

(³) By Pseudo-Isidore, ap. Gratian, Caus. iii. Qu. vi. c. 12 and 14.

CHAPTER XXXVIII.

ARCHBISHOPS AND METROPOLITANS.

1. THERE appears to be this distinction between Archbishops and Metropolitans, that Archbishops have a precedence of rank (¹) only, whereas Metropolitans have authority or jurisdiction to supervise the work of their fellow-bishops in a limited and canonical manner. Hence there may be and are Archbishops without suffragans, but never Metropolitans without suffragans. When an Archbishop does exercise control over Bishops, it is as Metropolitan, when over Metropolitans, it is as Primate or Patriarch (²).

Metropolitans existed before the Nicene Council, and are expressly recognised by it (³). The Council of Antioch (⁴) gives as the reason why jurisdiction is assigned to them, "because those who have business come from every quarter to the metropolis;" and it is ordered that their privileges be respected.

2. The Jurisdiction of a Metropolitan is not autocratic. He acts for and on behalf of the whole Episcopal Body. of

(¹) Archbishops alone use the pallium. Decret. Greg. IX. Lib. i. Tit. viii.

(²) See Owen's *Institutes of Canon Law*, p. 38.

(³) Canons 4 and 6.

(⁴) A.D. 341, Can. 9.

the Church ([1]), so that he acts (1) only conjointly with his suffragans or comprovincials, and (2) only in cases requiring such intervention for the good of the Church.

He acts always conjointly with his suffragans ([2]) since appeals are made to him in Synod ([3]), though for convenience they may be heard in Courts, which are then not so much his courts as Courts of the Province. Every Bishop of the province is therefore bound to attend the Provincial Synod ([4]), there to judge and give a voice with the Metropolitan ; and the sentence of the majority of the Suffragans prevails against his, and without their consent he cannot dissolve a Synod ([5]).

3. As no Bishop may intermeddle with the See of another ([6]), so a Metropolitan's interference in the Dioceses

---

([1]) ·Hence a Metropolitan is required not to consecrate a Bishop without the Primate's consent. Leo ap. Gratian I. Dist. lxv. c. 4. Concil. Carthag. ii. Can. 12, A.D. 390, *Ibid.* c. 5, and difficult matters go from the Metropolitan to the Primate. Boniface ap. Gratian, Caus. vi. Qu. iv. c. 8.

([2]) Martinus ex Concil. Antioch. Can. 9, ap Gratian, Caus. ix. Qu. iii. c. 1; Per singulas provincias oportet episcopos cognoscere metropolitanum suum, et ipsum primatus curam suscipere, nihil autem agere reliquos episcopos præter eum . . . Propter quod metropolitanus episcopus nihil praesumtive assumat absque concilio ceterorum.

([3]) Pseudo-Isidorus, ap. Gratian, Caus. ix. Qu. iii. c. 4. Concil. Carthag. iv. Can. 66, ap. Gratian, Caus. xi. Qu. iii. c. 30; Clericus qui episcopi circa se districtionem injustam putat, recurrat ad synodum. Decret. Greg. IX. Lib. v. Tit. i. c. 25.

([4]) So all bishops subjecti ordinationibus apostolicis were required to appear at Rome every year by Zacharias in 748. See Grat. I. Dist. xciii. c. 4.

([5]) Hence Comprovincials are Judges in the case of a Metropolitan. See authorities ap. Gratian, Caus. ii. Qu. vii. c. 44 and 45.

([6]) Nicolaus et Gregorius, ap. Gratian, Caus. xvi. Qu. v. c. 1 and 3.

of his Comprovincials is limited to the three cases, (1) of
visitation, (2) of negligence, and (3) of appeal.

4. A metropolitan may freely visit his province although
his suffragans are not negligent ([1]). In visitation the
Ordinary Jurisdiction of the Bishop is superseded by that
of the Metropolitan, who acts as the representative or deputy
of the Co-episcopate for the time being. Hence no visitations
may be held without the bishop of the diocese being first
consulted, and the Metropolitan's decision must be taken in
his presence ([2]).

5. In case of a Bishop neglecting ([3]) to do that
which by law or custom pertains to his office, the Metropolitan, having first monished him, may himself supply the
negligence ([4]), as by ordaining and instituting clerks,
excommunicating, absolving or condemning offenders. He
is then said to act by devolution. But he may not hear or
judge a case in the first instance in a diocese other than his
own ([5]).

6. A Metropolitan may, however, decide a case when it is
lawfully brought before him and his suffragans on appeal
([6]), after it has been first heard and decided upon by the
bishop to whose diocese it appertains.

A Metropolitan is appointed like any other Bishop with

([1]) Sext Decret. iii. Tit. xx.
([2]) Nicolaus ap. Gratian, Caus. ix., Qu. iii. c. 4 to 5.
([3]) Leo ap. Gratian, Caus. xxv. Qu. i. c. 2.
([4]) Decret. Greg. IX. Lib. i. Tit. x.
([5]) Romana Synodus, A.D. 381, ap. Gratian, Caus. iii. Qu. vi. c. 16.
([6]) The Council of Sardica, Can. 17, A.D. 347, ap. Gratian, Caus. xi.
Qu. iii. c. 4, sanctions appeals. Also the Concil. Carthag. ii., Can. 8.
A.D., 397, *Ibid.* c. 5. Also Concil. Milev. Can. 22, ap. Gratian, Caus. xi.
Qu. iii. c. 34, permits appeals to episcopi vicini.

the concurrence of the Clergy and Laity (¹) and consecrated by all his Suffragans (²). Later regulations require a Metropolitan to be approved by the Prelate above him, and invested with the pallium (³) by the Pope.

(¹) Leo ap. Gratian I. Dist. lxiii. c. 19.

(²) Pseudo-Isidore ap. Gratian I. Dist. lxvi. c. 1.   Decret. Greg. IX. Lib. i. Tit. xi. c. 6.

(³) Leo and Gregorius, ap. Gratian, Caus. xxv. Qu. ii. c. 1 to 8, 11, 12.

CHAPTER XXXIX.

THE OFFICIALS OF METROPOLITANS.

1. A METROPOLITAN is assisted in the administration of his Province by divers Courts and Officials separate and distinct from those who assist in the administration of his Diocese.

In the Metropolitan Province of Canterbury the Archbishop anciently combined in his person three distinct offices. He was (1) Archbishop of the See of Canterbury, (2) Metropolitan of the Province of Canterbury, and (3) Primate of all England, and born Legate of the Pope.

2. As Archbishop of the See of Canterbury he has a Court corresponding with the Diocesan or Consistorial Court of any Bishop, presided over by a Spiritual Judge corresponding with the Official-Principal or Chancellor of any other Bishop. This Judge is called the Commissary of the Archbishop, and discharges the duties of an Official Principal and Vicar General so far as his own diocese is concerned, and this Court is called the Court of the Commissary of the Archbishop.

3. As Metropolitan of the Province of Canterbury the Archbishop has the assistance of three different Courts for administering the affairs of the province :—

(1) The Court of Audience, or the Archbishop's *Personal* Court, in which at first were dispatched all such matters whether of voluntary or contentious jurisdictions as the Archbishop

thought fit to reserve for his own hearing ([1]).
Those who prepared evidence to bring before this
court were called auditors. In the Archbishop's
absence this Court was presided over by an
officer called the Master Official of the Audience.
This Court is now almost obsolete and is only
used on the rare occurrence of the trial of a
Bishop ([2]), when it appears to be the same as
a Synodical Council presided over by the Archbishop and acting according to set forms of law ([3]).

(2) The Court of the Official Principal ([4]), of
Judicial Representative of the Archbishop.
This is the Court of appeal in all contentious
matters from the Consistorial or Diocesan Courts
of the Province, and from the Court of the
Archbishop's Commissary. It is held usually
in Bow Church, commonly called S. Mary of
Arches, one of the thirteen London parishes
exempt from the jurisdiction of the Bishop of
London, and hence called peculiars. It is
therefore commonly called the Arches Court ([5]),
and is the most ancient Court and Consistory
of the Archbishop of Canterbury ([6]).

([1]) See Johnson 254. Phillimore's *Ecclesiastical Law*, p. 1204.

([2]) As in the case of the Bishop of S. David's, deprived by the
Archbishop of Canterbury in 1695. 14 State trials, 447. Phillimore's
Ecclesiastical Law, p. 84 and 1201.

([3]) See Chap. lxiv.

([4]) Gibs. 1004. Phillimore's *Ecclesiastical Law*, p. 1205.

([5]) Phillimore, p. 257, 1201, 1203, 1205.

([6]) The rules at present regulating procedure in the Court of Arches
were made 1 Jan. 1867.

(3) The Court of the Vicar General, or *Spiritual Representative* of the Archbishop. The chief function of this Court is to inquire into the regularity of spiritual acts done in the Province. Hence it takes cognisance of the Confirmation of Bishops (¹).

4. As Primate of all England, and born Legate of the Pope (²), the Archbishop has also other two courts :—

(1) The Court of Peculiars, which was the Court to which all exempt jurisdictions or peculiars in England were amenable. The Judge of this Court being constantly employed by the Official Principal as his deputy whenever he was absent on foreign embassies came to be considered as that Official's standing substitute or Dean, and was hence called Dean of the Arches Court, sometimes Dean of the Peculiars. His functions are now usually discharged by the Official Principal of the Archbishop's Court.

(2) The Court of Faculties, which has to do with the issuing of Faculties and Dispensations and the admissions of Notaries, the judge of which is called the Master of the Faculties (³).

(¹) Phillimore, p. 1201.

(²) See Owen's *Institutes of Canon Law*, p. 40.

(³) It is called a Court in Inst. Part 4 p. 387. By the Statute 28, Hen. VIII. c. 21, s. 2, it has all the powers of granting dispensations formerly exercised by the Pope. It would seem from s. 11 that an appeal lies from this Court to the Lord Chancellor, but this is by Statute not by Canon Law. See Phillimore's *Ecclesiastical Law*, p. 1234.

CHAPTER XL.

DIOCESAN BISHOPS.

1. A DIOCESAN Bishop is one who has been appointed to preside over the Clergy and Body of Christians dwelling within certain territorial limits, to rule and teach them as the Ordinary (¹) Representative of the Apostolic College, and to exercise among them the plenitude of the Priesthood.

The appointment of a Bishop is made by the Co-episcopate acting through the Bishops (²) of the province, and from it he derives both Jurisdiction (³) and Orders; but it is only made after the Clergy and Laity of the Diocese over which he is called to preside (⁴) have concurred in nominating a fit person (⁵).

(¹) A man must be in Holy Orders at the time of his appointment. See Urban II. ap. Gratian I. Dist. lx. c. 4. Gregorii Lib. vii. Reg. Epist. 118, ap. Gratian I. Dist. lxi. c. 1. Hormisdas, *Ibid.* c. 2 and 3. Innocentius Epist. xii. A.D. 416. *Ibid.* c. 4. Leo, Epist. lxxxv. (al. xxxvii. c. 1.) *Ibid.* c. 5. Martinus, *Ibid.* I. Dist. lxiii. c. 8.

(²) Leo, Epist. xc. (al. xcii. c. 1) ap. Gratian I. Dist lxii. c. 1. Calixtus, *Ibid.* c. 3. Capitula Caroli ap. Gratian I. Dist. lxiii. c. 84.

(³) On the share of the Emperor in the appointment of Bishops and of the Pope, see the authorities in Gratian I. Dist. lxiii. c. 9, 15, 16, 17, 18, 22, 23 : Concil. Toletanum xii. Can. 6, *Ibid.* c. 25, also 26.

(⁴) Concil. Nicæn. Can. 4, ap. Gratian I. Dist lxiv. c. 1. Concil. Antioch. Can. 16, A.D. 382, ap. Gratian I. Dist. xcii. c. 8 : Si quis episcopus vacans in ecclesiam non habentem episcopum, surripiens populos, sine concilio integri ordinis irruerit, etiamsi populus quem seduxit, desideret illum, alienum eum ab ecclesia esse oportet. Integrum autem et perfectum concilium dicimus illud, cui metropolitanus episcopus interfuit.

(⁵) There cannot, therefore, be more than one Bishop in any Church. Hieronymus ap. Gratian, Caus. viii. Qu. i. c. 41.

2. The concurrence of the Laity is generally expressed through the Patron (¹), and is given either before or after election, either by recommending a particular person for election, or by selecting one of several candidates proposed by the Clergy. In England the sovereign usually acts as the Patron through the Prime Minister, but formerly the Earls of Derby were the Patrons of the see of Sodor and Man, and the Archbishops of Canterbury the Patrons of the bishopric of Rochester. In other countries the Patronage is sometimes shared between the Pope and the Sovereign; sometimes it is exercised by individuals.

3. The concurrence of the Clergy is given by the formal election of the Chapter.

4. The appointment by the Co-episcopate is made by the act of confirmation, whereby actual jurisdiction or a right over the spiritualities is conferred. Confirmation is made by the higher Metropolitan as the representative of the Episcopal Body.

5. Investiture or Installation is the putting in possession of the lay fiefs or property belonging to the see. It confers only a right to the temporalities, and was at one time a matter of serious dispute between the ecclesiastical and civil authorities.

(¹) Concil. Carthag. iv. Can. 27 ap. Gratian, Caus. viii. Qu. i. c. 37.

CHAPTER XLI.

ELECTION OF BISHOPS.

1. BEFORE a Bishop can be appointed to a Diocese it is necessary that the concurrence of the Clergy and Laity of that Diocese shall first have been given to his appointment ([1]). In ancient times he was said to be elected by the Clergy and Laity. What the actual share of the Laity was in the election is not clear, nor whether it was more than simply assenting to what the Clergy had done ([2]). Their interference appears to have given rise to occasional irregularities ([3]). Subsequently when sees became endowed, the share of Clergy and Laity was a matter of frequent dispute, as in the struggle about Investitures. On the whole the Laity obtained a preponderating influence by the right of Patronage ([4]), and in return the Clergy excluded them from the formal election in Chapter ([5]).

([1]) Gregorius Lib. ii. Epist 19. ap. Gratian I. Dist. lxi. c. 11. Episcopus dum fuerit postulatus, cum solemnitate decreti subscriptionibus omnium roborati et dilectionis tuæ testimonio literarum ad nos sacrandus occurrat. See Leo ap. Gratian I. Dist. lxii. c. 2. But an election by non-Catholics is void. See Gregorius Lib. viii. Epist. 65, ap. Gratian Caus. ix. Qu. i. c. 6.

([2]) Cœlestini Epist. iii. c. 3, A.D. 429, ap. Gratian I. Dist. lxii. c. 2. Hadrianus in viii. Synodo Constantinopoli, A.D. 870, ap. Gratian I. Dist. lxiii. c. 1.

([3]) See Decret. Greg. IX. Lib. i. Tit vi. c. 2.

([4]) In England by Statute, 25 Henry VIII. c. 20.

([5]) See Lateran Council of 1139, Can. 28, and Decret. Greg. IX. Lib. i Tit. vi. c. 56.

2. The share of the Laity in the appointment of a Bishop is more usually exercised before the formal election by the Clergy by nominating an individual for election; sometimes by selecting one out of several candidates elected by the Chapter. A predominating influence is secured to the Laity in the appointment, by the temporalities being subject to the regulations of the Civil Government, and so requiring the elect of the Clergy to have the approval of the Laity.

3. With the Clergy alone, however, now rests the formal election ([1]), and it has to be held subject to particular customs which prevail and the agreement come to with the representatives of the Laity. It is moreover now confined to those Clergy who are regularly attached to the Diocese, *i.e.* the Chapter, no voice being allowed to the Clergy who are only attached to Parishes ([2]).

4. A regular election by the Clergy may take place in one of three ways ([3]). It may be :—

(1) By scrutiny ([4]), or voting by ballot, in which case

([1]) The formal election by the Clergy, may be regarded as the act of a Court called on to inquire and decide whether the proposed Candidate fulfils the Church's requirements, such as that he is not guilty of any crime punishable by Canon Law. See Gratian I. Dist. lxii. c. 18.

([2]) But used not so to be. See Innocentius ap. Gratian I. Dist. lxiii. c. 35, and Decret. Greg. IX. Lib. i. Tit. vi. c. 56.

([3]) Decret. Greg. IX. Lib. i. Tit. vi. c. 12.

([4]) In Acts i. 26, the earliest case on record, it appears to have been by votes given secretly ; καὶ ἔδωκαν κλήρους αὐτῶν, *i.e.* They (the electors) gave their votes (κλήρους or ballot votes as opposed to public voting). If the rendering is αὐτοῖς, the reading would be : they (the electors) voted upon them (the two candidates). It is far more probable that the Church in the 4th century followed the precedent set in the appointment of S. Matthias to the Apostolate, than that the Apostles should the greater and wiser part of the electors must agree ([1]).

(2) By Compromise.

(3) By Inspiration, when the electors simultaneously nominate one and the same person.

5. There are also two irregular modes of appointment :—

(1) By Postulation, when the electors demand one who is disqualified by the Canons of the Church or the Law of the Land. In this case the removal of the disqualification, which is done by a· dispensation, constitutes the appointment ([2]).

(2) By Nomination, as when two or more fit persons are presented to a third person, who finally makes choice between them.

6. The rules applying to an ordinary Election are the following ([3]):—

(1) Every one who has a right must be summoned ([4]).

have followed some Jewish or heathen practice in use more than 1000 years previously. Hence the onus probandi is on those who make ' κλήρους ἔδωκαν a different mode of election from that which the conservatism of the Church has ever since followed.

([1]) See Leo ap. Gratian I. Dist. lxiii. c. 36, by a great majority, Concil. Nic. Can. 6 ap. Gratian I. Dist. lxv. c. 1. Gregorius Lib. viii. Epist. 40 ap. Gratian, Caus. viii. Qu. i. c. 17, and Decret. Greg. IX. Lib. i. Tit. vi. c. 22, and 35, 36, 55, 57.

([2]) Disqualifications for a Bishop are all the things which disqualify for the Priesthood, besides which there are others, such as being advocates in a court of law, or holding a military command. Concil. Sardic. Can. 13. Having been a schismatic, Decret. Greg. IX. Lib. i. Tit. vi. c. 5. Certain disqualifications are not removable according to Decret. Greg. IX. Lib. i. Tit. v. c. 1, 2, 3, 4.

([3]) See Phillimore's *Ecclesiastical Law*, p. 198.

([4]) Decret. Greg. IX. Lib. i. Tit vi. c. 35.

The presence of non-electors does not vitiate an election (¹), but the protest of any omitted qualified elector vitiates the proceedings.

(2) Only those in Holy Orders can vote, and no votes may be received from unqualified persons.

(3) The election must be free from force or violence (²).

(4) Votes must be given absolutely.

(5) There must be no simony (³).

(6) Electors cannot change after the result is made known and the elected has assented thereto (⁴).

(¹) An election is not vitiated by the presence of non-electors. Decret Greg. IX. Lib. iTit. vi. c. 18.

(²) Gratian I. Dist. lxi. c. 13. Decret. Greg. IX. Lib. i. Tit. vi. c. 14.

(³) Gregorius Lib. viii. Epist. 40 ap. Gratian, Caus. i. Qu. vi. c. 3. Gregorius ap. Gratian, Caus. viii. Qu. ii., Decret. Greg. IX. Lib. i. Tit. vi. c. 59.

(⁴) Decret. Greg. IX. Lib. i. Tit. vi. c. 21 and 58.

CHAPTER XLII.

THE CONFIRMATION, TRANSLATION, AND RESIGNATION OF BISHOPS.

1. WHEN the Clergy and Laity have concurred in the choice of a Bishop ([1]), the actual appointment is made by the Metropolitan acting for the Co-episcopate generally ([2]). This appointment is called Confirmation ([3]), and is not permitted to be made by a layman ([4]). Before making it the confirming Prelate is bound to inquire into the fitness of the nominee ([5]), and not to confirm an unsuitable appointment on pain of being deprived of the power of confirming future elections ([6]). Once made, a Confirmation holds good.

By Confirmation Jurisdiction over the Diocese is committed to the Bishop Elect, even though the Episcopal Order be as yet wanting ([7]), since the administration of a

([1]) Hieronymus ad Titum c. 1. ap. Gratian, Caus. viii. Qu. i. c. 20.

([2]) Concil. Antioch. Can. 16, A.D. 332, ap. Gratian I. Dist. xcii. c. 8: Integrum autem et perfectum concilium [integri ordinis] dicimus illud, cui metropolitanus episcopus interfuit. Concil. Carthag. iv. Can. 27, ap. Gratian, Caus. vii. Qu. i. c. 37.

([3]) Greg. III. ap. Decret. Greg. IX. Lib. i. Tit. vi. c. 3. Decret. Greg. IX. Lib. ii. Tit. xxx.

([4]) Gregorius VII. ap. Gratian, Caus. xvi. Qu. vii. c. 12 and 13. Canones Apostolorum 31. Ibid. c. 14-20.

([5]) See Decret. Greg. IX. Lib. i. Tit. xii. and Tit. xiv.

([6]) Decret. Greg. IX. Lib. i. Tit. vi. c. 44.; Tit. vii. c. 1.

([7]) Decret. Greg. IX. Lib. i. Tit. vi. c. 15.

Diocese is a matter of Jurisdiction rather than of Order, and acts requiring Order may be done by a delegate who is in Episcopal Orders ([1]).

2. When a Bishop is removed from one see to another, it is called a Translation. Translations were strictly forbidden by the Council of Nicæa ([2]), and still more strictly by that of Antioch ([3]). Nevertheless, custom appear to have allowed them very generally ([4]), when they seemed to be advantageous for the whole Church, of which the Episcopal Body or their representative ([5]) must be the judge.

3. Renunciation or simple Resignation of a see is forbidden to a Bishop, except for one of the following reasons ([6]) :—

(1) When he has a sin on his conscience which hinders the execution of his office ([7]).

(2) On account of sickness or old age ([8]), or

([1]) Decret. Greg. IX. Lib. i. Tit. xxxiii. c. 10.

([2]) Can. 15 ap. Gratian, Caus. vii. Qu. i. c. 19.

([3]) Concil. Antioch, Can. 21 ap. Gratian, Caus. vii. Qu. i. c. 25 ; also by Evaristus ap. Gratian, Caus. vii. Qu. i. c. 11; by Concil. Carthag. v. Can. 5, A.D. 401, *Ibid.* c. 21 ; by Hilarius, A.D. 465, *Ibid.* c. 30; by Leo, *Ibid.* c. 31.

([4]) Pseudo-Isidorus ap. Gratian, Caus. vii. Qu. i. c. 34 and 35, and Concil. Carthag. iv. Can. 27, *Ibid.* c. 37, Gregorius, *Ibid.* c. 44.

([5]) Decret. Greg. IX. Lib. i. Tit. vii. and Lib. iii. Tit. iv. c. 1.

([6]) Commemorated in the following lines, ap. Decret. Greg. IX. Lib. i. Tit. ix. c. 10 :—

Debilis, Ignarus, Male Conscius, Irregularis
Quem mala plebs odit, dans scandala cedere possit.

([7]) Decret. Greg. IX. Lib. i. Tit. ix. c. 11.

([8]) Decret. Greg. IX. Lib. i. Tit. ix. c. 9 (and not always allowed then); Decret. Greg. IX. Lib. i. Tit. ix. c. 1.

(3) For lack of knowledge of spiritual things, or of skill to deal with the temporalities.

(4) When the people are incorrigibly disobedient.

(5) To avoid grievous scandal which cannot be otherwise prevented.

(6) On account of personal irregularity, such as having been twice married.

Instead of Renunciation, the Canon Law prefers the appointment of a Coadjutor or a Suffragan.

DIVISION III.

THE UNIT OF JURISDICTION—THE DIOCESE.

.

CHAPTER XLIII.

DIOCESAN JURISDICTION.

1. THE Diocese ([1]) is the unit of Church Government. It is the district committed to the spiritual oversight of one Bishop, together with his Clergy the Chapter, and administered by his and their officers ([2]).

The rule of a Bishop over a single Diocese ([3]) is a most ancient institution of the Church, and existed before the establishment of Provinces and Patriarchates and a graduated Hierarchy.

Within the Diocese the Bishop, as representative of the Apostolic College, is the superior Ordinary, and exercises a

([1]) Anciently called παροικια or Parish.

([2]) A Bishop is strictly forbidden from invading the Diocese of another Concil. Antioch, Can. 22 ; Concil. Constantinopol. i. Can. 2, A.D. 391, ap. Gratian, Caus. ix. Qu. ii. c. 7, 8, 9, 10 ; nor may the Clergy forsake their Diocese and go over to another, according to Concil. Nicæn. Can. 16, A.D. 825 ; Concil. Antioch, Can. 3, ap. Gratian, Caus. viii. Qu. i. c. 23 and 24 ; and Damasus, *Ibid.* c. 43.

([3]) Clergy without cure of souls are not bound to take the oath of obedience. See Decret. Greg. IX. Lib. i. Tit. xxxiii. c. 3, yet all within the Diocese are under the Bishop, *Ibid.* c. 4.

well-defined jurisdiction allowed by the Church (¹). Hence a Bishop's first duty is to visit his Diocese (²), in order that he may know it. Yet this he may do by deputy if unable to do it in person (³).

2. A Bishop's Jurisdiction is, nevertheless, not an absolute one. It is limited (1) by the Hierarchy from above, and (2) by the Chapter co-ordinately.

By the Hierarchy it is limited indirectly only, inasmuch as no Bishop is permitted to interfere in the Diocese of another save to supervise occasionally, as in visitations ; to set right what is complained of as a miscarriage of justice, as in appeals ; and to supplement what is neglected, as in cases of devolution.

By the Chapter it is limited directly, seeing that the charge of the Diocese is not entrusted to the Bishop alone, but to him jointly with the Chapter, of which he is the ordinary superior.

3. When a Bishop acts with his Chapter, their acts are acts of the Church and bind his successors. When he acts by himself, those acts are his own and not the acts of the Church, and are of force only during his lifetime. The Chapter cannot act without him in the Diocese, unless he

---

(¹) Synodus Regiaticina, A.D. 850, ap. Gratian I. Dist. xciii. c. 8 : Nulla ratione clerici aut sacerdotes habendi sunt qui sub nullius episcopi disciplina ac providentia gubernantur. Tales enim acephalos id est sine capite prisca ecclesiae consuetudo nominavit. See also letters of Clement and Anacletus, *Ibid.* c. 9 and 10. See Calixtus, ap. Gratian, Caus. xvi. Qu. vii. c. 11.

(²) Concil. Toletan. iv. and Concil. Tarraconense, Can. 8, A.D. 516, ap. Gratian, Caus. x. Qu. i. c. 9 and 10. ; Concil. Bracarense ii. Can. 1, *Ibid.* c. 12.

(³) Concil. Toletan. iv. Can. 35, A.D. 633, ap. Gratian, Caus. x. Qu. i. c. 11 ; Decret. Greg. IX. Lib. i. Tit. xxx. c. 16.

be dead or incapacitated, in which case it administers the Diocese through a Vicar-Capitular.

A Bishop's jurisdiction is to a great extent not exercised directly, but through intermediaries, some of whom have an ordinary jurisdiction under him. These are of three kinds : (1) Episcopal Officers, such as his Vicar-General and Official Principal ; (2) Diocesan Officers, such as the Archpriest and Archdeacon ; (3) Officers of the laity in Holy Orders, such as the Parochial Clergy.

4. The creation of new Sees as well as the subdivision or the union of old ones cannot be made without the assent of the Co-episcopate and of all the Bishops affected by the change ([1]).

([1]) Gratian, Caus. xvi. Qu. i. c. 48-54.

CHAPTER XLV.

THE Episcopal Officers appointed to assist in diocesan administration are of three kinds : (1) Coadjutor or Suffragan Bishops, who are consecrated to perform episcopal acts, as the Diocesan's deputies ; (2) the Bishop's Vicar-General, Official Principal, and Chancellor, who exercise the Bishop's Ordinary jurisdiction as and for him as principals and not as deputies ; (3) those who hold a special Commission limited by the terms of that Commission, such as Rural Deans.

1. A Coadjutor or Suffragan Bishop is one who is appointed to assist another Bishop in case of illness, age, or mental incapacity, by doing episcopal acts on his behalf ([1]). When he is appointed to preside over the same see during the Bishop's lifetime, with right of succession, he is called a Coadjutor Bishop ([2]). When he is appointed to preside over a part of a diocese and to act during the

---

([1]) Both Gregory and Nicolaus forbid a Bishop's being deprived because of age (ap. Gratian, Caus. vii. Qu. i. c. 1 and 3) ; but another may be appointed to assist him, *Ibid.* c. 13, and Concil. Toletan. xi. Can. 14, A.D. 675, *Ibid.* c. 15 ; also Zacharias, A.D. 784, *Ibid.* c. 17, and Pelagius, c. 18 ; Pseudo-Isidorus, ap. Gratian, Caus. viii. Qu. i. c. 1. Innocent III. in Decret. Greg. IX. Lib. iii. Tit. vi. c. 5. The Act 32 and 33 Vict. c. 111 secs. 3 and 4, sanctions the appointment of a Coadjutor Bishop in case of the incapacity of the Diocesan.

([2]) A bishop, however, cannot appoint his successor. See Gratian, Caus. viii. Qu. i. c. 3 to 7.

Diocesan's pleasure, he is improperly called a Suffragan Bishop (¹).

2. By Vicar-General (²) is meant one who is appointed by the Bishop with general powers to represent him. His proper work is the exercise and administration of jurisdiction purely spiritual by the authority and under the direction of the Bishop, such as visitation, correction of manners, granting institutions (³), and the like, with a general inspection of men and things, to the preserving of discipline and good government in the Church (⁴). As the Bishop's representative he can take cognisance of all cases belonging to his jurisdiction which still rest in him, notwithstanding the appointment of an Official. His tribunal is identical with the Bishop's, with whom he is considered to make but one person, so that there is no appeal from him to the Bishop (⁵). He is the Bishop's chief spiritual officer, having charge of all his voluntary jurisdiction (⁶).

(¹) Suffragan Bishops in this sense are a creation of statute 26 Henry VIII. c. 14. See Phillimore's *Ecclesiastical Law*, p. 96. In the usual sense all the Diocesan Bishops of a Province are called Suffragans.

(²) Anciently called Vicedominus, or Oeconomus. Concil. Chalcedon, Can. 26, A.D. 451 : ἔδοξε πάσαν ἐκκλησίαν ἐπίσκοπον ἔχουσαν καὶ οἰκόνομον ἔχειν ἐκ τοῦ ἰδίου κλήρου, οἰκονομοῦντα τὰ ἐκκλησιαστικὰ κατὰ γνώμην τοῦ ἰδίου ἐπισκόπου· See Gregorius, Lib. ix. Ep. 66, and Lib. i. Ep. 11, ap. Gratian I. Dist. lxxxix. c. 2 and 3, and Caus. xii. Qu. ii. c. 45 ; Gratian, Caus. xvi. Qu .vii. c. 21. Synodus vii. Can. ii. ap. Gratian, Caus. ix. Qu. iii. c. 3, authorises a Metropolitan to appoint an Oeconomus for a Bishop who neglects so to do. Ayl. *Par.* 161.

(³) In *Smith* v. *Lovegrove* (2. Lee's *Rep.* 169), it was ruled that by 14 Car. ii. c. 4, Chancellors or Vicars-General were debarred from exercising the power of a Vicar-General by licensing a lecturer.

(⁴) Gibs. *Introd.* 22 ; Gibson's *Tracts*, 108 ; Phillimore's *Ecclesiastical Law*, p. 1208.

(⁵) 1. Stillingfleet, 330. Phillimore's *Ecclesiastical Law*, p. 1209.

(⁶) Concil. Hispalens. ii. Can. ix. A.D. 619, ap. Gratian, Caus. xvi. Qu. vii. c. 22, forbids the appointment of a layman. Conf. *Ibid.* c. 23 to 25.

The chief temporal officer of a Bishop is his Official Principal ([1]), who is charged with the care of all contentious matters of temporal cognisance, such as wills, marriages, and the like. As the Vicar-General is the Bishop's spiritual representative, so the Official Principal is his judicial representative. Except in the case of the see of Canterbury, the offices of Vicar-General and Official Principal are usually but not necessarily united in all English dioceses in one and the same person, who is called the Chancellor ([2]).

[1] By a constitution of Archbishop Chichele, ap. Lind. 128, it is enjoined : " To remove the scandals brought upon the authority of the Church, we, following the footsteps of the holy canons, do decree that no clerk *married*, nor *bigamus*, nor layman, shall upon any pretence, in his own name or in the name of any other, exercise any spiritual jurisdiction ; nor in cases of correction where the proceedings are for the health of the soul, or where the judge proceedeth *ex officio*, shall in any wise be a scribe, or register, or keeper of the registry of such corrections : And if any ordinary inferior to the Bishop or other person having ecclesiastical jurisdiction shall admit or suffer any such person to exercise any such office as aforesaid, he shall be *ipso facto* suspended from the exercise of his office and jurisdiction and from the entrance of the Church ; and all citations, processes, sentences, acts, and other proceedings had or made by such clerks *married*, *bigami*, or *laymen*, shall *ipso facto* incur the sentence of the greater excommunication." This Canonical enactment appears never to have been repealed, notwithstanding that the Statute 37 Henry VIII. c. 17, permits otherwise, enacting : " That all and singular persons, as well lay as married, being Doctors of the Civil Law, lawfully create and made in any university who shall be appointed to the office of Chancellor, Vicar-General, Commissary, Official, Scribe, or Register, may lawfully execute and exercise all manner of Jurisdiction, commonly called Ecclesiastical Jurisdiction, and all censures and coercions appertaining or in any wise belonging to the same, albeit such person or persons be lay, married or unmarried, so that they be Doctors of the Civil Law as is aforesaid ; any law, constitution, or ordinance to the contrary notwithstanding."

[2] See Gibson's *Tracts*, 110.

3. A Rural Dean ([1]) is one who is appointed to supervise a group of the Parochial Clergy ([2]) as the Bishop's officer, and generally to keep the Bishop informed of all that transpires in his Rural Deanery. His duties are, therefore, the same as one branch of the Archdeacon's duties ([3]), but within a more limited district, and accordingly of ancient right the Archdeacon had a share in his appointment jointly with the Bishop ([4]). His present position is that of being the Bishop's Commissary for certain purposes, the precise nature of which depends on the terms of his commission. He has, therefore, no ordinary jurisdiction, and is not a prelate ([5]).

4. There are, however, certain Commissaries of the Bishop, or rather of his Official Principal, who do exercise an ordinary jurisdiction. Such are the Commissaries who used to be appointed to act for the Chancellor in places of the diocese far distant from the chief city. These were termed Officials of the Outplaces ([6]) in contradistinction to the Official Principal.

([1]) Anciently called Archipresbyter Ruralis. See Decret. Greg. IX. Lib. i. Tit. xxiv. c. 4.

([2]) See below chapters on the Parochial Clergy and Benefices.

([3]) The Archdeacon supervises the Parochial Clergy because of their holding temporalities.

([4]) In ancient times, however, the Rural Dean was an Officer of the Church and not of the Bishop only, and was appointed by the Archdeacon jointly with the Bishop. See Decret. Greg. IX. Lib. i. Tit. xxiii. 1, 7, 8, and Tit. xxiv. c. 4; and Gibs. 971. This ancient office appears in England to have been superseded by the Archdeacon's on the one hand, or to have survived in that of Deans of Peculiars on the other. At the time of the Reformation its jurisdiction appears to have declined to nothing.

([5]) Modern Rural Deans are only the Bishop's Commissaries. See Phillimore's *Ecclesiastical Law*, p. 257.

([6]) Officiales foranei. See Phillimore's *Ecclesiastical Law*, p. 1215.

CHAPTER XLVI.

DIOCESAN OFFICERS.

THOSE who hold a recognised office in the Church or Diocese, and do not simply act under the Bishop, are termed Diocesan officers ([1]).

1. There are two such officers in every Diocese, the Archpriest or Dean, and the Archdeacon ([2]). As to the relative rank of the two, there appears to have been some diversity of practice ; in some places the Archdeacon taking precedence of the Archpriest ([3]). As officers of the Church, these two have a well defined Ordinary Jurisdiction ([4]).

2. The Archpriest, or as he is more commonly called, the Dean, is the Head of all the Priests regularly attached to

[1] They were anciently elected by the clergy and people. See Isidorus ap. Gratian I. Dist. lxiii., c. 20.

[2] See the regulations of Urban II. A.D. 1095, of Calixtus II. at the 1st Lateran Council A.D. 1123, of Innocent II. at the 2nd Lateran Council A.D. 1139, as to the persons qualified for the several dignities of Archdeacon, Archpriest, or Dean and Provost, ap. Gratian I. Dist. lx. c. 1, 2, and 3.

[3] But he appears to have been under the Archdeacon. See the Concil. Toletan. ap. Decret. Greg. IX. Lib. i. Tit xxiv. c. 1. Innocent III., ap. Greg. IX. Decret. Lib. i. Tit. xxiii. c. 7 : Archipresbyteri autem, qui a pluribus decani nuncupantur archidiaconi jurisdictioni se noverint subjacere.

[4] Recognised in England by books on Common law. See Phillimore's *Ecclesiastical Law*, p. 239, and Gibs. 970.

124   *The Elements of Canon Law.*

the Diocese. His Jurisdiction, therefore, is over them ([1])
i.e., over the Chapter which they compose; and inasmuch
as the members of the Chapter are the only spiritual
assessors of the Bishop recognised by the Church, and the
Dean is the Head of the Chapter, he is styled the
Bishop's Vicar born in spirituals. After the Bishop he
has the greatest place in the Church, and is responsible
for all the ministrations in the Cathedral Church of the
Diocese ([2]).

8. The other Diocesan Officer is the Archdeacon ([3]),
one or more, the eye of the Bishop ([4]) to whom is committed the charge of all the temporalities of his Arch-
deaconry ([5]). He is, therefore, said to be the Bishop's Vicar
born in temporals. As such he appears to have Jurisdiction over the Parochial Clergy in respect of their temporalities ([6]), the Parochial Clergy being not so much officers

([1]) Lindwood says that the canons are under the Dean as to
the cure of souls, and make their confessions to him. God. 55, Lind.
327.

([2]) He is therefore required to reside. Can. 42 of 1603, requires a
Dean to reside 90 days. The Act 13 and 14 Vict. c. 98, s. 3 requires every
Dean to reside 8 months at the least.

([3]) On the duties of an archdeacon, see Decret. Greg. IX. Lib. i.
Tit. xxiii. Isidorus Hispalensis ap. Gratian I. Dist. xxv. c. 1 : Solicitudo
quoque parochiarum et ordinatio et jurgia ad ejus pertinent curam. Pro
reparandis Diocesanis basilicis ipse suggerit sacerdoti. Ipse inquirit
parochias cum jussione episcopi et ornamenta vel res basilicarum parochiarum et libertatum episcopo idem refert.

([4]) So called by Innocent III. in Decret. Greg. IX. Lib. i. Tit. xxiii.
c. 7.

([5]) Concil. Carthag. iv. Can. 17, ap. Gratian I. Dist. lxxxviii., c. 7 :
Episcopus gubernationem viduarum et pupillorum ac peregrinorum non
per se ipsum sed per archipresbyterum aut archidiaconum agat; but not
of the Cathedral. Decret. Greg. IX. Lib. i. Tit. xxxiii. c. 16.

([6]) Concil. Cabilonense, Can. 15, A.D. 813, ap. Gratian 1. Dist. xciv.

of the Church as of the Laity, and occupying the position they do by virtue of possessing benefices, but he has not Jurisdiction over the Chapter ([1]).

4. A Vicar-General, or other Official of the Bishop, exercising an ordinary Jurisdiction, becomes a Diocesan, and no longer simply an Episcopal officer, if his appointment is confirmed by the Dean and Chapter.

c. 3, forbids Archdeacons to exercise lordship over priests: for dictum est, quod in plerisque locis archidiaconi super presbyteros parochianos quandam exercent dominationem, et ab eis censum exigant, quod magis ad tyrannidem quam ad rectitudinis pertinet ordinem.

([1]) Decret. Greg. IX. Lib. i. Tit. xxxiii. 16, quoted by Gibs. 171.

CHAPTER XLVII.

PAROCHIAL CLERGY.

1. THE Parochial Clergy are not Officers of the Church of the Diocese, seeing they are not regularly attached to it like the Members of the Chapter. They have therefore no ordinary jurisdiction of their own, but in respect of jurisdiction are simply Vicars of the Bishop. Neither are they altogether officers of the Bishop although they are his Vicars, seeing that their ministrations are not for the whole Diocese but only for particular districts thereof called Parishes. But they are rather officers of the Laity by whom they are appointed to the places, (¹) within which they are deputed by the Bishop to exercise certain spiritual functions.

They have, therefore, a double character. They are (1) Officers of the Laity in respect of the places they hold and to which they have been appointed by them, and (2) they are Curates of the Bishop in respect to their spiritual ministrations.

2. Of ancient right they have no recognised ecclesiastical position in the Diocese like the Chapter Clergy. Nevertheless the possession of benefices has conferred on them a legal position, which by custom has come to be canonically acknowledged, so that they do not hold place like ordinary

(¹) Decret. Greg. IX. Lib. iii. Tit. v. c. 34.

Curates during the Bishop's life, or good pleasure, but, like others having an ordinary jurisdiction, continue to hold the office to which they are appointed until they are canonically removed from their benefices.

On the other hand their ministrations are confined strictly to the duties for which they are appointed, so that without the Bishop's license they have no authority to exercise others (¹).

(¹) Unless, therefore, they have the Bishop's License, or at least his cognisance, they have no authority to administer Penance.

PART III.

OF CERTAIN ESSENTIALS FOR THE HOLINESS AND MAINTENANCE OF THE CHURCH UPON EARTH.

CHAPTER XLVIII.

OF GRACES, GIFTS, AND CENSURES.

1. The Church having been planted in the world for the purpose of securing the holiness of its members by means of Christ's holiness, and its own continuous existence upon earth being necessary for all mankind to be partakers of so great a benefit, the means whereby these objects may be secured are of primary importance, and the rules for their administration occupy a large place in its laws.

These may be divided into three groups :—

(1) All those outward means provided in the Church whereby grace is conveyed to the souls of its members, including not only the Sacraments, but also Sacramental Acts.

(2) Certain states of life to which spiritual gifts are attached in the Church, whereby the means of grace are dispensed for the good of others, including not only Holy Orders, but also the Holy Estate of Matrimony.

(3) The powers of Discipline and Censure, both public and private, whereby the exercise of both graces and gifts is safe-guarded for the good of all.

2. The means of grace which Christ has committed to His Church are the two Sacraments of the Gospel, viz., Baptism and the Holy Eucharist; the first whereby new members are incorporated into the Body of Christ, the other whereby such as are already members of that Body are advanced in the way 'of holiness. Confirmation and Unction are also subsidiary means of grace. So also are Preaching and all the public Offices of the Church.

3. For the purpose of dispensing these graces Christ has established in His Church certain Spiritual Gifts called Holy Orders, inherent in certain classes of men. Of these there are likewise two, the Orders of Priests and Deacons; for Bishops and Priests are held to belong to one Order, although Bishops have a higher degree in the same (¹). A certain spiritual gift is likewise attached to those in another condition of life called Matrimony, when it is rightly contracted in the Church.

4. The dispensing of these graces and gifts is not left to the arbitrary will of individuals, but rests in the disposition of the Church, which alone has the power of determining not only how and by whom they shall be enjoyed, but also in what cases, and for what reasons they shall be withheld by way of censure. This is termed the power of Church Discipline.

(¹) Concil. Benevent, A.D. 1091, ap. Gratian I. Dist. lx. c. 4; Ordines qui auctoritate Christi et Apostolorum sacri fuerunt et sunt, qui sunt Diaconatus et Sacerdotium. See Owen's *Institutes of Canon Law* p. 42.

K

DIVISION I.

THE MEANS OF GRACE.

CHAPTER XLIX.

SACRAMENTS, SACRAMENTAL ACTS, AND PUBLIC WORSHIP.

THE Sacraments are the chief means of grace which Christ has committed to His Church for the maintenance of the Church's existence upon earth, and the edification of the faithful.

1. The essence of every true Sacrament consists in the use of an outward and·visible sign (¹) as the agency for conveying to man an inward and spiritual grace. That outward signs should be capable of conveying inward graces to the souls of men is a result of their being of divine appointment (²). Hence every true Sacrament must have a divine origin; and so Baptism and the Lord's Supper are

---

(¹) Augustin Lib. ii. de Doctrina Christiana c. 1. ap. Gratian III. Dist. iii. c. 33. Lanfranc ap. Gratian III. Dist. iii. c. 48. August. Tract. lxxx ad. c. 15, Joannis ap. Gratian, Caus. i. Qu. i. c. 54; Detrahe verbum et quid est nisi aqua. Accedit verbum ad elementum et fit sacramentum.

(²) Gregorius et Eusebius Emissenus ap. Gratian III. Dist. iii. c. 34, 35, and 36. Ambrosius, *Ibid.* c. 69.

the two great Sacraments of the Gospel because they were undoubtedly instituted by Christ Himself (').

2. Although in every true Sacrament the outward sign conveys the inward grace necessarily by virtue of Christ's appointment (²), there are, nevertheless, certain outward signs which ordinarily convey grace to the soul, and which are of the Church's appointment. These are called Sacramental Acts. Such are Confirmation and Unction.

3. Grace is received also by yet other means, as by hearing Sermons, or in the Public Worship of the Church.

(¹) Baptism in Matt. xxviii., 19., the Eucharist Matt. xxvi., 26.

(²) Augustinus in Psalm x. and Gregorius ap. Gratian, Caus. i. Qu. i. c. 88, 89, and 96, 97.

CHAPTER L.

THE SACRAMENTS.

THERE are two Sacraments of the Gospel ordained by Christ Himself, viz., Baptism and the Supper of the Lord.

1. Holy Baptism is the Sacrament of admission to the Christian life. By it the baptized person is grafted into, and made a member of the Body of Christ (¹), which is His Church, and is thus made partaker of Christ's holiness (²). He is thereby born again into a new life, and saved in and through Christ unless he forfeit his membership, and lose his union with the Head.

2. The Holy Eucharist is the Sacrament of continuance in the Christian life. By it the union of the individual with Christ the Head, and with the body of Christ the Church is maintained, and fresh grace is given to the Communicant to reproduce Christ's holiness in his own life. As the Church exists upon earth to promote the holiness of its members, so it excludes from its communion any member who either determinedly refuses to pursue this holiness or who, by carelessly neglecting to do so, hinders the holiness of others.

3. The Validity of Sacraments is not affected by the

(¹)   Rom. vi. 3.

(²)   Gal. iii. 37 ; ὅσοι εἰς Χριστὸν ἐβαπτίσθητε, Χριστὸν ἐνεδύσασθε·

worthiness of the Minister (¹). They are forbidden to be administered to those out of the jurisdiction (²), and in no case may fees be demanded for their Ministration (³).

(¹) Augustinus contra Hæreticos Tractat. v. ap. Gratian, Caus. i. Qu. i. c. 30 to 38. August. de corpore Domini ap. Gratian, Caus. i. Qu. i. c. 77. Augustin. contra Petil. Lib. ii. c. 8 ap. Gratian, Caus. i. Qu. i. c. 87 and 98. Nicolaus ap. Gratian, Caus. xv. Qu. viii. c. 5.

(²) Concil. Nannetense, Can. 1 and 2 ap. Gratian, Caus. ix. Qu. ii. c. 4, 5.

(³) Gelasius, A.D. 494, Epist. i. c. 7 ap. Gratian, Caus. i. Qu. i. c. 99. Baptizandis consignandisque fidelibus sacerdotes pretia nulla praefigant. Sexta Synod. Can. 23. A.D. 692, *Ibid.* 100 ; nullus episcopus aut presbyter aut diaconus, qui sacram dispensat communionem, a percipiente gratiam communionis aliquod pretium exigat. Concil. Toletan. xi. Can. 8, A.D. 675, *Ibid.* c. 101 : Concil. Bracarens. ii. Can. 4 and 7, A.D. 572, *Ibid.* 102 and 103. Concil. Eliberitan. Can. 48, A.D. 310, *Ibid.* 104. Concil. Tribur. A.D. 895, *Ibid.* 105. Concil. Cabilonens. Can. 16, A.D. 913, *Ibid.* 106.

CHAPTER LI.

BAPTISM.

BAPTISM is the Sacrament which cleanses from sin [1] by grafting the Baptized Person into the Church which is the Body of Christ [2].

1. The essentials of Baptism are the use of water in its natural state, and the use of words stating the purpose for which it is employed, viz., to baptize. It should be administered in the name of the Father, the Son, and the Holy Ghost, but it is not invalid if administered in the name of Christ only [3].

2. The proper mode of baptizing is by immersion. Single immersion suffices [4] but to immerse thrice is preferable [5] because it signifies belief in the Trinity and the

[1] S. Augustin, and S. John Chrysostom, ap. Gratian III. Dist. iv. c. 3 and 4; S. Boniface, *Ibid.* c. 136 to 137; See Decret. Greg. IX. Lib. iii. Tit. xlii; Clament, Lib. iii. Tit. xv.

In the New Testament, Acts ii. 38; βαπτισθήτω ἕκαστος ὑμῶν . . εἰς ἄφεσιν ἁμαρτιῶν Acts xxii. 16; βαπτίσαι καὶ ἀπόλουσαι τὰς ἁμαρτίας σου 1 Pet. iii. 21; ὃ (so. ὕδωρ) καὶ ὑμᾶς ἀντίτυπον νῦν σώζει βάπτισμα·

[2] S. Ambrose, Lib. i. de Sacramentis, c. 4 et 5, ap. Gratian III. Dist. iv. c. 9; S. Boniface, ap. Gratian III. Dist. iv. c. 131, and c. 133; Augustin, *Ibid.* c. 143; Rom. vi. 3: ἐβαπτίσθημεν εἰς Χριστὸν Ἰησοῦν. 1 Cor. xii. 13: εἰς ἓν σῶμα ἐβαπτίσθημεν·

[3] Pelagius, *Ibid.* c. 30.

[4] Fourth Council of Toledo in Gratian III. Dist. iv. c. 85.

[5] S. Augustin, ap. Gratian III. Dist. iv. c. 78; Zacharias, *Ibid.* c. 83; Apostolic Canons, *Ibid.* c. 79; S. Gregory, *Ibid.* 80; Decret. Greg. IX. Lib. iii. Tit. xlii. S. Jerome ap. Gratian III. Dist. iv. c. 81; See also Zacharias as to mistakes in words, *Ibid.* c. 86.

three days burial of Christ. The custom of the country determines the practice. It seems likely that S. Peter baptized by sprinkling or aspersion, when five thousand were converted in one day. Hence baptism by aspersion is also allowed.

3. The proper minister to baptize is a Bishop or a Priest ([1]) who thereby becomes the spiritual father of the baptized ; but a Deacon may baptize when no Priest can be had, and in cases of necessity a layman ([2]) but usually not a woman ([3]).

4. All men may receive baptism ([4]) because it is necessary for all ([5]), but in case of the baptism of children, ([6]) the Church requires god-parents, one or more, who must be Christians ([7]), and themselves confirmed to insure the proper education of their god-children afterwards.

5. Anciently the Church baptized only on Easter Eve, and Whitsun Eve ([8]) except in the case of sickness ([9])

([1]) Isidorus ap. Gratian III. Dist. iv. c. 19.

([2]) Augustinus, *Ibid.* c. 21 and 86; Edmund, Lind. 63.

([3]) Forbidden by Fourth Council of Carthage, ap. Gratian III. Dist. iv. c. 20.

([4]) Martinus, *Ibid.* c. 22.

([5]) Augustin. *Ibid.* c. 37.

([6]) Isidorus *Ibid.* c. 74; Augustin c. 76 and 142 ; Decret. Greg. IX. Lib. iii. Tit. xlii. c. 8.

([7]) Augustinus, *Ibid.* c. 77 and 105. In ancient times one was enough. See Leo ap. Gratian, *Ibid.* c. 101 ; God-parentage establishes a relationship closer than blood, so carrying with it all the duties and marriage-disqualifications of blood relationship. See the authorities, ap. Gratian, Caus. xxx. Qu. i.

([8]) Siricius ap. Gratian III. Dist. iv. c. 11. Leo Epist. iv. c. 5, *Ibid.* c. 12 and 18 and 14 ; Conc. Gerundense, *Ibid.* c. 15 ; Gelasius, *Ibid.* c. 17 and 18.

([9]) Third Council of Carthage, *Ibid.* c. 75.

or some other necessity when it was allowed at any time ([¹]).
Such baptism was called Clinical Baptism and carried with
it several disabilities ([²]).

6. The Place where Baptism is administered is only in
Churches possessed of fonts ([³]) hence called baptismal
Churches ([⁴]) and these are only principal Churches.
Baptism elsewhere is permitted in the case of princes, or
where access cannot be had to a baptismal Church without
peril, not otherwise.

Baptism once administered is in no case allowed to be
repeated ([⁵]) and is good by whomsoever administered ([⁶]).

([¹]) Leo Epist. iv. c. 6 ap. Grat. III. Dist. iv. c. 16; Si qui necessitat
mortis, aegritudinis, obsidionis persecutionis et naufragii urgentur, omni
tempore debent baptizari.

([²]) It disqualifies for Orders. See Concil Neocaesarense, Can. 12, A.D.
314, ap. Gratian I. Dist. lvii.

([³]) A stone font ordered in every Church by Edmund Lind, 241.

([⁴]) Ecclesiae baptismales. See Gratian, Caus xvi. Qu. i.c. 45; not
in monasteries, Gratian, Caus. xviii. Qu. ii. c. 7.

([⁵]) Not even when administered by a pagan, Isidorus ap. Gratian, *Ibid.*
c. 23; Nicolaus, *Ibid.* 24; Augustin, *Ibid.* 28, 31, 32, 33. Leo, *Ibid.* 88;
Beda, *Ibid.* c. 51; third Council of Carthage, Can. 38, *Ibid.* c. 87.

([⁶]) S. Augustin, *Ibid.* c. 25, 26, 39, 40; Gregory, *Ibid.* c. 44; Isidorus
ap. Gratian, Caus. i. Qu. i. c. 59; Augustin Tract. v. in Joan. ap. Gratian,
Caus. i. Qu. i. c. 46, Leo, *Ibid.* c. 57.

CHAPTER LII.

THE other Sacrament of the Gospel is the Holy Eucharist, called also the Holy Communion or the Sacrament of the Body and Blood of Christ, whereby such as are already members of Christ's Body are helped forward by grace in the way of holiness ([1]), by partaking of Christ's true Body and Blood ([2]).

1. The material forms of the Eucharist are Bread and Wine mixed with water ([3]); bread made of pure wheaten flour leavened or preferably unleavened ([4]), and wine the pure juice of the grape. Neither water ([5]) nor ale is allowed as a substitute. By the action of the Holy Spirit they become Christ's Body and Blood ([6]) to the receiver.

2. Three times a year every Christian is bound to com-

([1]) Prosper ap. Gratian III. Dist ii. c. 37. Leo, *Ibid.* c. 38.

([2]) Leo ap. Gratian III. Dist. ii. c. 38. Ambrosius, *Ibid.* c. 39, 40, 55, 56, and 91; Augustinus, *Ibid.* c. 41, 45, 46, 57, 58, and 92. Berengar, *Ibid.* c. 42. Hieronymus, *Ibid.* c. 49, 87, and 88.

([3]) Cyprian, Lib. ii. Epist. 2. ap. Gratian III. Dist. i. c. 2. Concil. Martini Bracarensis, Can. 55, *Ibid.* c. 4; Concil. Carthagen. iii. Can. 24, *Ibid.* c. 5. Ambrosius, *Ibid.* c. 83. Decret. Greg. IX. Lib. iii. Tit. xli. c. 13.

([4]) Authorities in Maskell's *Ancient Liturgy*, p. 48.

([5]) In early days those who used water were called Hydroparastatæ, and were condemned as heretics.

([6]) Augustinus, Lib. iii. de Trin. c. 4, ap. Gratian III. Dist. i. c. 60, 61, and 72. Ambrosius, *Ibid.* c. 74, 84, and 86. Hilarius, *Ibid.* c. 79.

municate, at Easter, at Pentecost, and at Christmas ([1]), the Easter Communion being absolute. Monks were required to communicate monthly, whence has probably arisen the practice of monthly communions ([2]).

3. The power of consecrating and offering the Eucharist, is given to every Priest at his Ordination ([3]). In early days the Bishop was the chief celebrant, the presbyters surrounding him and consecrating with him, as is now done at ordinations in the Roman Church.

4. A priest should not celebrate more than once a day, except in case of necessity or at Christmas ([4]). He should always communicate himself, and should not celebrate alone. Both the receiver and the altar should be fasting ([5]). Various rules are laid down as to the altar-vessels ([6]), the vestments ([7]), the proper hour to celebrate ([8]), the necessary preparation before ([9]), the ceremonies at ([10]), and the number of celebrations allowed ([11]).

5. By ancient rule the Eucharist was reserved ([12]), so

([1]) Fabian ap. Gratian III. Dist. ii. c. 16, Concil. Agathense, *Ibid.* c. 19. See Chapter lxxxix.

([2]) Clement. Lib. iii, Tit. x. c. 1.

([3]) Augustinus ap. Gratian III. Dist. ii. c. 26.

([4]) Decret. Greg. IX. Lib. iii. Tit. xli. c. 3.

([5]) August. ap. Gratian III. Dist. ii. c. 54. Concil. Africanum, Can. 8 ap. Gratian III. Dist. i. c. 49.

([6]) Which were not allowed to be of wood. See Gratian III. Dist. i. c. 41 and 45.

([7]) *Ibid.* c. 40 and 46.

([8]) *Ibid.* c. 48.

([9]) Gratian III. Dist. i. c. 49 ; Dist. ii. c. 21.

([10]) *Ibid.* c. 57 and 58.

([11]) Gratian III. Dist. ii. c. 53.

([12]) Ambrosius ap. Gratian III. Dist. ii. c. 43. See Justin Martyr's Apology i. c. 66 and 67.

that the communion might be ministered to the sick (¹). In the Western Church the practice grew of communicating in one kind only, for fear the Chalice might be spilt (²), or other excesses committed.

(¹) Concil. Wormaciense ap. Gratian III. Dist. ii. c. 93.
(²) Pius et Beda ap. Gratian III. Dist. ii. c. 27 and 28.

CHAPTER LIII.

SACRAMENTAL ACTS.

A SACRAMENTAL Act is the employment of an outward symbol or means, whereby ordinarily grace is conveyed to the soul. It differs from a Sacrament in not being of Christ's appointment.

1. The best known Sacramental Acts of the Church are two; Confirmation and Unction, or, as it is now more commonly used, extreme Unction.

2. The Churching of women (¹), the use of Holy Water, Public Prayers and the Hearing of Sermons may also be considered Sacramental Acts in so far as they are outward means whereby grace is often conveyed to the soul.

(¹) Decret. Greg. IX. Lib. iii. Tit. xlvii.

CHAPTER LIV.

CONFIRMATION.

1. THE Administration of Baptism in ancient times was followed by certain ceremonial rites (¹). Chief among these was the anointing or chrism (²), and the laying on of the Bishop's hands (³). When baptism was administered away from the Bishop's Church these acts could not be administered by the Bishop at the time (⁴). When they were subsequently administered by him and treated as a separate act, they received the name of Confirmation (⁵).

2. Confirmation is, therefore, a rite subsidiary to Baptism (⁶). As being the completion of Baptism it is not a separate Sacrament but only a Sacramental Act, whereby the baptized person is strengthened or confirmed (⁷) in his Christian membership, and voluntarily takes upon himself

(¹) Such as wearing a white garment. As to its meaning see Rabanus Ibid. c. 91. S. Ambrose, Ibid. c. 92.

(²) S. Ambrose on the symbolism thereof ap. Gratian III. Dist. iv. c. 87, 89, 90. Rabanus, Ibid. c. 88.

(³) Acts viii., 16, 17 ; οὔπω γὰρ ἦν ἐπ'οὐδενὶ αὐτῶν ἐπιπεπτωκὸς [Πνεῦμα Ἅγιον], μόνον δὲ βεβαπτισμένοι ὑπῆρχον εἰς τὸ ὄνομα τοῦ κυρίου Ἰησοῦ. Τότε ἐπετίθουν τὰς χεῖρας ἐπ' αὐτοὺς, καὶ ἐλάμβανον Πνεῦμα Ἅγιον.

(⁴) Pseudo-Isidorus, Ibid. c. 4.

(⁵) Leo Epist. lxxxvii ap. Gratian Caus. i. Qu. i. c. 51, orders those baptized by heretics to be confirmed.

(⁶) Pseudo-Isidorus ap. Gratian III. Dist. v. c. 3.

(⁷) Rabanus ap. Gratian III. Dist. v. 5.

the obligations which his godparents previously undertook for him.

3. The proper minister of Confirmation is the Bishop (¹). Nevertheless the Church permits Confirmation by a Priest with chrism consecrated by a Bishop (²), and this is the rule in the Eastern Church.

4. Adults should be confirmed as soon as possible after Baptism, and confirmed fasting (³). The old English rule enjoined Confirmation within three years.

(¹) Innocent ap. Gratian III. Dist. iv. c. 119. Gregorius, *Ibid.* c. 120.

(²) Council of Valentia ap. Gratian III. Dist. iv. c. 123. Gregorius Lib. iii. Epist. 26 ap. Gratian I. Dist. xcv. c. 1.

(³) Concil. Aurelianense ap. Gratian III. Dist. v. c. 6. Concil. Carthag. iv. Can. 86, *Ibid.* c. 12.

CHAPTER LV.

UNCTION AND EXTREME UNCTION.

1. THE Anointing of the Sick by the Presbyters of the Church was long regarded as an ordinance whereby, in answer to to the prayer of faith, sins were remitted and consequently bodily health was restored ([1]).

2. Unction was accordingly resorted to to fortify the receiver against any special attack of the ghostly foe. As such it was specially employed on the approach of death. When exclusively so used, as was the case after the 9th century, it was called Extreme Unction.

3. As a means for giving strength against the last assault of the ghostly foe, Extreme Unction may be considered a Sacramental Act, and a branch of Penance which is exercised upon them that lie in danger of death ([2]).

([1]) May be used by a Bishop. See Innocentius Epist. i. ap. Gratian I. Dist. xcv. c. 3. The Chrism must every year be fetched from the Bishop of the Diocese, according to Concil. Carthag. iv. c. 36. *Ibid.* c. 4. See Concil. Ticinens, Can. 8.

([2]) Thorndike's Works, Vol. v. p. 562, quoted by Owen's *Institutes of Canon Law*, p. 131.

DIVISION II.

OF SPIRITUAL GIFTS.

CHAPTER LVI.

HOLY STATES OF LIFE.

WHEN a spiritual gift or grace is permanently attached to a state of life, not so much for the good of him who exercises it as for the good of others, this is called either an Order or a Holy State of Life.

1. In so far as this result is brought about by means of outward and visible signs, the bestowal of such a spiritual gift may be considered to partake of the nature of a Sacrament. Hence the bestowal of a spiritual gift is usually treated as a Sacramental Act.

2. Spiritual gifts are attached to states of life in two distinct cases. There is (1) the case of the several Orders of the Ministry, and (2) the case of the Holy State of Matrimony. There is however this difference between the two that the several Orders of the Ministry have been endowed each with its spiritual gift for the well-being and continuation of the existence of the Church, whereas the State of Matrimony has been so endowed for the welfare and perpetuation of the family.

CHAPTER LVII.

ORDERS GENERALLY.

1. ORDERS are, properly speaking, classes of men set apart by the Church, and endowed with spiritual gifts for the good of others ([1]). They who are admitted to the privileges of these classes are said to be ordained, and the spiritual gifts which are severally bestowed on them are also called Orders.

2. Jesus Christ himself bestowed on His apostles certain spiritual gifts, and likewise gave to them the power to confer these spiritual gifts on those committed to their pastoral charge and to set them apart to be teachers of His truth. Hence Orders, like Jurisdiction, come from the Apostolic College through their successors in office. This is termed Apostolic Succession.

3. There are two kinds of Orders; (1) those which come from Christ through the Apostles, and have ever been in the Church, and which are called Holy Orders because they have to do with Holy things—the Altar and the vessels of the Altar; such are the Orders of Priests and Deacons ; and (2) those which are not of Apostolic origin, and to which the meddling with holy things ([2]) is forbidden ; these are

---

([1]) Ambrosius and Gregorius ap. Gratian, Caus. i. Qu. i. c. 83 and 84.

([2]) This is forbidden to Sub-deacons by the Council of Laodicea, Can. 21 ap. Gratian I. Dist. xxiii. c. 26, and to Readers by Concil. Bracarense ; Can 10, *Ibid.* c. 31 ; and to all the lower Orders by Concil. Agathense Can. 66, *Ibid.* c. 30.

L

usually called Minor Orders. In the Western Church there are four Minor Orders, those of Acolytes, Exorcists, Readers, and Doorkeepers. In former times Singers were also included among Minor Orders ([1]). In the Eastern Church there is only one, that of Readers ([2]). ·

4. All the Orders of the Clergy are forbidden to wear their hair long ([3]), or to meddle with secular business ([4]). They are, therefore, said to have the tonsure; and throughout all the Orders respect is due from the lower to the higher ones ([5]). Admission to the higher Orders is now only given after probation in the lower ones ([6]). Orders must not be given improperly, and ([7]) must be given without any money payment ([8]). Monks conducting themselves well in a monastery may be admitted to Holy Orders ([9]).

([1]) Conc. Carth. Can. 10 ap. Gratian I. Dist. xxiii. c. 20.

([2]) The duties of the several orders of the Clergy from the Bishop down to the Singing-man are fully given by Isidore in a letter to Ludifred ap. Gratian I. Dist. xxv. c. 1.

([3]) Concil. Agathense, Can. 20, and Gregorius II. ap. Gratian I. Dist. xxiii. c. 22 and 23., Martinus, *Ibid.* c. 32. Decret. Greg. IX. Lib. iii. Tit. i. c. 7.

([4]) Sext. Decret. Lib. iii. Tit. xxiv.

([5]) Romana Synodus, Can. 7. ap. Gratian I. Dist. xciii. c. 5., as it is from all inferiors to superiors, Gratian, Caus. xvii. Qu. iv. c. 37, 38.

([6]) See Zosimus, Epist. i. ap. Gratian I. Dist lix. c. 1 and 2, and Dist. lxxvii. c. 2; Gregorius, Lib. vii. Reg. Epist. 110, *Ibid.* c. 3.; Coelestinus, Epist. ii. c. 3., *Ibid* c. 4.

([7]) Leo, Epist. xc. ap. Gratian, Caus. i. Qu. i. c. 40. Leo, Epist. lxxxv., *Ibid.* c. 43.

([8]) Gregorius ap. Gratian, Caus. i. Qu. i. c. 117. See also *Ibid.* Qu. i. 1 to 29 and 107 to 116., also Gratian, Caus. i. Qu. ii. c. 4, Qu. vii. 1 to 6.

([9]) See the authorities ap. Gratian, Caus. xvi., Caus. i. c. 26, 27-35.

CHAPTER LVIII.

HOLY ORDERS.

1. The classes of men who are set apart for the service of the Altar (¹) and that which pertains thereto, are termed Holy Orders (²), and all the members of these classes are said to be in Holy Orders.

2. The bestowal of this rank (³) in the Church, is effected by means of a Sacramental Act called Ordination. Thereby a spiritual gift is conferred for the service of a spiritual office for the good of others (⁴). It is ordered that Bishops are

---

(¹) Clemens ap. Gratian III. Dist. ii. c. 23. Pseudo-Isidorus ap. Gratian III. Dist. i. c. 41 and 42.

(²) Urbanus II. ap. Gratian I. Dist. lx. c. 4: Sacros autem ordines dicimus diaconatum et presbyteratum. Hos siquidem solos primitiva legitur habuisse ecclesia; subdiaconos vero, quia et ipsi altaribus minis-trant, opportunitate exigente concedimus, si tamen spectatæ sint religionis et scientiæ.

(³) Symmachus, A.D. 500, ap. Gratian, Caus. i. Qu. i. c. 45: Vilissimus computandus est, nisi præcellat scientia et sanctitate, qui est honore præstantior. Women and unbaptized people are absolutely incapable of receiving Orders. Otho Athon, 16, states: Seeing it is dangerous to ordain persons unworthy, void of understanding, illegimate, irregular, and illiterate, we do decree that before the conferring of orders, by the Bishop, strict search and inquiry be made of all these things. Lind. 33: No simoniac, homicide, person excommunicate, usurer, sacri-ligious person, incendiary, or falsifier, nor any other having canonical impediment, shall be admitted into Holy Orders.

(⁴) Innocentius Epist. xviii. c. 3, ap. Gratian, Caus. i. Qu. i. c. 17: Qui perfectionem Spiritus quam acceperant perdiderunt, non ejus dare plenitudinem possunt, quae maxime operatur in ordinationibus.

L 2

not to lay (¹) hands suddenly on any (²), and only to ordain at the regular seasons (³), and after a suitable probation.

3. There are usually said to be two Holy Orders in the Christian Church, and no more; those of Priests and Deacons. Bishops together with Priests form but one Order (⁴), although they have a higher degree in the Priesthood. Subdeacons together with Deacons form only one Order, although they have a lower degree in the Diaconate.

4. Holy Orders once given ought not to be reconferred (⁵). Questions, however, may arise as to whether they have been validly given (⁶), or whether they can be exercised by heretics or schismatics (⁷), or those ordained by them (⁸), as to which divers regulations have been made in the Church.

5. The recipients of Holy Orders are subject to certain disabilities, and are allowed certain immunities (⁹) and

(¹) Two orders may not be conferred on the same day. Decret. Greg. IX. Lib. i. Tit. xi. c. 13, 15.

(²) Concil. Nicæn. Can. 2.

(³) Docret. Greg. IX. Lib. i. Tit. xi. c. 1, 2, 3, 8. Sext. Decret. Lib. i. Tit. ix.

(⁴) Gratian I. Decret. Dist. xcv. See Euseb. *Hist. Eccl.* i. c. 12.

(⁵) Decret. Greg. IX. Lib. i. Tit. xvi.

(⁶) Gratian, Caus. i. Qu. i. c. 108, 109, 113.

(⁷) Augustin. Lib. ii., contra Parmenian. c. 13, ap. Gratian, Caus. i. Qu. i. c. 97. Leo, *Ibid.* c. 112. The Reordination of Novatians. was required by Concil. Nicæn. Can. 8, ap. Gratian, Caus. i. Qu. vii. c. 8. Leo, *Ibid.* c. 19 and 21. See authorities ap. Gratian, Caus. ix. Qu. i., implying that ordinations by excommunicate persons are tolerated, unless they are excommunicated by name.

(⁸) Synodus vii. ap. Gratian, Caus. i. Qu. vii. c. 2 and 8.

(⁹) See Gratian, Caus. xvii. Qu. iv. c. 23, 30.

privileges ('). They are not required to surrender their patrimony at ordination ('), but they may not make a profit out of their ecclesiastical rank ('). In dress ('), conduct ('), and behaviour ('), they are required to act as becomes their order ('), not to bear arms ('), nor to take part in trials involving bloodshed ('), nor without episcopal leave to appeal to secular tribunals ('°).

A Bishop who has resigned may confer Orders on behalf of a Diocesan Prelate ('').

(¹) Gratian, Caus. xvi, Qu. i. c. 66, 67.

(²) See Gratian, Caus. xii. Qu. v.

(³) See authorities ap. Gratian, Caus. xii. Qu. iii. and iv.

(⁴) See authorities ap. Gratian Caus. xxi. Qu. iv. Decret. Greg. IX. Lib. v. Tit. xxxix. c. 45, and xxxiii. c. 27.

(⁵) See Gratian, Caus. xxi, Qu. iii. Decret. Greg. IX. Lib. iii. Tit. i. c. 15.

(⁶) Not harbouring women except relations. Concil. Nicæn. Can. 3, Decret. Greg. IX. Lib. iii. Tit. ii. c. 1 and 2.

(⁷) Decret. Greg. IX. Lib. iii. Tit. i. Sext. Decret. Lib. iii. Tit. i. Clement, Lib. iii. Tit. i. Extrav. Com. Lib. i. Tit. viii. and Lib. iii. Tit. i.

(⁸) Gratian, Caus. xxiii. Qu. viii.

(⁹) Concil. Toletan xi. Can. 6, A.D. 675, ap. Gratian, Caus. xxiii. Qu. viii. c. 30.

(¹⁰) See Gratian, Caus. xxi. Qu. v. Bishops are forbidden to appeal to the Emperor except by the advice of their comprovincials and the Metropolitan, by Concil. Antioch, Can. 11, A.D. 332, ap. Gratian, Caus. xxiii. Qu. viii. c. 27, also Decret. Greg. IX. Lib. i. Tit. xxxvii.

(¹¹) Decret. Greg. IX. Lib. i. Tit. xiii. c. 1. As to marriage, see e cret. Greg. IX. Lib. iv. Tit. vi.

CHAPTER LIX.

THE PRIESTHOOD.

1. The Priesthood is a spiritual gift once bestowed on, and ever afterwards inherent in, a class of men hence called Priests. The spiritual gift is defined to be a partaking or a sharing in the Priesthood of Christ, given to certain ministers of His Body, the Church, by the rite of Ordination, whereby they are set apart to offer His Sacrifice ([1]), to administer His Sacraments, and to teach and guide His flock in the way everlasting.

2. Every Priest upon his ordination is set apart for these duties; yet hath he not the actual exercise of them unless he be commissioned thereto by some one having the necessary jurisdiction. It has therefore been the rule of the Church ([2]) not to set apart anyone for performing ecclesiastical duties unless there be some vacant office requiring the performance of those duties, or as it is usually expressed, not to confer Orders except to fill an office requiring Orders. Such an office is called a title ([3]).

([1]) Augustin. ap. Gratian III. Dist. iii. c. 51 and 52., Ambros. *Ibid.* c. 53.

([2]) Concil. Chalcedon. Can. 6, A.D. 451 ap. Gratian I. Dist. lxx. c. 1 : μηδένα ἀπολελυμένως χειροτονεῖσθοι μήτε πρεσβύτερον, μήτε διάκονον, μήτε ὅλως τινὰ τῶν ἐν τῷ ἐκκλησιαστικῷ τάγματι· Decret. Greg. IX. Lib. i. Tit. xiv. c. 13., Lib. iii. Tit. v. c. 2. A Bishop who ordains without a title is bound to maintain his clerk. See Concil. Lateran iii., *Ibid.* c. 4.

([3]) Decret. Greg. IX. Lib. iii. Tit. v. c. 2-4, 16. Can. 33 of 1603

3. In the Priesthood there are two degrees (¹). There are (1) ordinary priests, or presbyters, called also ἐπίσκοποι in the New Testament, who then, and in after times, appear as a College or Body, all of whom jointly and severally possess the Priesthood in any Church (²). And (2) there are certain Priests chosen to preside over such bodies, and alone possessing the power of bestowing the Priesthood on others (³). These are called Bishops in the ecclesiastical sense of the term (⁴).

4. Admission to the Order of Priesthood is conferred by a rite called Ordination (⁵), which is a Sacramental Act, and

after mentioning seven varieties of titles continues : If any Bishop shall admit any person into the ministry, that hath none of these titles as ·aforesaid, then he shall keep and maintain him with all things necessary till he do prefer him to some ecclesiastical living. See Chap. xxxii.

(¹) Hieronymus ad Cap. i. Epist. ad Titum ap. Gratian I. Dist. xcv. c. 5 ; Olim idem erat presbyter, qui est episcopus. Postquam vero unusquisque eos quos baptizaverat, suos putabat esse non Christi, in toto orbe decretum est, ut unus de presbyteris electus superponeretur cæteris, ad quem omnis ecclesiæ cura pertineret. Concil. Carthag. iv. Can. 34, *Ibid.* c. 9 ; Episcopus in quolibet loco sedens stare presbyterum non patiatur.

(²) See Concil. Laodicens. Can. 56, A.D. 363 ap. Gratian I. Dist. xcv. c. 8. ; Concil. Neocæsarens. Can. 13, A.D. 314, *Ibid.* c. 12. See Chap. v.

(³) But an abbot in priests' Orders can bestow orders, Decret. Greg. IX. Lib. i. Tit. xiv. c. 11.

(⁴) Concil. Hispalen. ii., Can. 6, A.D. 619, ap. Gratian I. Dist. lxviii. c. 4 ; Quamvis chorepiscopis et presbyteris plurima cum episcopis communis sit dispensatio, quædam tamen . . . . sibi prohibita noverint, sicut est presbyterorum et diaconorum aut virginum consecratio, &c.

(⁵) Concil. Carthag. Can. 8 ap. Gratian I. Dist. xxiii. c. 8 ; Presbyter cum ordinatur, episcopo eum benedicente et manum super caput ejus tenente, etiam omnes presbyteri, qui præsentes sunt, manus suas juxta manum episcopi super caput illius teneant. The rite is not to be repeated, except in case of doubt as to its validity. See Gratian I. Dist. lxviii.

should not be conferred on an unwilling subject (¹), nor at improper times (²). Advancement from a lower degree of the Priesthood to the Episcopate is called Consecration, because it is not a change of Order, but promotion in a Holy Office.

5. Ordination as being admission within the ranks of the Priesthood of a particular Church (³) can only be given by the Head or President of each unit of the Church (⁴), *i.e.*, by the Bishop (⁵), and should only be given with the advice and consent of his presbyters (⁶). Consecration being admission to the Co-episcopate of the whole Church, requires ordinarily the act of more than one member of the Episcopal Body, and is not considered to be · regularly conferred unless at least three Bishops take part in it (⁷). Strangers are forbidden to be admitted to Holy Orders unless provided with a testimonial signed by five Bishops (⁸).

(¹) Gratian I. Dist. lxxiv.

(₂) Gratian I. Dist. lxxv and lxxvi. c. 12.

(₃) Strange clergy should not be received without full testimonials, Decret. Greg. IX. Lib. i. Tit. xxii.

(⁴) Therefore not by a stranger. See Concil. Sardicense, Can. 18 and 19, A.D. 344, ap. Gratian I. Dist. lxxi. c. 1.; Con. Nic. Can. 16, A.D. 325 : εἰ δὲ καὶ τολμήσειέν τις ὑφαρπάσαι τὸν τῷ ἑτέρῳ διαφέροντα, καὶ χειροτονῆσαι ἐν τῇ αὐτοῦ ἐκκλησίᾳ, μὴ συγκατατιθεμένου τοῦ ἰδίου ἐπισκόπου οὗ ἀνεχώρησιν ὁ ἐν τῷ κανόνι ἐξεταζόμενος, ἄκυρος ἔστω ἡ χειροτονία. Concil. Chalced., Can. 20, A.D. 451.   Concil. Carthag. i. Can. 5, A.D. 348. See other authorities ap. Gratian I., Dist. lxxii.

(⁵) Concil. Hispalense ii. Can. 6, A.D. 619 ap. Gratian I. Dist. lxvii. c. 2 ; Episcopus sacerdotibus ac ministris solus honorem dare potest, solus auferre non potest.

(⁶) Concil. Carthag. iv. Can. 22 ap. Gratian I. Dist. xxiv. c. 6, Episcopus sine concilio clericorum suorum clericos non ordinet. Urbanus ap. Gratian, Caus. xii. Qu. ii. c. 37.

(⁷) See Chap. xxix.   Decret. Greg. IX. Lib. i. Tit. xi. c. 6.   See Chap. lxiii.·2.

(⁸) Authorities ap. Gratian I. Dist. xcviii.

CHAPTER LX.

QUALIFICATIONS FOR THE PRIESTHOOD.

1. THE high dignity of the Sacerdotal rank, as composed of men called to share in the Priesthood of Christ, has from the first hedged that Order about with special care and watchfulness (¹). Hence it has been universally held that none should be admitted to that Order who laboured under any of the following defects, all of which are canonical disqualifications for the Priesthood :—

(1) Defects of mind, such as madness, epilepsy (²), or want of sufficient knowledge (³).

(2) Defects of body (⁴), such as being a dwarf, or blind, or leprous; defects of birth, such as being born out of wedlock, or the son of a priest (⁵), or the son of a slave (⁶).

(¹) See the authorities Symmachus, Hieronymus, Gregorius, Joannes Chrysostomus, Bonifacius, Augustinus, Ambrosius, ap. Gratian. I. Dist. xl. Gratian, Caus. viii. Qu.; c. 11-19.

(²) Pius ap. Gratian I. Dist. xxxiii. c. 3; Nicolaus, *Ibid.* c. 4; Gelasius, *Ibid.* c. 5.

(³) Zosimus, A.D. 418, ap. Gratian I. Dist. xxxvi. c. 2;. also the authorities in Dist. xxxvii., xxxviii. and lv. c. 3.

(⁴) Martinus Bracarensis ap. Gratian I. Dist. lv. c. 9; Gelasius, *Ibid.* c. 13; Decret. Greg. IX. Lib. i. Tit. xx.

(⁵) See the authorities for and against, ap. Gratian I. Dist. lvi.; also Concil. Toletan. ix. Can. 10, A.D. 655, ap. Gratian, Caus. xv. Qu. viii. c. 3; Decret. Greg. IX. Lib. i. Tit. xvii. A son is strictly forbidden to succeed a father in any office in the Church. See authorities, *Ibid.* Tit. xvii.

(⁶) Leo, Epist. i. ap. Gratian I. Dist. liv. c. 1; Concil. Tribur, A.D. 895,

(3) Defects of age, such as not being full 24 for a
priest ('), or full 30 for a bishop.

(4) Defects of moral character, such as being of ill
repute ; defects of moral position, such as being
a penitent (*), the husband of a second wife
('), or of a widow (*), or of a divorced woman
(*); defects of bloodguiltiness (*), such as having

Ibid. c. 2 ; Gelasius, *Ibid.* c. 12. As to slaves when ordained, see
Concil. Toletan. iii. Can. 6 ap. Gratian, Caus. xii. Qu. ii. c. 63 ; Concil.
Toletan iv. *Ibid.* c. 65 ; Decret. Greg. IX. Lib. i. Tit. xviii.

(¹) Concil. Carthag. iii. Can. 4, A.D. 397, ap. Gratian I. Dist. lxxvii.
c. 5 : Placuit, ut ante viginti quinque annos ætatis nec diaconi ordi-
nentur nec virgines consecrentur ; Concil. Agathense, Can. 16, A.D. 506 ;
Concil. Toletan iv. Can. 20, A.D. 633, *Ibid.* i. Dist. lxxvii. c. 6 and 7 ;
also fix 25 as the age for a deacon, and 30 for a priest. The same in
Bonifacius and Concil. Neocæsarense, Can. 11, A.D. 314 ; *Ibid.* Dist.
lxxviii ; but Zacharias (Epist. 6, A.D. 751) permits, in case of necessity, a
priest to be 25 ; See Gratian I. Dist. lxxviii. c. 5. Sext. Decret. Lib. i.
Tit. x. Clement. Lib. i. Tit. vi. c. 3. The English Canon 34 of 1603
fixes the age for a deacon at 23 years old, and for a priest at 24 years old
complete. This is also Statute Law by 44 Geo. III. c. 43, sec. 1.

(²) Gregorius, Epist. Lib. ii. 25 ap. Gratian I. Dist. xxxiv. c. 10 ;
Concil. Carthag. iv. Can. 68 and 69 ap. Gratian I. Dist. l. c. 55 ; Innocentius, *Ibid.* c. 60 ; Hilarius ap. Gratian I. Dist. lv. c. 3.

(³) Hieronymus ap. Gratian I. Dist. xxvi. c. 1 ; Augustin. *Ibid.* c. 2 ;
Innocentius, *Ibid.* c. 3 ; Gregorius ap. Gratian I. Dist. xxxii. c. 2 ;
Concil. Gerundense, Can. 8 ap. Gratian I. Dist. xxxiv. c. 8 ; Ambrosius,
Epist. lxxxii. *Ibid.* c. 14 ; Siricius, Epist. i. c. 15 ap. Gratian I. Dist. l.
c. 56 ; Gelasius, *Ibid.* c. 59 ; Decret. Greg. IX. Lib. i. Tit. xxi.

(⁴) Hilarius ap. Gratian I. Dist. xxxiv. c. 9 ; Innocentius, Epist. ii.
c. 5, *Ibid.* c. 13 ; Martinus, *Ibid.* c. 18 ; Siricius, Epist. i. c. 11 ap.
Gratian I. Dist. lxxxiv. c. 5.

(⁵) Concil. Neocæsarense, Can. 8 ap. Gratian I. Dist. xxxiv. c. 11 ;
Martinus, *Ibid.* c. 12.

(⁶) Joannes VIII. ap. Gratian I. Dist. l. c. 4 ; Nicolaus, *Ibid.* c. 5 and 6 ;
Martinus Bracarens. *Ibid.* c. 8 ; Concil. Ilerdense, Can. 1, A.D. 546, ap.
Gratian I. Dist. l. c. 36 ; Urbanus II. *Ibid.* c. 37 ; Nicolaus, *Ibid.* c. 39 ;
Concil. Ancyranum, Can. 22, A.D. 314, *Ibid.* c. 42 ; Concil. Eliberi-
tanum, Can. 4, A.D. 310, *Ibid.* c. 43.

slain another even in battle (¹), or having mutilated himself (²).

2. For the same reason the clergy are required to be sober (³), and hospitable (⁴), and quiet (⁵). They are forbidden to busy themselves with secular matters (⁶), or to frequent taverns, markets, or fairs, (⁷), to act as executors (⁸), or to hunt (⁹), although they are permitted to practice a handicraft and to farm a moderate quantity of land (¹⁰) in order to provide themselves with a livelihood (¹¹).

3. As to the Celibacy or Continence of the Priests, the mind of the Church is clearly this: that as S. Paul requires the use of wedlock to be forborne for extraordinary devotions (¹²), so they whose ordinary devotions ought to be

(¹) Innocentius, Epist. xxiv. c. 2 ap. Gratian I. Dist. li. c. 1.

(²) Canones Apostolorum, Can. 22 and 23 ap. Gratian I. Dist. lv. c. 4 ; Concil. Arelatense, *Ibid.* c. 7; Innocentius, *Ibid.* c. 8; Concil. Nic. Can. 1.

(³) See the authorities in Gratian I. Dist. xxxv and Dist. xli and xliv.

(⁴) See authorities ap. Gratian I. Dist. xlii.

(⁵) Non litigiosus. See authorities ap. Gratian I. Dist. xc.

(⁶) Many authorities ap. Gratian I. Dist. lxxxviii. and Caus. xxi. Qu. iii. See Decret. Greg. IX. Lib. i. Tit. xix.

(⁷) Concil. Laodicense, Can. 24 ap. Gratian I. Dist. xliv. c. 2; vi. Synod. Can. 9, A.D. 692, *Ibid.* c. 3 ; Concil. Carthag. iii. Can. 27, A.D. 397, *Ibid.* c. 4.

(⁸) Concil. Carthag. iv. Can. 18 ap. Gratian I. Dist. lxxxviii. c. 5 ; Cyprianus, Lib. i. Ep. 9 ap. Gratian I. Dist. lxxxviii. c. 14.

(⁹) See the very numerous authorities in notes to Chap. lxx.

(¹⁰) The English Statute Law, 1 and 2 Vic. c. 106, fixes the limit at 80 acres, and forbids trading.

(¹¹) Isidorus ap. Gratian I. Dist. xxiii. c. 3 ; Concil. Carthag. iv. Can. 52 and 49 ap. Gratian I. Dist. xci. c. 3 and 4.

(¹²) Concil. Eliberitanum, ap. Gratian III. Dist. iii. c. 21 ; Concil.

extraordinary in comparison with the people, should forbear it always ('). Nor is this mind impaired by the fact that individual branches of the Church considering the disadvantages of a celibate life to outweigh the advantages, have relaxed the rule of celibacy (²), seeing that continence is not in secular clerks essential to Order nor of divine right (³).

4. The Western and the Eastern Church alike agree in forbidding the Marriage of the Clergy after Ordination, at, first, however, without requiring their Celibacy ('). And in so doing they carried out the Canon of the Council of Neocæsarea (A.D. 314), and the views expressed at the Nicene Council (⁵).

Since the time of Pope Siricius, however, (A.D. 385) (⁶)

Carthag. ii. Can. 2 ap. Gratian I. Dist. xxxi. c. 2; also *Ibid.* xxxii. c. 13. See I. Cor. vii.

(') Decret. Greg. IX. Lib. iii. Tit. iii.

(²) .Perhaps this relaxation may be supported by the authorities for the rule attributed to Gregory: Pro diversitate rerum temperantur regulæ sanctorum, ap. Gratian I. Dist. xxix. c. 2. See the decree of the Council of Winchester, A.D. 1076, on this point, ap. Labbæus et Cossart xii. p. 593 : Decretum est ut nullus canonicus uxorem habeat : sacerdotum vero in castellis vel in vicis commorantium placet, ut episcopi, presbyteri, et diaconi, vel qui sacramenta contrectant, pudicitiæ custodes etiam ab uxoribus abstineant. Concil. Carthag. v. Can. 3 A.D. 401; *Ibid.* c. 4. The 32nd Article, which permits Bishops Priests, and Deacons, like other Christian men, to marry at their own discretion, would hardly seem to dispense from the rules as to forbidden persons any more than it dispenses from the rules as to forbidden degrees.

(³) Decret. Greg. IX. Lib. iii. Tit. i. c. 3, and Tit. iii. c. 6.

(⁴) Concil. Toletan. i. Can. 7, A.D. 400, ap. Gratian, Caus. xxxiii. Qu. ii. c. 10, provides for the case of the wives of the clergy falling into grave sins.

(⁵) Concil. Nic. Can. 3 ap. Gratian I. Dist. xxxii. c. 12, and Socrates, *Eccles. History,* i. 11.

(⁶) Siricius, Epist. i. c. 12, ap. Gratian I. Dist. lxxx. c. 31 : Feminas

a stricter rule has been unswervingly upheld (¹) in the West, forbidding not only the Marriage of the Clergy, but imposing continence on such as are already married (²). This view appears to have had the sympathy of the Eastern Church, inasmuch as for all the higher ecclesiastical offices only the regular or unmarried clergy are eligible.

non alias patimur in domibus clericorum, nisi eas tantum quas propter solas necessitudinum causas habitare cum iisdem synodus Nicæna permittit. *Ibid.* ap. Gratian I. Dist. lxxxii. c. 3.

(¹) See the various authorities in Gratian I. Dist. xxviii, xxxi, and xxxii; Decret. Greg. IX. Lib. iii. c. 13.

(²) Calixtus II. in Concil. Remens. A.D. 1119, Can. 5 et 1 Lateran, A.D. 1123, ap. Gratian I. Dist. xxvii. c. 8: Presbyteris, diaconis, subdiaconis et monachis concubinas habere seu matrimonia contrahere penitus interdicimus; contracta quoque matrimonia ab hujusmodi personis disjungi et personas ad pœnitentiam redigi debere, juxta sacrorum canonum definitiones judicamus. Concil. Carthag. v. Can. 3 ap. Gratian I. Dist. xxxii. c. 13; Concil. Carthag. ii. Can. 2, A.D. 390, ap. Gratian I. Dist. lxxxiv. c. 3: Omnibus in vicis habitantium, habentes uxores non cogantur ut dimittant; non habentes interdicentur ut habeant. Et deinceps caveant episcopi ut sacerdotes vel diaconos non præsumant ordinare, nisi prius profiteantur ut uxores non habeant.

CHAPTER LXI.

OF CLERICAL IRREGULARITY.

CERTAIN persons are disqualified from being admitted to
Holy Orders, or if already in Holy Orders are disqualified
from exercising their office on the ground that the exercise
of the ministry by them would tend to cause scandal. Such
persons are said to be *Irregular*, and the disqualifying
circumstance, which may not be a sin at all, is called an
Irregularity.

1. An Irregularity may, therefore, be defined to be a
canonical disability which either (1) prevents the reception
of Orders, or (2) prevents the exercise of an Order already
obtained, or (3) excludes from a Benefice or Ecclesiastical
Office. The dignity of the sacred ministry forbids one who
has been ordained against the rules of the Church, or who
has transgressed the rule of life of Christians in general or
of the clerical state in particular, from exercising his office
until he has put himself right with the Church.

2. An irregularity may arise from causes of two kinds;
either (1) those which are not of the individual's own
making, in which case the irregularity is called a *defect;* or
(2) those in which it is a result of his previous conduct, in
which case it is called a *crime.* To constitute an irregularity,
however, and to be a cause of scandal, a crime must (1) be
a very grave one, (2) be publicly known and not secret, and

(3) be a sin of actual commission and not of intention only.

3. All the canonical disqualifications for the reception of Holy Orders are disqualifications for their exercise also (¹), and in addition there are two other principal causes of irregularity, (1) ill-repute arising from public exposure in certain cases (²), and (2) the having been concerned in a case of blood (³).

Ill-repute is considered to attach (1) to public exposure in the case of one who has judicially confessed or been judicially convicted of murder, perjury, heresy, sodomy, adultery, robbery, or rape (⁴) ; and (2) to all who have exercised certain callings considered degrading in public estimation, notably those of actors, butchers, and publicans.

The having been concerned in a case of blood, or as it is called *Lenity*, includes not only the having actually killed another, but the having been concerned in any way directly in taking life, either as a judge or legislator, as an accuser or a clerk in court(⁵).

4. Irregularities may cease in one of four ways ; (1) by Baptism which takes away all previous faults and offences whatever ; (2) by the lapse of time or study, or absence, as

(¹) See Chapter lx.

(²) Gratian. Caus. vi. Qu. i. c. 17 ; Decret. Greg IX. Lib. v. Tit. xxxiv.

(³) See Chap. lviii. 5.

(⁴) It does not appear that irregularity is incurred by the confession of any offence less than the above, for instance, not of incontinency. For the causes of irregularity cannot be merely local customs, but must be defined by some general law of the Church. Nevertheless, as every man should be severe in his own case though lenient in the case of others, even lesser offences may be admitted as reasons for requiring a dispensation. See Decret. Greg. IX. Lib. v. Tit. xii. xvi. xvii. xxvi. xxxi. c. 4.

(⁵) Decret. Greg. IX. Lib. v. Tit. xii. c. 11 and 18 ; Tit. x v. c. 2. Tit. xxxi. c. 10.

in the case of one too young or too unlearned for Orders or who has owned to a lesser offence; (3) by entering a Religious Order; or (4) by Dispensation. Such a Dispensation cannot, however, be ordinarily granted by a Diocesan Bishop except in a few cases ([1]), or when the cause of the irregularity is not publicly known. In other cases it must come from the representative of the Collective Episcopate ([2]).

([1]) A Bishop in the case of his own subjects can dispense those irregularities which come from defects of birth or reputation, unless they have been exposed before a court of justice, and also those which spring from secret crimes. He may also dispense with a clerk guilty of fornication, although notorious, provided the clerk intermeddle not with divine service. See Bohie. sup. Decret. f. 46, and Decret. Greg. IX. Lib. v. Tit. xxvii. c. 10. Lib. i. Tit. xxi. c. 6.

([2]) In England this would be the Archbishop of Canterbury, through the Court presided over by the Master of the Faculties. See Chap. xxxix.

CHAPTER LXII.

BISHOPS.

1. A BISHOP is not only a Priest, or Participator in the Priesthood of Christ, but he is also one who has been advanced in the Priesthood to a share in its Plenitude. The Plenitude of the Priesthood consists in the power of transmitting the Priesthood to others. This power is latent in the Priesthood itself, but is developed into actuality by the rite of Consecration.

2. Without some lawful sphere requiring the exercise of this power, the plenitude of the priesthood would not only be useless but dangerous for the unity of the Church (¹). Hence no one can be advanced to the Episcopate unless there be some diocese vacant giving him a title thereto (²). Episcopal consecration is not therefore usually conferred unless on one who has acquired episcopal jurisdiction.

3. In respect of jurisdiction a Bishop is one who has been elected by his fellow priests to be their Head or

---

(¹) This was felt by the Council of Antioch, which by Can. 18, A.D. 332, ap. Gratian I. Dist. xcii. c. 5, provided : Si quis episcopus ordinatus ad parochiam cujus est electus minime accesserit, non suo vitio, sed quod eum aut populus vetet, aut propter aliam causam, non tamen ejus vitio perpetratam, hic et honoris sit et ministerii particeps, dummodo rebus ecclesiæ ubi ministrare cognoscitur, in nullo molestus existat. See also Concil. Ancyran. Can. 28, A.D. 314.

(²) See Chap. xxxii.

M

President ('), to preside over the unit of the Church to which they belong, to teach and to govern it as the representative of the Apostolical College upon earth, to perpetuate its existence by ordaining fresh clergy, and to be the ordinary means of its intercommunion with all the other Church units, which together make up Christ's One Holy Catholic Church upon earth.

4. A Bishop is, therefore, the Head Priest of some recognised Church-unit or Diocese, within which he alone has the plenitude of the Priesthood or power of conferring orders, subject nevertheless in this as in all other matters to the advice of his presbyters ('), for and on whose behalf he exercises the gift which they have latent within them.

5. As the Head or Representative of a Church-unit a Bishop is also a member of the Apostolic College, the Coepiscopate, the governing body of the whole Church ('), from which he derives his Diocesan Jurisdiction, with which he acts in legislating for the whole Church, and in and through which he rules and administers every part of the Church.

Within the part over which he presides, he has a direct jurisdiction; his authority over every other part is only mediate through the Collective Episcopate.

(¹) Hieronymus ap. Gratian. I. Dist. xcv. c. 5.

(²) See Chap. xliii.

(³) Urbanus ii. from Augustin, ad Psal. 44 in fine ap. Gratian I. Dist. lxviii. c. 6. Quorum vices in ecclesia habeant episcopi. . . Augustinus ostendit inquiens : Pro patribus tuis nati sunt tibi filii Quid est? Patres missi sunt apostoli; pro apostolis filii nati sunt tibi, constituti sunt episcopi.

CHAPTER LXIII.

QUALIFICATIONS FOR A BISHOP.

APART from jurisdiction, two things are required from those seeking to be advanced to the higher order of the Priesthood : (1) certain personal qualifications ; (2) episcopal consecration.

1. The qualifications for a Bishop, are thus laid down by the 4th Council of Carthage, possibly in S. Augustine's words : If he be by nature prudent, docile, chaste, sober, careful of his affairs (¹), humble, gentle (²), meek (³), learned (⁴), skilled in the law of the Lord (⁵), cautious about the sense of Scripture, versed in the dogmas of the Church (⁶), above all asserting in simple words the documents of the faith. If he satisfies these tests, let him be ordained with consent of the clergy and laity by the Synod of the provincial bishops and chiefly with the authority or presence of the Metropolitan (⁷).

A Bishop was required to be given to hospitality (⁸), to be

(¹) See Gratian I. Dist. lxxxix.
(²) Non litigiosum. See Gratian I. Dist. xlvi.
(³) Non percussorem. See authorities ap. Gratian I. Dist. xlv.
(⁴) Hieronymus ap. Gratian I. Dist. xlix. c. 2.
(⁵) Gregorius, Lib. ix. Epist. 48 ap. Gratian I. Dist. lxxxvi. c. 5.
(⁶) Not therefore a neophyte. See Gratian I. Dist. xlviii.
(⁷) Concil. Carthag. iv. Can. 1 ap. Gratian I. Dist. xxiii. c. 2.
(⁸) Gregorius, Lib. xii. Epist. 6 ap. Gratian I. Dist. lxxxv. c. 1. *Ibid.*

so far conversant with secular business that the Church under his control should not suffer (¹), but not to be avaricious or a usurer (²), to be in other respects worthy (³), and to reside at his cathedral (⁴).

He was required to be free from such bodily defects as would hinder the execution of his office. Hence the disqualifications for the Priesthood were *a fortiori* disqualifications for the Episcopal office, whether of mind or body, of age (⁵) or morals (⁶).

2. The Consecration of a Bishop is (⁷) a Sacramental Act, wherein, by the imposition of hands, power is given to exercise a gift already bestowed in the Priesthood and hitherto latently possessed.

lxxxvi. c. 6. Ambrosius, *Ibid.* c. 14 seq. Bishops shall have honest eleemosynaries, shall keep hospitality and hear the causes of the poor. Langton Lind. 67.

(¹) Gregorius, Epist. A.D. 600, ap. Gratian I. Dist. xxxix. c. i.

(²) See authorities in Gratian I. Dist. xlvii.

(³) See Gratian, Caus. ii. Qu. vii. c. 28, 29, 32, 34.

(⁴) Langton Lind. 130, Bishops shall be at their cathedrals on some of the greater Feasts, and at least in some part of Lent, as they shall find expedient for their souls' health.

(⁵) The English Church, (confirmed by 3 and 4 Ed. VI. c. 10; 5 and 6 Ed. VI. c. 1; 8 Eliz. c. 1; 14 Car. II. c. 4.) requires every man which is to be consecrated Bishop, to be full 30 years of age.

(⁶) See Chap. xli. 5 and xlii. 3 and the qualifications required by Concil. Nicæn. A.D. 325. Can. 4 and 5, and Augustinus ap. Gratian I. Dist. lxxxi. c. 4, 5 and 7 ; Decret. Greg. IX. Lib. i. Tit. xiii, c. 4, and the disqualifications for the Priesthood, Chap. lx. 1. and lxii. 3.

(⁷) Concil. Carthag. iv. Can. 2 ap. Gratian I. Dist. xxiii. c. 7 ; Episcopus cum ordinatur, Deo episcopi ponant et teneant evangeliorum codicem super caput et cervicem ejus, et uno super eum fundendo benedictionem reliqui omnes episcopi qui adsunt, manibus suis caput suum tangant.

Episcopal consecration may be, and has been, validly given by one Bishop : for the Chorepiscopi were consecrated by one Bishop (¹), and S. Athanasius is recorded to have alone consecrated several. Perhaps, however, as jurisdiction is involved, it is necessary in all such cases that the act should be subsequently ratified by the Coepiscopate. At any rate, such consecrations are irregular, the early rule holding good that a Bishop should be consecrated by not less than three Bishops (²) or by the Metropolitan and two neighbouring Bishops (³).

(¹) See Chap. ix. note.

(²) So Gregory writing to Augustin of Canterbury, A.D. 601, Ep. 64. 1. 11. ap. Gratian I. Dist. lxxx. 6. See Chap. xxix. and lix. 5.

(³) Innocentius, Epist. ii. c. 1, A.D. 404, ap. Gratian I. Dist lxiv. c. 5. Concil. Nicæn. Can. 4, *Ibid.* c. 8. Gelasius, *Ibid.* c. 6 ; Martinus, *Ibid.* Dist. lxv. 2. Concil. Antioch. Can. 19, A.D. 332, ap. Gratian I. Dist. lxv. c. 3.

CHAPTER LXIV.

A BISHOP'S DUTIES.

THE special duties of a Bishop are twofold ; (1) towards the Church at large, and (2) towards the particular part thereof entrusted to his care.

1. Towards the Church at large his duties are to attend all Councils and Synods (¹) that so he may take part in legislating for the whole Church, and, together with his comprovincials (²), assist in the regulation of the several parts thereof.

2. Towards the Diocese over which he is set to preside his duties are : (1) that of preaching ; (2) that of ordaining ; (3) that of presiding over the whole administration by visitation.

3. Preaching is specially regarded as the Bishop's function (³) because he is, or should be, the guardian of apostolic tradition, and from his relations with other Bishops the upholder of Catholic Orthodoxy. The right of preaching was gradually extended to Doctors, and subsequently in 529 A.D to all of the Priesthood (⁴). The Bishop is, how-

---

(¹) For not attending a Synod he might be excommunicated. Concil. Triburiense ap. Gratian, Caus. xi. Qu. iii. c. 43.

(²) This he may do by deputy. See Anacletus, A.D. 826, ap. Gratian Caus. v. Qu. iii. c. 3 ; Pseudo-Isidorus, *Ibid.* c. 1.

(³) See the authorities on preaching, ap. Gratian I. Dist. xliii.

(⁴) Clement. Lib. v, Tit. i.

ever, expected to abide at his Cathedral ([1]), and to preach on Sundays and Festivals so as to suit the capacity of the people.

4. It is exclusively his business to ordain Priests and Deacons for his own Church ; but before so doing he must ascertain that a title or office with maintenance attached is provided for them ; otherwise he himself is bound to maintain those whom he ordains, lest the clerical order should full into the disgrace of mendicancy ([2]).

5. As president of the whole administration and visible centre of unity of a Diocese it is specially his province to visit his Diocese at fit seasons ([3]), to admit outsiders and to reconcile penitents to the Church. Thus Baptism, or at least the completion thereof, Confirmation, is reserved to him, as also is the restoration of the lapsed, and the appointment of Church penances, in respect of which he is the sole Ordinary ([4]). He is, moreover, charged with the care of the poor ([5]) and the sick, widows, and orphans ([6]).

([1]) Otho Athon. 55 : Bishops shall abide at their Cathedral Churches and officiate on the chief festivals, and on the Lord's Day, and in Lent, and in Advent. See also Othobon Athon. 118.

([2]) Decret. Greg. IX. Lib. iii. Tit. v. c. 2, 4, 16 ; Concil. Chalcedon. Can. 6.

([3]) Otho Athon. 56 : Bishops shall visit their dioceses at fit seasons, correcting and reforming the Churches, and consecrating and sowing the word of life in the Lord's soil.

([4]) A bishop is specially ordered by Gregóry VII., A.D. 1078, to punish the incontinency of the clergy ; and on no account to wink at sin. See authorities ap. Gratian I. Dist. lxxxiii.

([5]) Langton Lind. 67.

([6]) Concil. Carthag. iv. Can. 108 ap. Gratian I. Dist. lxxxi. c. 84. Gregorius, Lib. xi. Epist. 29 ap. Gratian I. Dist. lxxxiv. 1, and the authorities ap. Gratian I. Dist. lxxxvii.

6. In all his duties he is assisted by his presbyters, sharers with himself in the one Priesthood of Christ. For the government of the Church is not a despotism. And as without the Bishop Priests should do nothing ([1]), so without the advice of his Clergy the Bishop's sentence is invalid ([2]).

([1]) Ignatius Ep. ad Eph. c. 3, 4, 5.

([2]) Concil. Carthag. iv. Can. 23 ap. Gratian, Caus. xv. Qu. vii. c. 6; Episcopus nullius causam audiat absque presentia suorum clericorum; alioquin irrita erit sententia episcopi, nisi clericorum sententia confirmetur. Canones Apostolorum, Can. 33.

CHAPTER LXV.

THE DIACONATE.

1. THE Diaconate is a Holy Order below that of the Priesthood. It is considered to have a share in the spiritual gift conferred by ordination, but what the extent of that share is, is not agreed upon by all. From the account given in the Acts of the Apostles it appears to have been an office carved out of the apostolate, and to have arisen from the desire of the Apostles to provide for the care of the temporalities of the Church in order that they might give all their energies to the ministration of the word and sacraments. A deacon is, therefore, one who has been set apart for the service of the Church, but who has not been ordained to the Priesthood.

2. The duties of a Deacon are the care of the secular concerns of the Church [1] and the charge and provision for the sick. In the absence of a Priest he may baptize, but he may not preach except with the Bishop's special license, and never offer the oblation [2],—a duty which pertains to the Priesthood only. A Deacon is ordained by the im-

[1] Hieronymus ap. Gratian I. Dist. xciii. c. 23.

[2] Concil. Laodicense, Can. 25, A.D. 363, ap. Gratian I. Dist. xciii. c. 16.

position of the hands of the Bishop only who blesses him (¹).

3. Brought in early times into close connection with the Bishop from the nature of their duties (²) and limited to the mystical number of seven (³) whilst the number of the other Clergy increased indefinitely, Deacons obtained great power in large cities, and their pretensions had to be restrained by several canons (⁴). At their head was the Archdeacon, who, as being the chief of those concerned with the temporal affairs of the Diocese, acquired a position much above that of his superiors in Order.

4. Their secular duties gradually gave way to spiritual ones, in which they appeared as ceremonial assistants of the Priest. The restriction as to numbers was evaded first by the institution of Deacons of a lower rank called Subdeacons (⁵), differing from them in little except in being

(¹) Concil. Carthag. Can. 4 ap. Gratian I. Dist. xxiii. c. 11 : Diaconus cum ordinatur, solus episcopus, qui eum benedicit, manum super caput illius ponat, quia non ad sacerdotium sed ad ministerium consecratur.

(²) Clemens, Ep. i. ap. Gratian I. Dist. xciii. c. 6 : Diaconi ecclesiae tanquam oculi sint episcopi, oberrantes et circum lustrantes cum verecundia actus totius ecclesiæ, et perscrutantes diligentius, si quem videant vicinum præcipitis et proximum esse peccato, ut referant hæc ad episcopum.

(³) Concil. Neocæsarense, Can. 14, A.D. 314, ap. Gratian I. Dist. xciii. c. 12 : Diaconi septem esse debent secundum regulam quamvis magna sit civitas.

(⁴) Concil. Nic. Can. 14, A.D. 325 ; Concil. Laodicense, Can. 20, A.D. 363, and Gelasius Epist. ap. Gratian I. Dist. xciii. c. 14, 15, 13 ; Concil. Toletan. iv. Can. 39, A.D. 633, *Ibid.* c. 20.   Hieronymus, Epist. lxxxv. *Ibid.* c. 24.   Cyprianus, Lib. iii. Epist. 9, *Ibid.* c. 25 ; Quinisexta Synodus, A.D. 692, *Ibid.* c. 26.

(⁵) Concil. Carthag. iv. Can. 5, ap. Gratian I. Dist. xxiii. c. 15 : Sub-

ceremonially their inferiors, and then was gradually relaxed and given up altogether.

There is at present no rule limiting their number ; and their position is simply that of Probationers for the Priesthood.

diaconus eum ordinatur, quia manus impositionem non accipit, patenam de manu episcopi accipiat vacuam et calicem vacuum ; de manu vero archidiaconi accipiat urceolum cum aqua, manile et manutergium. A subdeacon may act as the Pope's deputy, See Gregorius. Lib. i. Epist. i. ap. Gratian I. Dist. xciv. c. 1.

CHAPTER LXVI.

MINOR ORDERS.

MINOR Orders are classes of men set apart for some
service or office in the Church, but not permitted to meddle
with Holy things such as the Altar (¹) and what pertains
thereto. ' They are, therefore, not called Holy Orders.
Minor Orders may be conferred at other than the Ember
Seasons (²)

The Eastern Church knows only of one Minor Order,
that of Readers. In the Western Church there are usually
considered to be four; (1) Acolytes or Attendants, (2)
Exorcists, (3) Readers, (4) Doorkeepers.

The order of Acolytes (³) or Attendants still survives in the
Parish Clerks of Parochial Churches, whose business it is to
attend on the Priest in public worship and assist him by
their suffrages in celebrating the Divine Office.

The Exorcist's (⁴) office was to drive out evil spirits from

(¹) Concil. Remense, Can. 2 ap. Gratian III. Dist ii. c. 29.
(²) Decret. Greg. IX. Lib. i. Tit. xi. c. 3.
(³) Conc. Carth. iv. Can. 6 ap. Gratian I. Dist. xxiii. c. 16 : Acolythus
cum ordinatur, ab episcopo quidem doceatur qualiter in officio suo agere
debeat : sed ab archidiacono accipiat ceroferarium cum cereo, ut sciat se
ad accendenda ecclesiæ luminaria mancipari ; accipiat et urceolum vacuum
ad suggerendum vinum in eucharistiam sanguinis Christi.

(⁴) Concil. Carth. iv. Can. 7 ap. Gratian I. Dist. xxiii. c. 17
Exorcista cum ordinatur, accipiat de manu episcopi libellum, in quo
scripti sunt exorcismi, dicente sibi episcopo : Accipe et commenda
memoriæ, et habeto potestatem imponendi manus super energumenum
sive baptizatum, sive catechumenum.

those possessed with them. The office has disappeared, although the need for it appears not to have altogether vanished.

The Reader's (¹) duty was to read the prophets in the public meetings of the Church. That duty is now undertaken by devout laymen.

The Doorkeeper's (²) functions are now usually performed by the Churchwardens, or those deputed by them as Beadles in the larger Churches. Below these come the Singing-men, anciently called Psalmists. These are not now considered to belong to the Minor Orders (³) because they do not require to be appointed by a Bishop (⁴).

Other officials besides the above are the Sacristan and the Custodian (⁵). To those in Minor Orders marriage is permitted (⁶).

(¹) Concil. Carth. iv. Can. 8, ap. Gratian, *Ibid :* Lector cum ordinatur, faciat de illo episcopus verbum ad plebem, indicans ejus fidem ac vitam atque ingenium ; post hæc spectante plebe tradat ei codicem de quo lecturus est, dicens ad eum : Accipe et esto relator verbi Dei, habiturus, si fideliter et utiliter impleveris officium, partem cum eis qui verbum Dei ministraverint.

(²) Concil. Carth. iv. Can. 9, *Ibid* : Ostiarius cum ordinatur, pestquam ab archidiacono instructus fuerit, qualitur in domo Dei debeat conversari, ad suggestionem archidiaconi tradat ei episcopus claves ecclesiæ de altario, dicens : Sic age, quasi redditurus Deo rationem pro his rebus quæ his clavibus recluduntur.

(³) Concil. Carth, iv. 10, ap. Gratian I. Dist. xxiii. c. 20 ; Psalmista, id est cantor, potest absque licentia episcopi sola jussione presbyteri officium suscipere cantandi, dicente sibi presbytero : Vide ut quod ore cantas, corde credas, et quod corde credas, operibus comprobes. Gregorius, Lib. iv. Epist. 44, ap. Gratian I. Dist. xcii. c. 2, forbids deacons from usurping their functions.

(⁴) Concil. Martini ap. Gratian I. Dist. xcii. c. 3.

(⁵) Decret. Greg. IX. Lib. i. Tit. xxvi. xxvii. Extrav. Com. Lib. i. Tit. v

(⁶) Decret. Greg. IX. Lib. iii. Tit. iii.

CHAPTER LXVII.

MATRIMONY.

THERE is a distinct condition of life other than that of Holy Orders, to which a spiritual grace is attached in the Church. That is the Holy Estate of Matrimony [1].

1. Matrimony is not merely a civil contract, but is the foundation of a new family for the perpetuation of the human race. Hence when contracted between Christians it becomes invested with a sacramental importance. The bride and bridegroom are the ministers of a Sacramental Act. Their outward union is the visible sign whereby an inward and spiritual union between them is cemented such as is the union betwixt Christ and His Church.

Regular Matrimony is usually considered to be entered upon by two separate acts ; (1) the Betrothal, and (2) the Espousal.

2. The Betrothal [2], or promise of marriage, is a civil contract entered into between two persons capable of contracting. It is merely an engagement to proceed to Marriage, and may be made in a formal or informal manner. Its chief importance is that it removes civil impediments to

[1] See Decret. Greg. IX. Lib. iv. Tit. i.

[2] A vow of chastity is the opposite of a betrothal and is a valid bar to matrimony. See Gratian, Caus. xxvii. Qu. i. c. 1-3, Concil. Toletan. iv. Can. 8, *Ibid.* c. 7, Concil. Aurelian. Can. 3, *Ibid.* c. 16, Augustinus, *Ibid.* Qu. ii. c. 35, Decret. Greg. IX. Lib. iv. Tit. ii. iii. and v.

a valid marriage by securing those consents without which by civil law such a contract cannot be made (¹).

3. The Espousal, however, constitutes the real Sacramental Act. The essentials of an Espousal, which are also the outward signs of the Sacramental Act, are two ; (1) Mutual Consent (²), and (2) Sexual Union (³). When two persons mutually consent to live together after God's ordinance, whether this be done regularly before the Church or irregularly before God only, Marriage is said to be initiated. When that mutual consent is followed by sexual union, it is said to be consummated (⁴), and until sexual union it is no indissoluble marriage. The religious ceremony is not an essential (⁵) ; and even concubinage (⁶),

(¹) See Gratian, Caus. xxvii. Qu. ii. c. 35-46. This is most important in countries like France and Italy, in which no marriage is allowed by the law of the land without the consent of the parent or the family.

(²) Isidorus ap. Gratian, Caus. xxvii. Qu. ii: Consensus facit matrimonium. Ambrosius, *Ibid.* c. 5 : Non enim defloratio virginitatis facit conjugium sed pactio conjugalis. Consent cannot be given until seven years of age ; Nicolaus ap. Gratian, Caus. xxx. Qu. ii. c. 1; and must be given freely. See Gratian, Caus. xxxi. Qu. ii. c. 1 and 2 ; Decret. Greg. IX. Lib. iv. Tit. i. c. 25.

(³) Augustinus ap. Gratian, Caus. xxvii. Qu. ii. c. 16 : Non est dubium illam mulierem non pertinere ad matrimonium cum qua commixtio sexus non docetur fuisse. Leo, *Ibid.* c. 17. See Decret. Greg. IX. Lib. iv. Tit. xv.

(⁴) Hieronymus ap. Gratian, Caus. xxvii. Qu. ii. c. 37: quae sponsali conventione initiantur, et commixtione corporum perficiuntur.

(⁵) Concil. Carth. iv. Can. 13, ap. Gratian I. Dist. xxiii. c. 33, and Gratian, Caus. xxx. Qu. v. c. 5 : Sponsus et sponsa cum benedicendi sunt a sacerdote, a parentibus suis vel a paranymphis offerantur, qui cum benedictionem acceperint, eadem nocte pro reverentia ipsius benedictionis in virginitate permaneant.

(⁶) The Church allows marriage with a slave, and other unequal matches. See Gratian, Caus. xxix. Qu. ii.

so that it be sole and perpetual, is allowed by the Church as valid though irregular (¹), as being Matrimony according to the law of nature (²).

4. The spiritual gift is the inward and spiritual union between man and wife, whereby each is enabled to surrender his or her will to the other (³). This inward and spiritual union involves (⁴) : (1) that man and wife are no longer two but one person in the eyes of the Church, and as such claim no private property one against the other ; (2) that they live together for the mutual help and comfort of one another ; and (3) that their children are lawful, and no longer proof of lust on the one side and weakness on the other (⁵).

5. Hence polygamy (⁶) is not permitted in the Church, nor the rupture of the marriage tie (⁷) of those truly married (⁸)

(¹) See Gratian, Caus. xxx. Qu. v.   A divorced woman may not marry the co-respondent, Gratian, Caus. xxxi. Qu. i.

(²) Concil. Toletan. i. Can. 17, ap. Gratian I. Dist. xxxiv. c. 4 ; Isidorus *Ibid.* c. 5.   Conf. Augustinus ap. Gratian, Caus. xxvii. c. 51. Augustinus ap. Gratian, Caus. xxxii. Qu. ii. c. 6 ; but a man who has kept a mistress is exhorted to put her away and marry a wife by Leo ap. Gratian, Caus. xxxii. Qu. ii. c. 11.

(³) Urbanus ap. Gratian Caus. xxxi. Qu. ii. c. 4 : Quorum enim unum corpus est, unus debet esse et animus.

(⁴) Proles, fides, sacramentum.   See Augustinus ap. Gratian, Caus. xxvii. Qu. ii. c. 10.

(⁵) Augustinus ap. Gratian, Caus. xxxii. Qu. i. c. 11 : Alia sunt ad nuptias proprie pertinentia, quibus ab adulteriis nuptiae discernuntur, sicuti est tori conjugalis fides, et cura ordinate filios procreandi, et (quae maxima est differentia) bonus usus mali, hoc est bonus usus concupiscentiæ carnis, quo bono male utuntur adulteri.

(⁶) Concil. Meldens. Can 1, ap. Gratian, Caus. xxviii. Qu. ii. and Qu. iii.

(⁷) Authorities ap. Gratian, Caus. xxxii. Qu. vii. c. 3-10, Gregorius, *Ibid.* Qu. vii. c. 22.

(⁸) The marriage tie is not indissoluble unless there has been true marriage.   See Gratian, Caus. xxxiii. Qu. i. and Qu. vii. 2.

either by Divorce (¹) or by length of absence (²). In case
of adultery (³) the innocent person (⁴) is allowed, and even
required to put away the other until the expiration of the
time of penance. So difficult a law as that whereby a man
is tied to one woman for life could hardly have been
guarded so jealously by the Church were it not of Christ's
appointment. And as divorce is forbidden to Christians
in cases where it is allowed by the law of Moses,
so the Church's prohibition of marriage within certain
degrees of relationship (⁵) has other reasons to support it
besides the ceremonial law of the Jews (⁶).

To avoid fornication second marriages are allowed (⁷) but
discouraged by the Church, and involve certain canonical
disabilities. Vows of continence are not allowed except
with the willing consent of both parties (⁸).

(¹) Gregorius ap. Gratian, Caus. xxvii. Qu. ii. c. 19, also *Ibid.* c. 20-26,
Caus. xxxii. Qu. vii. c. 1, 2, and 25, 27.

(²) See Gratian, Caus. xxxiv. Qu. i.

(³) A man is required to put away an adulterous wife, and to receive
her back after penance at the end of three years; see Gratian, Caus.
xxxii. Qu. i., and Caus. xxxiii. Qu. ii. c. 2, 11-13, 16, but only after proof
of her adultery, Gratian, Caus. xxxv. Qu. vi. c. 10.

(⁴) Augustinus ap. Gratian, Caus. xxxii. Qu. vi. c. 1.

(⁵) Marriage between god-parents and god-children is strictly forbidden.
See authorities ap. Gratian, Caus. xxx. Qu. iii. As to the counting of
degrees of relationship see Gratian, Caus. xxxv. Qu. v., and as to those
marrying within them ignorantly, Gratian, Caus. xxxv. Qu. viii.

(⁶) See Augustin ap. Gratian, Caus. xxxv. Qu. i. c. 1, and Qu. ii. and iii
The general law of the Church forbade marriage up to the 7th degree of
relationship; in England the prohibition extended to the 4th and 5th
only. See Gregorius ap. Gratian, Caus. xxxv. Qu. ii. and iii. c. 20.

(⁷) See authorities ap. Gratian xxxi. Qu. i. c. 9 seq.

(⁸) See authorities ap. Gratian, Caus. xxxiii. Qu. v.

DIVISION III.

CHAPTER LXVIII.

JUDICIAL POWER OF THE CHURCH.

1. THE Christian Church, having the power of defining the doctrines of the faith and the power of making rules for advancing the holiness of its members, has also the power of judging all alleged offences against faith or morals committed by any of its members, and of punishing offenders by partially or wholly excluding them from its communion. This power has been committed to it by Christ (Matt. xviii. 15-18) for the purpose of keeping His Body in the unity of the faith, pure and spotless (¹).

2. The use of this power is termed Church Discipline, and its administration rests with those to whom the government of the Church has been committed by Christ. It is, therefore, exercised exclusively by authority of those possessing jurisdiction therein. The general rules of Church discipline emanate from the collective Episcopate,

---

(¹) Augustinus ap. Gratian, Caus. xxiii. Qu. vi. c. 1.

but their application in each diocese is under the charge of the Diocesan Prelate, or his special officers appointed for that purpose.

8. The Clergy are forbidden to bring suits against brother clergy before secular tribunals (¹). The crime of conspiracy amongst them is specially reprobated (²). In all cases obedience to the Bishop is enjoined (³), save when he invades a right (⁴) and respect for ecclesiastical censures (⁵) even when unjust.

(¹) See the authorities ap. Gratian, Caus. xi. Qu. i.

(²) Concil. Chalcedon, Can. 18, A.D. 451: εἴ τινες τοίνυν ἢ κληρικοὶ ἢ μονάζοντες εὑρεθεῖεν, ἢ συνομνύμενοι ἢ φρατριάζοντες, ἢ κατασκευὰς τυρεύοντες ἐπισκόποις ἢ συγκληρικοῖς ἐκπιπτέτωσαν πάντη τοῦ οἰκείου βάθμου. Also Concil. Toletan. and Concil. Aurelian. iii. ap. Gratian, Caus. xi. Qu. i. c. 24 and 25.

(³) See authorities ap. Gratian Caus. xi. Qu. iii. c. 11, 13, 14. Urbanus *Ibid.* c. 27.

(⁴) Decret. Greg. IX. Lib. i. Tit. xxxiii. c. 8, and Lib. v. Tit xxxi. c. 5.

(⁵) Joannes Chrysostom. Homil. iv. ad. ii. Epist ad Heb. ap. Gratian, Caus. xi. Qu. iii. c. 30 and 81.

CHAPTER LXIX.

SUBJECT-MATTER OF THE CHURCH'S JUDICIAL POWER.

THE Church has power over all matters which affect its members, and since these are either public or private matters, Church discipline is partly of a public, partly of a private nature.

1. A Christian's duty towards God in the Church and in the world is a private matter, and so the discipline concerning it is privately administered by a director or Licensed Confessor with the Bishop's sanction. He imposes censures privately, and privately reconciles. Private reconciliation is, however, allowed even in cases of public sins if the penitent be at the point of death (¹).

Private discipline may be administered by a Priest with the Bishop's cognisance (²).

2. When offences are of such a nature as to cause public scandal, the case is one for the exercise of the public discipline of the Church (³). The offence being public, the

(¹) Concil. Carthag. ii. Can. 4, ap. Gratian, Caus. xxvi. Qu. vi. c. 5. Martinus, *Ibid.* c. 6. Concil. Nicaen. Can. 13, A.D. 325; ὁ παλαιὸς καὶ κανονικὸς νόμος φυλαχθήσεται, ὥστε εἴτις ἐξοδεύοι, τοῦ τελευταίου καὶ ἀναγκαιοτάτου ἐφοδίου μὴ ἀποστερεῖσθαι. See also authorities ap. Gratian, Caus. xxvi. Qu. vi. c. 10-14.

(²) See Gratian, Caus. xxvi. Qu. vi. c. 4 and 14.

(³) But not without strict proof. See Evaristus ap. Gratian, Caus. xxx. Qu. v. c. 10.; nullum ante veram justamque probationem judicare aut

censure is public also and likewise the restoration after censure.

Public Discipline cannot be administered by a Priest ([1]) but only by the Bishop or Spiritual Judge.

3. The rule of charity requiring that Christians should be slow to believe the report of other men's sins, the public administration of discipline is hedged about by a strict code of rules ([2]) called rules of Procedure.

Hence the judicial power of the Church and its administration is seen to involve three points.—

(1) The private administration of censures—called Penance.

(2) The public administration of censures—called Church Discipline.

(3) The method of publicly administering Discipline —called Procedure.

damnare debemus, teste Apostolo qui dicit: Tu quis es qui judicas alienum servum? Domino suo stat aut cadit. Mala itaque audita nullum moveant, nec passim dicta absque certa probatione quisquam unquam credat ; sed ante audita diligenter inquirat, ne præcipitando quicquam aliquis agat.

([1]) Concil. Carthag. ii. Can. 3, A.D. 390, ap. Gratian, Caus. xxvi. Qu. vi. c. 1 : Reconciliare quenquam in publica missa presbytero non licere. Concil. Agathens. Can. 43 and 44, A.D. 506, *Ibid.* c. 3.

([2]) No one can be condemned unless after conviction, or on his own confession. See authorities for this, ap. Gratian, Caus. ii. Qu. i. c. 1 to 5, 11.

CHAPTER LXX.

ECCLESIASTICAL OFFENCES.—SINS VENIAL AND MORTAL.

1. EVERY fault whether of omission or commission is a sin against God; but it is not every fault that can or ought to be publicly noticed by the Church. A broad distinction is drawn between Venial and Mortal sins.

Venial sins (¹) are such as are light in themselves and spring from natural inadvertence or passing weakness (²), to which the will does not consent, and which are forgiven in the daily prayer of Christians. These are at most only noticeable in private Penance. Mortal sins are such as sever the soul from communion with God, and are hence called deadly.

2. In the early days of Christianity all discipline was exercised publicly, and its exercise was limited to the cases of the three deadly sins, viz., Idolatry, Murder, and Adultery. The sins of which these three are representative constitute the ecclesiastical offences of which the Church now takes cognisance. When committed privately, however, the Church deals with them privately in the administration of Penance, the rules for which are so varied that a special branch of Canon Law called Casuistry or Moral Theology is devoted to them.

(¹) See Gregor. Dial. Lib. iv. c. 39, on Venial Sins ap. Gratian I. Dist. xxv. c. 4.

(²) Immoderate license of the married is venial according to Augustin. ap. Gratian, Caus. xxxii. Qu. ii. c. 3.

3. The subject-matter of the Public Discipline of the Church consists, therefore, of the following classes of sins, when publicly committed :—

    (1) Sins which are offences against God and true religion, of which Idolatry is the type—such as Apostacy and Heresy ([1]), Simony ([2]), and Perjury ([3]).

    (2) Sins which are offences against fellowmen and natural justice, of which Murder is a type—such as Homicide ([4]), Stealing ([5]), False-witness ([6]).

([1]) Gratian, Caus. xxiv. Qu. i. and. ii. under which soothsaying is included, Gratian, Caus. xxvi. Qu. i. iii. and iv. and v., and Concil. Aurelianense i. Can. 32, *Ibid.* c. 9, and incantations and charms, Gratian, Caus. xxvi. Qu. vii. c. 13-18.

([2]) See the various authorities on simony, ap. Gratian, Caus. i. Qu. i. c. 1 to 29, 107 to 116, and 118 to 130, and Qu. ii. Qu. iii. iv. v. vi. Decret. Greg. IX. Lib. v. Tit. iii.

([3]) See Gratian, Cans. xxii. Qu. i and ii. particularly as to when false-speaking is allowed, and Qu. iv. as to when rash vows should not be kept, and Qu. v.

([4]) Gregorius. ap. Gratian, Cans. xxiii. Qu. v. c. 7, and August. Qu. viii. c. 33, including suicide, August. ap. Gratian, Caus. xxiii. Qu. v. c. 10 and 12, and procuring abortion after quickening, Augustinus, ap. Gratian, Caus. xxxii. Qu. ii. c. 8, and killing an adulterous wife, Pius ap. Gratian, Caus. xxxiii. Qu. ii. c. 7, aiding and abetting in so doing, see Gratian, Caus. xxxiii. Qu. iii. c. 23-28. Nevertheless military service is permitted to laymen, Gratian, Caus. xxiii. Qu. i., and Augustinus, *Ibid.* Qu. v. c. 9, and Ambrosius, *Ibid* c. 25 : *Ibid.* Caus. xxiii. Qu. viii. c. 9. Decret. Greg. IX. Lib. v. Tit. xii. and xxv. So too is capital punishment when administered by an official ;—See Innocentius and Gregorius ap. Gratian, Caus. xxiii. Qu. iv. c. 45-47, Qu. v. also Hieronymus ap. Gratian, Caus. xxiii. Qu. v. c. 31 ; Augustinus, *Ibid.* c. 41 ; or when directed against heretics, Urban. ap. Gratian, Caus. xxiii. Qu. iii. c. 47.

([5]) See authorities ap. Gratian, Caus. xiv. Qu. v. c. 14 and 15 : Qu. vi. c. 3 and 4 Decret. Greg. IX. Lib. v. Tit. 18. On stealing Church property, see Gratian, Caus. xvii. Qu. iv.

([6]) Concil. Agathens. Can. 37, A.D. 506, ap. Gratian, Caus. xxiv. Qu. ii. c. 20, Decret. Greg. IX. Lib v. Tit. xx.

(3) Sins which are offences against the Body of Christ, such as Adultery ('), Rape ('), and other acts of bodily impurity in a Christian (').

To these must be added—

(4) Offences purely Ecclesiastical, *i.e.* things innocent in themselves but forbidden to ecclesiastics because of their holy calling, such as Clerical Marriage ('), Hunting ('), and Trading (').

(¹) Augustinus ap. Gratian, Caus. xxxii. Qu. iv. c. 11: Nomine moechiæ omnis illicitus concubitus atque illorum membrorum non legitimus usus prohibitus debet intelligi. Hieronymus, *Ibid.* c. 14. See authorities ap. Gratian, Caus. xxxii. Qu. v. c. 13-23, and Qu. vii. c. 15. Decret. Greg. IX. Lib. v. Tit. xvi.

(²) Gratian, Caus. xxxvi. Qu. i. and ii.

(³) Ambrosius ap. Gratian, Caus. xxxii. Qu. vii. c. 12 : Minus est secundum naturam coire quam adversus naturam delinquere. Violence done to the body to which the mind does not consent cannot be considered immodesty. See authorities ap. Gratian, Caus. xxxii. Qu. v.

(⁴) On Clerical Continence, see Chapter lx. and the rules as to not having women under the same roof with the Clergy laid down by various authorities ap. Gratian I. Dist. lxxxi. c. 15-33.

(⁵) Concil. Aurelianense iv. ap. Gratian I. Dist. xxxiv. c. 2. See the quotations from Augustinus, Hieronymus, and Ambrosius, ap. Gratian I. Dist. lxxxvi. c. 8 to 13. Decret. Greg. IX. Lib. v. Tit. xxiv.

(⁶) Concil. Chalcedon, Can. 3, A.D. 451, ὥρισεν τοίνυν ἡ ἁγία καὶ μεγάλη σύνοδος, μηδένα τοῦ λοιποῦ, μὴ ἐπίσκοπον, μὴ κληρικὸν, μὴ μονάζοντα, ἢ μισθοῦσθαι κτήματα, ἢ πράγματα, ἢ ἐπεισάγειν ἑαυτὸν κοσμικαῖς διοικήσασι. Gregorius. Lib. vii. Indic. ii. Epist. i. ap. Gratian I. Dist. lxxxvi. c. 24. Can. Apostolorum 7, ap. Gratian I. Dist. lxxxviii. c. 3 : Episcopus aut presbyter aut diaconus nequaquam saeculares curas assumat : sin aliter, dejiciatur. Gregorius. Lib. viii. Ep. 11, *Ibid.* c. 4. This included any form of usury. See Gratian, Caus. xiv. Qu. iii. and Qu. iv. and v., and even taking money for defending a case. See Gratian, Caus. xv. Qu. ii., Decret. Greg. IX. Lib. iii. Tit. l.

CHAPTER LXXI.

PRIVATE DISCIPLINE.—PENANCE.

1. PENANCE is the name applied to the private administration of Church Discipline by a Licensed Confessor dealing with a Penitent, acting for and on behalf of the Bishop. Strictly speaking a penance is a canonical punishment or period of abstention from the Eucharist coupled with prayer and fasting imposed on one who should fall into sin after the washing of regeneration.

2. The discipline of Penance has been administered in more ways than one in different ages of the Church. In the earliest times it was always public. Such as had been guilty of Idolatry, Murder, Adultery, or any crime to which the civil law attached the punishment of death, were a known class. As penitents, they were put to open shame and had to go through years of Penance ([1]), before they were re-admitted to the communion of the Church.

3. When persecutions ceased whilst open Penance was still reserved for open sinners, it was found better for the avoiding of scandals that those guilty of secret sins should confess them privately to a Priest, who prescribed the time

---

([1]) See Concil. Nicæn. Can. 11 and 12, A.D. 325, also Leo ap. Gratian, Caus. xxvi. Qu. vii. c. 2. As to the time, see Gratian, Caus. xxxiii. Qu. iii. Dist. vii. During penance conjugal abstinence was required, Gratian, Caus. xxxiii. Qu. iv.

of abstention from Communion ([1]), and at its close restored them by absolution. Owing to the difficulties of the subject a special officer was appointed by the Bishop for this purpose, called a Penitentiary Presbyter ([2]), whose duties with certain reservations were in after times entrusted to all licensed Confessors.

4. In Mediæval times Penance ([3]) became the Ministry of Consolation rather than of judgment. Hence commutations of Penance ([4]) were admitted, and instead of being for years excluded from Communion, an offender was restored after a short period provided he substituted in their place certain charitable works ([5]), such as almsgiving.

These Commutations of penance were called Indulgences, and in them the prescribed works of charity ([6]) were considered substitutes for the old canonical penances ([7]).

([1]) Nicolaus ap. Gratian, Caus. xxvi. Qu. vii. c. 3, Communion is not to be denied to those who suffer the extreme penalty of the law. See Concil. Aurelian. ap. Gratian, Caus. xiii. Qu. ii. c. 32.

([2]) Evaristus ap. Gratian, Caus. xxvi. Qu vi. c. 4 : Presbyteri de occultis peccatis jussione episcopi pœnitentes reconcilient et infirmantes absolvant et communicent. Concil. Carthag, iii. Can. 31, A.D. 397, ap. Gratian, Caus. xxvi. Qu. vii. c 5 Pœnitentibus secundum differentiam peccatorum episcopi arbitrio pœnitentiæ tempora decernantur.

([3]) There can, however, be no Penance without restitution. See Augustinus and Gregorius ap. Gratian, Caus. xiv. Qu. vi. c. 1 and 2. On degrees and kinds of Penance, see Gratian, Caus. xxvi. Qu. vii. c. 7-10 ; and Gratian, Caus. xxxiii. Dist. iii.

([4]) Concil. Eliberitan, Can. 72, ap. Gratian, Caus. xxxi. Qu. i. c. 8 : Tempus pœnitentiæ constitutum est, sed conversatio et fides eorum tempus abreviat. Decret. Greg. IX. Lib. v. Tit. xxxviii.

([5]) See, Ambrosius, Augustinus, and others ap. Gratian, Caus. xxxiii. Qu. iii. c. 76-85, also *Ibid.* Caus. xxxiii. Qu. iii. Dist. ii.

([6]) Gratian, Caus. xxxiii. Qu. iii. Dist. ii.

([7]) According to Augustine ap. Gratian, Caus. xxxiii. Qu. iii. c. 84, the

The rules of Penance, the circumstances under which commutations are allowed, and the nature of the Indulgences permitted belong to a special department of Canon Law called Casuistry (¹).

5. As there is no clear authority that Christ appointed confession to be made to a Priest (²), so the discipline of Penance is not more than a Sacramental Act. The Canonical view of Private Confession is that it is obedience to a precept and as such a test of penitence (³), rather than a necessity for salvation or a means of pardon. It is conducive to humility, when it is resorted to for venial sins. In the case of mortal sins it is a substitute for and stands on the same footing as public Discipline.

6. The fourth Lateran Council (⁴) made it obligatory on all Christians once a year, lest any unwittingly should be abouring under mortal sin.

measure of grief rather than of time must be considered in apportioning penances.

(¹) See the long Tractatus de Pœnitentia ap. Gratian, Caus. xxxiii. Qu. iii.

(²) See Gratian, Caus. xxxiii. Qu. iii. c. 89, 90, and Qu. iii. Dist. vi.

(³) Ser authorities ap. Gratian, Caus. xxxiii. Qu. iii. c. 38 to 75, 89, also Caus. xxxiii. Dist. iv. also Dist. i. c. 37

(⁴) A.D. 1215, Can. 21.

CHAPTER LXXII.

PUBLIC DISCIPLINE.

1. THE Church now takes formal public notice only of offences which cause public scandal. This is called the judgment of the Outer tribunal. In the early days of Christianity there was no other, and for some time it was hotly debated whether the Lapsed—*i.e.*, such as after baptism had fallen into mortal sin—could be re-admitted to its Communion. This debate gave rise to the Novatian Schism.

A somewhat similar dissension arose in the fourth century respecting the treatment of the *Traditores, i.e.*, such as under stress of persecution had delivered up the sacred books. When Christianity became the recognised religion of state, other like points had to be settled.

2. The rules of discipline adopted by the Church were really a compromise between two opposing currents of thought, both of which, however, aimed at the same end—the holiness of the Church ; the one seeking to secure this end by cutting off great sinners as a source of contamination to the rest ; the other seeking to win back a sinner from the error of his ways. The former tendency gives rise to what is called Vindictive, the latter to Remedial discipline. Until offences have been actually

brought home to offenders, they should be charitably borne
with (¹).

3. The received rules of Discipline in early days allowed
only of one reconciliation to the Church after a lapse (²).
From the length of time which had to pass before
reconciliation could be permitted, and the severity of the
mortification to be gone through in the meanwhile, it is
seen how strictly the Church guarded its purity against
sham Conversions (³).

4. A distinction was also made between the case of the
Clergy and the Laity. Clergy were simply removed from
the ministry without public penance (⁴), whereas the Laity
did penance openly, and at its close were openly recon-
ciled by the Bishop with the imposition of hands before the
sanctuary.

(¹) See authorities ap. Gratian, Caus. xxiii. Qu. iv. c. 1-15, 18, 19, 22.

(²) See Gratian, Caus. xxxiii. Dist. iii. c. 34.

(³) Liber de vera et falsa pœnitentia ap. Gratian I. Dist. xxv. c. 5, also
Caus. xxxiii. Dist. v.

(⁴) Gregorius, Lib. iv. Epist. 17 ap. Grat. I. Dist. L c. 1, and Lib. vii.
Epist. 25, *Ibid.* c. 3, and Lib. iii. Epist. 26, *Ibid.* c. 9, Martinus i, *Ibid.*
c. 2 and 12, Concil. Agathense, Can. 50, A.D. 506, *Ibid.* c. 7. See also
Gratian I. Dist. lxxxi. c. 5 to 12.

That the Clergy may be restored after Penance, is maintained by
Calixtus I. Epist. ii. ap. Gratian I. Dist. l. c. 14, by Hieronymus, cap. 3
Malachiæ, *Ibid.* c. 15, 19, and 20. also by Gregorius, Lib vii. Epist. 53,
Ibid. c. 16. and Concil. Agathense, Can. 2, *Ibid.* c. 21. As to who may and
who may not be restored, see Isidorus ap. Gratian I. Dist. l. c. 28,
Hormisdas, *Ibid.* c. 29, Nicolaus, *Ibid.* 33, Rabanus, *Ibid.* c. 34, Concil.
Ilerdense. Can. 5, A. D. 546, ap. Gratian I. Dist. l. c. 52.

Clergy were restored without imposition of hands, see Concil. Carthag.
v. Can. 11, A.D. 401, ap. Gratian I. Dist. l. c. 65, Leo. Epist. xc. c. 2,
Ibid. c. 67.

CHAPTER LXXIII.

DISCIPLINE OF THE CLERGY.

1. THE discipline of the Clergy is necessarily vindictive, *i.e.* it is inflicted on unwilling subjects primarily for the maintenance of the purity of the Church and only secondarily for the soul's health of the offender ([1]).

2. In case of a charge being preferred against a Bishop or Priest, it should according to ancient rule be investigated by a provincial Synod ([2]). Ordinarily the presence of twelve Bishops ([3]) besides the Metropolitan was required for the trial of a Bishop ([4]); six for that of a Priest or Archdeacon; three for that of a Deacon ([5]).

3. No heretic, separatist, or criminous person, was per-

([1]) Sometimes only the latter. See Concil. Derdense, Can. 5, A.D. 546, ap. Gratian, Caus. xv. Qu. viii. c. 2.

([2]) Concil. Carthag. iv. Can 29, ap. Gratian, Caus. vi. Qu. ii. c. 1 : Episcopus si clerico vel laico crimen impegerit deducatur ad probationem in Synodum. See authorities ap. Gratian, Caus. xv. Qu. vii.

([3]) Pseudo-Isidore ap. Gratian, Caus. v. Qu. iv. Concil. Carthag. ii. Can. 10, A.D. 390, ap. Gratian, Caus. iii. Qu. viii. c. 2. Si quis episcopus in reatum aliquem incurrerit et nimia necessitas ei fuerit non posse plurimos congregare, ne in crimine remaneat, a duodecim audiatur episcopis.

([4]) Gratian, Caus. vi. Qu. iv. c. 5.

([5]) Concil. Carthag. i. Can. 11, A.D. 348, ap. Gratian, Caus. xv. Qu. vii. c. 3: A tribus vicinis episcopis, si diaconus est qui arguitur si presbyter a sex; si episcopus a duodecim consacerdotibus audiatur. Concil. Carthag. iii. Can. 8, A.D. 397, *Ibid.* c. 5.

mitted to give evidence against a Bishop on an ecclesiastical charge ([1]), but he might on another charge, provided he first stated in writing his willingness to bear the penalty should he fail to substantiate it.

4. Should the judging Bishops be divided in opinion, a neighbouring Metropolitan and some neighbouring Bishops were summoned to assist ([2]). To depose a Bishop the presence of all the Comprovincials was required as well as of the accused himself.

5. In the case of a Priest, punishment could only be enforced after a careful investigation by the Bishop ([3]) and suitable monition ([4]). Mere ill repute without evidence was not allowed to condemn a clerk, but in some cases it was enough to call on him to clear himself by compurgation ([5]). Should a Priest be deprived by the captiousness or party spirit of his Bishop ([6]), an appeal lay to a Synod of neighbouring Bishops, the majority of whom would cancel or confirm the sentence.

([1]) Concil. Const. Can. 6.

([2]) Concil. Antioch, Can. 14, A.D. 332, ap. Gratian, Caus. vi. Qu. iv. c. 1.

([3]) Gregorius ap. Gratian, Caus. xv. Qu. vii. c. 2. Concil. Hispalens. ii. Can. 6, A.D. 619, ap. Gratian, Caus. xv. Qu. vii. c. 7 : Nisi in Synodo canonica vocata sacerdotes damnari non possunt.

([4]) Decret. Greg. IX. Lib. iii. Tit. i. c. 16, and Tit. ii. c. 4 and 6.

([5]) Decret. Greg. IX. Lib. v. Tit. xxxiv. and xxxv.

([6]) Concil. Nic. Can. 5. A.D. 825.

CHAPTER LXXIV.

CENSURES ON THE CLERGY.

THE Censures (¹) by which the Discipline of the Clergy is enforced are of three kinds: (1) Suspension (2), Deprivation, and (3) Degradation.

1. Suspension is a temporary withdrawal of the authority to exercise clerical duties (²). As such it is called suspension *ab officio*. When to this is added a withdrawal of the right to receive clerical maintenance, it is called suspension *a beneficio*. Suspension ought not to be given without a previous admonition (³), and may be pronounced by a spiritual Judge (⁴).

2. Deprivation is a permanent removal from the clerical office (⁵), and may only be pronounced by the Bishop (⁶).

(¹) Decret. Greg. IX. Lib. v. Tit. xxxvii.

(²) Temporary suspension is not allowed by Concil. Carthag. iii. Can. 7, A.D. 891, unless the accused fails to appear. See Gratian, Caus. iv. Qu. v. c. 1. See Sext. Decret. Lib. v. Tit. xi. c. 1. Const. Clem. Lib. v. Tit. x. Extrav. Lib. i. Tit. xiii.

(³) Gibs. 1047, Phillimore's *Ecclesiastical Law*, p. 1376. See Sext. Decret. Lib. v. Tit. xi. c. 18.

(⁴) Phillimore's *Ecclesiastical Law*, p. 1375.

(⁵) No Deacon or Priest may be deprived of the clerical office without first having a hearing. Gratian, Caus. Qu. vii. c. 1.

(⁶) Phillimore's *Ecclesiastical Law*, p. 1375. Yet may be pronounced by the Judge of the Court of Arches without the presence of the Bishop or Archbishop. See legal authorities in Phillimore's *Ecclesiastical Law*, p. 1399.

It may be either *ab officio*, or *a beneficio*, the former ordinarily involving the latter. But a case is conceivable of one deprived of his spiritual office whom the law does not allow to be deprived of his benefice. Deprivation follows canonically *ipso facto* on the commission of certain crimes such as simony, heresy, sacrilege, homicide, self-mutilation, falsification of ecclesiastical documents, intrusion into another's benefice, sodomy, and spiritual incest. Nevertheless in all these cases a declaratory sentence must be given in the Spiritual Court, before an office can be considered vacant (¹).

3. Degradation or total removal from the exercise of Orders can only follow on the commission of some very enormous crime (²). Formerly it was enforced after a conviction for heresy.

(¹) Neither a Deacon nor a Priest may be deprived except he either pleads guilty or is proved guilty. See Nicolaus ap. Gratian, Caus. xv. Qu. v. c. 2. So it has been decided, too, in the Court of Arches. See the authorities in Phillimore's *Ecclesiastical Law*, p. 1401.

(²) See Sext. Lib. v. Tit. ix, c. 2.

O

CHAPTER LXXV.

CENSURES ON THE LAITY.

1. THE Discipline of the Laity has for its first object the amendment of the sinner. Hence censures are properly inflicted on the contumacious only, except in cases of grave public scandal. The public censures reserved for the laity are of two kinds, either (1) Excommunication or (2) the Interdict.

2. Excommunication (¹), which is often called the Bishop's sword, is of one of two degrees (²), either the lesser Excommunication or the greater Excommunication. The lesser Excommunication is the suspension of a Christian from communion and Divine worship for a limited period. Being remedial and applied for the good of his soul, it must be preceded by suitable admonition.

3. The greater Excommunication (³) involves not only exclusion from Communion, but separation from the fellowship and conversation of the faithful, its object being not so

---

(¹) One who is himself excommunicate cannot excommunicate another, Gratian, Caus. xxiv. Qu. i. c. 4, 36-42. Excommunications can only be pronounced on the living, Gratian, Caus. xxiv. Qu. ii. Decret. Greg. IX. Lib. v. Tit. xxxix.

(²) Hieronymus in Lib. Jud. Hom. ii ap Gratian, Caus. xi. Qu. iii. c. 21.

(³) As to the treatment of the excommunicate, see authorities ap.

much to reform a backslider as to prevent the contamination of others by a member corrupt past remedy. It is, therefore vindictive. To inspire awe the sentence used to be pronounced (¹) by the Bishop surrounded by twelve Clergy with lighted candles, who on its promulgation dashed them to the ground and trod upon them. Similar ceremonies attended the removal of the sentence (²). The name of a person so censured was not allowed to be mentioned (³) in the public prayers of the Church, nor might he receive any Sacrament. One who is included in this censure, but not *denounced* (⁴) by name, is called a *tolerated* person and several exceptions are made in his favour.

4. The Interdict or, as it is often called, the Anathema is a still severer form of punishment. It applies both to persons and places, and those to whom it applies are cut off from all the offices of the Church (⁵).

5. In all cases a sentence pronounced by one Bishop must be observed by others, until it is remedied on

Gratian, Caus. xi. Qu. iii. c. 16, 17, 18, 22-24, 26-29, 102-105, 110. Concil. Carthag. iv. Can. 73, *Ibid.* c. 19.: Qui communicaverit vel oraverit cum excommunicato, si laicus est excommunicetur, si clericus deponatur.

(¹) See Gratian, Caus. xi. Qu. iii. c. 106.

(²) See Gratian, Caus. xi. Qu. iii. c. 108.

(³) See Honorius, ap. Gratian, Caus. xi. Qu. iii. c. 20.

(⁴) Urbanus A.D. 1095 mentions those excommunicated but not *nominatim.* Gratian, Caus. ix. Qu. i. c. 5.

(⁵) Pseudo-Isidore ap. Gratian, Caus. iii. Qu. iv. c. 12. See Concil. Eliberitan. Can. 52, ap. Gratian, Caus. v. Qu. i. c. 3, also Decret. Greg. IX. Lib. v. Tit. xxxiii. c. 25.

appeal (¹). Yet a Bishop should not pass sentence in a case which concerns himself (²), nor except for grave reason (³) and according to law (⁴).

(¹) Concil. Nicæn. Can. 5. Concil. Antioch. Can. 6, A.D. 332, ap. Gratian, Caus. xi. Qu. iii. c. 2 and 3, 7-10.

(²) Ambrosius ap. Gratian, Caus. xxiii. Qu. iv. c. 27.

(³) Not for captiousness or party spirit. Concil. Nicæn. Can. 5.

(⁴) See Gratian, Caus. xxiv Qu. ii. c. 6-13, 16, 18, 19, 20-25, 37.

PART IV.

OF CERTAIN EXTENSIONS OF CHURCH ORGANISATION IN MEDIÆVAL AND MODERN TIMES.

CHAPTER LXXVI.

CHANGE IN THE CHURCH'S POSITION IN THE 12TH CENTURY.

1. A GREAT change came over the relations of the Church to the world in the West during the 12th century. Previously to the time of the first Lateran Council, A.D. 1123, the Church had held in Cis-Alpine Europe, the position of a Missionary Institution. After the fourth Lateran Council, A.D. 1215, it appeared as a powerful and united Spiritual Empire, the equal and the superior of the revived Roman Empire. It had everywhere obtained considerable property, and its hierarchial government was thoroughly well organized. On the other hand it included among its members many who had been hastily converted and who had forgotten or ignored its note of holiness ; and thus too often the end was sacrificed to perfect the means.

2. The change in its position affected principally three points :—

    (1) The Diocesan system, which was curtailed and .modified by the creation of a number of Sub-units of Jurisdiction such as Parishes, Colleges, Orders.

(2) Eucharistic Worship, since, as a sequel to the rise of the Parochial system, a Divine Office, Holy Places and Holy Times were set apart for regular observance away from the Cathedral Church and Episcopal superintendance.

(3) The administration of discipline, which was in many points remodelled to suit the altered state of things.

DIVISION I.

MODIFICATION OF THE DIOCESAN SYSTEM—SUB-UNITS OF
JURISDICTION.

CHAPTER LXXVII.

THE ENDOWMENT OF THE CHURCH.

1. ALTHOUGH the Diocese, as being the district presided over
by one Bishop, is the lowest unit of Church Administration,
yet the acquisition of property by several bodies within the
Church other than the Diocesan unit obscured in time the
knowledge of that fact. This it did in more ways than
one : (1) It prevented the natural increase in the number
of Dioceses by subdivision as populations increased ; for the
means necessary for the maintenance of new Bishops and
Chapters had been in other ways already disposed of : and (2)
it raised up within the Diocese a number of Sub-units, such
as Parishes (¹) and religious Foundations, some subsidiary

(¹) Kennet's Parochial Antiquities gives the following account of the
origin of the Parochial System : For the first six or seven centuries, the
Parochia was the Diocese or Episcopal District, wherein the Bishop and
his Clergy lived together at the Cathedral Church ; and whatever were the
tithes and obligations of the faithful, they were all brought into a common
fund, from whence a continual supply was had for support of the Bishop
and his College of Presbyters and Deacons, for the repair and ornaments
of the Church, and for other suitable works of piety and charity. . . .
While the Bishops thus lived amongst their Clergy. . . the stated

to, others more or less exempt from the Bishop's Jurisdiction, but all overshadowing the ancient rule according to which the Bishop of the Diocese, acting with the advice of his regularly attached clergy the Chapter, is the source and centre of Church Administration.

2. The several steps by which the Diocesan system was modified were, (1) the acquisition of property by certain bodies within the Church, other than the Diocesan Church unit, (2) the creation of Parishes as Sub-units within the Diocese in consequence thereof, and (3) as a further consequence, the foundation of Colleges and Religious Houses, claiming in all cases to be extra-parochial and in many to be extra-diocesan.

services or public offices of religion were performed only in those single Choirs, to which the people of each whole Diocese resorted, especially at the more solemn times and seasons of devotion. But to supply the inconveniences of distant and difficult access, the Bishop sent out some Presbyters into the remoter parts to be itinerant preachers, or occasional dispensers of the word and Sacrament. Most of these Missionaries returned from this holy circuit to the centre of unity, the Episcopal College, and had there only their fixed abode.

Yet some few. . . when they saw a place more populous and a people zealous, built there a plain and humble conveniency for divine worship. And while the necessities of the country were thus upon occasion supplied it did not alter the state of the ecclesiastical patrimony.

Sometimes the itinerant preachers found encouragement to settle amongst a liberal people, and by their assistance to raise up a Church and a little adjoining manse. . . . . But the more ordinary and standing method of augmenting the number of Churches depended on the piety of the thanes or greater lords ; who having large fees and territories in the country, founded Churches for the service of their families and tenants within their dominion. It was this gave a primary title to the patronage of laymen. It was this made the bounds of a Parish commensurate to the extent of a Manor. . . . and it was this distinct property of lords and tenants that by degrees allotted new Parish bounds by the adding of new auxiliary Churches.

CHAPTER LXXVIII.

CHURCH PROPERTY.

1. THE Church of Christ is a great Corporation. As such it would appear capable of possessing land and property like any other Corporotion which the Civil Law allows. The Church, however, cannot assume the rights of ownership without incurring the duties of citizenship and so bringing itself under the grasp of the Law of the land ; and inasmuch as it belongs to no nation or state in particular but to all, it is difficult to see how it can own land and property anywhere without detriment to its Catholic character, except where it is itself supreme temporal Governour.

2. On the other hand as Civil Governours can pronounce certain individuals disqualified from holding property under their protection ([1]), so they can, and usually do declare all Corporations disqualified to act as Persons unless they have previously obtained their approval. In England a Corporation must have been treated as such time out of mind, or it must have obtained a Charter of Incorporation, and even then its power of possessing landed property is strictly limited.

3. The Law of England has never recognised the Church

([1]) Owing to the vague use of the term Church, many of the questions arose as to changes of ownership which are answered by Gratian, Caus. xxiii. Qu. vii.

of Christ as a legal Corporation capable of holding property within this realm, partly perhaps because it conceived that although its members might as individuals own property in the world, yet the Church as a whole, being Christ's Kingdom not of this world, ought not so to do; partly also because the Church as being independent of any particular nationality was regarded as an alien body and the majority of its members as aliens. Neither has it allowed corporate rights until quite recent times [1], and then only in a limited way and under its own management even to the Branch of Christ's Church or National Church within the kingdom which is the aggregate of all the Church units or Dioceses therein.

[1] There are two Corporations known to English Law which in a certain way represent the Church of England. These are (1) *Queen Anne's Bounty*, (2) and the *Ecclesiastical Commissioners*. The former represents the Pope's interest in the English Church, viz: the right to first-fruits and tenths, which by 26 Hen. VIII. c. 8, were taken from him and annexed to the crown of England. These first-fruits and tenths continued to form part of the revenues of the crown until the time of Queen Anne, when she resolved to apply them for the augmentation of the livings of the poorer Clergy. Accordingly an Act was passed 2 and 8 Queen Ann, c. 20, authorising the Queen to establish a Corporation for that purpose. This Corporation according to its Charter consists of the Archbishops, Bishops, Deans, the Speaker, Master of the Rolls, Privy-Councillors, Lieutenants, and Custodes Rotulorum of the Counties, Judges, Serjeants of Law, Attorney and Solicitor General, Advocate General, Chancellors and Vice-Chancellors of the two Universities, Mayor and Aldermen of the City, and Mayors of other cities, to which certain others have been subsequently added, and its object is to augment the maintenance of the poor Clergy. The Ecclesiastical Commissioners are a Corporation established by 6 and 7, Will. IV. c. 77, and 8 and 4 Vict. c. 113, and subsequent amending Statutes with power to take the Estates of the then greater Church Corporations, and out of them after assigning Salaries to the present holders to make better provision for the cure of souls in parishes where such assistance is most needed.

4. There are, however, certain ecclesiastical Units and Sub-units which it allows to hold property, not, however, treating those units themselves as corporations, but those who represent them. Such are, the Church of the Diocese as represented by the Bishop and Chapter; the part of that Church within a County as represented by the Archdeacon; a Parish as represented by a Parson or Vicar; and a College or Foundation. Bishops, Archdeacons, Parsons, and Vicars are called Corporations Sole. So also is a Dean and each member of a Chapter in right of his Prebend. Chapters and Colleges are called Corporations Aggregate.

CHAPTER LXXIX.

PROPERTY OF THE CHURCH-UNIT.—THE DIOCESE.

THE Bishop and the Chapter together appear originally to have formed one Corporation, representing the Church of the Diocese. Gifts of land or money made to the Church, were made to them (¹), and they determined the application thereof.

1. The old rule required the Division of all Church revenues (²) into four equal parts, one for the Bishop, one for the Clergy of the Diocese *i.e.* the members of the Chapter (³), one for the fabric of the Church (⁴), and one for the poor (⁵).

When extensive gifts of land or benefices were made to the Church, and those lands were held subject to feudal duties, it was found more convenient that they should be in the hands of individuals capable of discharging those duties. Hence a division was made of the Church Estates into two

---

(¹) See Gratian, Caus. xvi., Qu. i. c. 55-57 ; Qu. ii. c. 8.

(²) It required all revenues to go into a common fund ; see Gratian, Caus. xvi. Qu. i. c. 55-58.

(³) Gregorius ap. Gratian, Caus. xvi. Qu. i. c. 68.

(⁴) As to the fabric, see Concil. Toletan. xvi. Can. 5, A.D. 698, ap. Gratian, Caus. x. Qu. iii. c. 8.

(⁵) Gelasius in Epist. ad Brulios c. 29, ap. Gratian, Caus. xii. Qu. ii. c. 27. Simplicius, *Ibid.* c, 28. Gregorius, *Ibid.* c. 29, and 80.

parts (¹), one of which was held by the Bishop as a Corporation Sole for his own use and that of the poor (²), and the other of which was held by the Chapter as a Corporation Aggregate for their own use and that of the fabric. The former were called Episcopal, the latter Chapter Estates, and a trace of the original joint-ownership survives still in the fact that neither Bishop (³) nor Chapter (⁴) can alienate without the consent of the other (⁵).

2. Although in the view of the Common Law, the Bishop and the Chapter are regarded as Corporations having the absolute ownership of their respective Estates, yet in the eyes of the Canon Law they are deemed to hold them for the use of the Church, and are considered bound to administer them as stewards for the good of the Church (⁶)

(¹) Concil. Aurelianense i. Can. 16, A.D. 511, ap. Gratian, Caus. x. Qu. i. c. 8 decrees, ut de his quæ in altario oblatione fidelium conferuntur, medietatem sibi episcopus vendicet, et medietatem sibi dispensandam secundum gradus clerus accipiat. Phillimore's *Ecclesiastical Law* p. 155 confirms the above.

(²) Concil. Aurelianense i. Can. 18, A.D. 511 ap. Gratian I. Dist. lxxxii, c. 1 Episcopus pauperibus vel infirmis, qui debilitate faciente non possunt suis manibus laborare, victum et vestitum, in quantum sibi possibile fuerit, largiatur.

(³) Authorities ap. Gratian, Caus. xii. Qu. ii. c. 18 to 20.

(⁴) Concil. Agathens. Can. 22, A.D. 506, ap. Gratian, Caus. xii. Qu. ii. c. 32, 35, 41, and 42.

(⁵) Alienation is allowed for the purpose of redeeming captives by the Universal Synod, Can. 15, A.D. 869, ap. Gratian, Caus. xii. Qu. ii. c. 13 ; also *Ibid.* c. 14, and 15. Concil. Carthagin. ap. Gratian, Caus. xii. Qu. ii. c. 51, 70, 73. In cases of doubt, the primate must decide upon the validity of the reason; see Concil. Carthagin. Can. 26, A.D. 409, ap. Gratian, Caus. xvii. Qu. iv. c. 39.

(⁶) See the authorities ap. Gratian, Caus. x. Qu. ii. and Qu. iii. c. i. to 3 ; also Gratian, Caus. xii. Qu. i. c. 13. Concil. Antioch. Can. 25. *Ibid.* c. 23, 24, 26, and 27. Decret. Greg. IX. Lib. iii. Tit. v. c. 3.

and not for themselves only (¹). They are therefore liable to give an account of their stewardship to a superior, which is one of the duties of Visitation, but in England the Visitor's legal power of controlling their administration is hardly more than a shadow.

(¹) Hence the gravity of the offence when Church property is given to laymen, Gratian, Caus. xii. Qu ii.

CHAPTER LXXX.

EFFECTS OF CHURCH PROPERTY.

THE acquisition of property by the several Church Officers permitted to hold it as Corporations Sole or Aggregate has had a twofold effect. It has (1) enhanced the worldly position of those Officers, and (2) brought them largely under the control of the Civil Power.

1. It has raised their worldly position by making them no longer almsmen living off the gifts of the faithful and dependent on the good-will of the laity, but free and independent land-owners, having fixity of tenure, invested with the rights and duties of feudal holdings, and as such ranking with laymen similarly placed ; and it has also to that extent made them more independent of their hierarchial superiors.

2. On the other hand it has brought the holders of all offices in the Church to which freeholds are attached (¹) within the purview of the laws of the realm, so that not only can appointments to them only be made in a way which the Law of the land allows, but removal from them can only be permitted upon proof of misconduct, such as the Law of the land recognises as sufficient cause, and none

---

(¹) Prescriptions are in England cognisable by the Secular Tribunals This is not contrary to the reason for a thirty years' prescription laid down by Gelasius, ap. Gratian, Caus. xiii. Qu. ii. c. 1.

of the implied trusts which the Canon Law lays down can be enforced against the holders.

3. So long as any temporalities are attached to Church offices, the State as supreme over all property must in cases of dispute be the ultimate court of appeal for determining whether its laws have been complied with or not whenever a charge is brought against any one for a supposed dereliction of duty (¹).

(¹) By the ancient laws of the Church a Bishop should not litigate for a temporal matter. See Gratian, Caus. xiv. Qu. i. c. 1. Other authorities, however, permit an appeal to the Courts rather than to force. Gratian, Caus. xvi. Qu. vi. c. 1.

CHAPTER LXXXI.

THE PARISH.

ONE of the first results of the possession of landed property by the Church in feudal times has been the creation of Parishes (¹).

1. A Parish may be defined in several ways. *Ecclesiastically* it is an arbitrary district or part of a Diocese belonging to one or more land-owners who have combined to build a Church and make an endowment. They who have done this are called Patrons. He who has it is called the Parson, and in respect of him it is called Preferment. *Spiritually*, it is the Parish, *i.e.* the district committed to the exclusive ministrations of one Priest called the Parish Priest, whose ministrations are locally supplementary to those of the Bishop and Chapter regularly attached to the Diocese. In respect of *Property* it is a Benefice, *i.e.* a district which supplies a maintenance for one Parish Priest who is thence called a Beneficed Clerk.

2. Apart from its Ecclesiastical Head the Parish is lost in the Diocese at large (²) Through him it becomes a Sub-

---

(¹) See Kennet : For the first six or seven centuries the term Parish meant the Diocese or Episcopal District, so that before the division of England into Parishes (as the term is now used) all tithes, offerings, and ecclesiastical profits did entirely belong to the Bishop and his Clergy for pious uses. See Phillimore's *Ecclesiastical Law*, p. 263.

(²) Dr. Lushington in *Braithwaite v. Hook*, Dean of Chichester, pub. by Elliott, Chichester, 1862, p. 8, S. C. 8 Jurist. N.S. 1186, observes : I

P

unit of the Diocese, a centre for the exercise of a certain
limited jurisdiction, and its head as representing· it is a
Corporation or Person in the eye of the law and therefore
commonly called the Parson.

In respect of his ministrations the Parish Priest is only
supplementary to the Bishop and Chapter (¹). Their
jurisdiction and ministrations extend over the whole
Diocese ; his only to one part thereof.

3. The Parish Priest owes his present position (²)
mainly to three causes : (1) the difficulty of subdividing

think that Cathedrals existed before the institution of civil parishes, and
Lord Coke, the highest of all legal authority, so declares. The course of
history seems to have been that originally the Bishop and the Priest
subordinate to him were resident in and about the Cathedral . . . that
these subordinate Priests were from time to time sent into the country
to discharge ecclesiastical duties, and this by the orders and under the
control of the Bishop ; that for the more efficient discharge of those
duties the country was marked out by the ecclesiastical authority into
parishes, and thus gradually arose Rectories, Vicarages, and Perpetual
Curacies . . . . It is not doubted that the same ecclesiastical authority
which marked out the boundaries of parishes for spiritual purposes could
in those days alter them. But in course of time . . . . the civil courts
came to determine what were the boundaries of the parishes. But this
exercise of such civil jurisdiction over parishes does not, according to
Lord Coke, date earlier than 1189.

(¹) Concil. Ilerdense, Can. 3, A.D. 546, ap. Gratian, Caus. x. Qu. i. c.
1 : Si ex laicis quispiam a se factam basilicam consecrari desiderat, nequa-
nam . . . a diocesana lege audeat segregare. Concil. Toletan. iii. Can.
19, A.D. 589, *Ibid.* c. 2, Concil. Cabilonense ii. A.D. 813, *Ibid.* c. 3 ;
Decretum est ut omnes ecclesiæ . . . . in episcopi potestate consistant,
atque ad ordinationem suam semper pertineant, Concil. Toletan. iv. c. 32
A.D. 633 ; Concil. Antioch. Can. 24, A.D. 332 ; Concil. Aurelianense i. Can.
17, A.D. 511, *Ibid.* c. 6, 5 and 7. Concil. Aurelianense i. Can. 19 aⁿ.
Gratian, Caus. xvi. Qu. vii. c. 10.

(²) Perhaps the origin of Parishes may be traced back to the ordinance
of Leo, Epist. lxxxv. c. 2 ap. Gratian I. Dist. lxxx. c. 4 : Volumus
canonum statuta servari, ut non in quibuslibet locis, neque quibuslibet

Dioceses, when this involved questions of property and therefore required the assent of the Civil Government, (2) the insufficiency of the Capitular Clergy to do the work of extensive Dioceses, both in respect of numbers and physical capacity, (3) the preference of the Laity for endowing local resident Clergy instead of contributing to the general funds of the Diocese (¹). Thus instead of Dioceses being sub-divided as populations increased, and the number of Chapter-titles being enlarged (²) as Chapter-property augmented, Sub-units of ecclesiastical administration were established within the Diocese called Parishes (³).

4. In respect of property a Parish Priest has not, like the clergy regularly attached to a Diocese, a fixed share or dividend from the general revenues of the Church as his maintenance, but a gift of land or landrights bestowed by the Founder or Patron of a Parish called a benefice ; and inasmuch as feudalism required benefices to be in the hands of those able to discharge the duties with which they were

castellis et ubi ante non fuerunt, episcopi consecrentur, cum ubi minores sunt plebes minoresque conventus presbyterorum cura sufficiat; but it would appear that the presbyteri referred to correspond to our members of Chapters from Concil. Laodicense, Can. 57, *Ibid.* c. 5, A.D. 363 : Non debere in vicis et villis episcopos ordinari, sed visitatores, id est qui circumeant, constitui ; hos autem, qui antehoc, ordinati sunt, nihil agere censemus sine conscientia episcopi civitatis.

(¹) This was permitted by the Bishop in return for certain services or money payments secured to himself. See Chapter lxxxii. and Gratian, Caus. xviii. Qu. ii. c. 30 and 31. Kennet observes : The division of a Diocese into rural Parishes, and the foundations of Churches adequate to them, cannot be ascribed to any one act, nor indeed to any one single age.

(²) Decret. Greg. IX. Lib. iii. Tit. v. c. 26.

(³) Gelasius ap. Gratian, Caus. xvi. Qu. xii. c. 26 and 27.

burdened, both Bishops and Chapters found it more convenient to follow the example of lay-Patrons by endowing Parish Priests with benefices in outlying districts, instead of serving them themselves, by members of the Chapter receiving dividends. Hence Chapters became diminished in numbers and Parishes rapidly increased, and they became nearly universal by the time of the third Lateran Council, A.D. 1179.

CHAPTER LXXXII.

THE Parish is a Sub-unit of the Diocese, which supplies one Priest with a maintenance, and is committed to his spiritual charge. In its corporate capacity it is represented by its spiritual officer, who is, therefore, called the Parson ([1]).

1. The endowments of a Parson are not Church property in the ordinary sense of the term, but private property given for the use of a local officer, the parochial minister or Parish Priest. They are not, therefore, subject to the Church's rule, requiring a fourfold division for four separate purposes, neither are they liable to maintain the fabric of the Parish Church, which is the duty of the Patron and his vassals, but they are a maintenance for a local Clergyman ([2]).

Inasmuch as the Endowment of Parishes withdrew tithes and land from the Church of the diocese, it was usual for the Bishop in consenting thereto, to reserve an annual quitrent for himself. This was called a *Cathedraticum*. It was ordered by several Councils that its amount should not be oppressive ([3]). It was usually collected

---

([1]) Lyndwood, p. 117, and Phillimore's *Ecclesiastical Law*, p. 262.

([2]) It is order that a Rector should have a sufficient maintenance, after paying the Bishop's and Patron's dues. Decret. Greg. IX. Lib. iii. Tit. v. c. 30.

([3]) See Gratian, Caus. x. Qu. iii. c. 1, 6, 7, 8; Caus. xvi. Qu. i. c. 62 Decret. Greg. IX. Lib. iii. Tit. xxxix. It is ordered by Concil-

by the Bishop when he made his Visitation and is better
known in modern times by the name of *Procurations* (¹).

2. With the consent of the donor or patron, as well as of
the bishop, a Parson may continue to hold these
endowments whilst otherwise employed than in his local
clerical work, provided he entrust the charge of the Parish
to the care of a competent deputy approved by the Bishop
and supply him with a proper maintenance (²). This he
may do either temporarily or permanently, and whether he
be an individual or a religious Corporation. The deputy so
appointed is called a Vicar (³).

3. When such an arrangement has been made as a
perpetuity, as in cases where a religious Corporation is
the Parson (⁴), it is called an Appropriation (⁵) ; and the
Corporation which retains the Parson's rights—now, how

Bracarense ii. Can. 2, ap. Gratian, Caus. x. Qu. iii. c. 1, that the amount
should not exceed two shillings. See Concil. Toletan. iii. c. 20. A.D. 589,
Concil. Cabilon. ii. Can. 14, A.D. 813. Concil. Toletan. vii. Can. 4, A.D.
646, ap. Gratian, Caus. x. Qu. iii. c. 6, 7, 8, also Leo. IV. ap. Gratian,
Caus. xvi. Qu. i. c. 62.

(¹) Sext. Decret. Lib. iii. Tit. xx., Clement. Lib. iii. Tit. xiii. Extrav.
Com. Lib. iii. Tit. x.

(²) A Vicar was supposed to have small tithes and other endowments
to the value of at least one third of the benefice. See Phillimore's
Ecclesiastical Law, p. 272, and the Statutes, 15. Ric. II. c. 6 and 4.
Hen. IV. c. 12.

(³) On Vicarages. See Decret. Greg. IX. Lib. i. Tit. xxviii ; Lib. iii·
Tit. v. c. 10.

(⁴) Gregorius, Lib. ii. Indict. ii. Epist. 17, ap. Gratian, Caus. xii. Qu.
ii. c. 75, permits Church property to be given to a monastery. Gratian,
Caus. xii. Qu. v. c. 8. Hieronymus ap. Gratian, Caus. xvi. Qu. i. c. 68.
See Decret. Greg. IX. Lib. i. Tit. x. c. 2 ; Decret. Greg. IX. Lib. iii. Tit.
xiii.

(⁵) See Decret, Greg. IX. Lib. v. Tit. xxxiii. c. 19. The Statute 15, Ric.
II. c. 6, provides : In every license to be made in the Chancery of the
Appropriation of any Parish Church, it shall be expressly contained, that

ever, limited by the appointment of a perpetual Vicar to discharge his duties, (¹)—is called the Appropriate Rector.

When an Appropriate Rectory passes into the hands of a layman (²), whereby its rights become still further shorn, it is called an Impropriate Rectory, and such an arrangement is called an Impropriation.

4. The Parson or Rector is a Corporation Sole, who ordinarily represents the Parish. When, however, the Rectory is appropriate, the perpetual Vicar, his deputy becomes also as such a Corporation Sole, and capable of possessing property (³).

the Diocesan of the place upon the Appropriation of such Churches, shall ordain according to the value of such Churches, a convenient sum of money to be paid and distributed yearly of the fruits and profits of the said Churches by those that will have the said Churches in proper use, and by their successors, to the poor parishioners of the said Churches, in aid of their living and sustenance for ever; and also that the Vicar be well and sufficiently endowed.

(¹) 4 Hen. IV. c. 12, provides: From henceforth in every Church Appropriated, there shall be a secular person ordained Vicar Perpetual, canonically instituted and inducted, and convenably endowed by the discretion of the Ordinary to do divine service and to inform the people and to keep hospitality there, and no religious shall in any wise be made vicar in any Church Appropriated.

(²) Such grants are forbidden as simony by Gregory VII. ap. Gratian, Caus. i. Qu. iii. c. 13. See also Hieronymus, Calixtus, and Damasus, ap. Gratian, Caus. x. Qu. i. c. 13 to 15. If this is done by lay authority, it deserves excommunication according to Nicolaus ap. Gratian, Caus. xii. Qu. ii. c. 22. Gregorius VII. ap. Gratian, Caus. xvi. Qu. vii. c. 1, 3. Appropriations to laymen, although legal, were strictly forbidden by the Lateran Council of 1179, see Decret. Greg. IX. Lib. iii. Tit. xxx. c. 19. which was incorporated into English Law; see Bishop of Winton's case, 1. Salk. 136; nevertheless they have been legalised in England by Statutes, 29 Hen. VIII. c. 28 and 31 Hen. VIII. c. 13, which granted to the King and his grantees the same interest that the Religious Houses had in them.

(³) See Clement. Lib. i. Tit. vii. and Phillimore's *Ecclesiastical Law*, p. 279.

CHAPTER LXXXIII.

PAROCHIAL BENEFICES.

1. A BENEFICE is an estate of land or other hereditaments held for life. Such estates are often held by Bishops and Chapters and go to make up the Episcopal or Capitular Revenues whence these ecclesiastics derive their dividends.

2. There are two kinds of Benefices, (1) those which are called ecclesiastical benefices or prebends, and (2) parochial benefices ([1]). Of these the former are much more ancient; the latter are a creation of Cis-Alpine Christianity and an outgrowth of the feudal system. Parishes had become universal in England by the time of the third Lateran council, A.D. 1179.

An ecclesiastical or Chapter Benefice is the perpetual right to a fixed share or dividend of the whole ecclesiastical revenues of the diocese available for this purpose, which share is attached to the holding of some ecclesiastical office there ([2]).

A parochial Benefice is an estate of land or other here-

([1]) A canon should be supplied with a prebend as soon as may be. Decret. Greg. IX. Lib. iii. Tit. viii. c. 8.

([2]) Such as Major pars Altaris, Tertia pars Altaris, in other cases by composition, such as the Prebend of Pattero and the like. It is ordered that every Canon shall have a Probend assigned to him so soon as may be after his election. See Decret. Greg IX. Lib iii. Tit v. c. 9 and 19.

ditaments which has been given by a founder of a Parish or
Patron to the Priest nominated by himself and ordained and
admitted by the Bishop to minister in the parochial
church there.

3. The effect of the establishment of a Parochial Benefice is threefold. Without taking the Parish out of the care
of the Bishop and Chapter it (1) gives to the Beneficed clerk
a life-holding subject to certain exceptions or canonical disabilities which the law of the land allows as just cause of
forfeiture. This is called a Freehold. (2) It gives to him
exclusive possession of the Church as being his freehold, so
that without his consent neither the Chapter nor any one
else can use his Church for their otherwise regular ministrations. This is the right of exclusive ministration within
his own Church. (3) It confers a right on the giver or Patron of determining who the Priest shall be that enjoys it (¹).
This is called the right of Presentation or Advowson (²).

4. Possession of a Benefice is obtained by becoming the
holder of the office to which the Benefice is attached.
Nevertheless it requires a separate act to give possession
of the Benefice itself. Thus in the case of any office
involving cure of souls, as that of a parish priest, possession
of the *office* is given by the Bishop or other ordinary

(¹) This right is secured by Concil. Toletan. ix. Can. 2. ap. Gratian,
Caus. xvi. Qu. viii. c. 32. The Patron has no right of depriving. See
Leo ap. Gratian, Caus. xvi. Qu. vii. c. 29 and 37. Concil. Cabilonens.
ii. Can. 42, A.D. 813, *Ibid.* c. 38., but he ought to keep up the church
which he has founded. Concil. Toletan. ix. Can. 1 ap. Gratian, Caus. xvi.
Qu. vii. c. 31.

(²) See Decret. Greg. IX. Lib iii. Tit. xxxviii. Sext. Decret. Lib. iii.
Tit. xix., Clement. Lib. iii. Tit. xii.

exercising episcopal rights, that of the *benefice* is given by
the Archdeacon or other person having charge of the
temporalities.

The putting of a priest into possession of any office is
called either Collation or Institution (¹). Collation is a
free giving by one who has the right to give, as when a
Bishop prefers a clerk to a parish in his own gift. Institution is a giving by one who has the right to give but is not
free in the exercise of his right, as when a Bishop institutes
a clerk presented to him by a patron.

The giving an office-holder possession of the temporalities
of the benefice attached to his office is called Induction and
is done by a symbolical act characteristic of the feudal incidents of a benefice.

5. There would seem to be no rule against exchanging
benefices within the same Church for any, even the slightest,
reason; but the changing from one diocese to another is a
thing strongly reprobated by the canons (²).

6. Residence (³) is absolutely necessary for continuing to
hold an office with a benefice attached, because it is necessary
in order to discharge the duties of the office; and as no one
can reside simultaneously in two places, so it is absolutely
forbidden for anyone to hold an office in two Dioceses (⁴).

(¹) Decret. Greg. IX. Lib. iii. Tit. vii.

(²) See authorities. ap. Gratian, Caus. xxi. Qu. ii.

(³) Decret, Greg. IX. Lib. iii. Tit. iv. c. 6, 11, 17.

(⁴) Concil. Chalced. Can. 10. A.D. 451; μὴ ἐξεῖναι κληρικὸν ἐν δύο
πόλεων καταλέγεσθαι ἐκκλησίαις κατὰ τὸ αὐτὸ· Synodus vii Can. 15 ap.
Gratian, Caus. xxi. Qu. i. c. 1. Decret. Greg. IX. Lib. iii. Tit. iv. c. 3.
Tit. v. c. 5, 7, 13, 14, 15.

7. Ordinarily the Founder or Patron retains such an interest in the Benefice attached to a parish or foundation, that in case he himself should fall into poverty, it is bound to supply him with a moderate maintenance (').

(') Concil. Toletan. iv. Can. 37, ᴀ.ᴅ. 633, ap. Gratian, Caus. xvi. Qu. vii. c. 32.

CHAPTER LXXXIV.

THE SPIRITUAL CHARGE OF PARISHES.

A PARISH being the district committed to the charge of one Priest, and his tenure of the Benefice being a freehold, the Parish Priest holds office for life unless he be deposed by canonical methods on grounds admitted by the civil authority as well as by the ecclesiastical authority to be valid.

1. Within the Parish he has a certain limited jurisdiction under the Bishop as Ordinary, whose Vicar he is in spirituals, as the Churchwardens are in temporals, and he is therefore entitled to the chief seat in the choir and the use of a stole in service time.

He is responsible (1) for the due performance of divine service, (2) for teaching the faithful by means of preaching and catechising, and (3) for reclaiming heretics or schismatics, heathens and infidels who may be resident within his Parish.

2. Although there can be only one Parish priest in a Parish (¹), yet a Parish may contain several subdivisions or Chapelries (²), each of which may have a priest or Vicar of

---

(¹) Concil. Toletan. ap. Gratian, Caus. xvi. Qu. i. c. 54: Plures baptismales ecclesiæ in una terminatione esse non possunt.

(²) A Chapel was not permitted to have bells. Decret. Greg. IX. Lib. v. Tit. xxxiii. c. 10.

its own, who occupies in his subdivision the same position that the Parish priest does over the whole (¹). There may also be Chapels and Oratories each with its own separate and irremoveable Clergy. All of these are called incumbents or perpetual Curates, and because they have some definite maintenance or benefice assigned to them, they cannot be removed without a trial or conviction.

3. Besides the irremoveable Clergy, there may be assistant Curates to aid a Parish priest in his duties. These are his deputies and entirely under his rule, and are permitted to assist him by a license from the Bishop which may be withdrawn by him at pleasure.

4. The rule that all clerks who faithfully serve the Church, shall obtain from the Church stipends according to their deserts (²) has reference to the several Chapter-places together with the share of revenues belonging to each one, over which the Bishop and Chapter have the control. It does not apply to Parochial Benefices not in their patronage. Bishops and Chapters are further charged to honour rank and learning in appointing to their Benefices (³), and to fill up vacancies within six

---

(¹) But ancient Churches may not be mulcted for the benefit of new foundations. See Gratian, Caus. xvi. Qu. i. c. 43 to 45.

(²) Concil. Agathens. Can. 36, A.D. 506, ap. Gratian, Caus. i. Qu. ii. c. 10; Clerici omnes qui ecclesiæ fideliter vigilanterque deserviunt, stipendia sanctis laboribus debita secundum servitii sui meritum per ordinationem canonum a sacerdotibus consequantur. Synodus Eugenii. A.D. 826, Can. 34 ap. Gratian I. Dist. xxxvii. c. 12. A Bishop is required not to show favouritism by Concil. Toletan. x. Can. 3, A.D. 656, and Pseudo-Isidore ap. Gratian I. Dist. lxxxix. c. 6 and 7.

(³) 2nd Lateran Council, Can. 16, A.D. 1139.

months. Otherwise the Superior will supply their negligence (¹). This is called Presentation by lapse.

5. Those living outside the bounds of a Parish have no claims on the services of a Parish Priest, who on the contrary is strictly forbidden to admit them to the Sacraments (²).

(¹) 3rd Lateran Council, Can. 8, A.D. 1179.
(²) See Decret. Greg. IX. Lib. iii. Tit. xxix. c. 2.

CHAPTER LXXXV.

THE RESIGNATION OF BENEFICES.

1. RESIGNATION is the voluntary surrendering or yielding up of a spiritual charge and benefice into the hands of the superior of whom it is held ([1]). It differs alike from Deprivation, which is the compulsory forfeiting for good cause, and from Spoliation which is the wrongful losing for no cause of a like interest. Every resignation must be made to the immediate superior ([2])

2. Anyone holding a spiritual charge is competent to resign that charge, provided it be done, (1) regularly ; (2) for good cause ; and (3) be allowed by the superior. The Church, however, looks on resignation with disfavour ([3]).

3. To be regular a resignation must be made ; (1) *pure et sponte, i.e.,* without consideration and willingly ([4]) ; (2) *absolute et simpliciter, i.e.,* without reserve and unconditionally ; and (3) without fraud or force. Otherwise a resignation is invalid ; and also one to which any reserva-

([1]) Deg. p. 1. c. 14. Wats. c. 4. *Fairchild* v. *Gair.* Dyer's Rep. 294 (a) n. 6 Godolphin, Abr. 284.

([2]) 1 Roll. Rep. 137. 2 Roll. Abr. 358.

([3]) Gratian. Caus. vii. Qu. i. c. 19, 23, 24, 32, 43. Decret. Greg. IX. Lib. i. Tit ix. c. 10.

([4]) So all the authorities. See *Gayton's* case, Owen 12, and and the judgment in *Fletcher* v. *Sondes.* See Decret. Greg. IX. Lib. i. Tit. ix. c. 5. and Tit. xl. c. 3 and 4 ; also Lib. ii. Tit. xiii. o. 2 and 8 ; and Lib. v. Tit. iii. c. 46.

tion or condition is attached save one made for the purpose of exchange ([¹]).

4. A resignation can only be made for good cause ([²]). The causes allowed are: (1) consciousness of guilt; (2) bodily ill-health; (3) deficiency of knowledge; (4) ill-will of the people; (5) grave scandal, which could not otherwise be avoided; (6) personal irregularity. Before accepting or refusing a resignation, it is the duty of the superior to satisfy himself as to its regularity and also as to the sufficiency of the cause alleged.

5. The acceptance of a resignation is a quasi-judicial act ([³]), and is essential to make it effective ([⁴]), and render it complete. So long as it is incomplete, it is a mere proposal

---

([¹]) Decret. Greg. IX. Lib. iii. Tit. xix. c. 7 and 8. God. 277. Gibs. 821. 1 Still. 33. The Canon Law strictly forbids a Resignation-Bond entered into to make a vacancy for another person. Nevertheless, the practice in England had been otherwise before the decisions in *The Bishop of London* v. *Ffytche* and *Fletcher* v. *Sondes*. All undertakings to resign being declared illegal by these decisions, the statute 9 Geo. IV. c. 94 was passed legalising Undertakings to resign, which fulfilled the three following conditions: (1) They must be made in favour of a particular person to be named in the undertaking; (2) The undertaking must itself be lodged in the Registry within two months of its being executed; (3) The resignation following must refer to the undertaking; and unless the person named in the instrument is presented within six months after notice thereof, the Statute declares the resignation null and void.

([²]) Phill. 519, Reiffenstuel, Lib. i. Tit. ix. n. 34, and the cause must be inquired into. See Decret. Greg. IX. Lib. i. Tit. ix. c. 5 to 10, and above Chap. xlii.

([³]) So it was decided to be according to English Law in *Hesket* v. *Grey*, Ambler 268, yet not such a judicial act but that it can be performed in camera according to the decision in *Heyes* v. *Exeter Coll.*, 12 Ves. 336.

([⁴]) Decret. Greg. IX. Lib. i. Tit. ix. c. 4: *Rockingham* v. *Griffith*, 4 Bac. Abr. 472; *Smith* v. *Foaves*, Noy. 147, God. Abr. 261, Cro. Jac. 63.

or tender, and may at any time be withdrawn from the superior's cognisance ([1]).

6. Inasmuch as resignation involves actual delivery of possession and is not effected by a mere contract to resign, it can only be made in person ([2]), and not by deed. Personal attendance before the superior may, however, be dispensed with, and personal attendance before a Notary Public substituted, provided actual delivery of possession is made in the Notary's presence ([3]), and a Proctor is appointed before him to present such possession to the superior ([4]). The Proctor so appointed must, however, be furnished with a notarial attestation that an actual surrender has been made before him embodied in a proper instrument called an instrument of resignation. Should this be found satisfactory, and that there is a good cause for resigning, the superior may decree acceptance. Resignation by deed only, unless followed by some act of surrender, is canonically in-operative. ([5])

([1]) Reiffenstuel. Lib. i. Tit. 19, n. 38-40 Decret. Greg. IX. Lib. i. Tit. ix. c. 5. Conc. Vien. in Const. Clem. Lib. i. Tit. iv. Conf. Decret. Greg. IX. Lib. i. Tit. xxxviii. c. 3, 4, 10, 13, and Tit. xl. c. 2-4, on Proctors

([2]) Gibs. 822, Deg. p. 1. c. 14, Wats. c. 4.   Otho. Athon, 82. Othobon, Athon, 96, Phillimore's *Eccles. Law,* 510, 512.

([3]) A witness, and much more so, a Notary, can only testify to what has personally come before him. See Calixtus, Leo, and Pelagius, ap. Gratian, Caus. iii. Qu. ix. c. 15, 16, 20.

([4]) See Decret. Greg. IX. Lib. i. Tit. xxxviii. c. 1, 3, 4, and 13 Clement. Lib. i. Tit. iv., Phillimore p. 518.

([5]) Petrus de Ancharano, sup. Sext. Decret. i. Tit. iii. c. 6, because a deed is only a contract until acted upon, and no contract or agreement to resign can be enforced. The only exception is that by statute 9 Geo. IV. c. 94.

CHAPTER LXXXVI.

FOUNDATIONS.

1. THE possession of property by the Clergy in right of their offices, besides giving to them fixity of tenure, and bringing about the creation of parishes, has affected in yet another way Diocesan Administration, in that it has rendered possible the establishment of Foundations more or less exempt from Diocesan rule ([1]) and in which the Founders retain a certain interest ([2]).

2. These Foundations are of three different kinds. They are either (1) simple houses serving as homes for groups of men living together under a common rule without necessarily having a common purse ([3]). In this case they are called *Societies* or *Congregations.* Or, (2) they are Corporate Foundations, whether recognised as Corporations by the Law of the land or not, instituted for the advancement of some religious or philanthropic work, but standing as units by themselves. These are called *Colleges.* Or, (3) they are groups of Foundations or Aggregates of

([1]) Gratian, Caus. xvi. Qu. ii. c. 1 and 6, 7 ; Qu. i. c. 9., Caus. xviii. Qu. ii. c. 1 to 4 ; and therefore may not be made without the Bishop's consent, Gratian, Caus. xvi. Qu. vii. c. 39, Decret. Greg. ix. Lib. iii. Tit. xxxv. Sext. Decret. Lib. v. Tit. vii. c. 4.

([2]) Romana Synodus, A.D. 826, ap. Gratian, Caus. xvi. Qu. vii. c. 33, 34.

([3]) Gratian, Caus. xvi. Qu. vii. c. 40 and 41.

affiliated Congregations combined under a common head and a common rule, situated in many dioceses and even in many lands, and ordered under a special hierarchy of their own. Such are the *Monastic and Religious Orders.*

Such Foundations when once made cannot be re-called at will, but they may be removed elsewhere with consent of the Bishop and their members (¹).

(¹) Decret. Greg. ix. Lib. iii. Tit. xxxvi.

CHAPTER LXXXVII.

COLLEGES AND SOCIETIES.

1. When a body of Clergy live together ([1]) not bound by vows of any kind, nor having a common purse, but free to come and go as they please, such a body is called a Society or Congregation. The approbation of the bishop of the Diocese is sufficient for the establishment of a new society ([2]). That approbation implies that the rule has the sanction of the Church, and that the superior has authority over the others. The Society thereby becomes a sub-unit of the Diocese and extra-parochial ([3]).

2. When on the other hand a body of Clergy living together have a common purse and form a Corporation, such a body is called a *College* ([4]). Such bodies are established within a Diocese for some religious work. They are quite independent of Parishes although they often

([1]) Sext. Decret. Lib. iii. Tit xvii., Clement. Lib. iii. Tit. xi., Extrav. Lib. i. Tit. vii., Extrav. Com. Lib. iii. Tit. ix.

([2]) Without that approbation monks are irregular, See Concil. Chalcedon. Can. 23, and Pelagius ap. Gratian, Caus. xvi. Qu. i. c. 17 and 18; Concil. Agathens. Cau 27 ap. Gratian, Caus. xviii. Qu. ii. c. 12, 13, 14.

([3]) See Decret. Greg. IX. Lib. iii. Tit. xxxvi.

([4]) Lindwood's definition given by Gibs., 172, is : A chapter is spoken in respect of a Cathedral Church ; a Convent in respect of a Church of Regulars ; a College in respect of an inferior Church where there are collected together persons living in common. See Decret. Greg. IX. Lib. v. Tit. xxxi. c. 14.

have the charge of them (¹). The best known Corporation of this kind is the Cathedral Chapter (²).

3. Societies and Colleges are of different kinds and bear different names accordingly. (1) When they have been established to assist the Bishop in the care of the whole Diocese, they are called Cathedral Chapters; when established for the service of a Parish or some educational work (³) they are called Colleges, and their Parish a Collegiate Church. The members of such societies are called *Canons* or Canonici from the rule which they are supposed to observe, and *Prebendaries* from the prebends or maintenance which they receive. (2) When the members forming such a Society or College are bound by monastic vows (⁴) they are called *Regulars* (⁵) when they are under no such vows, they are called *Seculars*.

All Cathedral Chapters are Corporations or Colleges, but in some cases they are Foundations of Regular Clerks (⁶), in others of Secular Clerks.

(¹) Decret. Greg. IX. Lib. iii. Tit. xxxv. c. 5 and xxxvii.

(²) The rule of common life for the Clergy was ordered by Leo IV. A.D. 826, See Gratian, Caus. xii. Qu. i. c. 3, also *Ibid.* c. 1-12.

(³) Monks were allowed to hold benefices by Innocentius, Gregorius, and others, ap. Gratian, Caus. xvi. Qu. i. c. 22-25.

(⁴) On the obligations of vows, see authorities ap. Gratian, Caus. xvii. Qu. i. and Caus. xx. Qu. iii. As to rash vows, Gratian, Caus. xxii. Qu. iv., Decret. Greg. IX. Lib. iii. Tit. xxxiv.

(⁵) The earlier monks were as a rule laymen, so much so that Gregory, Lib. iv. Epist. i. ap. Gratian, Caus. xvi. Qu. i. c. 2, wrote: Nemo potest et ecclesiasticis obsequiis deservire et in monachica regula ordinate persistere. They are permitted to be clergy by Ambrosius, ap. Gratian, Caus. xvi. Qu. i. c. 21, Decret. Greg. IX. Lib. iii. Tit. xxxi and xxxv.

(⁶) Decret. Greg. IX. Lib. iii. Tit. xxxi., Sext. Decret. Lib. iii. Tit. xvi. Clement. Lib. iii. Tit. ix. Extrav. Com. Lib. iii. Tit. viii.

CHAPTER LXXXVIII.

RELIGIOUS AND MONASTIC ORDERS.

1. RELIGIOUS Orders are associated groups of faithful men (whether clergy or laymen, whether men or women) established with a view to advance Christian perfection by a common life according to a rule approved by the Church (¹).

2. A Society or Congregation is the unit of an Order, the Order itself being an aggregate of affiliated Societies in many Dioceses having a common rule and a common purse, administered by one Head under a graduated hierarchy of its own.

3. Hence although the approbation of the Bishop of the Diocese is sufficient for the establishment of a Society (²) the approbation of a new Order must come from the collective Episcopate or its representative, as the Pope was in the Middle Ages (³).

4. The Religious Orders best known in the history of the Church are of the four following kinds :

(¹) A clergyman entering a monastery takes his property with him, Gratian, Caus. xvi. Qu. vi. c. 5. Sundry rules on this point are to be found in Gratian, Caus. xviii. Qu. ii. and Caus. xix. Qu. iii. and Caus. xx. Qu. i. Qu. ii.

(²) Concil Chalcedon, Can. 4, A.D. 451 ; τοὺς δὲ καθ᾽ ἐκάστην πόλιν μονάζοντας, ὑποτετάχθαι τῷ ἐπισκόπῳ· A Bishop is ordered not to deprive a Monastery of its property because of the abbot's misbehaviour, but to put him under another abbot, by Concil. Moguntiac, ap. Gratian, Caus. xvi. Qu. vi. c. 7.

(³) Sext. Decret. Lib. iii. Tit. xvii. Clement. Lib. iii. Tit. x.

(1) *Monastic Orders* or Orders of Monks ([1]), *i.e.* such as have withdrawn from the world to lead a life of devotion and work within the Cloister-walls ([2]). These orders consisted atfirst quite as much of laymen as of clergy, and comprised women as well as men. Their rule was to work and to pray in seclusion from the world. They were therefore called Cloistered Monks. Such was the Order of the Benedictines founded by S. Benedict of Nursia at Monte Cassino in 529, which developed into the four great Orders known as reformed Benedictines founded in 780 by Benedict of Aniane, Cluniacs founded by Benno of Clugny in 909, Cistercians founded by Robert of Molesme in 1098, Carthusians founded by S. Bruno, in 1086 ([3]).

(2) *Canonical and Military Orders, i.e.* Orders of Canons Regular and Knights, the former charged with the care of public worship, the latter with the conquest of the Saracens. Such were the Canons Regular of S. Augustine founded in 1038 near Avignon, and the Knights Templars and Hospitallers founded at Jerusalem in 1099.

([1]) See Decret. Greg. IX. Lib. iii. Tit. xxxi. and xxxv. c. 6, 7, 8. Sext. Decret. Lib. iii. Tit. xiv. and xvi.

([2]) Cloistered monks may not undertake ministrations outside, See Alexander II. ap. Gratian, Caus. xvi. Qu. i. c. 11.

([3]) Other reformations of the Benedictine rule were made at Hirschau in 1069, at Vallombrosa about the same time; at Bursfield in 1425. The English Benedictines were reformed by S. Dunstan c. 900, by Lanfranc in 1072.

(3) *Mendicant Orders* or Orders of Friars. The rule of these Orders was poverty. They were not cloistered. Their Mission was to wander about preaching, and to supplement the shortcomings of the Secular Clergy. Such were the Grey Friars or Franciscans founded by S. Francis of Assissi in 1210, the Black Friars or Dominicaus founded by S. Dominic (called Jacobins in France) in 1215, the White Friars or Carmelites founded on Mount Carmel in 1156 by Berthold of Limoges, and the Austin Friars founded in 1256 out of the union of eight minor monastic congregations.

(4) *Missionary Orders* or Orders of Mission Priests. Most of the post-reformation Orders have been of this kind. Amongst the most celebrated is the Order of Jesuits founded by Ignatius Loyola in 1540.

(¹) Extrav. Lib. i. Tit. xiv. o. 3.

DIVISION II.

MODIFICATION OF THE EUCHARISTIC WORSHIP.

CHAPTER LXXXIX.

SUBSTITUTION OF PUBLIC WORSHIP FOR THE EUCHARISTIC SERVICE.

1. THE Eucharistic Service or Divine Liturgy ([1]) is the oldest and most important public office of the Church, and for many centuries it was the only one which the Church possessed. Used daily in Apostolic times ([2]), it was likewise in daily use in mediæval times, in the principal or Cathedral Church of every See, and there celebrated every Sunday or greater Festival, by the Bishop himself in person, or in his absence by the Archpriest or Dean with the Clergy and assembled faithful, in commemoration of the death of Christ and the benefits thereby accruing to His Church. Attendance at this service was of obligation for all Christians ([3]); those who were absent without reasonable

([1]) See Chap. lii. and Maskell's *Ancient Liturgy of the Church of England.*

([2]) Concil. Agathense, Can. 47, ap. Gratian III. Dist. i. c. 64; Can. Apostolorum, 10, *Ibid.* c. 62; Concil. Aurelianense i. Can. 28, *Ibid.* c. 65.

([3]) Justin Martyr's *Apology*, i. c. 67. The account given by Pliny, Lib. x. 96, of the Christians' service is; Affirmabant hanc fuisse summam vel culpae suae vel erroris, quod essent soliti, stato die ante lucem convenire, carmenque Christo quasi Deo dicere secum invecim, seque

cause a certain number of times, being considered self-excommunicated.

2. The enormous extent of some of the early Cis-Alpine dioceses rendered it impossible for those living at a distance to attend the service at the Cathedral Church. Others who had been hastily converted or imperfectly instructed attended, but too ignorant to communicate fitly. Hence arose the demand for some public form of religious service, other than communicating attendance, and out of this grew the practice of being present at the Eucharistic Service without communicating, which was the great Mediaeval idea of Public Worship.

3. There were, however, other acts of worship of a less public nature, such as the administration of the Sacrament of Baptism, the services of Confirmation, Matrimony, and Burial. Above all there were the regular Hour Services recited at fixed times by the regular or canonical Clergy. All these gave to bystanders the idea of Worship without active participation, and led to the substitution in the popular mind of Public Worship for the Eucharistic Service of the Church.

sacramento non ad scelus aliquod obstringere sed ne furta, ne latrocinia, ne adulteria committerent. . . quibus peractis morem sibi discedendi fuisse, rursusque coeundi ad capiendum cibum, promiscuum tamen et innoxium.

CHAPTER XC.

PUBLIC WORSHIP AND THE PAROCHIAL SYSTEM.

1. THE permission granted to individual Priests not regularly attached to a Diocese to administer the Church's Offices in outlying localities away from the Cathedral Church and Episcopal supervision which the rise of the Parochial system brought about, necessitated the regulation of the circumstances under which, and the manner in which that permission might be exercised ([1]).

2. The rules made for this purpose apply to three points more particularly :—

(1) The proper form or order of divine service according to which the Eucharist should be administered in Parochial Churches, and also the forms for other permitted services ; these are called the Divine Office and the Hour services.

(2) The places in which the Eucharistic and other services are allowed to be used ; these are called Holy Places, and the rules for making such, are those for the Benediction and Consecration of Churches.

([1]) See Chap. xlvii.

(3) The days and times appointed for the use of the different offices, so that those dependent on the administrations of Parish Priests only might know how and when to present themselves for local worship. These go by the name of Holy Times or Feasts and Fasts.

CHAPTER XCI.

THE DIVINE OFFICE.

1. THE office or form of service prescribed by the Church for the public administration of the Eucharist as well in the principal Church of the Diocese as in subordinate or Parochial Churches, is called the Divine Office or *Liturgy*. It is set forth in the *Missal*, or Order for the administration of the Holy Communion which is in force in each particular Diocese.

2. The outline of this Office comes down from the earliest age of Christianity, but it has from time to time been added to and increased as local circumstances required (¹), until it has assumed the form in which it is known to us.

3. This Office is not therefore everywhere one and the same, but it differs from Diocese to Diocese. Its form is prescribed in every case by the Bishop with the consent of the Chapter, following the use which has been received in the Diocese. Neither the Bishop nor the Chapter may

---

(¹) Concil. Toletan. iv. Can. 12 ap. Gratian III. Dist. i. c. 54, orders hymns. The Angelic Hymn or Gloria in Excelsis is mentioned by Leo IX., and Nicolaus, *Ibid.* c. 55 and 56; standing during the reading of the Gospel by Pseudo-Isidore, *Ibid.* c. 68; the Sursum Corda by Cyprian, *Ibid.* c. 70; proper prefaces by Pseudo-Isidore, *Ibid.* c. 71. Probably the Liturgy which bears the name of S. Clement is the oldest form. It is given in Maskell's *Ancient Liturgy of the Church of England*.

make changes in it without the consent of the other ; but it is laid down that in making changes every Diocese should aim at uniformity by following the Metropolitan Church (¹).

4. The Divine Office in the Western Church is divided into two parts, which bear the names respectively of (1) the *Ordinary of the Mass*, and (2) the *Canon of the Mass* (²). The former consists of all that is invariable in the Office other than the Canon, and includes the variable part called the Proper of Seasons, which differs from Sunday to Sunday and from Feast to Feast, such as the Collect, the Gospel, and the Epistle. The Canon which is always constant consists of the commemoration of the living and the dead and the words of consecration only. The Ordinary of the Mass differs considerably in different Dioceses ; the Canon of the Mass is nearly the same in all the Western uses (³).

5. Among the best known of the uses prevailing in England previous to the year 1547, are those of Sarum, Bangor, Hereford, and York. That of Sarum, which is the most renowned, was arranged in A.D. 1085 by S. Osmund, Bishop of Sarum, who died A. D. 1099. Out of England that of S. Ambrose bears a great name next after the Roman, likewise those of Paris, Lyons and the Mozarabic.

(¹) Concil. Gerund. Can. 1 ap. Gratian III. Dist. iii. c. 31.

(²) Decret. Greg. IX. Lib. iii. Tit. xli. c. 6.

(³) Yet even the Canon of the Mass grew gradually. Beda II. relates that Gregory I. added to it three prayers : And dispose our days in Thy peace, and preserve us from eternal damnation, and rank us in the number of Thine elect, through Christ our Lord.

CHAPTER XCII.

THE HOUR SERVICES.

1. As early as the fifth century certain services other than the Eucharistic service appear to have been used by some of the Clergy (¹). In this use they appear to have followed the reported practice of S. Basil of Cæsarea. These services consisted chiefly of the Psalms which were arranged for recitation once in the week, certain canticles of the Old and New Testament, followed by readings from the Scriptures and Church writers and ending with a collect. (²)

2. When in the sixth century S. Benedict of Nursia founded the great Order which bears his name, and which has been the parent of all subsequent Western Orders, one part of his scheme was to have a perpetual service of praise and prayer upon earth which should represent the continuous worship of heaven. Hence services known as " the hours " were drawn up and appointed to be used by the members of his Society at the first, third, sixth, and ninth hours, as

---

(¹) Pelagius mentions " vigiliæ quotidianæ " circa 555 A.D., ap. Gratian I. Dist. xci. c. 1, and Hincmar of Reims, Cap. 9, orders all the hour services as of obligation on Clerks, *Ibid.* c. 2. Matins and Vespers were enjoined on the Clergy by Martin ex Concil. Tolet. i. A.D. 400, ap. Gratian I. Dist. xcii. c. 9.

(²) Concil. Agathense, Can. 30 ap. Gratian III. Dist. v. c. 13.

well as at the hours of sunset and sleep, at midnight and early dawn ([1]).

3. From S. Benedict the idea was borrowed by the Bishops and Capitular Clergy, and was embodied in a rule by Chrodegang, bishop of Metz who died A.D. 766. The clergy who lived under this rule were called Canons, and as it was usually adopted by most Cathedral establishments, the members of these were in consequence called Canons also. Other bodies of Secular clergy who likewise adopted this rule were the Austin Canons.

4. The Hour Services constitute a book called the *Breviary*, which is intended for the use of the Monastic Orders and the Clergy. ([2]) Out of it the Morning and Evening Prayer of the English Church have been compiled, which like the original are ordered to be recited daily by all persons consecrated to God ([3]).

([1]) The seven Day Hours are commemorated in the Old English rhyme :
At *Matins* bound, at *Prime* reviled, condemned to death at *Terce*,
Nailed to the cross at *Sext*, at *Nones* His sacred side they pierce ;
They take Him down at *Vespertide*, in grave at *Compline* lay,
Who thenceforth bids His Church observe her sevenfold Hours alway.

Besides these Day Hours there was also the night hour service called Lauds said at midnight.

([2]) See Decret. Greg. IX. Lib. iii. Tit. xli. c. 1 and 9.

([3]) See Hieronymus on heart-service ap. Gratian I. Dist. xcii. Decret. Greg. IX. Lib. iii. Tit. xli.

CHAPTER XCIII.

HOLY PLACES.

1. For the proper performance of the Public Worship of the Church (¹) a suitable building is necessary. Such a building is improperly called a Church (²) because it is the gathering place of the members of the Church.

2. Ever since Christianity ceased to be persecuted every Diocese and every Bishop has had its Church, which as being the place where the Bishop usually ministers, and where he has his *seat* or *cathedra*, is called his Cathedral Church. All the other buildings in a Diocese in which services are ministered are lesser or subsidiary Churches and none may be used as such without the Bishop's leave first had and obtained (³).

3. In the Cathedral Church (the arrangements of which have been followed in Collegiate and Parochial Churches to a great extent) a distinction is made between the part reserved for the use of the Clergy (⁴) and the part open for the use of the faithful generally. The former is called the

---

(¹) Concil. Aurelian. ap. Gratian III. Dist. i. c. 9, Concil Bracarense, *Ibid.* c. 10.

(²) Decret. Greg. IX. Lib. iii. Tit. xlviii. xlix.

(³) Concil. Aurelian. Can. 3, A.D. 824, ap. Gratian III. Dist. i. c. 33 ; vi. Synodus, Can. 31, A.D. 692, *Ibid.* c. 34.

(⁴) Decret. Greg. IX. Lib. iii. Tit. i. c. 1.

B

Choir in a Cathedral Church. In a Collegiate or Parish Church it is commonly called the Chancel because divided off from the rest by *Cancelli.*

4. In the earlier Cathedrals which followed the form of a basilica and had an apsidal end, the Clergy sat round the apse, the Bishop's seat being in the middle at the extreme end ([1]) whilst the Altar stood in front of the apse between the Clergy and the people.

5. In later times and in lesser Churches it was usual to divide the Choir or Chancel into two parts, called respectively the Choir and the Sanctuary, the Choir being the part in which the Clergy had their fixed seats according to their ecclesiastical rank, the Sanctuary being the place for the Altar and those there ministering. Within the Sanctuary the only rank allowed is that belonging to the officiator's office.

([1]) Concil. Carthag. iv. Can. 35 ap. Gratian I. Dist. xcv. c. 10. Episcopus in ecclesia et in consensu presbyterorum sublimior sedeat.

CHAPTER XCIV.

THE BENEDICTION AND CONSECRATION OF CHURCHES.

1. BEFORE a building can be used for the Eucharistic Service in any Diocese, whether permanently as a Parish Church or Parochial Chapelry, or temporarily in an emergency, it is necessary that the leave of the Bishop be first asked and obtained (¹).

In the case of a building which is only intended to be used temporarily, it is sufficient that the Bishop's leave be given by a simple License.

2. When such a building is intended to be used permanently as a Church, this may be done by a ceremony called Benediction, which is the dedication of the building to holy purposes (²). Benediction may be performed by a Priest properly authorised to perform it.

3. Consecration which should follow, though it was

(¹) Gratian III. Dist. i. c. 33, 34, 35. No money payment may be made for consecration. See Concil. Cabilonense. Can. 16, A.D. 813. ap. Gratian, Caus. i. Qu. i. c. 106. Concil. Bracarens. ii. Can. 5, A.D. 572, ap Gratian, Caus. i. Qu. ii. c. 1. Gregorius ap. Gratian, Caus. i. Qu. iv. c. 11 : Ecclesia quae pactione consecrata fuerit, potius execrata quam consecrata dici debet. Decret. Greg. IX. Lib iii. Tit. xl.

(²) Concil. Triburiense ap. Gratian III. Dist. i. c. 12. Missarum solennia non ubique sed in locis ab Episcopo consecratis vel ubi ipse permiserit, celebranda esse censemus. *Ibid.* c. 9, 11, 13, 14, 15, 25.

often deferred for a long time (¹), is a much more solemn rite (²). It is exclusively an Episcopal Act, and consists in anointing the building with Holy Oil, and it also requires the keeping of a Vigil or Wake and the Celebration of the Eucharist (³), and is ordered not to take place without relics (⁴). Twelve crosses are cut in the walls to mark the Dedication. By Consecration the ground and buildings are hallowed. And such is the effect of this hallowing that so long as any part of the buildings remain the place is still considered consecrated, nor is any new

(¹) By a Constitution of Othobon ap. Athon 7. it is enacted : " The dedication of Churches is known to have had its beginning under the Old Testament etc. . . Now because we have seen and heard, that so wholesome a mystery is contemned or least neglected by some ; having found many Churches, and some of those Cathedrals which although they have been built of old time, yet have not as yet been consecrated with the oil of sanctification ; therefore, being desirous to remedy so dangerous a neglect we do decree, that all Cathedral, Conventual and Parochial Churches which are now built, and the walls thereof perfected, be consecrated by the Diocesan Bishops or others authorised by them within two years ; and let it be so done within the like time in all Churches hereafter to be built." A constitution of Othobon ap. Athon 83 enacts : " The Rector or Vicar of an unconsecrated Church shall apply to the Bishop, if it can conveniently be done, otherwise to the Archdeacon that he may apply to the Bishop within a year after the building of the Church, for the consecration thereof ; upon pain that such Rector, Vicar, or Archdeacon making default shall be suspended from his office till he comply ; and the Bishop shall exact nothing therefor but the accustomed Procuration."

(²) Felix ap. Gratian III. Dist. i. c, 11. Concil. Meldense, *Ibid.* c. 18.

(³) Hyginus ap. Gratian III. Dist. i. c. 3.

(⁴) Gregorii Dialogus III. c. 30 ap. Gratian III. Dist. i. c. 22. Concil. Africanum, Can. 50, *Ibid.* c. 26. When a Church ceased to be used as such the relics were to be removed. See Gratian Caus. xvi. Qu. vii. c. 35 and 36.

consecration permitted unless it be polluted by bloodshed or other offence. (¹)

4. Certain privileges attach to consecrated places (²), which are considered so sacred that the remains of things consecrated to God, whether Church materials or vestments, are not to be diverted to secular purposes (³) but when done with to be burnt. No fee may be demanded for consecrating a Church (⁴)   .

(¹) Concil. Nicæn. ap. Gratian III. Dist. i. c. 20. Vigilius, *Ibid.* c. 24. Concil. Martini, *Ibid.* c. 29. Decret. Greg. IX. Lib. iii. Tit. xl. Sext. Decret. Lib. iii. Tit. xxi.

(²) See authorities ap. Gratian, Caus. xvii, Qu. iv. c. 82-86. Extrav. Com. Lib. iii. Tit. xiii.

(³) Hyginus. ap. Gratian III. Dist. i. c. 38.

(⁴) Concil. Bracarens. ii. Can. 5 ap. Gratian Caus. i. Qu. ii. c, 1. Conc. Cabil, c, 16, *Ibid.* Qu. i. c. 106. Decret, Greg. IX. Lib. v. Tit. iii. c. 9.

CHAPTER XCV.

HOLY TIMES.—FEASTS AND FASTS.

1. THE observance of certain days and seasons as Holy times ([1]) is a practice coeval with the existence of Christianity. The institution of some such times is of Apostolic origin, that of others is of ecclesiastical ordering. Sunday, Easter, Lent, and Pentecost have been kept from Apostolic times. Christmas and the Festival of the Trinity, the Feasts of Martyrs and Confessors, are of subsequent ecclesiastical appointment.

2. Sunday was kept as a Holy day ([2]) from the very first in weekly remembrance of the resurrection of the Church's Founder. It did not, however, at first supersede the Sabbath, which was kept as a day of rest by such Christians as still adhered to Jewish traditions. There was, however, this difference between the two, that Sunday was kept as a day of rejoicing or Feast day, whereas Saturday was kept as the Sabbath, as a day of asceticism and rest from work. Friday, too, was remembered as the weekly commemoration of Christ's death.

Easter ([3]) and Lent ([4]) were greater seasons of ecclesiastical observance. So, too, was Pentecost or Whitsuntide,

([1]) Concil. Lugdunens. ap. Gratian III. Dist. iii. c. 1.

. ([2]) S. Matt. xxviii. 1.

([3]) Gratian III. Dist. iii. c. 22 to 26.

([4]) Authorities, ap. Gratian III. Dist. iii. c. 6, 7, 8, 9-17, and iii. Dist.

all of which date from Apostolic times. Easter, as being the annual commemoration of the Christian's deliverance from the wilderness of the world to a new life through the resurrection of Christ, was kept as a time of rejoicing and as the greatest Festival of the Church. It was considered the Christian equivalent of the Jewish Feast of the Passover. Lent, being regarded as a season of mortification for sin and of preparation for the coming deliverance, was treated as a Fast. Whitsuntide was the Festival of Catholicism commemorating the outpouring of the Spirit on all flesh.

3. In addition to the above Feasts and Fasts (¹), a number of others were introduced into the use of the Church in the fifth and succeeding centuries. Such were the Birth Day of the Saviour or Christmas Day and the Epiphany, introduced in the Western and Eastern Churches respectively in the 4th century, the Festival of the Annunciation, of the Purification, the Assumption and other Festivals of the Blessed Virgin Mary, the feast of S. Michael and of the Trinity, the last named not introduced until the 14th century, and the several Festivals of Apostles, Martyrs and Confessors, all of which were established with the view of commemorating for the glory of God the great Saints He has caused to grow up in His Church. For this reason, too, the images of the Saints and relics were held in reverence (²).

v. c. 16-20, and i. Dist. iv. c. 4-6.   In case of necessity, not otherwise, warfare was tolerated in Lent. See Gratian, Caus. xxiii. Qu. viii. c. 15.

(¹) On the observance of Fasts see Decret. Greg. IX. Lib. ii. Tit. ix. and Lib. iii. Tit. xlvi.

(²) Gratian III. Dist. iii. c. 27-29. Sext. Decret. Lib. iii. Tit. xxii.

On the other hand the Rogation Days (¹), or days of intercession for a blessing on the fruits of the earth, and the Ember Days (²), or Four Seasons of Intercession for a

Clement. Lib. iii. Tit. xvi. Extrav. Com.Lib. iii. Tit. xii.

(¹) Concil. Aurelianense i. Can. 29. ap. Gratian III. Dist. iii. c. 3.

(²) Ember is usually supposed to be a corruption of Tempora. As to the Seasons for ordaining see Docret. Greg. IX. Lib. i. Tit. xi.

According to the use of Sarum in the 15th century Feasts were divided into:

1. Doubles which were of four kinds:

    (1) Principal Doubles—Christmas day, the Epiphany, Easter Day, Ascension Day, Whitsun Day, the Assumption, the Anniversary of the Place, and the Dedication of the Church.

    (2) Greater Doubles—Trinity Sunday, Corpus Christi, the Purification, the Visitation of the Blessed Virgin Mary, the Feast of Relics, the Name of Jesus, the Nativity of our Lady, and All Saints' Day.

    (3) Lesser Doubles—The 3 days after Christmas, the Circumcision, the 2 days after Easter and Whitsun Days, Low Sunday, Lady Day, the Invention of the Holy Rood; the Nativity of S. John Baptist, the Feas of SS. Peter and Paul, the transfiguration, Holy Cross Day, and the Conception of our Lady.

    (4) Inferior Doubles—The Feasts of SS. Andrew, Thomas, Thomas of Canterbury, Matthias, Mark, Philip and James, James the Great, Bartholomew, Matthew, Luke, Simon and Jude, Gregory, Ambrose, George, Augustine Apostle of England, Augustine Bishop of Hippo, Michaelmas Day, S. Jerome, the translation of S. Edward, King Confessor, the Chair of S. Peter at Antioch and All Souls' Day.

2. Simples which were either:

    (1) Moveable *i.e.* all feasts of Nine Lessons and certain feasts of three which occur in Eastertide, called three with Rulers, Octave Days, and Days in an Octave with Rulers.

    (2) Immoveable including all others.

3. Sundays which were again divided into:

    (1) Principal Sundays—Advent Sunday, Passion Sunday, Palm Sunday.

    (2) Greater Sundays—The 2nd, 3rd, and 4th Sunday in Advent, and all Sundays in Septuagesima and Lent to Passion Sunday.

blessing on those about to be admitted to the Church's
Ministry, were ordered to be treated as days of Abstinence
or Fast Days.

(3) Lesser Sundays—Those when Histories begin, and the 5th
Sunday after Easter.

(4) Inferior Sundays—The Sundays after the Octave of the
Epiphany until Septuagesima, those from the Octave of Low
Sunday, to the 5th Sunday after Easter, and all the Sundays
after Trinity until Advent.

CHAPTER XCVI.

OBSERVANCE OF HOLY TIMES.

1. In the Apostolic age, it was the daily use of Christians to meet together to shew forth the Lord's death by the breaking of bread and prayer (¹). At the beginning of the second century these regular meetings appear to have been confined to Sundays and other occasional days (²). After the cessation of persecution in the 4th century and the establishment of Christianity as the state religion, the aim of the Bishops and their Clergy was to re-establish the Apostolic use, and this practice gradually obtained in all Cathedral Churches in the West (³), with perhaps occasional interruptions caused by the unsettledness of the times or the worldliness of the Clergy.

2. It was otherwise in lesser Churches subsidiary to the Cathedral. In these the Eucharistic service was ministered on Sundays and certain Festival days, so far as was possible with the number of clergy available. When,

---

(¹) Acts ii. 42 : ἦσαν δὲ προσκαρτεροῦντες τῇ διδαχῇ τῶν ἀποστόλων καὶ τῇ κοινωνίᾳ καὶ τῇ κλάσει τοῦ ἄρτου καὶ ταῖς προσευχαῖς, and ii. 46 : καθ, ἡμέραν τε προσκαρτεροῦντες ὁμοθυμαδὸν ἐν τῷ ἱερῷ, κλῶντές τε κατ' οἶκον ἄρτον·

(²) See Justin Martyr i Apol. c. 67, and Pliny's letter x. 96.

(³) In the Eastern Church συνάξεις appear not to have been held daily but only on Saturdays and Sundays. See Socrates' *Eccl. Hist.* Lib. vi. c. 8.

however, Parochial Churches were founded, and became established sub-units of a Diocese with a limited ordinary jurisdiction of their own under the Bishop, it was ordered that their services should follow those of the Cathedral Church. In Collegiate and Parochial Churches where there were many clergy, a daily Eucharistic service became the practice. In those under the charge of a single Priest, it sufficed that the Divine Office was used on Sundays and the greater Festivals (¹).

3. The particular Feasts and Fasts to be kept and the manner of keeping them are matters within the administrative rule of each Diocesan Bishop with the advice of his clergy. Every Diocese in addition to the greater Feasts of general observance has its own Feasts of Diocesan observance. A Bishop cannot make any change therein without the advice of his Chapter; but every year on the first day of Lent a Pastoral should be issued by the Bishop to all the faithful of his Diocese, giving instructions as to the time and manner of keeping the appointed Feasts and Fasts.

4. It is a general rule that on the greatest Festivals all the faithful are required to attend the Eucharistic service either in their Bishop's Cathedral or in their own Parish Church, but not in a Parochial Chapelry (²); and

(¹) Decret. Greg. IX. Lib. iii. Tit. xxix. o. 3.

(²) Concil. Agathen. Can. 21, A.D. 506, ap. Gratian III. Dist. i. o. 135 : Si quis. . . . oratorium in agro habere voluerit, reliquis festivitatibus, ut ibi missas audiat propter fatigationem familiæ justa ordinatione permittimus. Pascha vero, Natali Domini, Epiphania Domini, Ascensione Domini, Pentecoste et Natali S. Joannis Baptistæ, et si qui maximi dies in festivitatibus habentur, non nisi in civitatibus aut in parochiis audiant. Gratian Caus. vii. Qu. i. o. 29.

whatever may be tolerated or excused in the case of the Laity, that all of the clergy and monks shall communicate at least once a month (¹). Ecclesiastical Courts are forbidden to hold their sittings on all the greater Feasts and Fasts (²).

5. Besides the general Feasts prescribed in the Diocese, two Festivals ought to be kept in every place with the highest solemnity. There are (1) the Dedication Feast of the Parish Church (³), and (2) the Feast of the Patron, Saint or Title.

(¹) Concil. Vien. ap. Clementin. III. Tit. x. c. i.

(²) Gratian, Caus. xv. Qu. v.

(³) Pseudo-Isidore ap. Gratian III. Dist. i. c. 16 and 17. See the language of Gregory to Augustine in Beda I. c. 30, respecting the day of the Dedication.

DIVISION III.

MEDIÆVAL AND MODERN ADMINISTRATION OF CHURCH DISCIPLINE.

CHAPTER XCVII.

EXTENSION OF THE CHURCH'S JUDICIAL FUNCTIONS.

1. WITH the acquisition of property and the growth of temporal power a very considerable extension of the Church's judicial powers· came about in Mediæval times, causing a large number of cases to be brought before ecclesiastical tribunals which had previously been elsewhere disposed of, and necessitating strict rules of procedure.

Such cases were divided either into (1) criminal and (2) civil cases ; or otherwise into (1) spiritual, (2) mixed, and (3) temporal cases.

2. Any offence against faith or morals is called a crime. Any dispute between Christians turning upon the rights and duties of one person towards another is termed a civil case ; such as a dispute between parent and child, between a bishop and one of his clergy, between a parish priest and one of his flock.

3. A spiritual case is one concerned solely with spiritual matters, of which there are usually said to be seven : (1)

cases concerning faith and morals; (2) cases concerning the granting or withholding of the sacraments; (3) cases as to the validity of Christian matrimony; (4) cases relating to public worship; (5) cases concerning the duties of clergy as clergy; (6) cases relating to regulars; and (7) cases relating to ecclesiastical censures. These as being spiritual are exclusively reserved for the spiritual judge.

A mixed case is one concerning a spiritual office to which temporal property is attached, such as the right to a benefice or tithes. In these cases, unless the civil authority recognises the action of the spiritual judge, many anomalies may result, such as one holding the spiritual charge of a Parish while another holds the benefice attached thereto (¹).

A temporal case is one concerning a temporal matter, although spiritual accidents may be annexed thereto. Such is the right of patronage. Albeit the spiritual judge claims to have cognisance in such a case, yet his judgment is usually disallowed by the temporal courts.

4. In all circumstances the procedure of the ecclesiastical tribunal involves three things :—

(1) That the matter be properly brought before a tribunal of competent jurisdiction.

(2) That it be duly heard and clearly established there.

(3) That a canonical sentence be passed and not appealed from.

(¹) In the 13th century the Church claimed the cognisance of many cases which are now disposed of in the temporal Courts. See Decret. Greg. IX. Lib. ii. Tit. i.

CHAPTER XCVIII.

COURTS CHRISTIAN.

1. In the first ages of the Church all judgments were summary, *i.e.* given without judicial forms. The Bishop was the judge, and his presbyters acted as accessors in dealing with any subject of his Diocese. In dealing with a Bishop the Metropolitan was the judge and his Comprovincials sat with him.

2. In later times the Bishop heard causes by his Vicar-General or Official Principal, and the Clergy ceased to act as his assistants. In like manner the Metropolitan and his Comprovincials appointed an Official to act for the Province before whom all cases were brought on appeal. Following their example Archdeacons appointed Officials to settle disputes respecting the temporalities under their charge. Hence there are Courts of the Province, Courts of the Bishop, and Archdeacon's Courts, each of them being presided over by its proper Official acting for and on behalf of the Prelate by whom he is appointed. These several Officials are called Spiritual Judges, and the Courts over which they preside Courts Christian or Ecclesiastical Courts, and they correspond in jurisdiction with the several ranks of the Hierarchy (¹).

(¹) Decret. Greg. IX. Lib. ii. Tit. i. Sext. Decret. Lib. ii. Tit. i. Clement. Lib. ii. Tit. i.

3. In proceeding in any of these Courts there are three principal persons (¹) concerned : (1) the Judge who hears the case, (2) the Complainant or promotor, (3) the Defendant or the accused (²). Witnesses are only accessories. To support proceedings in them, therefore, three things are necessary : (1) the Court must be one of competent jurisdiction, (2) the Complainant must have a *locus standi*, (3) the Defendant must be amenable to the Jurisdiction.

4. These requisites being fulfilled the Judge may decide the case in one of two ways, either (1) by the *Ordinary* procedure of the Court (³), or (2) *Summarily*. If he act summarily he must take care to inform himself of both sides of the question, so that his sentence may be a real sentence and not merely an opinion (⁴) to be set aside on appeal.

5. When the punishment is fixed by the Canon Law the Judge has no option but to award it. In other cases it requires prudence as well as charity to determine the sentence ; for often the Church were better served by admonition than by vengeance (⁵).

(¹) In civil cases the accuser and accused may appear by deputy, but not in criminal cases. See the authorities, ap. Gratian, Caus. v. Qu. iii.,

(²) It is not competent for one and same person to be both judge and accuser. See the authorities, ap. Gratian, Caus. iv. Qu. iv.

(³) Decret. Greg. IX. Lib. ii. Tit. i. c. 9.

(⁴) On rash sentences see authorities, ap. Gratian, Caus. ii. Qu. i. c. 20 ; Caus. xi. Qu. iii. c. 45 to 64, 66 to 73.

(⁵) Augustinus De Poenit, c. 12, ap. Gratian, Caus. ii. Qu. i. c. 18 ; Multi corriguntur ut Petrus ; multi tolerantur ut Judas. Augustinus, ap. Gratian, Caus. xxiii. Qu. iv. c. 24, Ambrosius, *Ibid.* c. 26.

CHAPTER XCIX.

JUDGES OF COMPETENT JURISDICTION.

1. An Ecclesiastical Judge is one who has lawful authority in the Church to hear and decide ecclesiastical cases. There are many varieties of such officers.

(1) Some are judges by *divine 'right*—This is the case of the Collective Episcopate in General Council assembled; others are of *ecclesiastical appointment* only, such as Diocesan Bishops.

(2) Some are *Ordinaries*, having authority to judge attached to the office they hold. Such is the Archbishop's Official Principal, and the Chancellor of a Bishop; others are *Delegates* acting for Ordinaries, as the Commissioners appointed to hold an inquiry under the Church Discipline Act.

(3) Some are Judges of *competent jurisdiction*, to whom a cognisance of a matter belongs by virtue of their office ; others are *Arbitrators* appointed by the sole will of the parties to decide a particular case.

(4) Some are Judges of *first instance* ; others are Judges to whom a case is brought on appeal.

2. For an Ecclesiastical Judge to be in a position lawfully to decide a case, two things are requisite : (1) He must be a Judge of competent jurisdiction; (2) There must

S

be nothing to disqualify him from adjudicating on that case, such as having been previously called in to advise upon it, having had a similar case of his own, or having an interest in the case ([1]).

3. For a Court to be one of competent jurisdiction ([2]), the matter in dispute or cause of action must have arisen within the local limits of the jurisdiction before which it is brought ([3]). This it may do in one of several ways:

    (1) The accused person's residence may be within the limits of the jurisdiction before which he is arraigned ([4]).

    (2) The cause of action may have arisen within those limits ([5]), as when a person not residing there has committed an offence or contracted an obligation within them.

    (3) The matter in dispute may be situated within them.

Should a person be cited to appear before a Court which cannot allege any one of these reasons, he may either decline to obey the citation, or obey under protest.

([1]) It has been decided in Ex parte Medevin and Hurst (1853) 1 El. and Bla. 609, that the fact of the Chancellor being able to award a Bishop his costs should the decision be given in his favour, does not give the Bishop such an interest in the case as to disqualify his Chancellor from hearing it at the suit of the Bishop. Gratian, Caus. iii. Qa. v. c. 15.

([2]) Decret. Greg. IX. Lib. ii. Tit. ii.

([3]) Pseudo-Isidorus ap Gratian, Caus. xi. Qu. i. c. 48. Sext. Decret. Lib. ii. Tit. ii. Clement. Lib. ii. Tit. ii.

([4]) Gratian, Caus. iii. Qu. vi. c. 2, 4, 17; also Caus. vi. Qu. iii., also Caus. ix. Qu. ii. Decret. Greg. IX. Lib. ii. Tit. ii. c. 1 and 18.

([5]) Gratian, Caus. iii. Qu. vi. c. 1 and 18. Decret. Greg. IX. Lib. ii. Tit. ii. c. 3.

No complaint therefore should be lodged except with a judge who has jurisdiction. If there are several such, the complainant may invite the assistance of any one of them.

4. An accused person may also canonically refuse a judge otherwise competent ([1]), on alleging a proper cause in writing at the time of receiving the citation. The principal cause for which such a refusal is allowed, is the personal enmity of the judge for the accused ([2]). If a judge is refused for a good cause, the Prelate must appoint a special commissary to try the case.

5. The duties of an Ecclesiastical Judge are fourfold : (1) To bring sufficient learning to bear on the hearing of a case ; (2) To expedite it without delay, and without fear or favour ; (3) To pass judgment according to law, and not according to his view of what the law should be ; (4) Only to accept as facts what have been satisfactorily proved to be such.

([1]) Infames judices esse non possunt. So Gratian, Caus. iii. Qu. vii. c. 1. There are three disqualifications for acting as judges : (1) natural disqualifications, such as blindness, deafness, &c.; (2) legal, such as being exempt : (3) moral, such as being women and slaves.

([2]) Gratian. Caus. iii. Qu. v. c. 15.

CHAPTER C.

PLAINTIFFS AND DEFENDANTS.—PROOTORS AND ADVOCATES.

1. Not all persons are capable of taking part in a suit as plaintiffs or defendants ([1]). Disqualified persons are the following :—(1) Infants, madmen, and lunatics ; (2) young people under fourteen, unless they appear by a Curator or next friend, or their evidence is absolutely necessary to prove a criminal charge ; (3) women, except by their own wish in civil cases, or in criminal cases to obtain redress for their own wrongs ; (4) persons excommunicate.

2. No one can be compelled to act as plaintiff against his will, but every defendant can be compelled to appear, or in default of appearance the case can go on and be adjudicated upon in his absence. Personal appearance cannot, however, be insisted upon, except when the Statute Law enforces it, or in criminal cases ([2]). It is otherwise sufficient that an appearance be entered by a proctor.

3. A Proctor ([3]) is one who stands in the place of his principal, having been by him properly appointed to that

---

([1]) Called technically Actor and Reus. Decret. Greg. IX. Lib. ii. Tit. xix., Gratian, Caus. ii. Qn. i. c. 14 ; Caus. iii. Qu. v. c. 4 ; Caus. iv. Qu. i. c. i. and Qu. ii. Sext. Decret. Lib. ii. Tit. i.

([2]) Governed in England by Stat. 3 and 4 Vict. c. 86.

([3]) See Decret. Greg. IX. Lib. i. Tit. xxxviii.

office (¹). A Proctor differs from an Advocate because he conducts a case, whereas an Advocate only advises upon it; he differs also from a Curator, or next friend, because the Curator is appointed by the Court and a Proctor by a Suitor. A Proctor may be appointed either generally to represent his principal, or specially for some particular business; and either with ordinary powers or with extraordinary full powers. Whilst his authority lasts (²) he represents his principal to all intents and purposes, and is said to be Master of the Case or *dominus litis* (³).

4. An Advocate is one learned in the Canon and Civil Law (⁴), who assists another with advice and counsel in any

(¹) Decret. Greg. IX. Lib. ii. Tit. xxviii. c. 48. Sext. Decret. Lib. i. Tit. xix. Clement. Lib. i. Tit. x. In the Report of the Ecclesiastical Commissioners, 1832, it is said: "Proctors in the ecclesiastical and admiralty courts discharge duties similar to those of solicitors and attornies in other courts." According to 2 Dom. 583, Proctors are officers established to represent in judgment the parties who empower them (by warrant under their hands called a *proxy*) to appear for them. A Proxy is an instrument signed by the principal, attested by two witnesses, accredited by a Notary Public, and deposited in the registry of the court. The proctor until such power be withdrawn is *dominus litis*.

(²) A Proctor's powers may be withdrawn, see Decret. Greg. IX Lib. i. Tit. xxxviii. c. 3, 4, and 13.

(³) Stat. 5 Geo. II. c. 18 s. 2 forbids a Proctor from being a Justice of the Peace; 33 and 34 Vict. c. 27 imposes a stamp duty of £25 on his admission to office. 53 Geo. III. c. 127 forbids Proctors from allowing their names to be used by unqualified persons. 10 Geo. IV. c. 7. s. 16 forbids Roman Catholics from acting as Proctors. Canon 129 of 1603 imposes restrictions on the exercise of their office by Proctors. 33 and 34 Vict. c. 28, s. 20 enables attornies or solicitors " to perform all such acts as appertain solely to the office of a Proctor in any ecclesiastical court other than the Provincial Courts of the Archbishop of Canterbury and of York and the Diocesan Court of the Bishop of London."

(⁴) According to the Report of the Ecclesiastical Commissioners, 1832: "No person can be admitted a member, or allowed to practise as an

judicial matter, and represents him in pleadings before a Tribunal. He does not, however, represent him generally as a Proctor does, nor elsewhere except before a Tribunal, so that his acts do not bind a client as the acts of a Proctor do. The duties of an Advocate are fourfold : (1) To possess sufficient knowledge ; (2) to decline to undertake an unjust cause ; (3) not to disclose his client's affairs to his adversary ; and (4) not to take more than a fair return for his assistance.

Advocate in the Courts at Doctors' Commons without having first taken the degree of Doctor of Laws in one of the English Universities." In former times the admission of Advocates was a papal prerogative. As such it appears to have been exercised in England by the Archbishop of Canterbury as the born legate of the Pope, and with him it now rests in England. There is a stamp duty of £50 on admission. As a matter of practice the functions of an Advocate are now often discharged by barristers. The Stat. 3 and 4 Vict. c. 86, s. 7 requires that in criminal proceedings instituted against a clergyman the Articles drawn up against him must be signed by an Advocate practising in Doctors' Commons.

CHAPTER CI.

COMPLAINANTS IN A CIVIL CASE.

1. THERE is this difference between a Civil and a Criminal case, that any person may be the Complainant in a a Civil case, whereas only certain persons can act as Complainants in a Criminal case (¹).

2. In a Civil case any person is competent to bring a complaint against another in the Courts Christian, provided he can fulfil two conditions. He must (1) be able and willing to carry the case through to a decision (²), and (2) he must be prepared to take the Oath of Calumny (³), whereby he pledges himself that his action is not malicious.

3. A Civil complaint is introduced by presenting to the Judge a writing or Libel (⁴) containing a short account of the matter complained of, and praying for a particular sentence by way of remedy. Having once been handed in the Libel may not be changed, but it may be amended at least once during the proceedings.

(¹) Decret. Greg. IX. Lib. v. Tit. i. c. 1. Si legitimus non fuerit accusator, non fatigetur accusatus.

(²) Pseudo-Isidore permits a man to withdraw from a suit, ap. Gratian, Caus. ii. Qu. vi. c. 18.

(³) Decret. Greg. IX. Lib. ii. Tit. vii. Canons of Otho, 1237. 2 Inst. 658 ; 12 Rep. 27.

(⁴) Decret. Greg. IX. Lib. ii. Tit. iii. Must be in writing. *Ibid.* c. 1

4. The effect of presenting a Libel is threefold : (1) It bars a claim by prescription ; (2) It points out a remedy, and so determines the sentence ; (3) It pledges the complainant to carry his case through to a decision.

5. Should the accused not plead guilty ('), the Court must before hearing the case administer to both parties the Oath of Calumny, whereby they pledge themselves that both action and defence are *bona fide*, and not prompted by malice (*).

(¹) It is the accuser's business to prove the case, not the accused person's to prove his innocence. See Gregorius ap. Gratian, Caus. vi. Qu. v.

(²) This oath may be required of a Bishop. Decret. Greg. IX. Lib. ii. Tit. vii. c. 7. Sext. Decret. Lib. ii. Tit. iv.

CHAPTER CII.

CRIMINAL PROCEDURE.—ACCUSATION.

1. THERE are three modes of proceeding criminally in ecclesiastical cases : (1) by publicly bringing a charge, called *Accusation;* (2) by privately giving information of an offence, called *Denunciation;* (3) by setting on foot inquiry where scandal exists, called *Inquisition.* All these methods come under the cognisance of the Outer Tribunal, and belong to the Bishop's Contentious Jurisdiction (¹).

2. The essential features of the mode of proceeding by Accusation are these :—(1) It is resorted to for the purpose of public vengeance (²), not for the amendment of the offender. Hence the accused must first have been warned (³). (2) The accuser takes upon himself the onus of proof (⁴). (3) Although anyone, conspirators and those excommunicated excepted (⁵), is competent to come forward as accuser, yet to

---

(¹) See Chap. xxxi.

(²) Decret. Greg. IX. Lib. v. Tit. i. c. 16.

(³) Decret. Greg. IX. Lib. v. Tit. i. c. 2 and 20. Concil. Lat. iii. in Decret. Greg. IX. Lib. ii. Tit. xxviii. c. 26, and Lib. iii. Tit. ii. c. 4 and 6.

(⁴) The accuser may not be an enemy by Decret. Greg. IX. Lib. v. Tit. i. c. 7, 10, 13, 19, 20, Gratian, Caus. v. Qu. v. Dig. Lib. xlvii. ap. Gratian, Caus. ii. Qu. i. c. 14. Prohibentur alii accusare propter sexum et ætatem ut mulier et pupillus; alii propter sacramentum ut qui stipendium merent.

(⁵) Gratian, Caus. iii. Qu. iv. c. 5.

guard against malicious prosecution an accuser is required by the common law of the Church to bind himself to submit to the same punishment which the offence charged would have entailed on a guilty person, in case he should fail to establish his charge ([1]).

3. Prior to the 11th century procedure by public Accusation appears to have been the course usually adopted. It was, however, then found to be attended by serious disadvantages, among which the following stand prominent : (1) a public accusation often causes more scandal, and so does more harm to the Church, than the offence itself ; (2) it often violates the rule of charity by aiming at vindictive punishment, when the amendment of the offender is both possible and probable ; (3) it publicly damages an offender's reputation for the future ([2]). Hence this mode of procedure is not allowed except in grave cases of public notoriety or when scandal exists ([3]).

4. An accusation is made by a written charge or Libel split up into Articles ([4]). The Libel must be in due form, giving the name of the Judge, the names of the accuser and

---

([1]) Concil. Eliberitan. Can. 75, A.D. 310, ap. Gratian, Caus. ii. Qu. iv. c. 4. : Si quis episcopum, aut presbyterum aut diaconum falsis criminibus appetierit et probare non potuerit, nec in fine dandam ei communionem censemus. Pseudo-Isidore, *Ibid.* Qu. 2. c. 2. Calumniator si in accusatione defecerit, talionem recipiat. *Ibid.* Caus. ii. Qu. viii. c. 4. Hadrianus, Epist. i. A.D. 361, Gregorius v. Epist. 30. ap. Gratian, Caus. v. Qu. i. c. 1 and 2, also Gratian, Caus. v. Qu. vi. Decret. Greg. IX. Lib. v. Tit. ii. and Tit. 1. c. 16.

([2]) S. Liguor, Lib. iv. n. 247: Delinquens jus habet ad servandum suam famam.

([3]) See Caisson Manuale, vol. iv. p. 118, and 3 and 4 Vict. c. 86. Also Decret. Greg. IX. Lib. v. Tit. i. c. 9.

([4]) Gratian. Caus. ii. Qu. viii.c. 1.

the accused, and the nature of the offence with full particulars thereof. By common right there ought to be appended thereto a bond by the accuser confessing judgment for the penalty incurred should adequate proof not to be forthcoming of the charge ; but in some countries this bond has fallen into desuetude. Hence the received practice of the tribunals must be followed.

5. The effect of a public accusation is to render the accused unqualified for promotion until it has been disposed of. By the common law of the Church there is no limit of time to bar offences being made the subject of an accusation. The Roman Law, however, did not admit a charge being lodged in respect of incontinence committed more than five years, or of any other offence committed more than twenty years previously (¹). The English statute Law disallows proceedings for the soul's health in respect of incontinence committed more than eight months previously (²), or any proceedings for public vengeance in respect of any offence of older standing than two years (³), unless a conviction in a

---

(¹) See authorities in Caisson Manuale, vol. iv. p. 119.

(²) By 27 Geo. III. c. 44: No suit shall be brought in any ecclesiastical court for fornication or incontinence after the expiration of eight calendar months from the time when such offence shall have been committed ; nor for fornication at any time after the parties shall have lawfully intermarried. It was ruled by the House of Lords that this did not prevent the ordinary from purging the Church of an incontinent clerk, and that it only referred to proceedings for his soul's health. See *Burgoyne* v. *Free.* Add. 405 ; 2 Hagg. 406.

(³) By 3 and 4 Vict. c. 86. s. 20 : Every suit or proceeding against any such clerk in Holy Orders for any offence against the laws ecclesiastical shall be commenced within two years after the commission of the offence in respect of which the suit or proceeding shall be instituted and not afterwards. It has been ruled by the Privy Council that the com-

Common Law Court has been subsequently obtained and then only within six months of such conviction ([1]).

mencement of the suit dates from the service of the citation upon the accused clerk and not from the date of the issue of a preliminary commission. *Denison* v. *Ditcher*, Deane and Swabey's *Rep.* 334 ; 11 Moor. P. C. 824.

([1]) 3 and 4 Vict. c. 86. s. 20 : Provided always that whenever any such suit or proceeding shall be brought in respect of any offence for which a conviction shall have been obtained in any court of common law, such suit or proceeding may be brought against the person convicted at any time within six calendar months after such conviction, although more than two years shall have elapsed since the commission of the offence in respect of which such suit or proceding shall be so brought.

CHAPTER CIII.

CRIMINAL PROCEDURE.—DENUNCIATION.

1. DENUNCIATION consists in giving private information of another's offence to his superior without undertaking the onus of proof. If the information be given to obtain redress for some private wrong, it is called a *Complaint* ([1]).

2. Denunciation is of two kinds : (1) Paternal, or that ordered by the Gospel, and (2) Judicial. Paternal Denunciation is the giving private intimation of an offence to a superior as a *Father*, that he may give fatherly warning and admonition to the offender to amend his ways for his soul's health, according to the Gospel precept which requires private warning to precede notice to the Church ([2]). Judicial Denunciation ([3]) is giving information to a superior as a *Judge*, so that he may be in a position to proceed against the offender for public vengeance.

[1] Querela.

[2] S. Matt. xviii. 15, 16, 17 : Moreover if thy brother shall trespass against thee, go and tell him his fault between him and thee alone ; if he shall hear thee, thou hast gained thy brother. But if he will not hear thee, then take with thee one or two more, that in the mouth of two or three witnesses every word may be established. And if he shall neglect to hear them, tell it unto the Church. See Decret. Greg. IX. Lib. ii. Tit. i. c. 13.

[3] Decret. Greg. IX. Lib. ii. Tit. i. c. 13. Decret. Greg. IX. Lib. v. Tit. i. c. 2. A denunciatione repellitur qui non præmonuit.

3. No one is *bound* to give information of another's offence, unless: (1) it be a mortal sin; (2) is certainly known to an informer; and (3) unless the giving of information is likely to lead to some spiritual good. Yet every one is *bound* to give such information, if the offence, besides being a mortal sin and known to the informer, is also one which does spiritual harm to third parties. Accomplices are not, however, considered third parties (¹).

4. When a superior receives a Judicial information, it is his duty to act wisely according to the rule of charity remembering that an offender has as much right to his reputation as a complainant has to consideration. Hence he should first warn the offender in private (²), then, if necessary, admonish him before witnesses, and not proceed publicly unless he be satisfied; either (1) that the reform of the offender can no longer be hoped for; or (2) that the offence is so injurious to others that warning is out of place; or (3) unless the offence be one of public notoriety (³). Should he act otherwise, he commits a grave breach of charity, though not such a wrong for which there exists a remedy.

(¹) See Caisson Manuale. Vol. iv. p. 125, neither is their evidence receivable. Decret. Greg. IX. Lib. ii. Tit. xx. c. 10.

(²). See Concil. Agathens. ap. Decret. Greg. IX. Lib. v. Tit. xxriv. c. 2; Si quis presbyter negligens vitæ suæ, pravis exemplis mala de se suspicari permiserit, et populus et episcopo juramenti seu banno Christianitates adstrictus, infamiam ejus patefecerit certique accusatores criminis defuerint, admoneatur primum scorsum de Episcopo, deinde sub duobus vel tribus testibus, et si non emendaverit, in conventu presbyterorum episcopus cum increpatione publica admoneat. Si vero nec sic se. correverit, ab officio suspendatur usque ad condignam satisfactionem ne populus fidelium in eo scandalum patiatur.

(³) Decret. Greg. IX. Lib. iii. Tit. ii. c. 4, 6 and 8, also Tit. xxviii. c. 26.

CHAPTER CIV.

1. INQUISITION is procedure by inquiry, and is undertaken to ascertain whether a certain person is guilty of an offence or not. It is usually confined to the case of Clergy who are suspected to be guilty of any crime (¹).

2. Before inquiry is undertaken there should be either (1) strong grounds for suspecting guilt; or (2) information should have been received from an informer, alleging an offence; or (3) there should be shewn to exist scandal.

3. When an inquiry is set on foot, it may be conducted either privately or publicly. The rule of charity and respect for another's reputation require that inquiry should be conducted privately whenever that is practicable. When that is not practicable it must be done publicly. In such a matter, however, much depends on the discretion of a superior. Public inquiry always causes scandal in the Church, and because of the serious consequences which may follow, affecting the accused's civil rights, it is in England strictly regulated by Statute Law (²).

(¹) See Decret. Greg. IX. Lib. ii. Tit. xiv. c. 8.

(²) By 3 and 4 Vict. c. 86, s. 3 : In every case of any Clerk in Holy Orders of the United Church of England and Ireland, who may be *charged with any offence against the laws ecclesiastical*, or concerning whom there may *exist scandal or evil report* as having offended against the said laws, it shall be lawful for the bishop of the diocese within which the offence is alleged or reported to have been committed, on the

4. When no adequate proof is forthcoming of a suspected offence, it is competent for the Judge to administer the Oath of Purgation (¹), and thus free the person suspected from the scandal caused by the public inquiry.

application of any party complaining thereof, or if he shall think fit *of his own mere motion*, to issue a commission under his hand and seal to five persons, of whom one shall be his Vicar-General or an Archdeacon or Rural Dean within the Diocese, for the purpose of making inquiry as to he grounds of such charge or report.

(¹) Decret. Greg. Lib. v. Tit. xxxiv. Gregorius II. A.D. 726, ap. Gratian, Caus. ii. Qu. v. c. 5 : Presbyter vel quilibet sacerdos si a populo accusatus fuerit, et certi non fuerint testes. . jus-jurandum in medio erit, et illum testem proferat de innocentiæ suæ puritate, cui nuda et aperta sint omnia. Concil. Agathense ap. Gratian, Caus. ii. Qu. v. c. 12. Leo scribens ad Carolum Magnum, A.D. 803, *Ibid.* c. 19. Concil. Wormaciense, Can. 10, *Ibid.* c. 26 : Si episcopo aut presbytero causa criminalis, hoc est homicidium, adulterium, furtum et maleficium imputatum fuerit, pro singulis missam celebrare debet et communicare et de singulis sibi imputatis innocentem se ostendere. Quod si non fecerit, quinquennio a liminibus ecclesiæ extraneus habeatur.

CHAPTER CV.

AMENABILITY OF THE ACCUSED.

1. A CASE may fall through, though properly introduced, owing to the Defendant not being amenable to the Jurisdiction. As a Bishop could not be cited to appear in an Archdeacon's Court, nor a Metropolitan in that of a Suffragan, nor a Prelate in his own Court ([1]), so in England the Sovereign would not seem to be amenable to any spiritual court.

2. Without an accuser no one can be condemned, however guilty he may be ([2]); nor can any accused person be punished unless he either pleads guilty or is proved to be guilty ([3]). A confession made before a secular judge cannot be used against a Clerk before an Ecclesiastical tribunal ([4]). A poor man does not deserve pity when he is in a bad case because of his own misdoing ([5]); neither is the Church to blame for using strict measures towards such as are proved guilty of heresy ([6]). The onus of proof is on the accuser, not of disproof on the accused ([7]).

([1]) Gratian, Caus. vi. Qu. ii.
([2]) Ambrosius ap. Gratian, Caus. xxiii. Qu. iv. c. 31.
([3]) Nicolaus ap. Gratian, Caus. xv. Qu. v. c. 2. Caus. ii. Qu. i.
([4]) Decret. Greg. IX. Lib. ii. Tit. i. c. 4. Nor are verdicts of Courts of Law admissable as evidence. 3 Hag. 260, 264, 292. But see Chap. cii. 5
([5]) Augustinus ap. Gratian, Caus. xxiii. Qu. iv. c. 34.
([6]) Augustinus ap. Gratian. Caus. xxiii. Qu. iv. c. 38, 39-42,
([7]) Gratian, Caus. vi. Qu. v.

T

CHAPTER CVI.

CRIMINAL PROCEDURE.—PROMOTING THE JUDGE'S OFFICE.

THE procedure in a Criminal Case before an Ecclesiastical Judge follows in a great measure the procedure usual according to the Civil Law. It may, therefore, be divided into three parts, each of which must be considered separately. These are : (1) The Introduction of the case, commonly called *Promoting the Office of the Judge ;* (2) the Hearing of a case, commonly called *the Trial ;* (3) the conclusion of a case, commonly called the *Judgment* (¹).

1. To promote the Judge's Office two things are requisite ; (1) There must be a Libel presented by a Complainant : and (2) a Citation issued by the Judge. As it is not compulsory for the Judge to allow his office to be promoted in a criminal case, so a Libel may be handed in without a Citation following. The Judge's Office is not, therefore, promoted until a Citation has followed on a Libel.

2. A Libel is a written document giving a brief account of the charge made and the person charged. It is the first step in every criminal suit, whether made by way of accusation or by way of information, and is absolutely necessary to commence proceedings. In a criminal suit it is usually called Articles ; in a testamentary case, an Allegation.

(¹) See note, page 275.

To be in proper form a Libel must contain the following particulars: (1) The Judge's name; (2) the name of the

(¹) The several parts of a complete Process are the following:—

The suit consists of the following parts.

A. PROMOTING THE JUDGE'S OFFICE

(1) The *Libel,* or *Articles,* or *Allegation*
- (a) The *nature* of a Libel.
- (b) *Requisites* in a Libel.
- (c) *Summary Information* to follow if it does not precede a Libel.

At this stage a suit may be settled out of Court by a *Composition.*

(2) The *Citation*
- (a) *Nature* of a Citation.
- (b) *Varieties* of Citation.
- (c) *Service* of Citation.
- (d) *Effect* of a Citation.

(3) *Admission* of the Libel after argument
- (a) *Exceptions* taken to the Libel.
- (b) *Objection* taken to the Judge.

B. THE TRIAL

(1) *Joining Issue*
- (a) *Nature* of Joining Issue.
- (b) *Varieties* of Issue joined. At this stage a case may be settled by a Judicial Confession in Court.
- (c) *Effect* of Joining issue.

At this stage it was usual to administer the Oath of Calumny.

(2) The *Evidence*
- (a) *Proof* of two degrees.
- (b) *Challenge* of the *witnesses.*
- (c) *Evidence* of the *accused.*

(3) The *Defence*
- (a) *Publication* of evidence for the *cross-examination* of witnesses.
- (b) *Defensive* plea and *evidence.*

C. JUDGMENT

(1) The *Sentence*
- (a) *Presumptions.*
- (b) *Sentences.*
- (c) *Requisites* in a Definition Sentence.

(2) *Execution* of the Sentence

(3) *Appeal*

Plaintiff; (3) the name of the Defendant; (4) the offence charged; (5) particulars of the circumstances under which the offence was committed.

Unless inquiry has gone before, a Libel must be followed by a *Summary Information, i.e.*, an inquiry whether a *prima facie* case has been made out for trial (¹).

3. On the receipt of a Libel, a Judge is in a position to allow his office to be promoted. He may, however, decline to do this; or at this stage of the proceedings the accused may admit his guilt, and the Judge may impose terms; should he do so, it is called a *Composition*, and the case is said to be settled out of court.

4. Should the Judge decide to allow his office to be promoted, a *Citation* is now issued (²). A Citation is a notice stating the nature of the charge and the time and place of hearing (³), and calling on the defendant to appear; and it may be either (1) simple, which, to be effective, must be thrice repeated; or (2) peremptory, which, once given, suffices. The Citation must be served at the instance of the Judge by some one acting for him (⁴). Any defect in the service of a Citation vitiates all subsequent proceedings.

The effect of a Citation is twofold: (1) It obliges the defendant to appear under pain of being pronounced *contu-*

(¹) According to the requirements of Stat. 3 and 4 Vict. c. 86, Summary Information is now obtained by a Commission of Inquiry, which precedes the institution of proceedings.

(²) Pseudo-Isidore ap. Gratian, Caus. v. Qu. ii. c. 1 and 2.

(³) Decret. Greg. IX. Lib. v. Tit. i. c. 24.

(⁴) Decret. Greg. IX. Lib. ii. Tit. xiv. c. 9.

macious ; (2) It actually commences proceedings. There is now a *suit pending* (').

5. The Citation having been issued, it is open to the accused to take exception (²) to the admission of the Libel, or object to the Judge.

Such an exception is in the nature of a Demurrer and may be either in whole or in part. An exception in whole or peremptory (³) as it is sometimes called, is one denying altogether the plaintiff's right of action or shewing that the facts stated, if true, would not warrant the demand made. A partial exception consists in raising objections to parts of the Libel, to some of the facts as irrelevant or as incapable of proof.

Objection may also be taken to the Judge (⁴), on the ground of his being either the Defendant's enemy or the Plaintiff's friend (⁵), or having acted as Advocate or Proctor in the same matter (⁶).

These objections are made and argued before the Judge, and his decision is taken on them, which is open to appeal.

(¹) Lis dicitur mota cum fuerit contestata, Decret. Greg. IX. Lib. v. Tit. xl. c. 30.

(²) Decret. Greg. IX. Lib. ii. Tit. xxv. Sext. Decret. Lib. ii. Tit. xii.

(³) Sext. Decret. Lib. ii. Tit. iii. c. 2.

(⁴) Gratian, Caus. iii. Qu. v. c. 15.

(⁵) Decret. Greg. IX. Lib. ii. Tit. ii. c. 4.

(⁶) Decret. Greg. IX. Lib. ii. Tit. i. c. 18.

CHAPTER CVII.

CRIMINAL PROCEDURE.—TRIAL.

THE Conduct of a case after a Judge has decreed the admission of the Libel or Articles is called the *Trial*. It consists in three things : (1) Joining issue, (2) Taking the evidence, (3) the Defence.   The accused must be present (¹) and the accuser in person (²) in a criminal case, and if the accused do not plead guilty, the question of proof must be gone into (³), and that upon oath (⁴).

1. The important thing in every Ecclesiastical suit is what is called *Joining issue* (⁵).   For this three things are requisite : (1) There must be an allegation by a plaintiff, and a reply by a defendant ; (2) the allegation and reply must be made in open court ; (3) the reply must be made with intent to bring the matter to a judicial decision.   The

(¹) Pseudo-Isidore, ap. Gratian, Caus. iii. Qu. iv. c. 2, c. 4, 5 to 8; also Qu. v. c. 6, 7.   A man who has failed on one charge cannot be heard on others ; Concil. Carthag. vii. A.D. 419, Can. 3, ap. Gratian, Caus. iii. Qu. x. c. 1.   Nor can the accused turn on his accusers until he has cleared himself.   Pseudo-Isidorus ap. Gratian, Caus. iii. Qu. xi. c. 1.

(²) Gratian, Caus. xv. Qu. iv. Decret. Greg. IX. Lib. ii. Tit. ix.

(³) Because no one may be deprived unless he either plead guilty or be proved to be guilty.   See Nicolaus ap. Gratian, Caus. xv. Qu. v. c. 2.

(⁴) The taking of oaths is permitted but perjury is forbidden, Gratian, Caus. xxii. Qu. i. Decret. Greg. IX. Lib. ii. Tit. xxiv. ; but not to those under fourteen, by Concil. Eliberit. ap. Gratian, Caus. xxii. Qu. v. c. 15.

(⁵) Called *Litis Contestatio*, see Decret. Greg. IX. Lib. ii. Tit. v. and vi. Sext. Lib. ii. Tit. iii.

issue may be one of three kinds; either (1) simple affirmative which is the same thing as a Judicial Confession, and ends the case; or (2) simple negative; or (3) qualified affirmative or negative.

Several important effects follow from joining issue. (1) With it the trial commences; (2) Time dates from it in all cases of prescription; (3) Demurrers and objections are now considered out of court.

Joining issue is followed by the *Oath of Calumny* (') administered to both plaintiff and defendant, whereby they declare that their respective actions are not caused by malice. It may be administered to a defendant in a criminal case, but the Bishop's Officer in taking proceedings against a clergyman is excused from taking it. It has now fallen into disuse.

2. The second part of the trial (') consists in taking the evidence of witnesses in order to furnish·*Proof* ('). Proof is of two degrees, complete or incomplete. For complete proof the evidence of two witnesses (') above all challenge is necessary, and complete proof is imperative in criminal cases('). The

---

(') *Juramentum Calumniæ.* On this, see Decret. Greg. IX. Lib. ii. Tit. vii., Sext. Lib. ii. Tit. iv.

(') This mode of procedure has for all practical purposes been entirely altered in England since the passing of 18 and 19 Vict. c. 41; which introduced *viva voce* evidence in place of written evidence taken before an examiner.

(') *Probatio,* see Decret. Greg. IX. Lib. ii. Tit. xix. Sext. Lib. ii. Tit. x.

(') Gratian, Caus. ii. Qu. iv. c. 1. S. John viii. 7.

(') A judge cannot pass sentence because an offence is known to himself; but must have proof. August. Serm. xvi. de verbis domini, ap. Gratian, Caus. ii. Qu. i. c. 19; Decret. Greg. IX. Lib. ii. Tit. xix. Julianus Lib. Constitutionum, ap. Gratian, Caus. ii. Qu. i. c. 11; Nemo episcopus, nemo presbyter excommunicet aliquem, antequam causa probetúr. Augustinus Ep. cxxxvii. *Ibid.* c. 12; Nomen presbyteri propterea non ausus sum de

evidence of one witness only makes incomplete proof which may suffice in civil cases. Should the witnesses disagree, or be equally balanced, the decision must be on the side of charity (¹).

. In conducting a case (²) only fit persons can be called as witnesses (³). Unfit persons are excluded, such as slaves (⁴), infants under fourteen (⁵), persons of ill-repute (⁶), and avowed enemies (⁷), and in criminal cases women also (⁸) unless prosecuting for wrongs done to themselves. Two witnesses

numero collegarum ejus supprimere vel delere ne divinæ potestati, sub cujus examine causa adhuc pendet, facere viderer injuriam, si illius judicium meo vellem judicio prævenire. Augustin De Poenit, c. 3, ap. Gratian, Caus. xi. Qu. iii. c. 75 ; Quamvis vera sint quædam, non tamen judici sunt credenda, nisi certis indiciis monstrentur.   Gregorius, *Ibid.* c. 74 ; Grave satis est et indecens, ut in re dubia certa detur sententia.

(¹)   See Eleutherius, ap. Gratian, Caus. xxx. Qu. v. c. 11.

(²)   Decret. Greg. IX. Lib. ii. Tit. x.

(³)   Decret. Greg. IX. Lib. ii. Tit. xx.   Witnesses can only state what they know of their own knowledge from having been personally present, Pseudo-Isidore ap. Gratian, Caus. iii. Qu. ix. c. 15, 16 and 20.

(⁴)   Pseudo-Isidore ap. Gratian, Caus. iii. Qu. v. c. 8.

(⁵)   Concil. Carthag. vii. A.D. 419, ap. Gratian, Caus. iv. Qu. ii. c. 1 Ad testimonium autem infra annos quatuordecim ætatis suæ non admittantur [testes].

(⁶)   Pseudo-Isidore ap. Gratian, Caus. i. Qu. vii. c. 23 ; Caus. iii. Qu. iv: c. 1 and 9, 11, and Qu. v. c. 9 ; Concil. Carthag. vii. A.D. 419, ap. Gratian. Caus. iv. Qu. i. c. 1 ; Omnes etiam infamiæ maculis aspersi, id est histriones et turpitudinibus subjectæ personæ, hæretici etiam sive pagani sive Judaei, ab accusatione prohibentur ; Caus. vi. Qu. i. Decret. Greg. IX. Lib. ii. Tit. xxv. c. 1.

(⁷)   Pseudo-Isidore, ap. Gratian, Caus. iii. Qu. v. c. 2, 4, 10, 11, 13, 15.

(⁸)   The evidence of women was by the Civil Law only permitted when they prosecuted for their own wrongs. See Gratian, Caus. xv. Qu. iii. c. 1, 2, 3. Decret. Greg. IX. Lib. ii. Tit. xx. c. 3, 4, 5, 6 and 9.

at the least are required (¹). A witness may be compelled (²) by ecclesiastical censures to give evidence in a civil case. Not so in a criminal case, where he can only be warned (³). Hearings are forbidden to be held on solemn or fast days (⁴).

The accused may himself give evidence (⁵) but is not bound to answer unlawful interrogatories, *i.e.* questions tending to criminate or degrade himself. Extrajudicial confessions may be received as evidence of the guilt of the person making them, if they are shown to have been made seriously at the time (⁶), but they are not evidence against an accomplice (⁷); nor can proceedings in a secular court be put in as evidence (⁸).

3. After taking the evidence the *Defence* is open to the accused. This consists in two things : (1) discrediting the plaintiff's evidence; (2) Statement of defence with evidence in support of it.

Should the evidence of the plaintiff's witnesses not have been given in open court, the *publication* of it now becomes

(¹) Concil. Bracarons. ii. Can. 8, A.D. 572, ap. Gratian, Caus. i. Qu. v. c. 1; Si quis aliquem clericorum in accusatione fornicationis impetet . . duo vel tria testimonia requirantur ab illo.

(²) Decret.Greg. IX. Lib. ii. Tit. xxi.

(³) Decret. Greg. IX. Lib. ii. Tit. xx. c. 45.

(⁴) Decret. Greg. IX. Lib. v. Tit. i. c. 15, and Lib. ii. Tit ix.

(⁵) Although this is contrary to the ordinary English rule in criminal cases, yet it has been ruled by the present Judge of the Court of Arches that the accused party is admissible to give evidence under 14 and 15 Vict. c. 99. See Phillimore's *Ecclesiastical Law*, p. 1326.

(⁶) Confessions may not be extorted by torture, Gratian, Caus. xv. Qu. vi.

(⁷) Pseudo-Isidore, ap. Gratian, Caus. xv. Qu. iii. c. 5 ; Decret. Greg. IX. Lib. ii. Tit. xviii. c. 1.

(⁸) Decret. Greg. IX. Lib. ii. Tit. i. c. 4. 3 Hag. 260, 264, 272.

necessary in order that the defendant may be in a position to traverse it by cross-examination (¹).

The Defendant has then a right to make a counter-allegation or his own *statement of Defence* (²) bringing forward witnesses in support of it (³), which may also be published if thought fit, but publication of this is not necessary.

(¹) Called *Articuli interogatorii*, or *Repetitio et Confrontatio testium*.

(²) *Processus defensivus*. See Caisson Manuale, vol. iv. p. 163.

(³) Decret. Greg. IX. Lib. ii. Tit. xx. c. 26 and 32.

CHAPTER CVIII.

THE Trial being over, Judgment follows. This includes not only (1) Passing sentence, but also (2) the Execution of the Sentence, and (3) Appeal.

1. In passing Sentence the Judge is guided not only by the evidence before him, but also by what are called Presumptions ([1]). These Presumptions are of two kinds, either personal or legal. Personal presumptions are personal considerations which no prudent man could ignore. Legal presumptions are general considerations which the law presumes, such as that an evil deed is done with an evil intent. Legal presumptions only ([2]) are not sufficient evidence of guilt.

([1]) Decret. Greg. IX. Lib. ii. Tit. xxiii. The following are instances of legal presumptions. See Caisson Manuale, vol. iv. p. 98. (1) Immorality is presumed si testes deponant se vidisse aliquem solum cum sola, nudum cum nuda in eodem lecto jacentem; (2) one who kills another is presumed to do so of malice aforethought; (3) boundary stones are presumed to be in place, unless it can be shown they have been changed; (4) the onus of proof lies on him who alleges incompetence for an ordinary position; not so for an extraordinary one: (5) a charitable interpretation is to be put on doubtful facts: (6) every one is presumed to be good, until he is shown to be bad. Decret. Greg. IX. Lib. ii. Tit. xxiii. c. 3 and 6 and 9; youthful conduct is a presumption as to conduct in old age, c. 4; he who seeks delay is guilty, c. 5: he who denies only one of two charges admits the other, c. 7 and 8. What is known abroad is known at home, c. 10; stronger evidence is necessary to establish an improbability.

([2]) Decret. Greg. IX. Lib. ii. Tit. xxiii. c. 14, by c. 15; a presump-

Sentences are of two kinds : (1) Interlocutory and (2) Definitive. An interlocutory sentence is a decision given on a point which has been incidentally raised during the hearing of a case. A definitive sentence is a sentence on the case itself (¹).

To be canonically valid a Definitive sentence must fulfil the following conditions : (1) It must be absolute not conditional ; (2) it must be in writing (²) ; (3) it must be according to Law (³) ; (4) it must be pronounced in presence of the parties or at least after they have been peremptorily cited to be present. And (5) it must be according to the Libel, and given after the strictest proof (⁴).

2. If no appeal is made (⁵), the Defendant in a Civil case has four months to obey the (⁶) Sentence; in a criminal case it takes effect at once. A sentence duly passed by a judge can be enforced anywhere, and it is the Ordinary's duty to see to its prompt execution. Payment of costs can be compelled by ecclesiastical censures.

3. An Appeal is a carrying the case to a higher Tribunal

---

tion of incontinence in old age will not hold against one who has been continent in his youth.

(¹) Clement. Lib. ii. Tit. xi.

(²) Gratian, Caus. ii. Qu. i. c. 8 and 9.

(³) On the invalidity of an unjust sentence see authorities ap. Gratian, Caus. xi. Qu. iii. c. 86 to 89, 94, 95. Decret. Greg. IX. Lib. ii. Tit. xxvii. c. 1. Sext. Decret, Lib. ii. Tit. xiv.

(⁴) Hence no action can be taken against a Bishop until his offences is proven. See Symmachus ap. Gratian, Caus. viii. Qu. iv.

(⁵) A number of Pseudo-Isidorian decretals on appeals ap. Gratian, Caus. ii. Qu. vi. c. 1-9.

(⁶) A sentence stands good until it is appealed against, although given on faulty data, Gratian, Caus. xxxv. Qu. ix.

(¹) for a rehearing in order that a sentence may be there altered or dissolved. Anyone who feels himself aggrieved may appeal (²), either (1) judicially or (2) extra-judicially; judicially to set aside a definitive sentence; extra-judicially to correct an interlocutory decision, or to remedy an injury caused by a mistake (³).

An appeal may be made either *viva voce*, when the Judge is sitting in court, or, if made afterwards, by means of a Libel.

The effect of an appeal is to suspend execution of the sentence until the decision of the superior court is known (⁴).

The forms of appeal are local and variable. So is the limit of time within which an appeal may be prosecuted (⁵).

(¹) Within a limited time, Gratian, Caus. ii. Qu. vi. c. 7 to 12, 22 and 28 to 31, 37 and 41, appeals should be prosecuted within a year. See Concil. Carthagen. v. Can. 12, A.D. 401, and Gelasius ap. Gratian, Caus. xi. Qu. iii. c. 36 and 37. Pseudo-Isidore ap. Gratian, Caus. ii. Qu. vi. c. 21. Sext. Decret. Lib. ii. Tit. xv. Clement Lib. ii. Tit. xii.

(²) Decret. Greg. IX. Lib. ii. Tit. xxvii. c. 9 and 22, and xxviii.

(³) Such as a sentence of excommunication given on a false certificate of citation.

(⁴) In England the Inhibition issued on appeal suspends proceedings in the court below.

(⁵) By rule 23 of the Rules in force since 1 Jan. 1867, in the Arches Court of Canterbury, notice of appeal must be given within 15 days of the date of the order or decree appealed from, and prosecuted within one month.

CHAPTER CIX.

STATUTORY LIMITATIONS OF COURTS CHRISTIAN IN ENGLAND.

ENGLISH Law has curtailed the jurisdiction of the Ecclesiastical Courts principally in two ways: (1) by withdrawing from them many things which once belonged to their cognisance, and (2) by creating a new supreme Court of Appeal.

1. The Act 53 Geo. III. c. 127 forbids Ecclesiastical Courts from passing sentences of Excommunication, save when such sentences are pronounced as spiritual censures for offences of ecclesiastical cognisance only, and in that case forbids Excommunication from being followed by any civil penalty or incapacity beyond a liability to imprisonment for a term not exceeding six months, this imprisonment to be enforced only through the Civil Authority by means of a Writ called *Significavit.* The Statute 20 and 21 Vict. c. 85 passed in 1857, withdrew Divorce and Matrimonial causes from the cognisance of the Spiritual Courts; and the Statute 20 and 21 Vict. c. 77 amended by 21 and 22 Vict. c. 95, abolished all the powers hitherto exercised by them in the granting of Probates of Wills and Letters of Administration, transfering these to a new Court called the Court of Probate, which is now a branch of the High Court of Justice.

2. The Act of Supremacy 26 Hen. 'VIII. c. 1. in substituting the Sovereign for the Pope as Supreme Head of the Church, without supplying him with the necessary ecclesiastical machinery, practically exempted the Bishops of the two English Provinces from the supervision of the Collective Episcopate, that supervision having heretofore in the intervals between General Councils been exercised by the Pope as the Representative of the whole Episcopal Body, and as the President of a permanent Committee of Revision of the whole Church.

3. In place of appeals to the Pope the Statute 25 Hen. VIII. c. 19, permitted appeals from the Archbishop's Court to the King in Chancery, the practice being for the Lord Chancellor on petition to appoint certain Delegates to hear the appeal, that body being called the Court of Delegates. Should their decision not be satisfactory, a commission of review might be granted under the great seal on petition to the King in Council, "to revise, review, and rehear the case."

4. The Act 2 and 3 Will. IV. c. 92 prohibited the granting in future of Commissions of Review and the Act 3 and 4 Will. IV. c. 41 transferred the powers and jurisdiction of the Court of Delegates to the Judicial Committee of the Privy Council. An entirely new Court was thus established as the supreme Court of Appeal in matters Ecclesiastical.

Strange as these results may seem, it is hard to see how any Civil Government could allow cases involving the property and civil rights of citizens within the realm to be carried on appeal before a body of mostly alien ecclesiastics; nor even how it could permit appeals to be settled by ecclesiastics at home, without affording the opportunity for their decisions to be revised by secular courts, should they be given contrary to the Laws of the realm.

CHAPTER CX.

STATUTORY REGULATION OF ECCLESIASTICAL PROCEDURE
IN ENGLAND.

1. The manner of proceeding in the English Ecclesiastical Courts is founded on the general method of ecclesiastical procedure, modified partly by decisions of the supreme Court of Appeal, partly by Statutes specially affecting it, the principal ones in modern times being the Statutes 1 and 2 Vict. c. 106, amended by the Pluralities Amendment Act 48 and 49 Vict. c. 54, and 3 and 4 Vict. c. 86, the latter being commonly known as the Church Discipline Act.

The Criminal suit is open to any one whom the Ordinary allows to promote his office, not excluding one excommunicated by sentence (¹). It is within the Ordinary's discretion to allow, or to refuse to allow, his office to be promoted (²); but having once permitted action to be taken he cannot subsequently interpose to stay proceedings without the promoter's consent (³). Criminal proceedings are, however, limited in case of procedure for the soul's health to offences committed within the previous eight months (⁴) in case of pro-

(¹) Privy Council, *Mastin* v. *Escott*, 2 Curt. 692, 4 Moore P. C. 104, 1 *Notes of Cases*, 552, 3 *Notes of Cases*, 387.

(²) See Notes, Phillimore's *Ecclesiastical Law*, p. 1320 and 1299, so that he may consider the fitness of the person to be made responsible for costs to the other party, *Carr* v. *Marsh*, 2 Phill. 204.

(³) *Reg.* v. *Archbishop of Canterbury*, 6 El. and Bl. 546.

(⁴) By 27 Geo. III. c. 44; No suit shall be brought in any ecclesiastical

U

cedure for purging the Church, to offences committed within two years (¹) before the service of the citation (²). A criminal case may be adjudicated upon either by the Bishop with Assessors, or sent by him by Letters of Request to the Court of the Province to be there tried (³).

court for fornication or incontinence after the expiration of eight calendar months from the time when such offence shall have been committed. In *Free* v. *Burgoyne*, 9 D., and R. 14; 2 Bligh N S. 65, where a clergyman was proceeded against for incontinence committed more than eight months previously a prohibition was awarded as to proceedings for reformation of manners, but a consultation granted for purging the Church of a criminous clerk.

(¹) By 3 and 4, Vict. c. 86, sect 20 ; Every suit or proceeding against any such clerk in Holy Orders for any offence against the laws ecclesiastical shall be commenced within two years after the commission of the offence in respect of which the act or proceeding shall be instituted and not afterwards.

(²) *Denison* v. *Ditcher*, Deane and Swabey's *Rep.* 334, 11 Moor, P. C. 324.

(³) The Statute provides for the trial of an accused Clerk in the following way:

1. By sec. 3. the Bishop may issue a Commission of Inquiry to 5 persons, of whom one shall be his Vicar-General or an Archdeacon or Rural Dean within the Diocese after 14 days previous notice of his intention so to do. If the Commission report that there is *prima facie* ground for proceeding,

2. The case may be adjudicated upon by the Bishop, either

    (a) Under sec. 9, by the Bishop or his Commissary summarily, if the defendant plead guilty, or

    (b) Under sec. 11 after a hearing by the Bishop with 3 Assessors, one of whom shall be an Advocate of 5 years standing or a Serjeant or a Barrister of 7 years standing, and another the Dean or an Archdeacon or the Bishop's Chancellor.

3. Or by sec. 13 the case may be sent by Letters of Request to the Court of the Province, either

    (a) In the first instance, or

    (b) *After* the Commission of Inquiry has reported and *before* Articles are filed.

The Civil suit is open to any one showing an interest ([1]).

2. In the case of the clergy a Criminal suit may be preceded by a commission of inquiry ([2]) to ascertain if there are any sufficient grounds for bringing it. Such a commission is however strictly limited in its inquiries to matters arising within the local limits of the Bishop's authority who issues it ([3]).

3. The actual suit is commenced by a Citation, which is issued by the Spiritual Court on the motion of a Complainant. The Citation calls on the Defendant, whom it cites by name, to appear on a certain day at a certain place before a Judge whose name is also given to answer to a charge, the nature of which is described. Such a Citation when issued by the Court of Arches is called a Decree.

4. The original charge or first plea is called a Libel in a Civil case, or Articles in a Criminal case. A Libel runs in the Complainant's name who *alleges* and *propounds* what is therein set forth; Articles run in the Judge's name who *articles* and *objects*. Every other kind of plea and every subsequent plea whether responsive or by way of rejoinder and by whatever party given in is called an Allegation. In a Criminal case the Court cannot go beyond the particular offence charged ([4]) nor can the Articles go beyond what is contained in the Citation ([5]). The promoter of the Judge's

([1]) *Turner* v. *Meyers*, 1 Consist. 415 note.

([2]) 3 and 4 Vict. c. 86, sect. 3.

([3]) *Homer* v. *Jones*, 9 Jur. 167.

([4]) The general words of Articles only include subordinate charges ejusdem generis. See *Bennett* v. *Bonaker*, 3 Hagg. 25.

([5]) *Breeks* v. *Woolfrey*, 1 Curt. 880.

office is, moreover, bound not only to give the substance but also a true copy of the Articles to the defendant (¹).

5. When the Defendant appears on the day and at the place named and hands in his answer, he is said to join issue, and the handing in of the answer is called joining issue, or *Litis Contestatio.* Issue may be joined in one of three ways; (1) by simply affirming the Libel or Articles, in which case the suit is at an end, or (2) by simply denying them, or (3) by admitting or denying them with qualification.

6. Before evidence can be tendered or a plea of any kind be admitted to proof, the court must first settle what pleas are admissible and what are not. It is open to either party to object to the other's pleas in whole or in part, and the arguments upon these objections have first to be heard and decided.

7. When the pleadings have been thus settled the case is ripe for evidence, if any of the facts alleged in the pleadings are in dispute. In giving evidence the Act 18 and 19 Vict. c. 41 allows *viva voce* examination and cross-questioning in open court in place of written evidence taken before an examiner out of court, as used to be the practice. In Criminal cases the Defendant cannot be called upon for answers (²). Nor is he in others bound to answer when his answer would criminate himself, or even tend to degrade him (³). The Defendant has nevertheless been allowed to

(¹) *Williams* v. *Bott,* 1 Consist. 1, and *Thorpe* v. *Mansell.*
(²) See *Stephen on Pleading,* p. 25.
(³) *Swift* v. *Swift,* 4 Hagg. 139.

give evidence (¹) by virtue of the Act 14 and 15 Vict. c. 99, in cases which have been taken on appeal to the Privy Council without any opinion having been there expressed as to the admission of such evidence (²).

8. From a sentence when given an appeal lies first to the Court of the Province and then to the Privy Council. But besides these appeals the High Court of Justice also interposes to set aside the sentences of Ecclesiastical Tribunals by Writ of Prohibition (³); in any case where they appear to have overstepped the limits of their Jurisdiction or where there has been an obvious denial of justice in the conduct of a case. Prohibition, however, is not usually allowed in cases in which justice could be obtained by appeal.

(¹) *Bp. of Norwich* v. *Pearse,* L. R. 2 Adm. and Eccl. 281.

(²) L. R. 3, P. C. 52.

(³) Something of the same kind is known to the Canon Law. See Decret. Greg. IX. Lib. ii. Tit. xxvii. c. 24.

CHAPTER CXI.

GENERAL REVIEW OF THE SUBJECT.

THE abiding impression left on the mind from a study of Canon Law is that of respect for its scrupulous care to guard against the smallest injustice and its extreme charity.

1. Whilst it lays down strict rules for the government of those enlightened by the knowledge of God in the face of Jesus Christ, it never forgets that we have this treasure in earthen vessels; and that although the soul soars upwards to higher things, the body has not lost its human instincts.

2. Whilst it teaches that by the Incarnation the Church's Founder has rescued humanity from its low estate and sanctified it, and that the Christian's Body is a temple of the Holy Ghost, it still makes allowances for the strength of human passions surprising the unwary and carrying them to excess at times, remembering that the simple gratification of the primary instincts of human nature such as eating, drinking, sexual intercourse, and the like, is not wrong *per se* (¹) but only becomes so when indulged in excessively, unlawfully, or unnaturally.

3. Far from confounding religion with morality, it owns that the Church itself exists through grace, and hence rejoices in every triumph of grace over human weakness.

(¹) Augustine. ap. Gratian, Caus. xxxii. Qu. i. c. 11. See Chap. i.

Ever merciful, that where sin has abounded, grace might much more abound, it trusts to its supernatural power to raise up them that fall, and finally to beat down the power of evil, and has none of the world's timidity in the face of acknowledged wrong-doing ; this it has anticipated, with this it is prepared to deal.

4. And thus it confers a quiet dignity on the society which is under its rule, such as no association possesses which repudiates its sway. For it represents no sudden thought nor spasmodic action, but the accumulated wisdom of centuries, dealing under the guidance of the Holy Ghost with human nature which is ever the same, which has still the same instincts, the same temptations, the same aspirations, hopes and fears, and the same complicated problems to solve as it had in mediæval or Apostolic times, or in the yet remoter ages of waiting till the coming One should come.

Of it may, therefore, be said in the words of Solomon : Happy is the man that findeth wisdom and the man that getteth understanding ; and in the words of One greater than Solomon : Wisdom is justified of her children.

INDEX.

1889.

NEW CATHOLIC PUBLICATIONS

OF

THOMAS BAKER,

1, SOHO SQUARE, 1,

LONDON,

.W.

ST. JOHN OF THE CROSS.—The ASCENT of MOUNT CARMEL, written in Spanish by St. JOHN OF THE CROSS, of the Order of our Lady of Mount Carmel, *newly translated and corrected from the last Spanish Edition*, (1885) by DAVID LEWIS, ESQ. (Author of " Life of St. Theresa, &c.), with an entirely new LIFE OF THE SAINT, by the Translator. Thick handsome 8vo, cloth extra, (pub. 12s), **9s** nett; postage 6d   1888

> " The writings of St. John of the Cross possess the same authority in Mystical Theology that the writings of St. Thomas and the Fathers possess in Dogmatic Theology."—*Bossuet Instruct. sur les etats d'oraison, liv. 1, No. 12.*

St. Philip Neri recommended the perusal of books whose Authors names were prefaced by the letter S, that is, saint, and no better opportunity of following his counsel can be found than by having recourse to the volume just published by Mr. Baker. It contains Mr. David Lewis' *Life of St. John of the Cross*, and the priceless *Ascent of Mount Carmel*........ ....Mr. Lewis' life of the Saint is full in fact of matter which will amply repay thoughtful and careful study ; and it can be warmly recommended to all persons who are not already cognisant of its import. The volume is brought to a close by a translation of St. John's "*Ascent of Mount Carmel*," that of course requires no review ; the writing of a Saint —and of such a Saint—calls only for reverence and appropriation to the personal needs of the reader.—TABLET, April, 1889.

LIFE OF ST. MONICA, by the ABBE BOUGAUD, *Vicar-General of Orleans.* Translated by E. A. HAZELAND. Crown 8vo, cloth extra, **2s 6d** nett ; postage 5d

> "A History such as this should not be written, but sung ! For it is a poem : a poem of the most beautiful love that perhaps ever existed, the most tender, the most noble, and most pure, which for twenty-five years never for an instant wearied, and triumphed at last."—*Introduction.*

> "Read Monica's Life, you will see her care for her Augustine and find much to console you."—*St. Francis de Sales.*

> This translation by Mrs. Hazeland deserves a warm welcome in all English speaking Countries. There is not an unreadable sentence from beginning to end.—*Dublin Review.*

DALGAIRNS.—LIVES OF THE FATHERS OF THE DESERT, translated from the German of the COUNTESS HAHN HAHN. With an Introduction on the Spiritual Life of the first Six Centuries, by the Rev. J. B. DALGAIRNS, *of the London Oratory.* **New Edition.** thick crown 8vo, cloth extra (pub. 5s) **3s 9d** nett ; postage 6d   1888

> The admirable introduction by Father Dalgairns............ ..Treating of the Spiritual Life of the first Six Centuries greatly enhances the value of the book, which is by far, the fullest and best picture of the Primitive Monks, which has appeared in English.—"*Ave Maria.*"

> The narrative is direct and charmingly simple—The translation good. Father Dalgairns Introduction ....is of singular excellence, erudite, profoundly thoughtful and scientific.—*Dublin Review.*

TAULER (John, *D.D.*, *Dominican Friar and Mystic, circa* A.D. 1360) MEDITATIONS on the LIFE and PASSION of our Lord JESUS CHRIST, translated from the Latin by a Secular Priest. NEW EDITION. (640 pp.), cr. 8vo, cloth extra, **3s 9d** nett ; postage 5d   1889

> Full of heartfelt piety, which still speaks to the inmost longings and noblest wants of man's mind.

> The translation of Tauler's Meditations is in a quaintly antique style that lends a charm to the simple outpourings of a loving prayerful heart. Some chapters strike us as being singularly pathetic and devotional. — *Dublin Review.*

THE SPIRITUAL CONFERENCES OF ST. FRANCIS DE SALES, *Bishop and Prince of Geneva and Fonnder of the Order of Visitation of Holy Mary.* Faithfully translated from the French, with preface by H. E. CARDINAL WISEMAN, 12mo, cloth let., **2s 6d** nett ; postage 3d

THE MISTAKES OF MODERN INFIDELS: comprising a Complete refutation of COLONEL INGERSOLL'S "MISTAKES OF MOSES" and of the Objections of Voltaire and others against Christianity, by Rev. **G. R. NORTHGRAVES,** *of Ingersoll, Ont., Canada, new English edition,* cr. 8vo, cloth let. (pub. 4s 6d) **3s 6d** nett ; postage 5d

> SKETCH OF CONTENTS : Liberty and Licence; Religious and Political Liberty; Existence of God ; Creation and Providence ; Insufficiency of unaided Reason : Necessity of Revelation ; Authenticity and Integrity of the Pentateuch ; The Creation ; Fall of Man ; The Deluge ; Origin of Man, etc.

WISEMAN (Cardinal) LECTURES on the PRINCIPAL DOCTRINES and Practices of the Catholic Church. *New Edition.* (570 pp.) Handsome crown 8vo, cloth extra (pub. 4s 6d) **3s 6d** nett ; postage 5d   1888

> "This is the *third complete edition* in one volume of this celebrated series of Lectures by the great Cardinal. *It is faithfully re-printed from the edition which received the last corrections at the hands of the Author,* and as such it will always remain a Catholic Classic among English speaking peoples."

> It is not without a feeling of reverence that we gaze on these pages that come to us with the authority and love of a great pastor, to whom multitudes owe countless blessings through the instrumentality of his preaching .... These Lectures contain much that is most useful for the present day, and we heartily welcome their re-appearance.—*Catholic Times.*

> WE WELCOME very cordially the reprint of Cardinal Wiseman controversial Lectures............ The present volume is neatly bound, compact and well printed on good paper .... As for the matter of the work, commendation on our part would be out of place.—*Month.*

WISEMAN's (Cardinal) ESSAYS on VARIOUS SUBJECTS (A new Selection.) With a Biographical Introduction by the Rev. JEREMIAH MURPHY, *C.C.*, of Queenstown, Co. Cork. (Upwards of 550 pp.) Thick handsome large 8vo, cloth extra, gilt top, (pub. 12s) **9s** nett ; postage 6d   1888

> *Contents :* Biographical Introduction—Catholic Versions of Scripture—The Parables—The Miracles and the Actions of the New Testament—Two Letters on 1 John, v. 7—Ancient and Modern Catholicity—The High Church Theory of Dogmatical Authority—Christian Art—Account of the Council of Constantinople—Pope Boniface VIII.—Early Italian Academies.

—— Another smaller edition *(containing all the same matter)*, sm. 8vo, cloth (pub. 8s) **6s** nett

—PRESS NOTICES.—

A Republication of some of Cardinal Wiseman's best Essays, we are cordially glad to welcome it. . . . . The Introduction by Fr. Murphy give us an excellent account of the late Cardinal's Life.---DUBLIN REVIEW.

It gives us real pleasure to see that Cardinal Wiseman is not Forgotten, and Father Murphy has done us a real service for which we are grateful. . . . . A Biographhy of Cardinal Wiseman has long been a desideratum, and Fr. Murphy in his introduction has gone a long way towards supplying this want.---THE MONTH.

We heartily thank the editor and publisher for giving us this useful volume.--- CATHOLIC TIMES.

Fr. Murphy's biographical introduction has been executed in a manner which reflects the highest credit on the writer, &c.—THE NATION.

Cardinal Wiseman's writings need no recommendation. . . . . . There is no writer in the English language who may be read with greater profit. Fr. Murphy gives, in a pointed and pleasing style, an excellent account of the Cardinal's Life. . . . . It is excellent as to type, paper, and binding, and we wish all success to this welcome and most useful volume.---CORK HERALD.

The Essays range over a variety of subjects, and illustrate the versatile genius of the writer quite as much as his deep learning and polished style. . . . . . What manner of man the great Cardinal was is well told by Fr. Murphy. . . . . . The book is a handsome well printed volume and we hope it will speedily find a place in every Catholic Library.--- CATHOLIC PRESS.

All who appreciate a clear, dignified, and captivating style of exposition and controversy in religious matters, will feel deeply indebted to the publisher and to Fr. Murphy for his splendid edition of the Essays.---IRISH ECCLESIASTICAL RECORD.

THE ESSAYS contained in the volume are in the Cardinal best style, clear and logical, and with a wealth of illustration that illumines the subject which he is treating. None of them are of ephermal interest. They are all of permanent value and may be read now with as much profit and pleasure as when "they first appeared."—AMERICAN CATHOLIC QUARTERLY.

SWIFT AND CO.

2, NEWTON STREET, HIGH HOLBORN

LONDON, W.C.

www.ingramcontent.com/pod-product-compliance
Lightning Source LLC
Chambersburg PA
CBHW031341070726
47496CB00017B/1412